T21
media

something new is
breaking through

To Kerry

Awake In The Dark

Paul Laville

Enjoy

www.t21media.uk/awdk

Text Copyright © 2014 Paul Laville
All Rights Reserved

First published in paperback 2015

Cover Design by Ed Thomas, Doubleshot.tv
Cover Image 'Dark Mask 03' by Tanja Hehn

The moral right of the author has been asserted

All characters and events in this novel, other than those clearly in the public domain, are fictitious and any resemblance to real persons, living or dead, is purely coincidental.

Published by T21Media
info@t21media.uk

No part of this novel may be reproduced, stored in a retrieval system, or transmitted, in any form or by any means, without the prior permission in writing by the publisher, nor be otherwise circulated in any form of binding or cover other than that in which it is published and without a similar condition including this condition being imposed on the subsequent purchaser.

ISBN: 150239541X
ISBN-13: 978-1502395412

All quoted extracts within the novel remain the property of their respective authors and/ or publishers.
Used here by kind permission.

To all the special people in my life: past, present and future.

Opening

They pulled the corpse from the Thames when London was still dark and frozen around me.

I was standing on the mudflats at low tide. Standing amongst all the shit washed up by the river, my shoes sinking into the filth.

Watching. Waiting.

Along the bank a mobile spotlight was mounted onto a tripod. Next to it stood a brooding silhouette: Detective Inspector Hershey, hands in the pockets of her long coat, face forward, her breath forming wispy shapes in the harsh light. A diesel generator rumbled and whined nearby, powering the spotlight.

Out on the river a police boat ghosted on the low tide, its engine idling in counterpoint to the generator. Onboard, two police angled spotlights down at the water.

It seemed an age was passing. Maybe they wouldn't –

The water bubbled and broke where the beams of light converged. A radio crackled and there was motion suddenly.

Hershey jerked into life. She lifted a radio to her mouth and barked into it. "Just bring it up the south bank if you can. We've got about ten minutes left on the tide."

My breathing stopped for a second, then quickened as the monstrous shapes of two divers – rubber suits, tanks and pipes rising like a pair of Giger's demons – emerged from the river with the corpse between them.

With a slow, methodical calm and ease, they pulled the dead thing from the river, across the mud and up the bank. Then they carefully laid it to rest like a tribute to the tripod, in front of which an open bodybag had now been spread.

Hershey beckoned me over with a flick of her head and I walked forward, struggling to breathe. The spotlight on the tripod buzzed and sang with energy, and the light was so bright it bleached the shadows away.

I looked down.

Caught my breath.

The corpse seemed over-exposed as the forensics guys carefully, delicately, pulled weeds and silt away from its mouth and eyes to reveal a fish-bitten face.

"Oh God..."

It hurt, it physically hurt to look.

The face of the body was pale, spoiled by blue veins fat with river-water. Hair shaved right down. A face I knew well.

Looked just like me, as though it was my own face I was looking at.

Hershey glanced at me for confirmation but I don't think she needed it. I nodded, and then my legs just gave way.

Hands caught me, just about keeping me upright, and two uniformed police steered me away. I didn't resist as they walked me towards the ladders they'd set down over the wharf.

"Hey. Take a breather," said one of the coppers.

I climbed up. Didn't need him telling me what to do.

The motion was purely mechanical. One hand over the other, hauling myself back into the world. There was a policeman behind me, making sure my feet didn't slip.

"She shouldn't have taken him down there," a policewoman was saying when I came up. She stopped when she saw me, and then she and a colleague helped me up the last few steps.

"I'm OK," I said.

But I wasn't.

I'd thought I could handle this, I mean you saw it on the TV enough times, right? Body dragged up from the river? No big deal. And it wasn't like I wasn't expecting it.

But still... When it happened and your worst fears were confirmed...

Someone threw a blanket or a coat or something over my shoulders.

"Come on. Sit in the car. Stay warm."

It was the policewoman.

"I don't want to sit in the car," I told her.

"Jason," she said. "You've had a shock. You need to –"

I pushed her away. "Get off me!" I shouted.

And now her male colleague stepped forward. "Hey!" he barked.

I backed away from them, blood pounding in my ears, adrenaline burning me up. I had to get out of here. I couldn't be with these people. They couldn't help me because they wouldn't understand.

A moment ... then I made my decision. I turned, I threw off the blanket and I ran.

The police called after me. "JJ! Jason!"

I heard footsteps chasing but I didn't turn back.

On the opposite bank of the river I wouldn't have stood a chance of getting away so easily. Canary Wharf was lit up like Vegas and it was full of security guards and CCTV. The roads were wide and there was nowhere to run. But on this side of the river it was Deptford, and Deptford was old and dark, a place of rundown flats, wire fences guarding suspended renovations and narrow, high-walled alleyways. The subways were badly-lit, and I ran into one of them as fast as I could. All the cameras were broken and no one stopped me. There was no one around apart from a few guys sitting on cardboard mattresses who laughed at the police chasing me down. "Go on, mate!" one of them shouted. Pig noises and manic laughter echoed behind me.

It was a warren of weird light and shadow down there but I kept on running, turning left, then right, right again, looking for an exit.

I emerged cold and shivering in the middle of a silent, sudden canyon where towering, derelict warehouses rose on both sides of me. Contractor notices were everywhere, hanging off broken metal fencing.

Where to now? Had to hurry. The police couldn't be far behind.

I wiped my eyes and ran on, finding a gap in the fence that I could squeeze through. Once on the other side I stumbled across a wasteland of rubble, then into a towering derelict of dark concrete and scaffold, a warehouse which could have been slated for demolition as easily as renovation.

Inside there were rows of archways on my left. I plunged into one at random and Christ it was dark.

Stumbling, breathing hard, almost blind even, I picked my way through the warehouse and I buried myself deep inside, finding a stairway going down down down.

I stumbled into a room within a room, with what felt like old bricks piled up inside it. I folded myself into the darkness, knees up to my chin, head in my hands, and then I cried for the first time in such a long, long time.

That was this morning.

Now I just feel numb.

DI Hershey won't find me in here and she knows it. I heard them earlier, clattering around elsewhere in the building, their radios crackling while I slunk into a corner and held my breath. But it's dark and it's dangerous in here. It stinks of piss, it's full of old shit and there are a dozen other ramshackle buildings I could have dropped into; so now, if she's looking at all, she's looking somewhere else.

Who am I kidding? Hershey is relentless and she hates me. She'll hunt me down and dig me out. Eventually. Maybe I'll even let her. But not yet, not just yet. There are some things I have to do first.

Tonight, on New Year's Eve, I'll slip out into the streets, just one more face in the dark, and then I'll bring this thing to a close. But first I need to get my head into gear. I need to pull myself together and figure out how I came to be in this mess. How I came to stand on the bank of the Thames like a ghost to watch someone who looked like me being hauled from the river; how I became a man with no friends, no home, no identity. Hunted by a murderer.

Someone made this happen and I think I know who and I think I know why. But I have to be certain before I set out to find him and do what has to be done. I just need some time alone to think things through.

Trouble is that time is one thing I don't have. The clock is ticking down to midnight and he's still out there. My enemy.

So I ask myself, where might it all have started? Two bony boys? No, not quite so far back as that. Sometime, not so long ago. A day at the market perhaps, a day which began just like any other.

My memories focus on the day…

1

Impressionism

The life of our city is rich in romantic and beautiful subjects. We are enveloped and saturated, as though in an atmosphere of the marvellous; but we do not see it.

The Salon of 1846: On the Heroism of Modern Life.
Charles Baudelaire 13 May 1846.

1.1

Camden Market, North London. A freezing, grey afternoon the middle of October.

Place was packed.

I remember I was standing in the queue at Stan's burger van on the edge of the market, reading up on the scores inside the back pages of *The Mirror*. Most times I was oblivious to the racket all around me but today it seemed busier than usual, like something was going on and I hadn't been told about it.

So many people.

They were crowding the stalls, moving like pigs snuffling for truffles, paying well over the odds for any pretentious old tat they could lay hands on. Visitors all wanted something they could say they bought at Camden Market, while the locals, few and far between in a place like this, might have just popped over to rifle through the second-hand books and DVDs or say hello to a mate.

They used to buy paintings and prints off me but I'd packed up my stall for the last time a while ago. Crunch came when a bunch of kids dived into the stall and threw ink at the paintings, spoiling them all. So I sold my pitch to Harriet and helped her out instead.

Anyway I paid Stan his four-quid for the burger, then shoved the newspaper under an armpit while I loaded up with ketchup. Once that was all done I made my way round the back of the stalls munching down on the hot, greasy mass between my fingertips.

Pretty soon I found myself up against a wall of sound: the bouncy beat of Meghan Trainor's ridiculously catchy *All About That Bass* booming out the back of a white Transit. The van's doors were open to show crates full of cheap CDs flanked by two monstrous speakers jumping in time to the bone-shaking bass line. Jhavesh Patel, wearing a Superdry jacket and NY baseball cap, stood outside the van swapping CDs for cash. Flicking away his cigarette he waved me over while his cousin, a silhouette in a hoody, carried on taking the money. "JJ, man. How you been? Did you find him?" he shouted.

"Who?"

It was a struggle to chat with all the noise.

"Your mate."

"Huh?" No idea what he was talking about.

"...wiv a skinhead," he elaborated, then turned away to argue with someone.

"Stephen?"

Jhavesh looked up and shouted something else but I'd no idea what it was. Didn't matter. I turned to leave then, remembering something, I bellowed at him: "Don't forget tonight!"

He cupped a hand to his ear. "Huh?"

"Harriet's stuff?"

"Huh?"

"Later!"

"Huh?"

He was grinning when I showed him the finger and walked away.

"Your horse-burger stinks," Harriet said when I reached her stall. "Go away." She was wearing a red, woolly scarf which matched her gloves and a black duffel coat buttoned right up to her chin. I didn't think it was that cold but she was sniffling.

"That's no way to talk to a mate," I said to her, mouth full of burger and bread.

"You're scruffy and you smell."

"It's the bohemian look."

"It's the twenty-first century," she reminded me, "even for 'artists'?"

Hated the way she did that, with the fingers either side of her head and ending with an inflection that turned her statement into a question. Arnold, my agent, did the same thing. Very Annoying.

"You want something from me though, right?" I said, sucking ketchup off my fingers.

Harriet looked at me, puzzled for a minute, long black lashes over her bright, green cat's eyes. Then they opened wide. So did her mouth: a perfect smile.

"*Please* let me borrow your lock up to dump all my shit in tonight? Pretty please?"

She fluttered her lashes jokingly. She had amazing eyes.

Harriet Brisley was a twenty-seven year-old vegetarian who wished she was still nineteen. She hated 'getting old' and the closer she got to thirty the more uptight and worried about it she became. Thirty was history for me, though. I'd passed that milestone years back and was half way from there to forty.

"It's all sorted, H," I told her. "Jhavesh said he'd give us a lift so we can pack up all this crap in his van later and – What's this?" I asked, dumping the newspaper to pick up a silver pendant and chain with my greasy fingers. It was a tiny silver snake curling round to eat its own tail. She sold all kinds of crap like this – and she hated it when I called it that, but it was. She used to work the stall with a pagan-chick friend of hers who had vanished into the city a few months ago, so now the stall and its eclectic mix of jewellery, crystals, scented candles, birth-charts, whale-music and Tarot cards was hers alone.

Still, people seemed to buy it so what did I know?

"Are you buying?" she asked.

I shook my head and tossed it back. "No."

Finishing off my burger I leant against one of the poles holding up the stall. Harriet didn't like this either so she grabbed the newspaper I'd dumped on her counter and threw it at me. "Thought I told you to go away?" she said.

I caught the paper and tried to straighten it out, trouble was the grease from the burger made the headline ink smudge and spread. So I wiped my fingers on my coat. The dainty little napkin I'd been given by Stan had died in a gory mess on the way over.

"You didn't mean that."

"How do you know what I meant?" Harriet said. "What are you reading anyway? *The Mirror*? Jesus. I thought you creative types all read *The Guardian*?"

"It's teachers wot read the Guardian," I told her, slightly mockingly. "We 'artists'…" I did the thing with the fingers, at least with one hand, "… are far more low-brow."

She grabbed the paper off me, scanned the headline and threw it back.

"Trash," she said. "You know all this plays into the hands of this lunatic?" she said.

"What?"

She flicked the newspaper with her hand. "This. It's just a – a publicity platform for the Camden Killer. All the newspapers. They're all the fucking same."

Must be bad if she swore.

I shook out the front page. Alongside images of bikini-clad celebs and something about the EuroMillions, the smudged headline for the lead story claimed 'Camden Killer Victim Four'.

Then she looked at me properly, by which I mean that her eyes narrowed and her brain started ticking.

"That's why you bought the paper."

"What?"

"You! You're obsessed with him!"

"There's a double-page spread inside," I told her. "It shows all the locations where the bodies were found."

"You're sick."

"I'm not the Camden Killer."

"The guy's a murderer."

"And a celebrity. Big on Twitter right now." I said. "And not always in the way that you think."

"You're sick."

"Check it out." I shoved the paper into my armpit and dug out my phone. I tapped up Twitter and pointed the screen at her face. "See. Trending at number three. Was number one this morning…" I scrolled through the newsfeed. "It's like there's a whole online community that's built up around him. Have you seen the way Sky News introduce their Camden Killer features? They've given him his own theme tune."

She wasn't listening. A young girl covered in piercings and tattoos had drifted over to her stall and so Harriet moved towards her.

As she served her customer I had a quick scan through the keywords on the news feeds scrolling up my phone:

Police confirm serial killer in North London…

Fourth victim…

Female, undisclosed age…

Extravagent deathmask …

Found in a locked room in a North London church…

The phone rang. Incoming call replacing the text.

It was Jenny's hospital. They'd been trying to call me for a while but it wasn't the kind of conversation I wanted to have right here so I rejected it. Got grease on the LCD so I scraped it down my coat, which probably just made it worse. I guess I'd need to wash my hands at some point. Maybe treat the phone to a screen cleaner as well.

"Who is it?" Harriet asked, finishing up with her customer.

"Oh, so now you're interested."

"Is it Stephen?"

I put the phone back in my pocket. "No."

"Have you heard from him?"

I shook my head. Grunted.

"Have you called him?" she asked.

"No," I lied.

"You're rubbish, JJ," Harriet told me. "It's a wonder you've got any friends."

"I've got you."

"For now."

I raised an eyebrow. "You going somewhere?"

"Maybe," she said. "You could come with me. We could take off right now. Buy a ticket for the first plane out of Stansted and see where it takes us."

"You'd never do that."

She looked offended. "How do you know what I'd do? You don't know me. You don't know the first thing about me."

Appearances were deceptive. No matter how small and fragile she looked Harriet Brisley was full of fire and confidence. But she did look upset, and now she was deliberately ignoring me.

So maybe I'd gone too far with that comment. "Sorry," I said.

She shrugged. "Just don't forget about the lock up," she said. "I'm relying on you."

1.2

Back home I ran upstairs to the studio, which took up the whole second floor of my house. Cat was asleep on the top step of the middle landing and there she stayed, unruffled, as I vaulted over her. I guess she might have half-opened an eye to signal her annoyance, but I didn't see it.

The paint-splashed MacBook sat on a desk at the front end of the studio and I fired it up. While it booted I rang the hospital back on the mobile. There was no answer and I didn't have the patience to keep trying. Jenny was my sister and she'd been in St Cecilia's for about five years. The last conversation I'd had with Doctor Pandghani, her consultant, had mostly involved him trying to persuade me that Jenny should come and live with me. But I couldn't do that. I just ... Maybe one day, but not right now.

I cut the call, switched on a desk light and twisted it up at the wall behind the desk.

This was where I pinned all my newspaper cut-outs, articles and blogs on the Camden Killer. I just called it The Wall.

There was a baseball bat on the desk, an unwanted present from Stephen from his trip to the US, and I knocked it to the floor with a clatter. Then I spread the newspaper out and opened it up to pages five and six.

The spread was a Google Earth print of North London, focusing on Camden Town, Chalk Farm, Kentish Town – with Hampstead Heath to the north and the top corner of Regents Park to the south. Box-outs with photographs and text were linked by arrows to the locations on the map where the bodies of the Camden Killer's victims had been found. On the following pages was a long, 'story so far' of the Killer's progress. It told me there was an interactive version on their website.

Content with the paper copy I spent the next ten minutes removing the pages and pinning them up on The Wall, moving the other stuff around into a new configuration.

The MacBook had already chimed and when I was done with the paper I sat down, opened up Safari and clicked through to my Twitter homepage.

The Camden Killer was the number one UK trend again. Grief junkies and moralistic armchair guardians loved to tweet. As did the jokers.

@Jonny_Sticksmith: this guys a nutjob! String the fcker up!

@MallonSexxy: Another girl dead. My thoughts go out to her mum & dad. CK must be stopped

@Justinfan_Billy: I heard this one was wearing a mask like no2? Is this true?

@TheRealCK: Your all gonna fckn diieeeee!!!!!

@Justinfan_Billy: its so sad. police need to find this dick

@Sh1tPolice: check this out: bit.gl/QXWooj ... anyone been selling roses to the freak

@JLK121: @Sh1tPolice is that true?

@TheRealCK: yeh is troo an Ill do it again motherfckers

@welshgardener: prick

@LJK121: why would you put a nail in her head? I wish I hadn't read this

@Sh1tPolice: and this one the police dont want u to see goo.gl/c.3p

@derek_hammer: CK for prime minister!! LOL!

A hundred and fifty new Tweets arrived in while I spent a few seconds scanning through the crap. @Sh1tPolice was a regular on the CK Tweets. He (or she I suppose) kept finding stuff which the real police never published, and posted a lot of links to various blogs and rumour sites. I wondered if he actually was a police.

I clicked through one of his links and found a blogger who went on about how the police hunt was lacking motivation.

> I mean they've only just acknowledged publicly that they have a serial killer on their hands. What they need to do is look at the geography, look at the victims and find out what they all had in common because there must be something that each one had that has marked them out as a target...

"No no," I whispered under my breath. "They're all different."

I wrote this on the comments below the blog then I clicked through the previous comments. There seemed to be a general agreement that victim number three had had a nail hammered into her forehead. There was something about flowers too: irises or roses stuffed into her belly.

There was nothing on the recent fourth victim yet, but I guessed that there'd be something on the blogs by the end of the day. I'd keep an eye on it.

The Mirror's double-page spread took centre place in The Wall. I leaned back in the chair and looked at it.

The locations were all centred on Camden Town. So it seemed obvious he lived or worked here somewhere. But if that was true, why hadn't the police found him yet?

I went back into Twitter and entered the conversation with:

> *Every victim is different. Other than the fact that he killed them, these people have nothing in common*

The responses came in seconds later:

> @Tranny_Pam: nothing in common that WE know about...

> @Sh1tPolice: The police don't know either.

> @Bryan_Proctor: @JJX - are you saying the killings are random?

> *Maybe. Whoever the Camden Killer is, he's no ordinary serial murderer*

> @TheRealCK: That's right mthfckers!! Im 1 craaaazee cnt!!

> @Sh1tPolice: Someone switch that prick off

I went back into the blogs, keeping an eye on the tweets coming in, sending out new ones whenever I found something interesting.

I hadn't realised how much time had passed until my phone pinged with a text from Harriet:

Market closing in 1hr. U coming or do I come beat you up for bein a loser?

1.3

The landlord Harriet rented her storage from in Kentish Town had decided he wanted to knock the units through and sell them off to a coffee shop franchisee willing to pay him a ton of cash for the freehold. He'd given her notice but Harriet, being Harriet, had left it until the last minute to sort something out and now it was too late to get anything decent for what she could afford. She didn't have much stock but her flat was already crammed wall-to-wall, so I'd said she could use my old lock up in Tufnell Park to put it all in. Before the debacle at Lambeth and when I ran the stall, when I actually had a career, I used to store some art in there.

Jhavesh drove us up when the market closed down at six. It was cold and dark when we set off. Smell of fireworks in the air.

"Where is it, Jay?"

"Under the bridge, mate," I said. "Straight on."

The van rattled towards the bridge and mounted the kerb just as a high-speed train screamed over the top.

I stepped out as the last of the train disappeared and its echoes rumbled away above us.

"Love this place," Harriet said sarcastically as I helped her out, almost lifting her to the pavement. She'd been sucking on extra strong mints in the van and her mouth was so close I could almost taste them.

"Do you want to put your stuff in here or not?" I said.

The door on Jhavesh's side crashed shut, its noise booming down the street like a gunshot.

He joined us, lighting up his first cigarette since Harriet had objected to him smoking in the van. "It's my bloody van!" he'd told her in outrage. He'd had to wait nonetheless.

"All right I'm grateful," she said. "If it's safe for you then it's safe for me, right?"

Jhavesh mumbled, "Place is prob'ly full of crackheads, man."

"No. It isn't," I said. Harriet stared at me. "Seriously, it isn't! Look, I've been storing my art here for years, even when I had the stall and nothing's ever gone missing. It's safe. All right?"

"With all due respec', JJ," said Jhavesh. "Who's gonna teef your paintings?"

"Funny."

He grinned. "Come on," he said, moving to the back of the van. "Let's get this stuff out before the zombies come for a look."

The lock up was one in a row of arches built into the ancient bricks of the bridge. The road was blocked off for development on the other side of it and no one came here now.

Illumination drifted slowly down through isolated cones of light cast by a line of street-lamps. A thickening, evening fog seemed to make the light-cones solid and the artist head in me wondered, if I touched one, could I phase into a slow universe of crystallised light?

"Does it always stink like this around here?" Harriet's voice pulled me back into the real world.

"That's what I was finkin," called Jhavesh. "Place is rank, man."

I walked towards the lock up, pulling the key from my pocket.

"'fraid so. Not usually this bad though. There's probably a – " I looked down to where the padlock on the lock up door was dangling loose. A fat, lazy fly sat on it, seemingly half-dead in the cold. "Shit."

Jhavesh came up behind us with the first few boxes. He dumped them on the pavement by our feet, cigarette flapping on his lips. "'sup, crew? Shit, mate, seriously… Smells bad."

"Someone's broken into his lock up," Harriet told him nervously. "I said it wasn't safe didn't I?"

Jhavesh pulled the fag out of his mouth and vented smoke. He looked unsettled and in truth so was I.

I pulled on the lock up door and it scraped along the ground. When it was open far enough the smell really hit us. So did the flies, disturbed by the door.

"Oh my *Lord*!" swore Jhavesh, who was standing full on.

I covered my face with my hand and turned away for a minute.

"Jesus!" gasped Harriet, backing away.

I looked into the lock up but it was too dark to see anything. The light-switch had never worked. "Jhavesh, give me the torch."

"Mate, you don't want to go in there. Someone's *dog's* died, man!"

"Just get me the torch!"

"What torch?"

"I said to you make sure you got a fucking torch!"

"Just wait, man! *Jesus*!" he sounded hysterical but he went back to the van nonetheless and returned a minute later with a naff plastic torch.

"Is that it?"

"It's a torch! Sorry it ain't up to your *exacting* standards."

I took it off him, switched it on and moved into the lock up, pulling my coat collar over my mouth and nose with my other hand.

"Jason, don't go in," whispered Harriet. I felt her tugging at my sleeve.

The dead thing wasn't a dog. It was a man with a blood-soaked sack over his head.

"*Shit..!*" I gasped, almost jumping out of my skin.

At first I thought it was someone just standing there. In my lock up, in the dark. Hands behind his back.

I pinned him down with torchlight and moved in closer. Flies buzzed and dive-bombed my ears as I walked towards the body. They crawled over the figure, lending it a creepy animation. Eventually I was able to keep my hand steady and I could see that he was covered in streaks of dark, dried blood. It had run from head to toe to describe a chaotic landscape, like the satellite map of an ancient river system etched into his skin.

I guess most people would have turned around by now but I had to see more. It was just a body, right?

Lengths of wire were looped around it, tying it to a pillar, keeping it upright. It was pierced by arrows. Must have been twenty of them? *Thirty?*

No. More than that. Christ they were sticking out everywhere: from his neck, his arms, legs, his chest and his belly, creating shadows that wheeled around him as I moved the torch to get an idea of what exactly I was looking at. There was something weird going on around his belly so I shone the torch at it and saw that his guts were spilling out, crawling.

Fuck. That was nasty.

I caught my breath and I stepped closer.

They weren't arrows.

They were... I leaned inwards... *Paintbrushes?*

Paintbrushes honed to knife-sharp points and rammed deep into his flesh. Bristles sticking outwards.

It was horrible to look at. Like overkill from a slasher movie.

I flicked the torch upwards.

The sack covering his head had a clown face painted on it: Xs for eyes and a sad, sad mouth like some kind of suicidal Pierrot. I let go of my collar. I held my breath and reached out to the mask. I gripped it and started pulling it.

It gave easily at first, sliding over the crown fluidly. Then it seemed to get stuck, snagging on something.

"Jason!" called Harriet, her voice cutting harshly into my world.

I ignored her. The only thing that mattered right here and now was that I was sharing a space with someone who had been killed amongst my old art. Stuck with paintbrushes and tied to a post so that he looked like the Biblical martyr Saint Sebastian.

So who the hell was it?

The flies got agitated. Diving into my face and crawling over my hands and wrists. Trembling, I slid the hood up as far as I could and shone the torch right into the face.

"Fuck me...."

I tried to step away. Tried to pull my eyes away from the face but the ground seemed to give and I ended up stumbling and crashing to the ground, knocking things everywhere.

I dropped the torch and I ran out of the lock up choking, gasping for air, shaking off flies both real and imaginary.

Jhavesh was by his van smoking vigorously, finishing a call to 999 and his hands and face were shaking like mad. First time I'd ever seen him this rattled. Harriet was closer to the entrance and she was just staring into the lock up, frozen in place like a pale statue.

I leant against the side of the van as another train screamed above us, making me jump.

"Aw shit! Shit shit *shit*!" I hit the van. *Boom*!

Jhavesh walked up to Harriet and took her gently by the shoulders. He was still shaking and I wondered who was comforting who.

Harriet turned, broke away from him, and then came at me with an expression like she was accusing me.

"That's Stephen!" she said, sounding hysterical. "Jason, that's *Stephen Craine?*"

I think I nodded as I bent and panted for air, hands on my knees, face aimed to the ground. "Yeah," I gasped. Don't know if she heard me with all the sirens going on, getting really loud now.

Yeah... that was him all right...

That was Stephen Craine.

1.4

The police swooped down in cars and vans. Blue lights filling up the space under the bridge. They taped off the street, split the three of us up and started asking each of us questions. I saw Harriet looking in my direction a few times when she was being quizzed. Jhavesh too. An hour later the two of them were free to go but for some reason the police thought it was worthwhile taking me to the station.

1.5

DC Burrows was an arsehole and I didn't like him from the start. He was a youngish, red-haired CID copper with an intensely freckled face. His white shirt was too short on the arms so his skinny, hairy wrists poked out a good few inches from the cuffs. His stainless-steel D&G watch looked good but it was too big for him. And from the way he talked I got the impression he was trying to impress the woman sitting next to him.

She was his senior: Detective Inspector Hershey. A tall woman around late-thirties wearing a faded trouser suit and a white blouse in need of a good ironing. Her face was dominated by a pair of big, bulging blue eyes. They were quite intense to look at, but cold. Unlike Burrows' ginger crewcut, Hershey's hair was dark and straight, tired-looking. It hung like curtains around her head and she kept pushing it back over her ears while she studied the contents of a folder full of papers.

I got the feeling that everything about her was considered, calculated, misleading, and I didn't trust her an inch.

Burrows and I were going through the formalities.

"... you don't know where his parents live?" Burrows was saying.

I shook my head. "No."

"You said Stephen has a brother?"

"David, yes." I cleared my throat.

"Do you know where he lives?"

"No."

"Got a phone number?"

"No."

"Did Stephen have any other family? Any cousins? Uncles, aunts, great aunts?"

I was shaking my head.

Burrows continued, his voice increasingly sarcastic. "Anyone else we could contact that you know about?"

I shrugged. "Sorry, I don't know."

"Any other friends?"

"Sure. I guess so. I never mixed with his immediate social circle, so I don't know them."

"Work colleagues?"

"Probably."

"Where did he work?"

"He was an accountant?"

"Yeah but do you know the name of the company he worked for?"

"No."

Burrows sighed. "All right. So he was an accountant. Was he a supervisor? A clerk? A department head..?"

"I don't know."

"Big office? Small office?"

"Don't know."

"And he was a friend of yours?"

"Yes."

Burrows raised a ginger eyebrow. "Doesn't sound to me like you knew him that well."

"I guess not," I croaked in response.

We went through the sequence of events. What time did I leave the market? What time did we get to the lock up? At what point did I notice the lock had been opened?

And so on...

But then it turned sinister.

"... you said you were at home last night," Burrows was saying.

"I was."

"Alone?"

"Yes. Apart from my cat."

"OK. Did anyone call on you at any time? Did you have any visitors?"

"Why?"

"What about the night before? Where were you then? At home again...?"

"No, I was – why are you asking me?"

"Just routine," Burrows said. "No need to get worked up. Sorry if this is difficult for you."

Difficult? They had no fucking idea.

"OK," Burrows went on. "So tell me about something you do know. Tell me about the last time you saw Stephen Craine. When was that?"

I rubbed my face. "A month or so," I answered. "Hampstead Heath."

"Good. What were you doing there?"

"What does anyone do in Hampstead Heath?"

Burrows shrugged.

"Nothing sordid," I went on. "We were just walking... Talking."

"That's all?"

"We had a bust-up. Nothing major."

1.6

"What do you mean you don't want to see me again?" Stephen was angry. Set to explode.

"I'm not like you, mate," I told him.

"Not like me? What the fuck, JJ?"

"I'm not gay," I said. "I can't do this."

He'd laughed at me. Piercings on his tongue flashing. "Took you long enough to figure that out after everything we've done together," he said. "So what are you?"

"I'm just not..."

"You're dicking me around," he'd shouted. "And fine. Fine for you if you're not gay. You go play your games with some other poor bitch."

"It's not about playing games," I said to him.

"Well it's not a game for me either!" he'd said. "This is real. It's me. It's who I am."

"Stephen-"

"And it's *Steve*!" he'd snapped. "Always *Steve*! Never *Stephen*! I fucking hate being called *Stephen* and you always call me *Stephen*. Dickhead!" He'd sighed heavily and looked up at me, and for all his bluster and swearing, there were tear-trails down his cheeks. "I'm done, mate. I'm out of here. You've done nothing but fuck me about and that ain't what I need right now. See you around... Prick!"

At long last he'd walked away, down the hill into the strong sun, fading in the light, and I'd breathed a sigh of relief.

1.7

"He was gay, right?" asked Burrows.

"Is that important?"

"Dunno. Are you gay?"

"Not really."

"But you were in a relationship with him."

I nodded. "I guess. But I'm not gay. Not really…"

"So … what? You were just … *curious*?" Burrows said with a grin.

I let out a long sigh. "Does it matter?"

"Not to you obviously. You're not a fussy bloke then?"

"What do you mean?"

DI Hershey stepped in. "I think Detective Burrows' point, Mr Jones," she said, and I noticed a very slight northern accent – Sheffield or Derbyshire, somewhere like that – "is whether Stephen might have known anyone within the gay community who had some kind of a grudge against him."

"A grudge?" I repeated. "I don't know. I don't think so…"

It went on…

They talked then about whether some murderous homophobe might have lured him or followed him to the arches. But if it was someone who hated gays, why not just beat him up and stab him? Why all the theatre of puncturing him with paintbrushes? Burrows asked whether Stephen had a key to the lock up.

"Why would he?" I asked. Stephen hadn't even known about the lock up.

"The padlock wasn't forced," Burrows told me. "Key was found *inside* the body, rammed up his-"

"Did you give him the key, Jason?" Hershey interrupted.

"No," I said weakly. My head was spinning, trying to figure out the connections. Had he stolen it off me? Had he actually known about the lock up all along? Why would he go there anyway?

Why would anyone want to kill him in this way?

"You've been in here before haven't you?" said Burrows. "You told us before that you were getting a load of death threats on your Facebook page."

"Not that you lot did anything about it," I said. "And it was on my Wordpress page, not Facebook."

"What?"

"I used to write a blog. Wordpress. Totally different to Facebook."

Burrows and Hershey looked at each other, exchanging a silent *'whatever!'* between them. Hershey smiling slightly.

She looked back at me, her big blue eyes bulging even further, and she faked a bigger smile, even going so far as to show her teeth. "Was he really your friend, Jason?"

I remembered going blank on them, like my head was moving into another space and all they were was noise, rattling away in the background.

Stephen's body was in sudden sharp focus. The rotten dead smell was with me again and the flies and his mashed-up face stared right through me as I lifted the sackcloth hood from his head and I backed away and stumbled and fell and—

"Fucking hell," I swore. Then I puked.

1.8

They let me out. No more questions after all that explosive vomiting – I'd never seen two coppers leap backwards off their chairs so fast – and so within the hour I was walking home. It was around two in the morning, freezing, and I was shivering, with the aftertaste of puke in my mouth, stressing over everything that had happened in the last twelve hours. When I got home I smoked a joint, brushed my teeth and went for a sleep.

It didn't help. I woke up around ten o' clock more stressed than before.

Bella wanted feeding and she was being very vocal about it. Kept miaowing and wrapping herself round my legs while I went for a piss, texting Harriet with the other hand.

"I'll feed you in a minute," I told the cat.

H. You ok? Call me. JJx

Up in the studio, as the cat chomped noisily at some food I'd put down for her, I built another joint and spent the next twenty minutes smoking that down, hoping it'd make me feel better.

The smell outside the lock up... the scrape of the door along the ground... the torch picking out his intestines ... his face under the clown-face sacking... Stephen dead...

My head was a mess.
I walked upstairs.
I walked downstairs.

I couldn't settle in the lounge, couldn't settle in my bedroom. I couldn't even make myself a cup of tea. Think I boiled the kettle about a dozen times.

I decided in the end that I had to open some doors, let some air in. So I went up to the studio and pushed open the big French windows that led out onto a little balcony overlooking my garden of nettles. I took a final drag on the smoke and then flicked the butt down into the swamp.

I raked a bit of air into my lungs, breathed out slowly and looked around to kind of reestablish myself in the world.

My house was in a terrace. That was solid enough. It was a three-storey house with what I thought of as a 'lantern' on top of it where I sometimes went to think about stuff. There were fifteen houses on each side of mine and they were just as old and solid. Mine was the only one which had this lantern in the roof, a bizarre but welcome weirdness added by some previous inhabitant before planning permission was ever invented.

An alley ran along the back of our gardens and on the other side of that was the Church of St Leonard, a decrepit Gothic ruin standing high on a hill of rubble and stone. It was a wasteland, a desolation surrounded by a high-wire fence advertising the name of a security company I'd never been able to find on the internet. The fence was broken in so many places it was never going to keep anyone out of it.

Which I thought was ironic.

St Leonard was a patron saint of prisoners. It was said that if a prisoner invoked the saint's name in prayer then his chains would break and he'd be free to go. Over the years I'd lived here the place had become a haven for tramps and crackheads who gathered to light fires in the big metal drums dumped in the churchyard. I'd hear them sometimes, swearing and cursing. Singing. Some of them even managed a quick fuck in the dark. Don't know what with mind…

I shivered. Maybe it was more of a shudder. Whatever, it was cold and I was only wearing my boxers and an old t-shirt.

So I walked back into the house. Closed the doors behind me and padded barefoot across the wood flooring of the studio.

And then I stared at The Wall.

It was him wasn't it?

The Camden Killer had murdered Stephen Craine.

1.9

The Camden Killer's first victim — at least as far as anyone knew — was an old man: Benjamin Grace, who used to be a judge and whose son was also a judge.

He'd been flayed, expertly skinned from neck to toe. His face might have been taken off too but his head was nowhere to be found and police were still looking. The only way they'd been able to confirm that it was him was from the serial number on his pacemaker.

Judge Grace had been discovered one morning on the crest of Hampstead Heath, strapped down, headless and skinless, to an old, wooden bench facing the city of London.

I was on the internet, looking into this one again, and I found a link to some images which purported to show the flayed old judge sitting on his bench at dawn the morning he was discovered.

I clicked through the links, got through to the webpage, and then my finger tapped on the mouse... hesitating...

Did I really want to see?

Rumours were that the bench had been covered in the old man's skin. Pinned to the back of this macabre upholstery were hundreds of photographs of the old man's son going about his day, unaware he was being papped by a serial murderer.

Fuck it. Let's have a look. I clicked for the images, my heart in my mouth.

A trio of red crosses appeared on screen, together with the words: 'These images have been removed and are no longer available'.

I actually breathed a sigh of relief. I guess I didn't really want to see them. It was just...

The second victim was beautiful. A twenty-one-year-old girl transformed into a bejewelled corpse then left hanging by a rope off one of the tall lampposts on Blackfriar's Bridge. The jewels stuck into her skin weren't real. They were the kind of thing you'd buy off the internet or from Claires if you wanted to make a cheap mosaic or something. But that didn't lessen the effect. Her glittering, almost insect-like deathmask was like a stunning work of psychotic art.

There *had* been pictures of this one. People had snapped her dangling, bejewelled corpse on their phones, uploaded and shared the pictures with their friends instantly. Seemed most people had thought at the time that it was some kind of stunt, even though the bridge had been closed for half the day while the fire crews cut her down.

Victim number three was Rachael Clarke and she'd been twenty-seven years old.

For three nights a week she was a lapdancer at a club in Kentish Town, a job she did to pay for her University fees. Before she was killed she'd been studying a fifteen-month MBA at the London Business School.

This much had been released and reported on by the press.

She'd had an American fiancée. A guy called either Dan or Dom, Trelow or Teller. The reports and blogs were unsure but I could find that out later on. For a while he'd been a suspect because it was said that he used to beat her up.

One windy night in July Rachael disappeared. Turned a street corner, her face captured in grainy CCTV, and then she just vanished. There was a search but it started too late and nothing turned up. When her body was eventually found, two weeks later in a dirty, concrete trench behind the Sainsburys on Camden Road, the police were slammed for their apathy.

One thing all the reports and blogs I read were dead certain about was that a six-inch nail had been hammered into Rachael's forehead, carefully and very precisely so as not to crack the skull. Some sources said this was what had killed her, others said she had been strangled first.

The second fact that the reports were all agreed on was that there was no sign of any sexual abuse. They also now seemed to agree that Rachael's torso had been filled with flowers. Most said it was red roses, but others reckoned it was carnations or lilies. It made little sense either way. Why would you do that? Nail in the forehead? Red roses or whatever? Flowers? I mean… why?

Some kind of fantasy the killer was playing out?

There was nothing more on body number four yet, but it seemed that the world was waiting.

Holding its breath.

Was Stephen going to be announced as victim number five?

The doorbell rang loudly and I jumped out of my skin.

"I know you're in," a voice hollered though the letterbox. "Come on, open the door. I'm gonna change your life."

I took a breath, closed the MacBook, and composed myself before heading down to open the front door.

It was Arnold Evans, my agent, wearing a dark suit under his long raincoat and a Trilby hat that might have been in fashion in the 60s.

"Jesus, what have you been smoking? It stinks in here," he said when I let him in.

Bella, ran out, escaping between his legs like her tail was on fire.

"You look like shit. And seriously, it reeks. Come on, let's go for a drink."

"I don't have time —"

"Drink. Now!" he barked. "If I come into your house I'm going to have to get my suit cleaned. And this, my young friend, is a *very* expensive suit. Added to that I'm cash-strapped. So come on. Grab your shit and let's go. I've got some big news that's going to change your life and make us both ridiculously rich."

1.10

He took me to *The Prince Albert*, a nasty old pub on the corner of Arlington Road.

I didn't like the place. Prices were high and the staff were just plain rude. The tourists didn't seem to care about this since they thought it was just a typical English pub, but the locals knew better. Arnold wasn't a local and this was exactly his kind of place. To be honest it worked OK because I didn't want to be in sight of anyone who'd recognise me.

We sat at a table in the corner. It was still wet with beer spills, dusted with peanut fragments and bits of crisps. Arnold mopped it up with a napkin he'd brought over from the bar. "Well, what's the big news?" I asked him as he fussed.

"So you just want to cut to the chase, is that it? None of this, 'Hi Arnold, how's it going? Been busy lately? How's the house?'" He finished mopping and put his Fosters down on a beermat. "You really do have some kind of social deficit, Jason, you know that? And put your bloody phone away!"

I tossed the phone onto the table and slumped back in the chair. Nothing from Harriet. "Hi Arnold," I said. "How's the house? Been busy lately? Haven't seen you in ages. Have you got any work for me?"

"I'm not a job centre and I'm not doing your work for you."

"Well you should, considering your fee."

"All right. Enough of the small talk. We tried it and it doesn't work. Have a look at this."

He threw a pamphlet across the table. It had been screwed into a dog-eared roll from having spent too long inside his jacket pocket.

I took it and unrolled it.

"What is it?" I asked. Then, when I straightened out the cover, I saw one of my paintings printed on it. It was *St Rita at the Wasteland*. A kind of sci-fi, Giger-inspired take on a medieval subject that had been done a few times over the last half a century. It wasn't my favourite work since it was massively derivative. But I'd always been interested in the lives of the saints, and I'd been a fan of HR Giger too, so this had been my way of putting the two things together by way of homage. Bizarrely it was one of the images people instantly associated with me, having become a kind of signature piece. But it had been a while since I'd done paintings like this. A while since I'd done anything. Since the disaster at Lambeth things had taken a definite downturn.

Who was I kidding? Since Lambeth I'd done fuck all work. Every time I tried I was slammed by the press, shunned by the galleries and had shit thrown at me in the street, so now I didn't bother.

But, back to the pamphlet.

Above the cover art were the words 'A Plastic Odyssey', and down at the bottom was the stylish and somewhat futurist logo of Gallery21.

I glanced up at Arnold. "Is this from Brian Cavendish?"

He nodded. "Go on. Read it. There's all the usual pretentious bullshit in there, but basically it's a big fat commission, which is going to relaunch your career and propel you, my boy, into the heavens."

I raised an eyebrow. Arnold was at his most dangerous when he spoke like this. But I opened up the pamphlet anyway, straightening out the first page, and read through Brian's 'manifesto'.

"This isn't a commission," I told Arnold.

"All right. No. It isn't – not yet anyway. It's a proposal for a massive exhibition of new artists which Brian wants you to lead." He hesitated, seemed to consider something. Then he shrugged and said: "Which is close enough in my opinion."

I read out from the pamphlet. Putting on my best sarcastic voice.

"'It is the intention of the Organisers of this Exhibition to group together an exciting New Wave of talent in the plastic arts and document a vision which has arisen from the birthing pains of the Twenty-first Century like a dark phoenix. This is The Odyssey, the journey from mankind's humble beginnings to the advent of the Third Millennium.' This is typical Cavendish," I said. "Does it go on like this?"

Arnold sighed and reached over, snatching the pamphlet out of my hands. "Cut to the chase right?" he muttered, then handed it back with a new page open.

"'It is our intention to lead into the Exhibition with a recreation of Jason Jones' 2004 Environment, *Systems of Response in a Startled World*, in which human psychological states are represented by a series of everyday images in juxtaposition with organic and machine materials seemingly at odds with the biological systems of human motion and emotion.' "

Arnold was grinning. "Well?"

I looked up. "All right," I said. "Despite all the bullshit and hyperbole it sounds interesting."

"*Interesting?*" howled Arnold. "That's a fucking understatement. This is more than just 'interesting'. This, my friend, is what is known as a game changer. This is the project that will raise you up from way below the mass of mediocrity and let your talent shine like nothing else before it."

"Sure. So when is it happening?" I asked, looking over the pamphlet for a date and finding only TBCs. "And what do they want from me? Just resurrect my old work and stick it in a gallery with a load of rehashed Pop-Art for the likes of – "

"No, you idiot," Arnold snapped, interrupting me. "They'll lead with *Startled World* but they want something new from you, something they can use as the centrepiece of the whole thing. And it's in December – to be ready for the New Year in fact."

He might as well have punched me in the face. "What? *December?* You've got to be joking!"

He shook his head. "Jason. This will be the biggest thing to happen in your life since meeting me."

My face must have given my thoughts away. Arnold looked apologetic, and he caught himself. "I'm sorry... I know you've been through a lot recently. But life goes on, right? You and I have got to make a living and right now Brian Cavendish is the most influential mover and shaker in the business. He's like the Alan Sugar of the art world and for him to choose you, for him to come to us, especially since that *shitstorm* at Lambeth ... Jason, this here, this invite from G21 is *unprecedented.*"

I took a swig of my beer, all kinds of thoughts going through my head, not least of which was how the hell could I get something in place for New Year's Eve? I didn't have anything new – I mean there were a few ideas I'd been playing around with, but it was all far from finished. Most of it far from started.

"Brian wants to meet you right away," Arnold said. "He wants to whisk you off on a tour of the Dreadnought Gallery so you can look at the space he's giving you and talk to him about 'The Vision'." He did the thing with his fingers.

"He's holding the exhibition at the Dreadnought?" I said.

"It starts on New Year's Eve and there'll be a simultaneous event going on in New York to which there'll be a live feed. It's all very technical and state of the art, apparently. Right up your street."

Then I asked him who else was going to be represented. "I mean it's not just me, right?"

"Back page," he said, grabbing his Fosters, drinking it down like he was in some kind of rapture. Then he slammed it down and sat forward, leaning across the table. "Jason, this is an incredible opportunity," he enthused as I read down the list of proposed and confirmed artists. "After Lambeth this is exactly what we need to get you back on the radar. Resurrection, dear boy. That's what it is. That reference in there to some dark phoenix? That's you: a demagogue amongst a coven of new wave artists. Your art will be given a name. What would we call it? New – no! *Nu*. N–U! Ha! Yes! Nu… Nu-*something*… needs an ism… Expressionism? No. Old hat. Reflectionism? Interesting – has there ever been a Reflectionist movement in art?" He drank, thinking on this.

At the head of the 'confirmed' group were the names Theo Collins and Paula Laurie.

I threw the pamphlet back at him and stood.

"You can call it what you want," I told him flatly. "I'm not doing the exhibition."

He stared at me hatefully for a second, like I'd just poured his Fosters over his head. I swung my coat over my shoulders and shrugged my arms down the sleeves. "I won't be exhibiting alongside anything of Theo's at Gallery21," I told him. "It's either Theo or it's me. It's *never* the both of us."

1.11

"So what is it between you and this Theo Collins," Harriet asked me when I talked to her about it the next day. It was hot and sunny for once, and the two of us walked alongside the canal, ducking under low bridges hand in hand.

After I'd finished up with Arnold I'd gone round to her flat where she'd been in a real state. She'd known Stephen too, probably better than I had. We spent the night drinking wine and beer, talking about stuff, and we'd purged our feelings. I'd stayed over, sleeping on the sofa, ignoring Arnold's calls whenever his name floated up on the phone.

He'd sent me his first Angry Text around midnight. More followed throughout the rest of the night and although the words varied, slightly, the tone was pretty much the same.

> You're not fucking Rembrandt you know
> Call me in the morning!!!

"Long story," I said.
"What's he like? Some kind of nemesis?"
"Who Arnold?"
"Theo."
"Oh. I dunno. He used to be my best mate."
"And now..?"
I shrugged. "And now he ain't."
"It's that simple is it?"
"It really is."
"Nothing's ever that simple. Not with you." She slipped her arms into mine so that we walked the towpath like a couple out of a Richard Curtis film. "Or is it just that you're throwing away the only chance you have of restarting your career purely because of a luvvy-strop?"

I was looking behind us, certain I'd seen someone. The same someone who I reckoned had been following me all morning.

"Hey!" snapped Harriet.

I came back to her. "Sorry," I said. "I just thought... Never mind."

It was happening a lot lately, this feeling of being stalked. I'd catch a glimpse of someone at odd moments, hovering on a street corner, watching my house from the church, stepping out of view whenever I turned to look at them. Usually it was when I was stressed or anxious, or doped up on weed. So I was prepared to accept I could have just been paranoid and it was entirely down to my imagination.

She looked behind us then back again.

"No one there now," she said. "Maybe it's Theo."

1.12

As undergraduates at the London School of Fine Art, when the Twenty-First Century was a bold new thing, Theo Collins and I were initially middle-ground, so-so students who might as well have been invisible. I wasn't looking for friends and nor was he. The both of us were too wrapped up in our dark worlds to really see what the other was doing. It was a tutor who first understood that our work as individuals could be exponentially enhanced if we collaborated. We tried it but it didn't work. I felt like he was getting in the way of what I wanted to achieve and he felt that I didn't understand his vision.

In the end it was the horror of 9/11, at the start of the second year, that catalysed the process of dark fusion which finally bound us.

From then on we excelled and became best mates. We were popular. We were hip. We were invited to every party and we screwed every girl, often the same one at the same time. We were Star Students, prize winners inseparable from each other, inseparable from our art – for which we lived and breathed without exception.

The stuff we fired into the world was the product of violence, energy and high-octane drama. It was explosive. It was big. And it was Fucking Good.

The art press were writing about us before we'd even passed our exams and we thought our future was assured.

But there came a moment, one single point in time that rose and fell, in which that future was destroyed and it all started going wrong.

Maybe that moment was here...

I remember Theo sitting on a wall on the South Bank one night, feet dangling over the river.

It was three in the morning... ish... and after a quick meet at the National Gallery in Trafalgar Square we'd spent the day getting stupidly, horrifically drunk. The game was that we chose a single square from the London A-Z. We chose it blind, like pinning the tail on the donkey. Once selected we travelled out towards that square, and then took one drink in each pub we discovered inside its boundary. This square had been a beauty, covering the square mile or so of streets between Charing Cross and Embankment. Seemed like there was a pub on every street corner.

Afterwards we'd hit a couple of clubs, then walked down to Waterloo looking for a train back to the East End. At least, that was the plan.

Out of a party of fifteen only Nugent Fry and Lucy Stapleton were still with us, and Nugent was on his way out. He was vomiting into the river, and Lucy, I remember, was consoling him. Not that he wanted her to.

"My arm!" he kept shouting, which he always did when he was drunk. "Leggo of me fucking arm!"

When he was sixteen Nugent had almost lost his right arm in a skiing accident. He'd showed me the distinctive zig-zag scar the Austrian surgeons had left him with after they'd stitched it back on. He'd shown me this many times, each time embellishing the whole grisly story of how he'd had to hold onto it during the helicopter ride to the hospital, keeping it pushed into the rest of his upper arm whilst high on morphine.

"This is one of the best views in London," Theo said to me as we stared at the distant, floodlit dome of St Paul's Cathedral across the water and way down to our right. "But it's ironic," he added, "that you can see it best from one of the ugliest examples of civic architecture known to the good people of London Town."

He meant The Royal Festival Hall, which always came in for a slating but which I'd always liked. The South Bank complex was a place of criss-crossing concrete stairways and walkways upon which you could set off in one direction and end up coming back on yourself from another.

"Oh fuck," I heard Nugent gasping, before another surge of alcoholic vomit sluiced down from his mouth and into the river.

Both Theo and I had drunk ourselves almost sober. We'd entered into the calm, fuzzy and philosophical state of mind that follows a successful binge. Earlier in the day we'd had our moments, especially me. It had been a hard day and I'd had some decisions to make.

"JJ," he said, his voice a croak.

"What?"

"You OK?"

I shrugged.

"Still thinking about that letter from your mum?"

I nodded. It had arrived this morning.

"Don't worry," he said. "I'll take you up there tomorrow. OK?"

I nodded again. Mumbled a swift, "Cheers, mate," and lit up another cigarette. I offered Theo one.

"Change of subject, JJ," he said, taking the cigarette.

"Go for it."

When you leave college, mate."

"Yeah?"

"You gonna stick with the art scene?"

I leaned over the wall, elbows next to Theo's legs. "I hope so, mate. It's what I want to do, y'know? When I was little I wanted to be either an artist or a footballer. I reckon I'll never play for Liverpool so it'll have to be the art."

"Even though art is full of dickheads and ponces?"

I shrugged, took a toke on my fag. "Ponces are everywhere, mate. You know that."

"More so in the art world than anywhere else I think," he said. "You should've been a footballer."

This might have been true. By "ponces" I was assuming Theo meant the population of milk-blooded critics, soft-bellied pedants, pompous, petit bourgeois housewives, and self-important and pretentious pseudo-intellectuals that inhabited the art world, rather than its smaller constituent of gay men and women. But you could never tell with Theo.

He said, "When I was little, JJ, I wanted to build cars like my dad."

I laughed. "My dad was a middle management executive for British Rail," I told him.

Theo went on, "I was happy that my dad made cars," he said, "because I liked cars when I was a kid, and I liked cars when I was a teenager. Cars were the great escape. Fast, stylish and they looked great with naked birds posing on them."

I nodded, wondering where the conversation was going.

"My dad was hard as fucking nails, mate," he said. "Used to kick seven tons of shit out of me twice daily."

"And you're a better man for it eh?" I said sarcastically. Fact was I had my own problems. Theo's shit with his dad was trivial compared to what I'd been through.

He stared down at me.

"No, mate. I hated it. He made me want to kill him. I used to lie awake on a night, my face hot and bruised, and so wet with tears ... I used to dream up different ways of killing him, all the detail – what I would do, what I would say. One day was all I would need with him, J, just one fucking day. I would take him apart, bit by bit by bit. I'd tie him down and bleed him slowly, and somehow I would break him."

"Shit..." I mumbled. "That's grim."

"Pipe dreams," said Theo. "Fact is I'm frightened of the old cunt. He could look at me and I'd literally piss in my pants I was so scared."

I felt awkward. It wasn't often Theo opened up like this. "Sorry, man," I mumbled.

He looked out across the dark river again, and I wondered whether he might slide off into it.

"Cars," he said, and supped on the fag. "The great escape." He blew the smoke from his lips, sighing, and then looked back at me. "Except they're not. Know why?"

"Na."

"Because *he* makes the cars."

"Your dad?"

"Yup. He's in there, in the metal, in the petrol as it burns through the engine, in the smell of the seats and the oil and the paint and the rubber. He's in every component, every single piece of that car and every car, and no matter what I think I'd like to do to him, he'd always be in the car, laughing at me, calling me a useless piece of shit."

He looked out across the Thames while I pictured his art in my head, and now all the biomechanical nightmares he'd constructed seemed to make sense; then I said to him, "Does this mean you won't drive me to Anglesey, mate?"

He laughed, breaking the tension, and shook his head. "It's fine, JJ. I'll take you up to Anglesey. Don't worry about it."

1.13

"We don't get on anymore," I told Harriet. "The last time we exhibited together we had a fight. I mean a proper fight. It wasn't staged – we wanted to kill each other. That was with Gallery21 so it's even more surprising that Cavendish wants to me lead his new project. Anyway I've only ever seen Theo once since then and he looked a mess. He's fucked-up."

"So he really is your nemesis then?"

"He's a racist, Harriet. Nasty with it. He's got baggage – a lot of anger and a lot of hatred. His art spills over with it."

"I don't think I've ever seen his work."

"Google him," I told her. "But don't expect anything that isn't full of death, depravity and horror."

"That sounds strong…"

"He got involved with fascists years ago. He goes to their marches, their rallies and God knows what else. I can't be associated with him, I can't have my art in the same room as his."

"Apart from the bit about fascists it sounds like you could be talking about your own stuff."

"Bollocks."

"Remember Lambeth?" She took hold of my hand and forced me to look at her. "People who don't like your art. Why do you think they're so vocal about it?"

"What's that got to do with anything?"

"Take a look at yourself sometimes, Jason," she said. "Try to see yourself as others do. You're a nice person, you're a good guy, but you've got all this darkness going on around you. I'm your friend so I can see through it and I know that you're cool underneath. But if the only thing you put out into the wider world is all this dark stuff in your art, then what is there that separates you from your mate Theo in the eyes of those who 'don't get it'?"

There was a lump in my throat and I took hold of her hands. They were so small. I said, "You are … the best mate an idiot like me could ever hope for."

She laughed.

We walked to my house from the back, crossing the wasteland of St Leonard's which smelled all at once of gas, piss and burnt stuff.

When we got to my back gate I saw that someone had scrawled new abuse on the garden fence.

"Look at this," I sighed.

'Peadophile' spelled incorrectly, and then, just to make sure people understood it, they had also written, 'Child Mallester' beneath it.

I shoved the gate open and let Harriet through the wildlife. "That's disgusting," she said. "Is it yours?"

"What?"

She pointed to a Sainsburys bag bursting with dogshit.

"Fuckers. I'll get rid of it later."

My hands were shaking so much I could hardly get the back door key in the lock. Flashbacks to the arches.

"Don't let them get to you," Harriet said, hand on my elbow as we pushed into the kitchen.

I ran a hand through my hair, although really I wanted to tear it out, and if I'd been here on my own then maybe I would have. "Tea?" I asked her, my voice all nervy. "Cup of tea? Do you want one?"

"Tea sounds good," she replied. Then, "Hello, you!"

I turned round and saw Bella rubbing herself against Harriet's legs. They seemed to like each other.

Harriet sat on a stool at the table and lifted the cat onto her lap.

There was purring and some cooing.

"You found somewhere for your stock yet?" I asked Harriet, lifting the kettle and checking the water inside it. Full of scale and down to the dregs so I took it over to the sink and switched on the tap.

I looked up through the window at the garden. Saw someone standing outside for just a second… staring at me…

The kitchen window exploded suddenly, shards of glass flying everywhere as a brick smashed through it. I swung my head away but the glass ripped into my cheek. I dropped the kettle with an almighty crash and stumbled away from the window, head down.

Harriet leapt up and the cat shot into the corridor, scratching Harriet's hand on her way out.

I turned and ran for the back door screaming, "Fuck! Fuck! Fucking *bastards*!"

"Jason!" called Harriet, as I tore open the kitchen door. "Leave it!"

I ignored her. I ran out after the fucker who'd thrown the brick and caught hold of some lanky kid running across the alley behind my garden wall. He was struggling to squeeze through a break in the metal fence between the alley and St Leonard's Church. Looked like his trousers were caught so I helped him out. I grabbed hold of him and I pulled him away from the fence, and then I swung him round so hard that I lost my grip and he hit the ground with his face. He rolled over in the chalky dirt and the weeds growing up from the cracks in the concrete.

"What are you doing, you nutter?" he spluttered, scrambling to his feet.

I kicked him in the stomach. Maybe twice.

Then I grabbed him by the collar of his coat, pulled him back onto his feet and ran him against the outside of my garden wall. There was a big "Hummph!!" as his lungs expelled their baggage.

"I'm sorry!" he gasped. "Sorry sorry! I didn't mean it!"

I didn't give a shit. I turned him round to face me then I headbutted him square on the bridge of his nose, flattening it down. I'd meant to shout first and ask him where he'd got my address from, why was he stalking me and why he thought I was a bad guy, but in the end I just punched him to the floor and kicked the shit out of him. I was so enraged I hardly saw Harriet coming up behind me, tearing me off the bloke.

"Stay the fuck away from me!" I yelled at the guy. "You get that? And tell all your fucking idiot mates to do the same! You keep away from me or I swear I'll fucking kill you all!"

He scrabbled away and I walked back to the house.

"I guess he was lucky you showed up," I said to Harriet.

"Yeah..." she whispered. "I guess he was."

1.14

History stems from our memories. Things experienced become things remembered, written down and stored away. Or painted, sculpted… tweeted: moments composed, compressed, repackaged, then frozen in time. My life story lies not in words but in pictures. It's there in my art, and it's who I am. If you want to know me look at my art. Look at my successes, and my failures.

I remember at college I once painted a picture called *Two Bony Boys*. It was very simple, and Expressionistic, like Munch's *The Scream*. I doubt Harriet would have liked it.

"What's this, JJ?" my tutor asked me.

I answered him: "It's a fight in a playground. Can't you tell?"

He'd shrugged. "It's derivative bullshit," he told me. "You can do better than this."

The Scream

Zero down from the edge of space towards the dead centre of your target.

What do you see as you dive into the vast, bright disc of our galaxy and the dust separates into billions of stars? Choose one star. Focus on it and keep going. Keep zooming in.

There it is: our Solar System.
The Earth.
England.
London.
Faster.
Closer.
And then —
Lambeth.
A gallery.
A circular room at the heart of the gallery.
A chair.
A girl on the chair.
She's tied to the chair and her mouth is open in a wide 'O'.
Dead centre.
The girl is screaming.

Zoom right back out, as quick as you like, as far as you can it doesn't matter.
You can still hear the scream.

2

Voyeurism

To become truly immortal a work of art needs to smash through all human limits: logic and common sense will only interfere. Once these barriers lie shattered and broken, then it will enter regions of childhood vision and dream.

Mystery And Creation
Giorgio de Chirico
The London Bulletin. No.6, October 1938

2.1

Two bony boys circle each other, moving around the rings of a simple, circular maze painted onto the tarmac of a primary school playground.

A pack of feral, baying children form a tight, dense ring around them.

One bony boy wipes his bloodied lip with the back of his hand.

The other squints through a blackened eye.

One looks at the other, sees his anger reflected in his opponent's eyes and posture. The adrenaline surges, the rush comes, and with an unspoken word the two boys run into the rings and crash together.

"Fight fight fight fight fight fight fight fight fight!"

Blood colours each face, fists are blurring, describing a typhoon of energy and motion. One boy grabs the V-necked jumper of the other and swings him round by it so that he falls into the crowd which parts like the Red Sea for Moses. He walks in after him and calmly, methodically launches strategically-placed, brutal kicks into the sack of his victim's body. The punchbag on the ground rolls over, protecting his face with his hands, curling into a foetal position, taking the beating, gathering his strength, turning his mind away from the physicality of the pain. When the moment is right, when his opponent's confidence causes him to over-balance, he jumps to his feet. No time for this to register. He lays into the other boy, punching his face hard and fast with one hand, holding his throat by the other, making every contact hit as hard as it can. There is nothing human, nothing even remotely childlike about the fight. The boys are out to kill each other, nothing less than that.

The fight may have started slowly, with each boy weighing up the other, deciding on strengths and weaknesses. Testing and probing. But now it's nothing less than brutal, savage primitivism.

Close quarters. Both boys are locked together, landing punches wherever they can. The time for thinking is over, now it's down to pure physicality.

"Fight fight fight fight fight fight!"

One of the boys suddenly delivers a vicious knee to the other's testicles. They part ways briefly and then, in pain and rage, the other boy lunges forward, grips his opponent's head in both hands and slams it down onto his upward-thrusting bony knee.

There is a horrific crunch, a scream and the crowd turns strangely quiet.

The boy staggers back, blood flowing from his shattered nose while the other boy slips slowly down the wall, crying and clutching his balls with both hands.

"James Gordon and Jason Jones, come here *this instant!*" booms a deep, Welsh voice from somewhere behind and above the crowd.

Big, bearded Mr Evans appears on the horizon like a sudden storm front. He looks down at the two injured fighters and shakes his giant grey head sadly.

"My God…! You boys never learn do you?" He picks James up first and inspects his nose. "Come here, let's see… Hurts… right?"

He gives James a handkerchief to hold. "Could be broken. Here, lift your head back and hold this over your nose. Try not to choke on your blood."

He then looks over at me. I'm curled into a foetal position against the wall, pain exploding from my loins, flowering throughout my battered body. "Well," he says, "I know that that hurts."

Mr Evans, with help from a couple of distraught teachers, orders the crowd to return to their lessons.

Playtime over.

2.2

We grew up in Anglesey, and the place we lived in was called Llangefni, a small town which lies deep in the heart of the island. James Gordon and his twin sister Jane had moved up a few years ago from Barnstaple, in Devon. They talked differently but we had a lot in common. Our birthdays, for one thing, were only two days apart and we usually celebrated them together. Jane loved her new home but James didn't.

He was a grim boy, moody and sulky and prone to sudden violence. We used to fight loads.

It's almost a cliché but I remember one sunny spring day, years ago. I was ten … maybe eleven. I was walking with Jenny and Jane. James had been with us but had vanished. He tended to vanish a lot so the two girls and I picked our own way through a sunken wood, following the route of a wide, gushing stream right at the edge of the town boundary.

Jane ran along the stone bank of the stream just a little way ahead of Jenny and me. Her bright yellow dress, stained green in places with grass, reflected and magnified the intense sun that shone in dappled patterns through the trees. The silver snake torc on her neck gleamed like a star, eating its own tail, and her white-blonde hair shone with energy and life.

"Look," she cried, pointing into the grass. "There's another one."

Dressed in jean-shorts and a white T-shirt, Jenny (my sister) treaded the stone wall that embanked the stream, arms out by her sides to keep balance. "Where?" she called, eyes down at her painted toes. Jenny was older than us by three years. To us she had a woman's figure and she seemed very tall. Her legs were long and her shoulders were on the same level as my nose. Whereas my hair fell in long, loose curls over my eyes and down around my throat, hers was short around the ears, spiky-wavy on top, and died jet black right through. I thought it looked gorgeous, very fashionable, but our mum and dad always used to joke that our scalps had been swapped at some point in our infancy so it was me who had the girls hair.

"Here!" Jane cried, pointing to a soiled condom half-hidden in the grass. "I'm winning now!" she sang and danced happily on her toes. "You've only seen six, and I've seen seven. How many have you found, JJ?"

I wasn't playing this game, I told her. Instead I was playing Locate and Destroy, scanning the woods for signs of James. He had to be around somewhere, watching us.

Excited by her find, Jane Gordon skipped further along the stream. My sister jumped down off the bank and ran after her. "Jane, wait," Jenny called, running through the trees.

With the two girls gone I was alone for a moment. The woods were filled with birdsong and the sounds of the stream. It was eerie, the feeling of being watched by James. I had a big, heavy branch in my hand. If James tried to jump out on me, my plan was to smack him across his head with the stick. As long he didn't have something similar planned for me then I'd crack his brains open.

Anyway, he didn't show and I couldn't see him. Truth was James was too good at this game, too good at hiding and stalking.

So I ran after the girls.

Jenny was alone when I caught her up. She was pacing. "What is it, Jen?" I asked her.

"It's Jane," she answered in a tiny voice. "I can't find her."

My heart missed a beat. I looked around. Had James captured her? His own twin sister?

"Jane?" I shouted. "Jane!"

There was no answer except for the weird echoes off the trees.

"Shit," Jenny cursed, and set off to look for her. I followed with my big stick. If anyone had hurt Jane, even if it was James, I'd kill them.

The sunken wood had grown wild around an abandoned railway, the broken track of which was visible only through a few gaps in the weeds and wildflowers. The railway ran at an angle across the stream over a square, stone bridge which I walked under, hoping that Jane was hiding there.

The light was always strange under the bridge. Shafts of blazing, green brilliance stabbed down through holes in the track, into a dank, wet space that had the air of a grotto about it. Reflections from the stream cast ripples of half-light onto the bridge's stone interior. Garlands of greenery tumbled down from the railway sleepers above to trail in the water.

Jenny followed me under the bridge, her sandals squelching in the squashy turf.

"She ain't in here," I said.

Swearing, Jenny pushed past me and went out the other side. She climbed up the bank. Stood on top of the bridge and looked around. I joined her, clambering quickly up in the baking summer heat.

Dragonflies fluttered around her like darts of iridescent light. Jenny was looking along the decrepit railway track which curved through the wood ahead of us, and she decided she would set off in that direction, careful not to put her foot through the rotting sleepers. "She *must* be in the tunnel," I heard her say.

I followed her, still keeping my eyes peeled for signs of James.

The forest built up rapidly around the old railway track as we walked along it. Thick brambles and nettles grew from the banks and from between the sleepers. On our right was a high rock wall, sheer and topped with dangerously overhanging trees, while on our left the weeds and bushes grew thick and almost impenetrable. The sun was hot on my face out here in the open. Sweat crawled down the contours of my back.

Jenny and I arrived at the old station house, a picturesque ruin of pitched roofs and arched windows standing on a cracked, concrete railway platform, boarded up and covered in creeping plants.

Just along from the station house was the high wall leading back up into town. A black, stone arch was cut into it, and through here the train track we'd been following vanished. It curved away inside the tunnel to the right, so that its depths were impenetrable from where Jenny now stood, just at its gaping mouth. Her hands tugged at the top of her shorts, the movement betraying her anxiety.

Catching my eye was a glint of metal, just inside the tunnel entrance. Jenny must have seen it too. She bent down and picked up the silver torc which Jane had 'borrowed' from her mum. The clasp was loose, I saw, coming up close to my sister. No wonder it had come off.

I looked behind me for a moment, again keeping my eye out for James as Jenny clipped the circlet onto her wrist, moving it right up her arm, onto her shoulder. Then I walked into the tunnel proper. "Jane?" Jenny called from behind me, her voice echoing around the dark stone arch. "Are you in there?"

It was cold inside the tunnel, and I felt as though the darkness was generating its own wind. There were strange symbols on the walls: swastikas and pictures of cartoon penises, logos and legends inscribed by youths not much older than Jenny. When she and I were younger we used to play on the edge of this tunnel and tell each other stories about what went on inside.

"Mr Michael lives in the tunnel," I told Jenny once. "Right down at the very back, where it's so dark you can't even see your own hands."

"Who's Mr Michael?"

"He's a child killer isn't he? He lives in the tunnel and he kills people who go too far in. Dad says he used to work on the train and he was a chef. But one day he burnt all the fingers on his hand in an accident while he was cooking and he lost his job and then he went mad and now he lives here. In the tunnel."

Suddenly there was a squeal from the darkness.

"Jane!" Jenny shrieked, and ran past me, almost throwing me out of her way. She stopped when she saw Jane crouched down and holding up her yellow dress, just on the edge of the light, having a wee.

Jane smiled, finished what she was doing and then stood up.

"I stung my bum," she explained, her voice echoing around the tunnel. She trod down the brambles that had been dragged into the tunnel by her dress.

"You shouldn't come in here," Jenny told her.

"Why not?"

As they walked back towards me, I glimpsed something lying on the ground, tucked between a clump of brambles and the wall of the tunnel. "Look at this, here!" I said, poking the thing with my big stick. Jenny and Jane approached it cautiously. It was something in a see-through plastic bag, which I'd first suspected to be another used condom.

"Eurgh! What is it?" whispered Jane.

It was a bag of blood, that much I could tell, and there was something inside the blood, a big, round shape. "I dunno," I said. I reached down with my hand and pulled at the bag, dislodging a nest of flies which flew up suddenly in our faces. The shape inside it was revealed to be half a baby's head crawling with maggots.

Jenny cried out, backed off, and Jane screamed, running from the tunnel.

Laughing, I picked up the bag. "It's just a doll!" I said, holding it on the end of my big stick. That was all. Just a doll in a bag with something mushy inside the head, an old peach or something which the flies had been feeding on.

Jenny was staring at the bag, her back against the wall of the tunnel. Her eyes were wide and her hands were shaking.

"If you ever do that to me again, Jason Jones," she hissed, "I'll fucking kill you I will!"

She walked outside to join and console Jane, who was crying.

Behind me I heard a low chuckling noise. James stepped into the green-tinged light. "Well done, JJ," he said, walking past me.

I watched as he joined Jenny and his twin sister, putting his arms around them both as they walked away from the tunnel.

"It was only a doll," I said to myself, feeling upset at how I had now been cut out of their company. It occurred to me that our roles had suddenly reversed, so that now I was the outsider, watching the three J's walk away from me, and James was the comfort, the third person holding the others together. "Just a bloody doll," I hissed, following them.

But what if it really had been a baby, I wondered? The image haunted me for a long time, even though I was the one who had laughed it off. It gave me nightmares I still have right now. Nightmares which seem frighteningly real.

2.3

Sunday night, just over a week since we'd found Stephen in the lock up. It was quiet and dark. I was in my 'lantern' at the top of the house, toying with a packet of cigarettes whilst looking through the windows at the brooding, gothic gable of St Leonard's church.

The lantern was the highest point of the house. It pushed up out of the pitch of the roof – a large, octagonal rotunda with a window on each face. When lit, from outside it looked like a fancy lighthouse standing high above the trees that screened my house from the road.

Tonight I had left the lights off, so no one could see me.

I moved in the darkness to sit on the window ledge, pondering the guy I'd hit and wishing I hadn't over-reacted like that. I felt ashamed because I wasn't a kid anymore. I could have killed him. As it was, he might be talking to the police right now, preparing to crucify me for assault or something. Also, I wished Harriet hadn't seen me do that. It wasn't me, I didn't…

What the hell. It was done now, right? Another stupid act from JJ-the-Stupid.

It's just that I thought he'd been stalking me. It was definitely him who'd thrown the brick through my window. So he deserved a beating didn't he?

With shaking hands I fished out a cigarette lighter from the pockets of the big old cardigan I was wearing which used to belong to my dad. I was naked underneath it. Naked except for my grey slipper-socks – not a great look I know but there was no one else in the house so I didn't care.

Lighting up my cigarette I glimpsed a ghost of myself reflected briefly in the eight dusty windows surrounding me. They vanished when I cut the flame, but even from that ephemeral reflection I still felt as though my past was watching me. Questioning and accusing.

Fuck me… My head does this sometimes… It's why I'm an artist right? I look at things this way. It's why I'd had to go into the lock up even though I knew there was a body in there.

I had to see it, record it, feel it, store it away for future use.

Didn't know it'd be Stephen, though. *Christ!*

I took another drag on the fag and forced my head back to happier times. Not many of those and even this one had turned sour…

My eleventh birthday. Children in the house all singing "Happy Birthday to you…" as three cakes were brought into the room and put in front of me, Jane and James. When we got older we used to say that because of our shared birthday parties and our shared 'J' we shared the same mind, that we were fragments of the same consciousness drifting in-between each body at different moments. We reckoned you could replace any one of us with the other, and I remember asking them once, one night when we were totally drunk, "how do I know that today I'm me and not you?"

But on that day, my eleventh birthday, I remember I was watching Eve Gordon, transfixed by the beautiful symmetry of her curves and by the utter perfection of her face: her sharp, green eyes, her dark brows and her long, long, beautifully-braided, raven-black hair. A real contrast to her porcelain-white skin.

But James hated her.

I remember that day she kept telling him to blow out his candles while he stood there sullenly in the flickering gloom. Jane and I blew ours out but James just wouldn't do it. I've no idea why not.

"Come on, Jamie," ordered his mum in her musical voice. "Give the candles a big puff."

Some other boys and girls at the party laughed. "Big poof! Ha ha!"

James glowered. And it seemed to me that the shadows in his eyes grew deeper and darker.

"*James*!" Eve hissed. "Blow out your damned candles!"

James scanned the room, and as I followed his eyes I saw that he was looking for Jenny, who stood in the darkness staring at him with mute sympathy.

Eve was getting short on temper now. "James," she snapped. "If you don't blow your bloody candles out I'm going to smack your arse."

James didn't like that. He grabbed the cake and flung it to the floor, candles and all. "You fucking blow them out!" he screamed.

Something in the room snapped, I felt it in my ears like a shift in pressure. Eve lunged at James, caught him by the scruff of his neck. She swung him round and threw him up against the wall. "You're not too old for a bloody smack, boy!"

"Get off me!" he screamed, turning away and falling to the floor.

Dimly I saw Jane putting out the candles with a damp cloth, and then the curtains were open and we were all blinking in the glare. I was acutely aware, as James must have been too, of just how many other children there were in the house. All of them seemed to be laughing, Gareth Evans more than most.

James was hauled to his feet, then his trousers and underpants were pulled savagely down to his ankles even as he tried to wriggle away, his bollocks flapping. The laughter increased tenfold.

With a struggle, but showing how strong she was, Eve held onto him, shoved his face into the floor and smacked his pale backside with the flat of her hand; so hard it must have stung like hell. With each blow the laughter increased and James's face, almost lost in the carpet, burned first red and then black, humiliated in his own house. Eventually he whipped out of his mum's grasp and stormed from the room, stumbling as he tried to pull his pants up. We all heard his footsteps pounding upstairs and the door to his bedroom slamming shut.

Standing next to me Jane held my hand. I could feel heat radiating from her skin as it pressed into mine, like she was willing us to fuse together in some way. She was holding me so hard it hurt.

For her part Eve was staring at the interior door. She was as still as a marble statue and just as suddenly cold. It seemed to me, thinking back now, that James could have turned on her and hit her back. She knew that, and she also knew that she would never be able to hit him like that again.

Moments frozen in time…

2.4

I pulled the cardigan tighter over my chest as the birthday party vanished into silence and darkness, an echo of voices and strong emotions dwindling to nothing.

History.

That's what we all are in the end, isn't it? Everything we do closes down. Our relationships cancel each other out and at the point of death we are nothing.

I looked down along the alleyway running behind the terrace. Wondered if some girl was alone taking a short cut home. I wondered if the Camden Killer was waiting for her. What would he do? How would he approach her?

What would I do if I was him?

Ask her the time?

She'd start running wouldn't she? Or at least quicken her walk. I guess she'd know it was futile because here was a man who had already decided that he was going to take her life. And everything that she was and everything that she had ever been, to herself and to anybody else, would suddenly, in just a short space of time become ... nothing.

Best to just jump out and grab her. Put a hand over her mouth and do what had to be done.

Or did he trick them somehow? Did he get to know them? What was the term they used...? Did he 'groom' his victims first? Pretending to be someone else on Facebook or some kind of MMORPG?

Tweets from @Sh1tpolice:

It's like a giant farmyard of victims for the Camden Killer

I replied to it with a question:

Do you think he's working alone?

To which he answered almost immediately:

No

And I guessed he was right. After all, knocking a nail into someone's forehead and filling a body with flowers wasn't the kind of thing you could do in the back of an alley just minutes before someone came along.

Made sense that he had to have an accomplice.

So who did what? Who did the killing, and who watched... or listened... or closed the door on the screams and pretended it wasn't happening?

I remember the girl in the chair screaming. So loud that the sound infused the walls of the gallery and left its mark inside them.

That was Lambeth, and I didn't ever want to go back there.

2.5

Monday:

"Mate, where'd you get all these TVs?" Jhavesh asked, looking round my studio.

He'd walked in without knocking, which meant I was going to have to get the back door fixed again. And yes the place was full of televisions of all shapes and sizes, from big wooden cabinets to flat screens small and large. They were up the stairs, stacked in the hall and on each landing, filling one of the bedrooms completely.

"Glad you came," I said to him.

"Mate, what happened to your face?"

Glass cuts from the window a few days ago. Most of the stitches were out now.

"Don't worry about it," I said. Then, "Jhavesh, I need your help."

"You want me to dump these TVs?"

"Dump them? Why would I want you to dump them? I just got them in."

"You paid money for all this shit?"

"Not all of it," I told him. "No. I need your IT skills."

"*My* IT skills? What makes you fink I'm good wiv computers?"

"You told me."

"Oh."

"'I'm wicked with computers and shit' you said. More than once. And now I got the shit, I need a computer. Importantly I need someone who knows how to knock up some kind of system that'll make all these tellies work with each other."

Jhavesh was looking around. "It's a lot of TVs and some of these are old, man."

"Are you just gonna stand there and make pithy comments or do you want to hear me out and help?"

"What's pithy mean?"

"It means stop being a cock for once and listen up."

He grinned. Took out a packet of Marlboro's and lit one. He offered me one but I shook my head. I'd smoked too much the night before and my mouth was like the inside of a box of old Weetabix.

"So why do you want all these tellies linked up?"

"Art."

"Art?"

"You wouldn't understand."

"Hey! I understand. You want to make them into a sculpture?"

"No. I want to put images on all of them. I want to create a constantly-baffling, visually dynamic and metamorphic cyclorama of paranoia, fear and bewilderment."

He nodded and puffed away. Stared at me. "You're a weirdo, man. Same image?"

"Maybe," I said. "Sometimes. Or I might want to show aspects of the same image. Like from different angles on different TVs. Or completely different images."

He was looking at me.

"I want to mix it up a bit." I sniffed. Brushed loose hair out of my face.

"Right..." he said. But it didn't sound like he got it.

So I explained it to him. "Like, say for example, there's a face against a plain coloured background. On one TV that background is blue, and on another TV it's red. Or maybe the background is a picture of a forest. Or the inside of a torture chamber. Or maybe both on top of each other. Or maybe on one TV the same face is replicated right across the screen and there is no background image. Maybe on another TV the face is just a silhouette. Maybe different faces in different TVs."

"And this is art?" He took another puff.

"You with me?" I asked.

"You gonna pay me?"

I nodded.

"Cool," he said with a bright grin. "I'm wiv you. I'm in."

I nodded again. "It's going in a gallery. So I need something, some kind of system that can work the displays for at least twelve hours a day."

"Right."

"I don't want stuff on a loop. I mean, we can have a bank of images – I'll take care of those – but I need a random element built into it. I want video cameras placed around the gallery inside and out, taking pictures of people coming and going. Then the system needs to superimpose those images, those people, onto the prerecorded stuff. Can you do that?"

"Yeah, man. I got a mate at the BBC. He does all that shit."

"Really?" I was surprised. Seemed like Jhavesh knew everyone.

"Nah, man! I'm messing. I don't know no one at the BBC." He laughed. "You're fucking crazy and this is way out of my league. When I said I was good at IT I just meant I could set you up with some hooky laptops"

"You son of a bitch," I said, getting stressed. "Do you know someone who can do this or not?"

"Easy, guy. There's my cousin Hari. He can sort summink out for you."

Was he taking the piss again? "Your cousin Hari?" I said.

"He's good, man. He works on big rigs for like The X-Factor Roadshow and all that."

I looked at him suspiciously.

"He did Kylie's tour," Jhavesh protested. "Does a load of bands. Straight up. All these dudes which have like massive AV rigs on their stage-shows. Massive screens. Computer-generated imagery. Crowd grabs. That stuff you want? It exists. You can do it – Hari can do it for you. But it ain't cheap, man. Seriously I hope you got some cash to spare."

"I want it in here first."

"Here?"

"In the house. Small scale – just to see if it'll work."

"Makes sense."

"Then, if it works, we'll take it to the Dreadnought."

"The what?"

"The gallery."

"Oh." Then. "When's that?"

"New Year's Eve."

He stared at me. "New Year's Eve? *This* New Year's Eve?"

I nodded. "How long can it take?" I said to him. "That gives us a couple of months to film it, trial it and fix any wotchacallits … gremlins."

"And install it," he said. "That ain't gonna be easy."

"Your cousin just needs to build the electronics and design the software to run it," I told him. "That's all. The gallery will use their own contractors to put the thing up and anyway that's down to me to design. We can do it."

"And how much you gonna pay?"

"Jesus Christ!" I turned on him. "Look, I'll pay whatever it costs. Just … just don't take the piss. Remember we're mates."

He grinned and hunted around for an ashtray. I handed him an old dinner plate I'd been eating some fruit off earlier and he stubbed his fag out on that. Then he blew the remains of the smoke into my face.

"Don't do that again," I said. "We good?"

"Yeah, man. We're good. I'll call up Harish."

"Brilliant. Like you said, there isn't much time."

He stared at me. Then: "You want me to call him now?"

"Thought you'd never ask!"

He gave me a look, then slipped out his iPhone and messaged his cousin. "He's in bed," he said a minute later. "I told him to get his lazy arse over here right away."

"Cool," I said. Then wondered immediately why I'd done that.

I never said 'cool' to anything.

Jhavesh nodded and looked around the TVs. "So this is what is art nowadays?"

"Yup."

"And I thought it was just paintings of flowers and fruitbowls."

"I've never painted flowers and fruitbowls."

"Maybe you should," he told me. "You could sell it in the market and make some cash. People like that shit."

"Thanks. I'll bear it in mind."

"You never done graffiti?"

"Graffiti isn't art."

"Tell that to Banksy."

"Graffiti isn't art."

He was grinning again. "You don't like Banksy?"

"I never met the guy."

"No one has. He's good though."

"If you say so."

"Whatever. You got any cup of tea on the go?"

"You want a cup of tea?"

"Mate, I'd murder my missus for a cup of lovely tea."

I only had Earl Grey – it was the only tea I drank but he didn't complain, he knew me well enough. His cousin Harish arrived twenty minutes later. He was a tall, lanky-limbed twenty-something wearing his jeans halfway down his arse with bright green Nike hi-tops on his feet. Laces hanging over the sides like he couldn't be bothered to tie them up. A dark grey Animal hoodie completed the outfit.

Jhavesh let him in when I was on the phone to Arnold.

"You sure?" I said to Arnold.

"He wasn't happy, not by a long chalk, Jason. Brian had already approached Theo to be in the exhibition and Theo had agreed to it. Now Brian's got to tell him he's no longer included. For one minute I thought he was going to tell me to forget about you."

"But Theo's out, right?" To be honest it was all I cared about.

There was a pause on the line. "Yes, Jason," Arnold said. "You want me to spell it out so I will. I'm good like that so here you go: Theo is no longer participating in *The Odyssey Exhibition*. You got your wish. I just hope you've got something worthwhile to exhibit because Brian Cavendish is putting a lot of faith in you right now. Be seeing you."

The call ended and I walked back into the room where Jhavesh and Harish were discussing the project.

"Well?" I asked.

Harish looked at me. Mumbled something.

"Pardon?" I said.

"He says do you want wi-fi?"

"Do I need wi-fi?"

"He says it'd be easier if you didn't," Jhavesh continued.

Harish nodded under the hoodie. I caught a glimpse of a round, brown nose and some facial hair below it.

"More reliable if it's hard-wired," muttered the 'tache.

"Fine," I said, "no wi-fi."

"But it'll cost more."

"Ok," I said. "You two guys know what I want to do, right? So you cost it up for me, whatever kit you need as long as you can get it ready by the end of the week. And if it works, then like I said, we do it again but on a much bigger scale – and you get paid more."

Jhavesh was grinning. "Mate," he said. "I hope you insured your house."

"Why? You think someone's going to break in and steal all these old TVs?"

"Nah, man," he said with a grin. "It's just that when you plug them all in you're going to overload your supply. And old houses like this don't have modern circuit breakers. You could go up in flames, mate. Whoosh! Fatal death just like that."

Seriously. I was going to kill this mouthy little fucker.

2.6

But…

Houses burning. Memories again. I remember a house burning.

I wasn't there to see it but it made the BBC local news and it was in all the papers the next day. I drew a picture of what it might have been like for the people trapped inside it: screaming faces mingling with the smoke and bubbling in the heat. Desperation and loss in their eyes.

It was a good drawing but when she saw it my mum ripped it up and threw it away.

It was two weeks or so after our eleventh birthday and the house was James Gordon's house. The people trapped inside it were Eve and Jane Gordon. They were rescued by the firemen and taken to hospital. I remember that Jane was treated for smoke inhalation. Smaller lungs, I suppose. Eve had minor burns and she'd broken two finger bones in her right hand trying to break the double-glazed window of the master bedroom with her fists.

After the fire James and his dad, Adam, had come to live at our house, and this had made me furious, especially when I was told by my mum that James would be sleeping in my bedroom. "He can't!" I wailed. I remember I was angrier than I had ever been.

"Get used to it and start acting your age, Jason. And clear this mess up by supper, I want to have the camp-bed down for James by then."

"No!" I screamed, set to explode.

But my mum left me to it. She walked out of the bedroom and closed the door behind her.

I sat on my bed and I plotted James's death. If he was coming here then so be it. I'd wait until he was snoring, then I'd stuff an old sock right into his mouth, so far down that it filled his throat and he wouldn't be able to scream. Then I would put my kit-bag over his head, pull the string tight and knot it. Kneeling on his chest so that he wouldn't be able to fight back I'd pound his ugly head into bony pulp inside the kit bag. It wouldn't take long.

Or I could stab him.

I could bring a kitchen knife up from downstairs and stab him while he was asleep: just press the point of the knife against his skin, right over his heart, and then slide it in, right between his ribs, right into his heart. He wouldn't feel it. Wouldn't even scream as it went in. I could put my other hand over his mouth just to be sure.

I fell asleep dreaming of James' death and sometime later I awoke to the sound of crying.

At first I was confused, I didn't know what was going on.

I looked over at the alien shape the camp-bed made in the darkness, at the outlines of white blankets glowing in the moonlight from behind the curtains. Sitting up I saw a deep shadow, a silhouette - a short-haired head with big, round ears sticking out either side.

At first I thought it was a mirror, a reflection of me come alive in the moonlight, then it hit me who it was.

"James?"

James was crying and muttering under his breath, rocking himself backwards and forwards on his bony arse.

"James!" I hissed again. "What are you doing?"

"She shouldn't have done it," James muttered in his thick Devon accent. "She shouldn't have done what she done."

"Who?"

"My mum. She shouldn't have pulled my pants down in front of everyone."

I could have laughed. Until now I had forgotten about that. James obviously hadn't.

"I didn't know Jane was in there too!" James blubbed. "I didn't know she was in there, in the house. I didn't know she would have died as well. But she shouldn't have done it should she? Mum shouldn't never have hit me like that, not in front of Jenny, not in front of no one."

He was crying again.

"No," I answered then, sitting up in bed. "No she shouldn't."

James, snivelling and weeping, shaking and shivering, crawled up onto my bed. "JJ," he whispered, his voice thick with emotion. "Promise you can keep a secret?"

"Promise," I answered seriously.

James told me then how he had started the fire.

2.7

"So what are you calling it?" asked Arnold, looking around at the televisions that were all over the rooms downstairs in my house. Wires everywhere.

"Castle Mechanics," I told him.

He didn't look impressed.

"What?" I said, sensing he wasn't exactly on a par with me here.

"Nothing."

"No. Come on. What's wrong with it?"

He turned towards me. Sighed and gave me a despairing look. "You've done castles before," he said.

"But not like this. Not using televisions."

"It isn't… very original."

"The *presentation* is original," I said defensively.

"No it isn't. You've used televisions before."

"Not to make a castle out of."

He raised an eyebrow. "But it's not 'actually' a castle is it?" he said, doing the thing with his fingers again.

I copied him. "Correct. It's not 'actually' a castle, it's a 'metaphor'. You know what that is right? Being an agent and all."

"Like no one's ever thought of that before," he mumbled. "Y'know… *Castles*," he said. "Look I'm glad you've got your mojo back. It's good to see. Really it is. But I just don't think this is… It's probably not what Brian was looking for."

"Has he told you what he wants from me?"

"Not in so many words, no."

"Did he give you a checklist?"

"What? No."

"So he's left it up to me, right? He wants something big and adventurous. Something which is quintessentially Jason Jones. Like you said, he likes my art. He *gets* me. I'm a demagogue – your words."

He threw his hands up. "All right. Do your bloody castle. See if I care. You'll meet him tomorrow anyway – I've made us an appointment at the Dreadnought so you can see the space and talk to him yourself. And if he likes it then fine. What the hell do I know anyway?"

"If he likes it then you get paid."

Arnold stared at me like he was going to kill me. He was really rattled by this.

"He'll like it," I said, calmer. "Don't worry."

"Your choice, I guess."

"I guess." Then I said to him, "Can you get me a model?"

"If you like."

"Seriously. I want a model."

"Male or female?"

"Female. Mature – ish. Late twenties early thirties. No teenagers who've never done this before."

"Good. We don't want another Lambeth disaster."

He was still in a mood.

Then he said to me, "What is it with you and castles anyway?"

"I like castles. Always have done."

2.8

I remember the summer after the fire, watching our two sisters playing in the surf. Both sets of parents were down on the beach lazing behind a colourful windbreak up against the base of the small, ragged cliffs that James and I sat atop of.

This was Rhosneigr, a shoreline on the south side of Anglesey at the bottom end of Cymyran Bay, a place surrounded by Official Designated Areas of Outstanding Beauty. The people who lived here had to fight hordes of bustling holidaymakers every summer for a place on the beach, a ground battle reflected in the air by the fierce aerobatics of the screeching seagulls wheeling overhead.

I used to wish that they'd all go away and leave me alone. For years I'd coveted the island, I wanted it all to myself: Its shallow green vales and golden beaches, its ancient castle ruins, Celtic burial chambers, standing stones and cairns, its lush parks and water meadows, sparkling, winding rivers and beautiful lakes. All would be mine and mine alone.

Sitting on the clifftops that day I confided in James. I remember telling him how I wanted to wake up one morning and discover that the people of Anglesey had gone over to Ireland, or retreated to mainland Wales. Better still, they'd all been infected by a killer virus to which we alone were immune, and now they were all dead.

After destroying the bridges which connected the island to Wales, I told him, I would build a castle that covered the whole of Anglesey with a wall of stone impregnable to any attack, its exterior and interior bristling with weapons and traps.

James took the idea and ran with it. "We should have a labyrinth in it," he suggested, "running underneath the whole castle so that when we'd finished torturing the prisoners we could put them in there if they was still alive. We would tell them there's a way out, see? And say if they find it they're free to go. But there would be wild animals in there, like lions, bears and wolves. We could use mirrors to make false corners. They'd look different from each direction so nobody would know where he'd come from, let alone where he was going. The only real path would be one that leads him right back to the centre. So there ain't no way out, not really."

"Sounds good," I agreed enthusiastically. I wasn't going to be outdone so I added in my own horrors. "We could have like giant saw blades falling down from the roof, and massive pits filled with poisonous snakes or acid, and walls that close in and crush you flat."

James was quiet for a minute. "Maybe we should let the girls into the castle as well," he suggested.

"What girls?" I asked.

He nodded down at Jenny and Jane.

The idea horrified me. "No," I said. "No girls."

"Why not?"

"They'll be running around the place getting under our feet."

"Jane doesn't run around so much now," he told me. "Not since the fire. She's still got smoke in her lungs."

There was a terrific scream in the sky. From the west two low-flying, military aircraft shot across the bay, trailing parallel lines of vapour in their wake.

James traced their path across the bay with his hand shading his eyes.

"I'd love to fly one of those," he told me. "We could have one to protect the castle."

As he fantasised about the aircraft I looked down at the two girls flirting in their bathing suits with the gentle surf, Jane with her blonde hair spinning in the sunlight, Jenny with her wet ponytail falling forward over her shoulder to dangle between her wobbling breasts.

"What about mum and dad?" I asked softly, watching as my fat dad stalked the girls with a bucket of seawater.

"No," said James darkly. "They won't be here. Don't forget they'll have been wiped out by the virus."

Down on the beach my dad threw the bucket of seawater over Jenny, who squealed and shivered and stamped her feet rapidly in the surf. Jane giggled and laughed, then started to cough and retch. Suddenly Dad whipped her away from the sea and ran back to the windbreak holding the girl in both his arms where Eve readied Jane's inhaler. I wondered where my mum and Adam had gone.

It would be sad if they were all killed by the virus, but it went against the original plan to let my mum or dad inside the castle. "We would have to get lots of tellies in," I told James.

"Yes."

"Because otherwise we won't be able to watch the footie."

James scoffed. He looked sideways at me and said, "There's more to life than football, J."

"Like what?" I challenged him.

He nodded down at the girls on the beach. "Them for starters."

2.9

Gallery21 was a massive corporate entity. A living example of the money-making power of art and the media, born out of the millennial anxiety of the 1990s and flourishing in the aftermath of 9/11.

Of the original six founders, only Brian Cavendish remained. He was a giant 'Rutger Hauer' kind of figure with a shock of blond hair and a face like a wall of stone. Cavendish had spent most of the 80s and 90s out in the Far East, tuning his soul into mountain music and polishing his karma. He believed that the future would find expression via the impersonal hives of the vast Asian Megacities rising in Korea, China and Japan. Fusing with Western paranoia and civil war in the Middle East it would take form as a global shadow of anxiety and fear, ruled over by a powerful mass media which controlled belief systems in ways that would make the Vatican envious. The G21 entrepreneurs advocated an art that both expressed this and was produced by it.

Theo and I exhibited with them once but that was a one-off and it ended in disaster – for us at least, if not for Gallery21. With additional funding from a mystery investor, Brian and his directors all grew rich and fat, setting up media companies around the world, buying and selling business and doing all the stuff that companies did when they wanted to expand.

Brian Cavendish remained in London, raking it all in. Saying all the right things to all the right people so that his empire grew large and he could drive up and down the Thames in his expensive boat. Now they were looking to pay me a fortune to exhibit at the Dreadnought.

The total sum was in the millions. The advance alone would be more than enough to cover the cost of building *Castle Mechanics*.

First though, I had to meet with Brian. Listen to his ideas and explain to him what I wanted to do for his 'Odyssey' project. I still had to get his approval.

"I'm serious," said Brian as he took me around the empty, white spaces of the Dreadnought. "It's time to pilot this ship and you're the man I want at the helm. No more mister nice-guy. These days I'm big enough and badass enough to take them on from the inside," he said. "No more been-there-done-that."

I glanced at Arnold who mouthed the word 'badass' and raised an eyebrow.

The Dreadnought Gallery extended partway across the Thames from Artillery Wharf on the north bank with a view of the O2 the other side. The building was shaped like a battleship and looking down through the giant, wedge of windows at the river flowing below my feet I could believe I was aboard one.

"I want *New!*" Brian suddenly bellowed, throwing his hands up. His mass of white-blond hair flaring in the sunlight. "I want *dangerous*. I want future-noire and tales of the unexpected. I don't want stencilled fucking graffiti and I don't want shit on a bed. I don't want spots or spinners or cows sliced in half and I don't want lyrical lines and forms suspended in 'non-space' whatever the hell that shit means. But then nor do I want anything retrograde. I don't want any whatisitcalled fucking 'Stuckist' bullshit either. This gallery, JJ, is not about what has been or even about what is. G21 has always been about what could be, what might be or must be. It's about the beast under the bed. It's about the far side of the sun. The dark side of the Moon. Dark matter and dark energy, it's about the ninety-percent of the Universe we know nothing about but which we all carry within us. Somewhere. Somewhere deep down. You get me?"

I nodded.

"I want you, Jason Jones," he said, taking both my shoulders in both of his hands. "I want everything you have here and now in this space at this point of change."

I nodded again.

"Because you know where we are, right?" he asked.

He didn't give me time to answer.

"Look down," he instructed me.

I looked down. At the floor.

"You see it?" he enthused.

"Um…"

"We," he hissed, "are standing on the Prime Meridian, my friend. That's what *this is*." He tapped the toe of his expensive brogues on a thin metal strip in the wood. The strip ran down the length of the room and between my feet. "Zero time," Brian enthused. "Night ends here. Daytime starts here. The world spins at a thousand miles per hour and every rotation starts and ends right here. Everything begins, everything dies… Right *here*!" he finished, eyes burning.

I nodded. I got it.

"Time," he said. "New Year's Eve. Point Zero," he whispered.

His giant hands squeezed my shoulders hard. Felt like he was going to crush them. I noticed he was smiling a thin-lipped smile.

"You've been with us before haven't you?" he asked me softly.

"Once," I answered. "It … didn't go so well."

"I remember," he said. "You had a *fight*."

"Yes."

"With Theo Collins."

"Yes."

"In front of all the papers."

"Yes," I said again. "I don't think I ever apologised to you – "

"No need," he hissed, interrupting. "No need… A drop off the cock."

"A what?"

He let me go and turned back to his giant windows. Leaned against a railing at his hips and looked out at the blinding sun like a sea-captain contemplating his next great journey.

"No fighting this time," he said. "If I'm paying you four and a half million pounds for this then –"

Arnold interrupted. "Actually, Brian," he said, "I don't think we've fully settled on –"

Brian interrupted him. "Four million, five, ten or twenty million. It doesn't *fucking matter!*" He rounded on Arnold. "It's still got six zeros on the end of it and for that, my friend…" he pointed right at me: "… no fights. Understand? Fight when *you're* paying *me*."

"Understood."

"Good," he said. Then, "So what do we do with Theo Collins?"

"What do you mean?"

"It's either him or you, this agent told me. And he convinced me why it should be you. In truth he needn't have bothered. If it was ever a choice, JJ, then it would always be you. Theo's work is… different…" he said. There was a long pause and then he added, "Still… I'd rather have the two of you together. Fuck me, Jason. Do that and I'll pay you double. What do you say to that?"

Arnold stepped up. "Erm… Brian…?"

"Shh!" he snapped. "I'm talking to the boy."

"Theo and me," I said. "I… No. It can't happen."

He was quiet. Glowering.

Then he turned back. "Whatever you want," he said. "I trust you. So. Tell me. What have you got? What is it?"

"What?"

"The New Thing that's going to fill this empty fucking space. What is it? What's it called?"

"I'm calling it *Castle Mechanics*."

Brian turned back to stare out of his giant windows, hands gripping the railing tightly. He said nothing but I thought I heard a strangled groan from Arnold behind me.

"Castles?" Brian said eventually. Quietly.

I nodded.

"I fucking *love* castles!" he boomed. Then laughed.

Loudly.

"*Brilliant!* Why has no one brought me castles before? It's always about line, and form, and volume and weight. Aesthetics and fucking bland, beige pissing pastels. If I see one more floating free-form self-expressive fucking stick on a wire I'm going to build a plank right through this window and march the talentless fuckwit off it with a spike up his arse."

And then he said, "I'm assuming it's a metaphor? I mean it's not really a castle; you're not going to build a fucking castle right here in my gallery?"

"Yes," I told him. "Yes it's a metaphor."

2.10

Brian explained more about this event he had in mind for New Year's Eve. He told us how it would link up live by satellite to a similar event in New York.

"Two New Year's Eves," he'd enthused. "One five hours later than the other. Almost like a re-run, a second chance right? Ha! You don't get many of those in life."

There'd be street music, a stage, drinks and food outside in the concourse. Video screens and fireworks. "It will be massive," he said.

Arnold and I walked out of the gallery when we'd finished, emerging into the sunshine. I didn't know about him but I felt like my brain had been sucked out of my head, chewed up and spat back at me with a splash of vodka.

The concourse outside the Dreadnought was long and straight, following the Prime Meridian north into the heart of East London. Sculptures lined the long walk at well-spaced intervals. Despite the sunshine there was water in the air, and the pavements were slick and dark from a recent rainfall. Everything was polished and gleaming but the light was odd. Weird. I looked up and saw why. A cloudbank loomed like a wall of sheer darkness behind the towers of Canary Wharf directly opposite the sun. An arc of colour disappeared between them. A partial rainbow at world's end.

"So this is where it's all going to happen?" I said to Arnold.

He nodded but said nothing.

"Brian's simultaneous event. With a five-hour time difference."

Arnold remained quiet.

"I like the element of time," I said. "I hadn't thought of that. I could use it."

I ran out of conversation-starters. Arnold was lost inside his own world of quiet.

He'd been moody all day and I was going to ask him what was wrong but actually I didn't need to. Brian Cavendish was the sort of guy who chewed up agents and I guess Arnold was feeling it. He was a strong character, Arnold, but I guess Brian was stronger, at least inside his own gallery.

"You know why this is such a strange place?" I asked.

"Why?" Arnold answered, breaking his silence at last.

"All this newness," I said, "in the middle of a place so old and full of history. Steel and glass apartments. Concrete and white stone where there used to be slums and workhouses. Long roads and pavements still dusty from having just been built. And no one around," I said. "No one but us."

"There's a Starbucks up ahead," Arnold said morosely. "There'll be people there."

"You sure about that?" I said to him.

He just looked at me. I expected a torrent of sarcastic abuse but none came. Which meant that he really was in a bad mood.

Truth was that I had been massively inspired by Brian Cavendish. My art-gene was now completely switched on, it was turned up to eleven and now I was seeing possibilities and connections everywhere. So walking along this wide, empty concourse I felt as though I was walking in a Surrealist's painting, maybe something by Giorgio di Chirico where strange mannequins inscribed with mathematical symbols haunted a sepulchral city of receding arches and wide piazzas; where the sails of distant ships rose like ghostly sheets over the city walls, and odd towers out of proportion with the rest of the town peeped around the weirdly-angled corners of empty buildings.

And then I saw something which brought the whole thing crashing down around me.

Rearing high to my left was a gleaming chromium disc facing south that bounced light back onto the concourse, almost blinding me when I looked at it. It was ten metres in diameter, leaning back at an angle to face the sky, its surface inscribed with arcane symbols, all of which were variations on a circle: the Yin Yang, the Celtic Cross, a pentagram and a swastika.

I knew the sculpture. It was called *Elliptical Time in a Slow-moving Universe*. And I knew the artist. We used to be friends.

Arnold, as if realising the danger of an outburst by me, came up behind me and put his hand on my shoulder. "You see?" he said quietly. "I told you his stuff had changed."

I shrugged. "Maybe."

"Theo wants to be a part of this Exhibition, Jason. I really don't see how you have the right to exclude him from it. Especially if Brian's going to double our fee."

"Did you find me a model?" I asked him, turning away from the shining bright disc.

"I've got a few possibles. Come on. Let's grab a Starbucks and I'll go through them with you."

We walked on through this empty street towards a parade of shops covered in dark glass façades. They were brightly-lit, but behind them all loomed this wall of sheer darkness, gathering body.

And it was so quiet.

2.11

We started building our castle in James's dad's garage. It was made out of everything: Lego, cardboard, polystyrene, Meccano, egg-boxes, you name it. But we never finished it. It was one of those structures which could never be finished.

I remember I asked James one day, while we were adding to the castle, "Why is your mum and dad called Adam and Eve?"

As usual he shrugged. James had a way of shrugging that was unique to himself. I picked it up after a while and my dad kept ticking me off for it, told me my shoulders would go funny and I'd end up like a hunchback.

But I persisted. I asked him, "Did they get together because their names were Adam and Eve, or was it just coincidence?"

"I don't know! And to be honest I don't fucking care."

"I was only asking."

"Well don't ask! Because I don't give a shit!"

Jenny asked James about his anger, and his broody mood swings once. He told her he missed his old house, and what I think of now as the autumnal bleakness of the West Country moors - the prehistoric crags and forests of Exmoor that reared up against the skies like some kind of Tolkien-esque vista.

In my mind, from his descriptions, the landscape of his home assumed a haunting darkness I've since always associated with James's deep moods. I used to paint pictures of it in my mind, imagining the moors falling into the bleak horizon like a dark sea of unfulfilled dreams of escape. It was a stark contrast to the lush beauty of Anglesey, which was a place of light and colour and endless movement.

At school, *Ysgol Gyfun Llangefni*, James never joined in at games. He showed nothing but contempt for the things which I enjoyed the most: football, rugby and cricket, and he rarely turned up to any lessons.

History, English, Welsh even, all were anathema to him. He despised them all.

Except maths.

He was a genius with numbers, and the delight on his face when he peered into the worlds they opened up to him was a joy to see.

As we entered our teenage years we would talk about girls, music, families... all kinds of things, and although James would seem bright and attentive his eyes were always looking up to the sky, to the horizon. They only ever returned to earth when the subject in some way touched on maths.

James was the only person I knew who could talk for hours about something called pi. He showed me pages of maths once, an entire exercise book crammed with impossible numbers and strange symbols. When I asked him what it all meant he said, "It's a circle. Moving through time, turning on an axis, building a sphere. It spins from one point to another, and the direction it moves in is determined by the direction of the spin. But it can only turn in one direction once."

"So eventually," I said to him, just to prove that I wasn't a total idiot, "it will stop."

He shook his head, smiling, his eyes burning bright like fire. My remark had been anticipated, invited even. "No," he answered. "It will carry on into infinity, because there are an infinite number of directions in which the sphere can move. There is always a place between two points. Trouble is it doesn't go anywhere. It stays put, spinning forever and ever, wasting all that energy."

That was about the gist of it, and the rest of what he actually said was Dutch to me. He ended up describing what patterns would appear if he were to plot his sphere and its movements through space and time onto a graph. Then he went on to delve into Chaos, at which point I switched off and it was my eyes which looked to the horizon.

This was a boy who was fourteen years old.

However, he was reasonably happy helping me build my castle in his dad's garage, and I was happy when he was with me doing it. Usually we were peaceful when we were involved in it, much to the amusement of our parents who were pleased to see that we were getting on with each other.

But what really made the castle were our dreams.

It was our secret place, and although it may have been small in actuality, filling only one corner of a poky little garage, in our minds it was vast. In my mind it assumed artistic dimensions: I pictured it from various angles against stunning backdrops, seeing huge gothic windows, enormous, crooked spires approached by foggy, cobwebbed stairwells. I heard screams echoing down long halls, saw bedchambers crowded with shadows and haunted with memories. I wallowed in the electric potential of its dark imagery.

James saw it in mathematical terms. There were ratios and proportions. There were tidy little formulae worked into the towers and keeps. There were dimensions and sub-dimensions, an endless breakdown of space.

In the castle, as in his sphere, I think James glimpsed infinity.

Perhaps his vision was as dark and dangerous as mine. Combined, the castle was not a place you would ever want to visit.

But our parents thought it was fun.

2.12

Arnold sat down in the corner of Starbucks with a green tea as gusting sheets of rain smashed against the window next to us. Looked like we'd got inside just in time.

He pulled out his iPad. Opened up a gallery of gorgeous women, none of whom interested me in the slightest.

Except for one.

"Her," I said, enlarging the picture and wheeling it around with my finger.

He stood the tablet up on its case and nodded approvingly. "Liselle Duchamps," he said.

"Duchamps?"

"Yes. She's French."

"She's the one, Arnold."

"Very attractive girl," he said. "Very much in demand." He looked at me as I took hold of my espresso and blew on it. "She won't be cheap."

"Brian's paying," I said. Then, "Jesus, Arnold! Four and a half fucking million! How the hell can he afford to pay that much?"

"You're not complaining are you?"

"No! But I mean… How?"

"G21 isn't just a gallery, Jason, it's a media empire," he said. "It makes money every minute of every day: Advertising, sponsorship, investments, deals with broadcasters and agencies you name it. It's a self-generating windfall, and with an event like the one he's proposing Brian stands to make ten times what he's paying you. People don't invest in goods anymore, Jason. They buy space. Empty space. And the more of it they have the more they can fill it, the more people will engage with it. Success is measured in mindshare and its vessel is the geometry of a brand logo."

I stared at him. Then, "That's pretty fucking deep, Arnold," I said.

He smiled. "It was wasn't it?"

We clinked our cups. "So come on," I said. "What's on your mind?"

Arnold sat back in the comfy chair and turned his face to the window. He stared through it for a while, his face as dark as the weather outside, clouds seeming to drift over the surface of his watering eyes. Then he cleared his throat and tried a smile. He looked right at me. "I guess I haven't been much company today right?"

"You've been a miserable shit all week."

He took a sip of his tea, then said, "It would have been Gareth's birthday today. He'd have been your age."

Instantly I felt bad. "Sorry, mate," I said. "I didn't know."

He shrugged. Sighed. "Don't worry about it. I'll make you pay for it later."

"If I've been a dick then I'm sorry."

He stared right at me and the pain in his vivid green eyes was easy to see. Looked like he was either going to explode or cry. Then he seemed to pull it all in, gather it up and lock it down for another year.

He picked up his iPad.

"So," he breathed, then cleared his throat. "Liselle Duchamps is the lucky girl who's going to be trapped inside your TV castle. I hope this isn't going to be another Lambeth, Jason. For your sake as much as mine. I want to be a millionaire as much as you do."

2.13

Back here. Back in the warehouse on New Year's Eve. Thinking about beautiful Liselle Duchamps.

"Don't worry," she said to me the first time we met. "You can do what you want with me. I won't scream."

Fucking goosebumps!

Even now, here in the dark, looking back through time…

2.14

Goosebumps.

Like when Jane Gordon first kissed me. Like when she squeezed my thigh under the desk during a history lesson at *Ysgol Gyfn Llangefni*, and carried on squeezing, giving me an erection that threatened to explode.

Jane Gordon...

Beautiful Jane Gordon as she turned from little girl to long-legged – almost gangly – teenager. Tall. Blonde. A strong chin and a stronger, challenging gaze from two huge blue-green eyes. She was confident and she was hungry for knowledge. She took to history lessons like a predator hunting for food. She ate it all up, bones and blood; every civil and international war, every political shift, every war crime the Royal Family ever committed. She tore into our past voraciously and I loved her for it.

Unlike her brother – who would have been in the same class had he *ever* turned up.

Still, Mr Horton shouldn't have taken it personally. James Gordon hated High School and History was no exception.

History was on a Friday morning that year, when James preferred instead to wander the old town alone. But I never wanted to be anywhere else. Jane and I sat side by side at the back while Mr Horton scribbled dates and difficult words on the blackboard.

I remember one of those days he was telling us, in his Wrexham accent, all about the life and works of:

"Giraldus Cambrensis," (spelling it), "who was also known as Gerald Of Wales. Born around 1146, died around 1223. For dates like this where we are unsure we use this little c to indicate our uncertainty, which means *circa*, which means *thereabouts*. So we write c.1146, c.1223. Are you writing this down? Good. Now, Giraldus wrote fictional stories, folk tales mostly, whilst travelling around Ireland and Wales. However, he also wrote on what he saw of the people and places he visited, and when he visited Anglesey in 1191 he wrote in his chronicle of Wales: *Itinerareum Cambriae* - don't worry about learning that, it's just Latin for An Itinerary of Wales - he wrote that Anglesey, which was then called Mona, was 'incomparably more fertile in corn than any other part of Wales.' Easy right?"

Silence. A few kids exchanged glances between themselves as if to question the teacher's sanity.

"*'Mon mam Cymbry'*, he wrote. Which means...? Anyone..?"

Nothing.

"God help us. It means 'Mona, mother of Wales'," he said, and wrote that on the blackboard too.

"Right. So I want you all to turn to page seventy-one of the blue textbook where you'll find some extracts from Gerald's chronicles. Has everybody got that? *Blue* textbook, Martin. OK. Good. Now. Who'd like to read out? Hmm? Jane Gordon."

She squeezed my bollocks hard, then slipped her hand off, leaving me almost gasping.

"Sir," she whispered, her eyes staring right at the teacher.

Mr Horton looked disconcerted for a moment, and all eyes in front of us turned around to stare at us both. Donna Llewllyn and two of her cronies stared daggers at Jane. There'd been a whisper going round that Donna wanted to beat Jane up for some reason. She could try it, I remember thinking. If she came close I'd give her to Jenny to use as a punchbag.

Then Mr Horton broke the tension. He said, "You can read the first couple of paragraphs, perhaps read them to your brother when you get home eh? Just so that he doesn't feel entirely left out."

There were sniggers in class. Someone muttered, "James is a gayboy," under his hands and all eyes turned back to the front.

"Ready Jane?" asked Mr Horton.

She nodded, and began to read from the textbook in her clear bell-like, regal tenor: "'The island of Mona contains three hundred and forty-three vills, considered equal to three cantreds…'"

2.15

At lunchtime – might have been that day, might have been a different day – I found James smoking a cigarette in town. He was looking in the window of the TV rental shop. It was quarter-past twelve by the town clock standing tall behind us and the place was filling up with schoolkids invading the chippies, bakeries and sweet shops.

James was watching his image on a television screen, an image being relayed to it by a huge video camera pointing right at him from a shelf just above the television. Both James and I had been trying for months to get our parents to rent or buy the video camera, but none of them had seemed interested, my dad saying it was far too expensive, and far too heavy for two lads to be messing about with.

I was about to ask James what he'd been doing all morning when a voice from across the road made him grit his teeth, and four reflections swam into view across the window of the rental shop. I saw them more clearly when they entered the frame of the television screen.

"Gordon!"

It was Ian Butler, Gareth Evans, Barry O'Connell and Hywel Jones.

"Why aren't you at school, Gordon?" asked Hywel in his singsong Welsh accent.

James shrugged, still looking at the television image in the shop window. Coolly smoking his cigarette.

"Give us a fag," said Gareth, holding his hand out.

James turned away from the window, then stared at Gareth, looking him up and down. These two had never got on together, and I wondered what Gareth was doing here. He wasn't spoiling for a fight. Was he? I looked at his face: long nose, dark eyes, slightly canine teeth and black floppy hair that made him look like a young Hitler. James just eyeballed him.

Gareth was a rich kid, popular and easy in the company of his mates. We didn't know why his dad had put him in our school but there'd been rumours that he'd put some kids in hospital at his previous posh school in England. Anyway, right now he matched James's gaze with a slight, tense smile. His hand was still outstretched. "Cigarette?"

It was there in the tone of his demand – a challenge. The words could have been anything, the intent behind them would have been the same.

I swore under my breath.

So he *was* here looking for a fight.

James smiled, took a drag on his own cigarette and blew the smoke sideways, keeping his eyes on Gareth.

Gareth said, "I'm seeing your sister at the weekend."

Which was a lie.

"James," I said, moving towards him. "Let's go."

Gareth looked at me. "What are you his fucking girlfriend?" he said. "Look at you. You're a fucking queer." Then back at James, "And you. Gayboy Gordon."

"Fuckoff," said James.

It was all he needed.

Suddenly Gareth Evans threw a punch at James, it was wickedly fast but he saw it coming. James was lightning quick when it came to fights, after all he had been practising against me for most of his life. He ducked, then stood upright and smacked Gareth hard on the chin, busting his lips. James, cigarette still in his mouth, kept on punching him, timing his blows just quickly enough to stop Gareth coming back to his senses, and loading them with as much weight as he could for maximum impact.

Gareth fell back under the force of each jolting blow, unable to get his wits together to reply, and eventually he fell against the shop window, where he cowered and bled and sobbed and begged James to stop. "I didn't mean it! I was only joking!" he screamed. Blood poured from his nose and lip. He held his hands over his head to protect himself and lifted one of his knees pathetically. James looked at him for moment, and I thought he was going to stop there.

He could have done. Gareth was beaten.

But then James punched him again – harder this time. Then, quickly, again – and again – and again – wilder now – faster. Gareth was quiet as he fell to the pavement, his long nose spilling blood.

Then James stopped, he just switched off and glanced down at what he had done. He waited for the others to step in and help their friend but they didn't.

Gareth Evans was on the pavement crying, curled up like a baby. His face was split and bruised. Bleeding. James took a last toke on his cigarette, then flicked it away before walking off, pushing past Barry and Hywel.

The video camera in the shop looked on impassively. I ran after James.

When I went home later that same day, I found Jenny sitting on my bed wearing her black dressing gown. Her hair was wrapped in a blue towel piled high on her head. She'd dyed her hair with streaks of dark red.

"You should have seen it, Jenny!" I hissed, barely able to contain my excitement. I took my school shirt off and shadow-boxed an imaginary Gareth Evans. "He kicked the shit out of him. Bam!" I threw a left, two right jabs: "Bam bam!"

"Watch your language, JJ," Jenny admonished, occupied with painting her nails black while I slid my trousers off and threw them across the floor.

"Are mum and dad out tonight?" I asked, flexing my shoulders.

Jenny, blowing her toenails gently, nodded. "Aren't they always?" she said. "What do you want for tea?"

In my undies I leaped onto the bed. It bounced, making her tut as she slipped varnish across her toe. "Whatever you've got," I told her. "I don't mind."

Jenny at last lifted her attention away from her toenails. She raised an eyebrow and smiled expansively, showing her gorgeous big and straight white teeth. She laughed. "Really?"

I shuffled forward on my knees, holding her gaze with my eyes.

"As long as I can have you for afters," I told her.

She leant forward to brush the hair from my eyes and kiss my forehead. "Wait and see," she said, then stood up and left the room.

2.16

It's still dark inside the warehouse. Pitch black in places. Outside it's daylight. I venture cautiously outside, onto the rooftop to see whether there's any sign of Hershey and her police, but there's nothing.

Looking across the cityscape of London I can see the big, white dome at Greenwich, the O2 Arena shining in the distance like the Emerald City.

I need to sleep but I can't. Too much going on in my head, keeping me awake in the dark.

I walk back inside, out of the cold and then I'm pacing. Upstairs, downstairs. Top floor, bottom floor. Basement level. My head is alive with memories and emotions. They're literally fizzing into life around me and it's as though I'm walking from one scene to another, each one in a different space in the warehouse, playing itself out.

The old station house back in Anglesey...

I'm fourteen, fifteen then sixteen again, with my sister off to work as a waitress in a tea-room, while Jane, James and I study hard for our exams. In the last year of school James had pulled it together and he never missed a day. Top of the class in six months – like that was all the education he'd needed in the last five years.

In the old station house Jane and I sat together one summer afternoon, sharing the warmth of our bodies in the summer heat, swapping stories on who was doing what to whom, and what our plans would be when we left school. It seems so far away but I cling to the memory because it's all that I have. Old timetables, like memories themselves, unused for many years turning yellow and crisp, looked down on where we sat while shafts of golden sunlight sifted in through the grimy windows.

I used to think that James's sister glowed with sunshine. She laughed so loudly and energetically, her eyes sparkling, her mouth open wide and her teeth flashing, her hair so blonde it was almost white; and she seemed so full of life that it was hard to remember that she had nearly died in that house fire, years ago.

"Jane Gordon…" Listen at me, an idiot mumbling away, muttering a name over and over again, relishing every syllable, every sound of that name as though I could bring her close to me again.

The cramp in my stomach seems to worsen, and even a long piss in the corner of a room which probably used to be a toilet (it certainly is now), doesn't help. I'm hungry, cold and sore. Alone and angry.

As adults we laugh at children's games and maybe tease them for their naiveté when they think they know better than we do – especially teenagers. But it's a serious place, with long days marking out a sense of time unfettered by experience. *Our* teenage world, the one which belonged to the four Js – myself, James, Jane and Jenny – was closed off to all outsiders. We let nobody in.

"Are we normal?" Jane asked me once, naked, sweat-covered and radiant with heat in our makeshift bed in the dusty ticket office. "Is there something wrong with us?"

I remember hugging her close to me, comforting and soothing her, kneading her bare shoulders with my knuckles. Secretly I wondered the same.

A closed world, and the old station house standing by a train-line that would never be used again, which ran into a tunnel blocked at the far end, was our universe. A universe going nowhere.

One day Jane was with my sister in the room upstairs, drinking some vodka they'd brought in and smoking cigarettes. Jane was dressed only in a pink cardigan buttoned between her small breasts, and a pair of white cotton knickers. Jenny, I remember, was wearing ripped jeans and a grey Nike halter.

I was outside taking a piss in the brambles and James was nowhere to be seen.

It was raining that day, the droplets falling through the canopy of trees, hissing on the leaves as they filtered down into the wood. The rain brought up the smell of the earth under my feet, mingling with the steamy urine smell I'd just made. When I was done I buttoned up and walked around the wall of the station house, careful not to expose any patch of skin to the nettles that grew in profusion around it.

At first I thought the giggling sound was coming from Jane and my sister upstairs, then I realised that in fact we had intruders who had sneaked in from the platform.

"Shh," hissed a voice behind me as I crept into the station house entrance.

Whipping round I saw James, holding a finger to his lips.

"Who is it?" I asked in a whisper.

He said he didn't know but we crept up on them nonetheless, readying ourselves for a fight as they went up towards the old living quarters. We saw that it was three girls, three pairs of white socks and pale legs making their way up the dangerous stairs hoping to catch Jane and Jenny engaged in some sexual act which they could then expose to their friends at school.

The three girls hissed and whispered, giggled and shushed each other as they crept onto the landing at the top of the stairs.

Donna Llewellyn put her hand to the doorknob and pushed.

James and I ran up behind them; James clamped his hand over Donna's mouth and pushed his bulk up behind her, pushing her into the room. He threw her in as the other two girls screamed and turned, running down past me. They were too fast and I couldn't catch them, not that I really wanted to. One of them tripped and almost fell down the stairs in her terror, I hoped she was all right.

"JJ!" shouted James as I entered the room to see Jane pulling on her cardigan. "Why did you let them go?"

I shrugged, closing the door behind me.

"Sorry," I said, meekly.

The rain outside drummed against the boarded windows and we heard thunder mumbling overhead. The room was lit by a giant miners' lantern. It shone into Donna's terrified face, showing her up as white and pale, ghostly against the deep, deep shadows.

Jenny looked furious. She strode up to Donna who'd been thrown against the wall by James. Her backside was pressing up against it and she looked terrified. You didn't mess with my sister.

"I know you," Jenny said. "Donna Llewellyn. What were you doing spying on us?"

"I wasn't spying," Donna replied, trying to regain her composure. "We was just coming up here that's all. This place don't belong to you."

Jenny reached forwards, put her hand on Donna's blue hairband and pulled it off with a sharp tug. Donna's fine, blonde hair fell across her face. "Get off me!" she cried. "I'll call the police! What you lot do is sick!"

Jenny rolled the fabric hairband into a ball. She reached forward and stuffed it deep into Donna's mouth. Gagged, Donna uttered an animalistic, guttural cry and snot bubbled from her nostrils. She thrashed and tried to hit back but Jenny was stronger. My sister grabbed the girl by the chin and smacked the back of her head against the wall.

Just once. Didn't even look that hard.

Donna went quiet instantly. She lost her balance and buckled, as though her legs had just switched off. Jenny caught her and lowered her to the floor.

"Whoa! Gently! There you go," said Jenny. "All over now, see?"

Standing in the shadows I felt a hot hand pressing into my palm. It was Jane, quiet and warm beside me. Together we stood and watched.

Donna started shaking. You could see it in her shoulders and her hands and knees. She tried to fold herself up into as small a space as possible.

"What shall we do with her now?" asked James, hunkering down and shining the miners' lantern at their captive. He reached out and touched the girl's bare knees, frowning. "Should we keep her? Tell her mum she's gone missing?"

"We can't keep her," I blurted. "Let her go."

In my mind Donna hadn't done anything wrong. We could let her go and close the doors and everything would be as it was before, safe and secure, shut off from the outside world.

They ignored me.

"We could put her in the tunnel with the dead things we killed earlier," James continued.

There was nothing in it. He was just making it up. But it had a terrifying effect on Donna. She visibly flinched, began shaking harder and breathing harshly though her nose.

I felt sick in my stomach.

Jenny moved round so that she was behind Donna. She supported her against her bosom, cuddling her like a baby. "Don't worry," Jenny whispered, her lips in Donna's ear. "We won't do you in the tunnel. We can kill you here just as easily."

Sounded like Donna was choking She squeezed her eyes tightly shut.

Jenny began stroking Donna's hair away from her eyes. "Shhh…" she whispered. "We can't let you go. You do know that, don't you?"

Then she looked across at James who seemed fascinated by Donna's knees. He was running his fingernail round one of them, then the other. Donna kept flinching. "You should go first, James. Fuck her or kill her.

Both if you want. If you could do anything with her, what would you do first? Where would you start?"

A high-pitched whining sound issued from deep within Donna's throat.

"Well?" Jenny challenged James with a smile. "Why not go straight in?"

She reached down and pulled Donna's skirt up her legs so that James could see the girl's knickers. There was the smallest of struggles from Donna, like she knew it was pointless.

Jenny took hold of James' hand and moved it up between Donna's thighs.

Donna opened her eyes and they flashed across at James.

I felt the sickness in my stomach. This wasn't over yet. *Please let her go*, I was thinking to myself. *Please, Jenny, please let her go.*

Jane Gordon's hand tightened in mine.

Now James and Donna's eyes seemed locked together, like a predator and its prey.

Then –

"No," he whispered. "I don't want her."

"You don't *want her*?" asked Jenny, sounding shocked. Then, in a slightly mocking tone: "Isn't she pretty enough for you? I think you're very pretty, Donna. We could use you in one of JJ's paintings. He likes drawing girls, did you know that? He likes drawing them naked and dead. Lying in the ground."

James pulled his hand away and then stood up, leaving the miners' lantern on the floor to shine upwards at the girls' faces.

"James?" snapped Jenny, her dark eyes clouding over.

He seemed to melt into the shadows.

"Let her go," he said quietly.

Jenny was disappointed – angry. "*She was spying on us!*"

"It doesn't matter – does it?" James said.

"So why did you bring her in here?" Jenny shrieked.

None of us could see James's face, the shadows were too deep, but Jenny's expression was all too exposed. It was filled with hatred.

Suddenly she grabbed Donna's chin and twisted her face round. "I'll fucking kill you if they won't!" she yelled, nose-to-nose with Donna Llewllyn. "Hear me? I'll do it myself!"

"Jenny!" I cried out, leaping forward. "Jenny, leave her!"

James grabbed me from behind and pulled me away, yanking me backwards.

83

Jenny tore Donna's school blouse down at one shoulder to reveal her bra. "If you won't have her, I will."

She looked up at James and me. "Still don't want her?" she cried.

I shook James off me and stepped forward; but at that moment there was movement in the darkness. Jane stepped into the light of the miners' lantern and knelt down next to my sister.

"Jenny," she said softly, reaching out a hand to touch her arm and lift it away.

Jenny stopped and looked at Jane, eyes wide open.

"Leave her now," said Jane. "She's learned her lesson." In the grim light shining upwards the three girls looked very different, as if the angles and colours of their faces were wrong.

Jenny looked back at Donna, then again at Jane. "She was spying on us," she whispered. "You know what she's like this one. She's evil. She wanted to kill you enough times."

"She's just a gossip," said Jane softly. "That's all. She never hurt me. And what does it matter anyway? We don't need no one else do we?"

She touched Jenny's other hand and pulled it gently away.

At that point I stepped forward and helped Donna to her feet, taking the gag from her mouth. It was full of spit and her jaw was trembling. I tried to help her set her bra and blouse to rights but she shrugged me off. Even though her hands were shaking so violently she couldn't fasten a button, she still refused my help.

While Jenny and Jane cuddled on the floor - Jane looking up at me - I walked Donna to the door.

I took her downstairs, then when we were outside I pulled her back by the shoulder and whispered close in her ear: "If you tell anyone what went on in here today, we'll come for you." I was shaking when I said it, but for that moment I was James — as dark and threatening as he could be in his deepest mood.

Donna ran into the rain, pulling her clothes back into shape as she stumbled through the wet greenery.

I watched her go and for a few, long minutes I stood still, letting the rainwater soak my hair and my clothes, my skin and my bones. It dripped from me; from my nose and my eyebrows, my ears and my fingertips. It soaked me utterly from head to foot but I did not move.

Didn't want to move.

With the organic smells and textures of the earth so vital, alive and thick in every direction, it felt as though the planet itself was breathing through my lungs; living through me. Every atom of my being was spinning in synchronicity with the entire planet Earth.

I breathed deeply and shivered, totally awestruck by this… *epiphany*. It meant that no matter how bad things became, the world was with me. I could do no wrong. *We* could do no wrong. Us four Js were elemental, and we worked to a higher order than people like Donna Llewllyn, Gareth Evans and their idiot friends.

I remember laughing and crying at the same time. Shaking so hard, literally shivering. I knew that something powerful in my DNA had been switched on that day and it was the most potent thing I'd ever felt at that age.

Standing there.

In the rain.

Centre of the universe.

The four of us.

I didn't even think how it might all end…

The Persistence of Memory

Years later...

Jenny leans forward to kiss me on the forehead. We're at one end of a vast room which smells of sickness and bleach. There's a carpet as blue as the sea, stretching out from wall to wall, and people sail leisurely upon it. They've no idea where they're going, where they came from, or even where they are. Occasionally it takes an orderly or a nurse to pilot one of them into harbour, and sit them at a reading desk or a comfy chair by the windows.

This is a lost place for lost people. I feel like one of them, staring at the rain running in chaotic streamers down the window while outside the dark sky splits with bursts of lightning as apocalyptic as the end of time itself.

Shush," Jenny whispers in my ear, her face a mask. "I've dragged our secrets through Hell and back, and they're here to stay." She taps her scarred forehead with a shaking forefinger. "They're going nowhere."

3

Symbolism

Without monsters and gods, art cannot enact our drama.

The Romantics were Prompted...
Mark Rothko.
Possibilities. New York. 1947

3.1

There were TVs all over the house.
 Wires everywhere.
 Laptop and TV screens glowed with dead, grey light in standby, or flickered and guttered ceaselessly with white noise, making weird-angled shadows dance on the ceiling.
 Walking downstairs in the middle of the night, wandering through the electric glow that suffused the house, I'd enter a room filled with vivid colour and electric silence. Inside this kaleidoscope of fizzing beauty I'd see Liselle's face multiplied on the screens. Sometimes she was screaming, sometimes just silent and watching. Always mouthing unknowable words while the backgrounds behind her changed.
 Night-time was best for walking the halls of my TV Castle.
 However, the system was in its infancy, and sometimes the images would collapse into garbage. Or a fatal error message would flash up – white text against a black background.
 Which, actually, I kind of liked…
 I asked Harish to build computer error messages into the random video. They didn't have to be genuine. As long they gave the appearance of 'fatal error messages' it was fine.
 And soon it would be perfect.

Jhavesh and Harish were both round the house one day, lugging huge drums of cables into the house, rolling them up the front door steps and down my hallway like Laurel and Hardy in a calamitous sketch.
 "Where you goin', man?"
 "This way! No no! What the fuck you doing?"
 "Oh my word!"

"You fool!"

"It was you dropped it, man!"

"I never drop nuffink. You let go!"

"Mind the walls, bro!"

There was plenty of banging and I figured if I didn't help them out then I'd have no front door left.

I went downstairs but they'd done the hard work by then. They'd left the front door wide open so I closed it. It was freezing out there.

"JJ! Mate, you gotta see this! It is *sick*!"

That was Jhavesh, calling out from the front room.

I joined them, and there on the biggest TV in the room, a seventy-something-inch Sharp Aquos, I saw Liselle's face and bare shoulders. Blue background behind her, onto which the system would overlay the pre-recorded backdrops.

"Check it out!" said Jhavesh.

Harish was sitting on a beanbag. Laptop on his knee, hoodie right over his head. He didn't look up much.

"Check what out?" I asked Jhavesh.

"Move around," he told me.

I moved around, walking up and down in front of the giant TV. I shrugged, but Jhavesh was bouncing up and down, doing stuff with his hands.

"What am I supposed to be looking at?" I asked.

"It is well-creepy," said Jhavesh. "Keep looking at the screen, man."

"But keep moving," added Hari.

I turned to the screen and then crabbed sideways. Liselle's eyes followed me from the TV.

I moved the other way and they followed me that way too. The movement was subtle, but when I moved all the way to the right her head turned and her eyes were still looking at me.

"Oh that's good," I said to the guys.

"You like that innit?" said Jhavesh.

"How do you do it?" I asked him.

"It's all on motion trackers, mate," he said, pointing upwards. "Three cameras pick up movement in a room, pinpoint the position of the thing that's moving and lock onto it."

"Relays all that info back to the system which triggers pre-recorded movements from Liselle," added Harish from somewhere under his hood.

"No delay?" I asked.

"There is a delay, at first," said Harish, "but you wouldn't notice it unless you was looking for it. You don't expect a face on the TV to be looking at you, right?"

"Guess not."

"And when you move around, the system predicts your movements."

"And if I suddenly stop?"

"Slight delay," said Harish. "But then this happens."

He hit a key on the laptop, and on the TV Liselle's face smiled and she arched her left eyebrow.

I nodded.

"Like this," I said, thumbs up.

Harish and Jhavesh exchanged high-fives, but Jhavesh knew better than to get one off me. I was shit at high-fives.

"You gonna record anymore stuff?" Harish mumbled from under his hoodie.

I nodded. "Few still things on the Mac," I answered. "And some more prerecords I gotta reshoot."

"You editing on the Mac as well?" he asked.

"That's the plan. Is it a problem?"

It's possible there was a shrug under the hoodie. Then he said, "Nah. S'cool, man."

3.2

"You're *seriously* weird," Harriet told me. She was at the market and it was busy.

I was taking pictures of her, snapping away on the brand new Nikon D4 and 50mm f/1.8 lens I'd treated myself to with some of Brian's advance.

"Yeah I thought you'd be chuffed. I'm thinking of publishing a series of 'market life' happy snaps on the side. You can be the hero."

"I'm pleased you got your mojo back," she said wryly.

The camera shutter made a beautiful, satisfying noise.

"You could be the most wonderful model that ever walked the land, Harriet," I said to her, luvvy-style as I checked out the pictures I'd taken on the camera's LCD. I meant it too. There was a kind of vulnerability in her large green eyes, she had great teeth when she smiled, and I loved her dark fringe of bobbed hair – cut straight just over her slanted,

'Elvish' eyebrows. She looked great in these black and white shots. Retro-chic!

She was chuffed, I knew she was. Trouble with Harriet was that although she came across as confident and sharp, all that brazenness masked a deep insecurity and lack of self-belief. I didn't know why Harriet, at her age, was content looking after a shitty market stall when she could be so much more.

All thoughts of Harriet disappeared when Liselle arrived, walking gracefully through the market like an angel parting a sea of lesser species.

I grinned. Lifted my camera and snapped her approach.

Harriet *was* a pretty girl, but Liselle was ... *stunning*. She knew it, and this gave her an air of confidence that just made her more attractive. She sailed towards the camera and when she reached me I stood and we did the celebrity kiss on both cheeks.

Harriet didn't seem impressed. She glowered at Liselle when I introduced them to each other. Her cheek-kiss was half-hearted and awkward, and she had to stand on tip toes, but Liselle was unfazed.

"He talks a lot about you," Liselle told her.

"Gotta go," I said to Harriet, pushing my errant model away from the stall.

"I won't wait up for you, don't worry," Harriet muttered darkly.

When we were out of earshot Liselle stopped giggling and asked how long Harriet and I had been together.

"Couple of years," I answered. Then, when I realised what she'd actually asked I said, "We're not 'together'. That was Harriet. Joking. She was joking."

Liselle raised a fine blonde eyebrow and squeezed my waist.

"Oh really?" she said.

3.3

I'd been to a party. Harriet was there and I remember chatting to her most of the night. It was the first time we'd met.

I woke up in a stranger's bed the morning after. I was naked and Harriet was naked too.

She was lying on top of me, and my hands cupped her pert and incredibly firm little arse-cheeks while we talked. She was the first person I'd really talked to in a long, long time. I didn't tell her everything about me but she knew more than most. It was easy talking to her, and listening while she told me her stories too.

We didn't have sex.

We just talked. And it was perfectly fine and natural for us both to be there: best mates totally naked, our genitals pressing together warmly, my hands on her arse, her head on my chest.

Just talking together.

3.4

One day, early October, the electric Castle was finished… at least the version of it that had rooted itself in my house was finished.

It was a monster.

Whichever room I walked into, whatever time of day or night, the screens would come alive with unsettling images. They flickered into life rapid-fire: dark faces, ethereal shapes, demonic and disturbing things, white noise, haunting landscapes and backgrounds of furious energy. Splashes of milk and blood. Fatal error messages and … yes, she was in there:

Liselle Duchamps.

Her face… her watching eyes…

Her lips.

"Well," Harish said to me one day. "For the most part it works. You like it?"

"Yeah…" I said, softly.

It was the most painful thing I'd ever expressed with my art.

3.5

"It's done," I told Arnold, pouring milk into my takeaway Starbucks. "The TV thing. *Castle Mechanics*. It's good to go. Everything works."

He looked at me. "And….?"

"Huh?"

"You don't sound convinced."

"What do you mean I don't sound convinced?"

"The tone of your voice," he said. "It lacks conviction."

"Which bit?"

"All of it. So what are you hiding from me?"

"Shut up," I said, exasperated.

I put the lid on my cup and walked out into the rain on Tottenham Court Road. He followed me out, pushing through the crowd of miserable faces, raincoats and scratching, poking, prodding brollies.

The street rumbled and shook with the perpetual thunder of endless traffic and footsteps. Headlamps and traffic lights shone bright and vivid in the hissing rain which turned the embankments of roadside snow into black slush. The pavements were flooded with people.

Arnold and I became part of that flood, diving underground with the masses.

We took the tube to Camden Town and on the way out Arnold stopped, suddenly turning to face the magazine stands of WHSmith.

I spun on my feet and doubled back to join him.

I didn't need to ask what he was looking at. A magazine with a brutal, tattooed man's face leered out at us from the cover. Rings hung off his cracked bottom lip. One gold tooth on the right.

"Look it's your mate," Arnold said.

"As I live and breathe," I muttered. It was Theo.

He picked up the magazine and leafed through it. It was called *The Art Tabloid*.

"Looks like they've had their publicity pack through," Arnold said. "Good... good good." Then: "Excellent!" There was a feature on *The Odyssey Exhibition* inside. Some of my old work was printed alongside the story and my name was mentioned.

But so too was the event at Lambeth, and looking at the picture of the girl on the chair surrounded by giant video screens a shiver snapped up my spine.

Arnold took the magazine and went inside to buy it.

While he did so I picked up another copy and flicked through to the interview with Theo. The interview had been written up by Hugh Donovan-Smith who used to edit the magazine years ago, and who was now a freelance bastard.

We'd never got on. Actually I'd never met the man, but he'd always had a lot to say about me:

'There are dark things uncovered in the harsh light of contemporary art,'

he'd written after Lambeth

'whether it's the cross-section of a cow and its unborn foetus, or splashes of semen turning crisp on the carpet. These things push the boundaries of artistic vision out towards whole new horizons. Which is just as it should be.

New lands are out there, awaiting exploration. But a horizon is a line nonetheless, and if you want to stay on the planet you don't step over it. Even within art there are subjects so dark and taboo that an artist simply cannot go there. With his destruction of a young model at Lambeth Gallery Jason Jones has not only crossed that line, but bounded over it with the fatal irresponsibility of an exuberant serial killer. Jones is not an artist, and his offerings are not art. They are butchery plain and simple. He has no eye, no vision. No talent. He may have partnered with Theo Collins at the London College many years ago, but it's clear to anyone viewing these early works exactly who was leading the cutting edge and who was holding the other back.'

Yeah, I remember that one. Memorised it word for word. He went on in the same piece to demolish everything I'd ever done. Even my paintings.

In a sudden fit of pure infantilism he'd gone on to say: 'Jones couldn't whitewash my West Country holiday cottage without messing it up.' After which I'd gone out and whitewashed his West Country holiday cottage. Inside and out, including the furniture.

Actually no. Not quite everything.

Arnold came back from the till, pocketing his wallet.

"You gonna show me this TV Castle thing then?" he said.

I put the magazine back. From a quick scan of the interview it was clear that Theo wasn't best pleased at being booted out of an exhibition he could have made a few million from.

"Why are you buying magazines from WHSmith?" I asked him as we walked out.

"Huh?"

"Don't you have *people* who do this for you? Isn't your office covered in art magazines? You know… aren't you a top-five trending agent or something?"

"It's not for me," he said, and slapped the magazine into my chest. "I'll bill you later. Come on."

3.6

"Jason! Arsehole! Wait!"

"Pissoff, Theo!"

He ran after me.

It was the LCA graduation ceremony, years ago now at the Barbican Centre in London.

Summer time.

Outside, in a windy-sunny concrete courtyard splashed with water-fountains and rainbows, I lit up a cigarette. Or tried to. I had to stop walking, cup the lighter right into my hand and shove my face into it with my back to the wind. Which was blowing fiercely, snapping at the ridiculous black gown I'd had to wear during the interminable ceremony.

Theo caught me up.

"I ain't going back inside," I said, blowing smoke from my lips.

"Didn't ask you to," he said. "I don't give a shit what you do."

I shrugged.

"What's up, bro'?" he asked me. I remember his bleached blond hair whipping across his grizzled and rugged face. Big eyes. Theo had big, blue eyes with very long lashes. No tattoos or lip-rings in those days.

"Don't worry about it," I told him.

"Fuckoff. Come on," he said, producing a packet of cigarettes from under his gown. "You don't get on with your mum?"

"It's not my mum that I'm pissed off with," I told him. "It's who she's with."

"So you don't get on with your old man then," he said, pulling a cigarette from the packet with his lips the way he always did. "At least he turned up. My dad thinks I'm some kind of gay wanker doing all this stuff."

"That fucker is *not* my dad!"

Puffs of smoke from Theo's cigarette whipped past my face as he lit up. He raised an eyebrow then steered me over to a bench by one of the ornamental fountains while I swore at him.

"*My* old man," he began cheerfully as we sat, "didn't even know I was going to be here."

"You didn't tell him?"

"Nup. None of his fucking business."

"Has he seen your art?" I asked him.

"No. What about your lot?"

"Only what's on display inside. I think my Mum likes it but… I dunno. She was looking queasy."

"And what about wotsisname? Him? The other feller? He seemed keen."

"Adam's a prick. He wouldn't understand it."

Theo sucked on his cigarette. "Well, it's only for today eh?"

I felt something then, as though someone or something had just walked right over my grave. I glanced upwards but saw only the grey face of the Barbican towers, the slim concrete tower blocks seeming to lean in towards us, crowding out the sky and enclosing us completely. "I fucking hate this place," I told Theo. "It's a shithole. Evil made manifest in concrete."

"I thought that was the RFH?"

I gave him a glance, and I laughed despite myself. What the fuck? We were art students and we had opinions on things that nobody in the real world cared about or actually gave any thought to whatsoever. In my head, at that time of my life, the Barbican was a topographical nightmare, like one of Escher's perplexing courtyards. The Barbican wasn't an emotional place. It was impassive. Dead stone. Cold and unseeing.

But inside it, inside the actual Centre itself, there was my Mum. Powerful and alive she stood among the students like a goddess, dressed in a stark, black-and-white outfit with hat and gloves to match.

She'd been standing near to the bar when I'd emerged from the presentation ceremony. A bunch of people had gathered around her and she was laughing, throwing back her head, lifting her face to the spotlights. Her lipstick was bright red, her hair was loose and a glass of Dry Martini sparkled in her long, silk-covered fingers. She was glamorous, alluring, and she inhabited her own space fully, demanding more besides. Like everyone else I was drawn towards her.

"Jason, my baby. There you are. I'm so proud of you. You look beautiful in that gown." Her eyes were on fire it seemed, as she smiled right at me and gave me a kiss on the cheek.

Jenny wasn't with her. Instead she'd brought Adam. He'd held out his hand and said, with an awkward smile on his gawky face, "Congratulations, son. We're both very proud of you."

I didn't shake his hand. I wanted to kill him there and then. So I'd hurried out in search of fresh air and Theo had seen me.

"It's rubbish out here, mate," he said. "Come on. Let's go back inside?"

"No," I told him, blowing hot smoke from my lungs.

"Up to you," he said. "But I'm going back in. There's still a few prizes to give away, and I heard on the grapevine that you and me are tipped for the Diane Carslake Award."

I'd heard it too. "We won't get the award."

"Who else are they going to give it to? Nugent?"

I laughed. Shook my head. Nugent Fry was a dick.

"Even if we did get it, it's a kiss of death right? No one who's won that award has ever gone on to do anything useful with their lives. If we're up for the Diane Carslake award then I don't want it."

My thoughts go back, right back now to a dusty lecture hall and there I am staring up at a portrait of some mad-looking old woman surrounded by foliage with what looks like a parrot on her head. Diane Carslake: student, model, painter, junkie, whore – got lost in the rainforest, went native with some of the tribes there, developed a liking for plants with hallucinogenic properties when boiled up in a pot, returned to civilisation with an art-demon on her shoulder firing off some mad stuff, and was shot dead in 1973 by a crazed evangelist who thought she was preaching Satan to the masses. Her treatises had been popular, once, long ago. She'd been something of a posthumous rebel martyr, but these days she was barely known outside the London College.

She was recognised only for one massive remaining portrait: *Jungle Nude* – which hung at the back of the stifling lecture hall, and for the annual award of a two-thousand pound grant to the 'most promising' student of the year, most of whom disappeared from trace within a year of receiving their cheque.

The kiss of death. The Curse of the Carslake Award.

Theo ground his cigarette out under his foot and started talking about the things he was going to do with the prize money.

A dark shadow fell over us suddenly.

Looking up I had to shield my eyes to make out a tall man wearing a black suit and black bowler hat who had walked into my light. The sun was bright, like a fire behind his head, and his face was narrow and long. He had green eyes, and a goatee beard immaculately trimmed against a strong, pointed chin. I put him in his late forties, maybe fifty. A few lines on his face around the eyes and mouth, but his hair was light, not as blond as Theo's but touched with grey and there was plenty of it. It curled down from the brim of his hat to slide behind his ears. At his lean neck was a stiff, white shirt collar with a perfectly knotted red tie hanging from it.

Aside from the hair he looked as though he'd just come from the Bank of England, or like Rene Magritte's *Son of Man*, but without the apple hiding his face. In this crazy concrete castle anything could have happened.

"Spare me a cigarette?" he asked.

To my surprise Theo reached into his gown and produced a cigarette for him.

The guy sat down between us and we shuffled sideways to let him in. He thanked us both and then lit the cigarette, shielding it expertly from the wind.

"Aah!" he breathed, enjoying the smoke and leaning his head back. "That does feel good."

Theo and I exchanged glances over his head:

- *Who the fuck is he?*

- *No idea!*

The man looked straight ahead. "Sorry, boys," he said brightly. "My name is Arnold Evans." With a flourish he pulled two business cards out of his breast pocket and handed one each to both of us. "I'm a ten-percenter, though I don't expect you two really know what that means. It's a quaint old term and anyway my fee is considerably higher. But you get what you pay for." He took a drag on his cigarette, and then said, "I'm an agent - for all kinds of things: musicians, actors, writers, dancers, artists. I've been looking in there," he nodded towards the glass doors of the Barbican, "trying to figure out whether any of this LCA factory fodder is worth any effort on my part. I mean I'd have to be a special kind of idiot to pass up a talented youngster fresh out of college right?" He chuckled under his breath, then tapped his cigarette ash to the ground. "Unfortunately there's nothing in there worth getting over-excited about. Genuine talent is rare these days, even at the London College. We live in an age where mediocrity is celebrated and banality exalted, encouraged by fools who, let's be honest, really should know better."

His exact words. I remember them as though he'd said it only yesterday.

Theo stood up. "I'm going inside," he said. "You coming or what?"

I nodded. "Yeah, hold up." I finished the last of my cigarette and flicked the dog end into the rainbows behind us.

Arnold looked offended. "You aren't leaving me out here alone are you?"

"Yes," snapped Theo, looking angry. He turned away and started marching back towards the Barbican.

Arnold laughed. "Off you trot then," he said. And then he made a circle with his right thumb and forefinger, held it to his eye and snatched it away in a mock salute. "Be seeing you, Jason," he said with a smile.

I forced a smile in return, then turned and walked across the courtyard back to the hall. When I reached the glass doors I looked back at the bench and saw that the agent had gone, disappearing as suddenly as he had appeared. How the hell had he known my name, I wondered?

Must have seen my picture next to some art.

He still looks the same – maybe a bit wider around the waist, but not fat, you could never call Arnold fat. His longish, wavy fair hair is mostly grey and he rarely wears a hat or a tie these days. And he's lost the beard. But he always had extremely good skin. I remember telling him once that I was impressed with the colour tone of his skin. He'd spent a few years in America he told me, on a course that dealt with his depression. "Like a fat camp," he'd said, "for manic depressives with suicidal urges. We spent a lot of time getting in tune with nature."

"What? Like singing to the trees or something? I can imagine you doing that."

"Not quite," he'd said.

"So..."

"They took us into the woods – big fucking forests up in the country. Giant trees, but we didn't sing to them. We went hunting."

"Hunting?"

"Bears, rabbits, deer. We used old Indian – sorry, *Native American* – methods. Camped out, tracked the beasts down then killed, skinned, butchered, cooked and ate them. I learnt how to skin an animal – actually got quite good at that. I could whip the hides of a rack of rabbits and turn the buggers inside-out ready for the barbecue faster than you could light up the grill, and as for identifying animal tracks... I was the undisputed Big Bear Sitting Bull."

"Bullshit," I said. "What was it really like?"

"Bedlam," he answered, laughing. "Bedlam with councillors, therapists, discussion groups and healing tutors instead of crazy surgeons trying to vent your brains out through your ears."

"Did *you* have a healing tutor?"

"Oh, Lordy, yes."

"And what did he heal?"

"You mean she? Nothing."

"Nothing?"

"Nothing ever truly heals, Jason. Nothing ever goes away. The only thing that got me through the camp was the searing heat of revenge." He said it so casually it was funny, and I tried hard not to laugh.

He told me once that he'd taken his millionaire actress wife – his second or third wife? The porn star anyway. He'd dragged her kicking and screaming through the courts to get back everything that she'd taken off him and more besides.

He'd lived a messy life from the sounds of things.

"She got what she fucking deserved," he said to me, politely but utterly drunk. He owned a lodge up in the wilds of Scotland which he hid inside every Christmas and for two years running I'd gone up and joined him for a couple days, once over Christmas, once over New Year. Each night getting stupid-drunk on the malt, during which time he'd shared his innermost feelings. "Yeah I made sure of that," he said, this one particular time. "It took a long old while, Jason, a very long time before I was in the best position to strike that crucial, final blow. You have to be patient."

He told me how he'd stalked one of his ex-wife's boyfriends, then one night he decided to take matters into his own hands.

"Could've killed the fucker," he said, and left it at that.

Theo and I gracefully accepted the Diane Carslake Award. "Thank you, all of you. We're really grateful," Theo had said into the mic. No mention of Mums or Dads from either of us, and when I looked for her afterwards, my mother had gone without a single goodbye and the Barbican Centre was cold once again.

So what the fuck? Why should I care? Theo and I had one and a half thousand pounds each to get our careers off the ground and a party that was just getting started when we got to our shared house in Bethnal Green along with a load of friends from the LCA.

But nothing happened. The morning after lasted for months and the hangovers replaced the honeymoon like white birds merging into black, one horrific day into the next. As many artworks were destroyed as created, torn apart in frenzies of explosive stress by both of us. And boy did we argue! Bottles were thrown at the street, canvas-frames through the windows. The neighbours complained about us shouting and fighting constantly.

Work after work was rejected, glanced over, laughed at, pissed on, and the money ran dry.

The Curse of the Diane Carslake Award.

Obscurity threatened us both like a giant black hole leaching away our creativity, our energy and talent, crunching it all up and hiding it away in an unreachable singularity.

Theo's way of dealing with it was to fuck himself over with drink and drugs, while mine was to take a job, any job I didn't care as long as it brought in some money to pay the rent, get some food in, buy some paint and canvases. I got a job as a gardener for Brent Council, mowing roundabouts and roadside verges on the other side of London only for that fucker to take the cash and piss it up the wall, burn it in a spoon, flush it down the toilet when the police burst in one dark and rainy October morning and dragged him away.

The blond, blue-eyed boy faded in time, and in his place grew someone who lazed around the house watching the television in the dark, or who would disappear for days at a time to mingle with dealers and prostitutes.

One day he told me that his dad was dying of cancer, and he was finding it difficult to reconcile the terror of his childhood with the bald, skeletal wretch fighting for every breath in a hospital bed over in Hammersmith. "He's still the same racist, bigoted bastard he always was," Theo raged one night when he came home from the hospital. "And he still tells me that I am less than a man! Less than *that?*" He paced the room. "I wish he'd get on with it, you know… I wish he'd hurry up and fucking die," he cried. Then he stopped in mid-stride, his eyes narrowed. He turned to me then and said, coldly, "Maybe I should speed it up. Maybe I should kill the fucker myself. I mean I *could* couldn't I?"

"Theo," I warned him.

"No, JJ. We could both of us kill him. You know how easy it is don't you, to kill a man in that condition?"

"Theo!" I snapped, shaking.

As his dad was pulled closer to death's gaping maw, Theo crawled closer to insanity. He would literally tear his hair out on a night while he rampaged about the house, asking himself what it was to be a man. And then one day he disappeared completely, for weeks, and I didn't know where he'd gone. Was he lying in a ditch somewhere, stabbed to death – or had he actually done what he'd always promised and pulled the plug from the machine that fought to extend the life of his dying father?

He came home one December night and I hardly recognised him. He'd shaved his hair off and had had a swastika tattooed behind his left earlobe. His face was cut and his lips were cracked and dry, his eyes bloodshot.

"Jesus, Theo! What have you done?"

"He's dead, Jason," he cried. "The old cunt's dead."

"Your dad? I'm sorry, mate. I'm so sorry."

3.7

So … what if I died?

Who'd notice I was gone?

Theo hated his dad utterly but he still cried like a baby, sobbing in my arms after his old man had expelled his last breath into the world.

So I'm thinking maybe it'd be better if I went right here, quietly, alone. Today. Nobody to see it. Nobody to hear it.

I'm up on the roof. Outside in the cold. Thinking too hard maybe.

I'm not going to kill myself. I don't give in that easily.

Still... There's a killer wind blowing over the Thames and that might even do it for me. Ice-cold knives blowing hard enough to strip my bones clean and toss what's left over the edge.

Tarpaulins flap and snap around me, threatening to fly off as the wind picks at their bindings. On the roof there are a dozen old, stone chimneys jutting skyward like ancient towers, wrapped in tarpaulin-covered scaffolding for the sake of preserving the brickwork. Between them run these huge, silver-clad heating and air-conditioning ducts which impose their own parasitic geometry upon the original architecture.

And I'm perched on the edge, between the chimneys, pitches and pipes like a giant Lovecraftian raven with my big coat flapping like wings out behind me.

On the opposite bank of the river rises the hallucinatory glamour of Canary Wharf. And down there to the far right, searchlights sweep along that ceiling of great, fat cloud. Blue, green and purple beams are shining up from the O2, AKA the Millennium Dome, AKA the Big White Elephant of the Nineties. The jutting angles of the Dreadnought Gallery can't be seen from here but I know that that's where he'll be.

Down there.

Tonight.

When I'm good and ready I'm out of here. I'm not going to jump. I'm not going to kill myself. I just need a sleep and I need to build up some strength. I'm starving and I need to eat but I can't go out like this, stinking of piss and filth, looking like something that crawled out of a tomb. I can't go out uncertain and unsure. I can't go out without belief or a plan.

I'm starting to figure it out see? Just remembering stuff and putting all the pieces together points to only one possible person who could have manipulated my downfall.

I think Arnold had a point about revenge. It can be a very powerful motivator and I'm feeling it right now.

So I tell myself to wait. Be patient.

"You have to choose your moment exactly," Arnold had said to me during one of those crazy drunken nights in his lodge up in Kyle of Lochalsh. "Planning and patience is key."

And he should know, considering what he did to his ex-wife and her husband.

"Horrible, Jason," he told me, drunk as fuck that night. "But they'll never know I did it."

"Why not?"

He lifted a finger and tapped the side of his nose. "Planning," he said.

So yeah. That's what I need to do.

I need to plan.

3.8

They used to call us twins, Theo and me. At the London College of Art we dyed our hair the same colour, wore the same kind of clothes, and our art was powered by a shared creative vision. We worked on everything together, which was why the Carslake Award had been upped by a grand and split between the two of us. But after college that explosive synergy collapsed – The Curse of the Carslake Award.

Theo joined some extreme right-wing organisation and our house in Bethnal Green soon filled up with hideous literature, stuff that condemned anyone who was not pure-bred white-English to a lifetime of brutality and persecution.

At that time I was already out looking for somewhere else to live, and I found a place I could afford in Kilburn, West London.

The night before I was due to move out, Theo slipped into my bedroom. He sat down by the side of my bed and shook me awake.

The first thing I smelled when I opened my eyes was beer, but there was something else as well, a coppery animal smell that made me feel sick and cold all over.

"Jason, you asleep, mate?" he asked.

He shook me roughly when I didn't reply.

"Jason!" he barked. "Are you asleep?"

"What do you want, Theo?"

He sat in a slim rectangle of pale yellow light which fell across my bed from the open door. Otherwise everything else was black.

"I know you're moving out, Jay, and I can't blame you. There's a monster inside of me, and I don't know what to do about it."

That took me by surprise. And when he said it I thought I glimpsed a flash of the blond student I'd shared everything with.

He asked me, "What's that word, when it means a dying soul has passed on into another body?"

"Reincarnation?" I suggested.

"No, but it's that kind of thing. The transmigration of the soul," he said, "that's what it means."

"Metempsychosis," I said, the word flashing before me in letters of fire. It had been inscribed into my brain alongside its dictionary definition by an exuberant lecturer of English Literature, which Theo and I had studied as a minor field at the LCA.

Theo nodded. His scarred, shaved head glowing like a small moon.

"That's what it is," he muttered. "Metempsychosis. I remember it now. Yeah."

"Did you wake me up just for that?" I said to him.

He stood, laughed and ran the palm of his hand over his scalp. "Do you believe it?" he asked me as he sat down in a chair, his legs spread wide, one of them jiggling rapidly on its heel. "D'you think there is such a thing?"

"Once. A long time ago. I used to think… No…" I whispered.

"So you believe," he said, "that when you die you really die? That there's no soul, no spark of life that can transfer itself from one host to another at the point of death?"

"Do you?"

His leg stopped moving, and he leaned forward, elbows on his knees, hands together. "When we went up to that house," he said to me, "that big house up in Scotland, I was hoping I would see some sign of it, and lately when I saw my dad… well … I've been trying to figure out why he hated me. I was thinking that maybe if I learned to hate people as much as he hated me then I'd be able to understand him. But I asked myself why would I even think that? Why would I even *want* to start thinking like my dad? I never hated people before, JJ. Never hated no one. So why now, after he's dead and buried six-feet in the ground?"

There was a silence. I didn't want to answer, so he did it himself.

"Then I remembered what we learned about this transmigration of the soul," he growled. "This metempsychosis."

"So you think your dad's soul has migrated across to you?" I said.

He shrugged.

"Theo, it's bullshit. There's no God, there's no soul. No one is responsible for your actions but you. You're not your dad, you're not me, you're not a fucking Nazi. What's happened to you, mate, is whatever you brought on yourself, and you've got to dig yourself out of it. If you want to that is. If you don't then fine; I don't give a shit."

"Some mate you are," he said. "After all we been through I thought you might understand. I thought you of all people might get it and help me out. I can't do it on my own."

"Mate," I said. "You need to pull yourself out of this rut and get on with your life. You never used to be like this. Before —" I stopped.

I stopped because I got it. I got what he meant.

His eyes flashed up at me darkly. He said, "Before you and me went up to Anglesey to sort out that business with your girlfriend and your sister? Yeah," he added sadly, "it was that that changed me, Jason. It wasn't my dad's soul that passed into me, but something from *you*. Some kind of dark contagion. And I can't get rid of it. I don't know what to do."

"Forget about it," I said. "It's what I do. Just bury it away, somewhere deep and dark. Cover it over and don't ever dig it up." I was sweating I realised.

"I can't forget what I saw. Wish I could but…" He tried laughing but it was a strangled choke that escaped from his mouth. "I'm dead inside, mate," he whispered. "Dead inside."

He paused, looked at the black window for a moment, then back at me.

"When I was in that room downstairs I saw some terrible things." He looked me straight in the eye. "The things that nutter had done to her…" he whispered. "To take someone so full of life and…" He couldn't finish it. The guy was wrecked.

I shook my head. "Theo…"

His eyes flicked downwards. "Too late to change, my friend," he whispered. "I wanted to know what could make people think like that, why some people commit these atrocities. I've looked into the darkness, and now it's part of me. The damage is done."

And it was all my fault, I remember thinking. But he could have said no. He should have said no.

He stood up off the chair, walked over to me and kissed my hand. Then he turned and walked away. I sat in the dark thinking only that I had to get out of here, away from Theo and his demons before they destroyed me too.

3.9

The next day couldn't come round quick enough. I remember I packed all my clothes into suitcases and then went out to hire a van. When I got back, ready to start moving my stuff out, Arnold Evans was sitting in the living room talking quietly with Theo.

They both looked up when I entered, and Theo whipped up a remote control to turn the video off. I wondered what they might have been watching. They looked like two guilty schoolboys, flushed red at being caught in the act.

Arnold was dressed in smart contrast to Theo's unwashed denim. Yet another black suit and red tie, but this time the combo was complemented by a Trilby which overshadowed much of his face. No more bowler hat. Seemed he'd evolved.

"Jason Jones," Arnold said, clearing his voice when I came into the room. "Good to meet you again." He stood and offered out his hand.

"It's Arnold isn't it? Arnold Evans?"

We shook hands.

"You have a good memory, young man," Arnold said quietly. "Much more so than that of your dozy friend here."

"Cut to the chase," drawled Theo from the chair. "Tell him what you want."

Arnold and I sat down on the sofa, one at each end turning to face the other.

"As you know," he began, "I am an artistic agent."

Theo snorted from the chair.

"Go on," I told Arnold.

Arnold went on to say how he had been scanning the pages of an LCA review catalogue in which was an examination of one of our College works with which he had been very impressed. I knew the one he meant, and I was quick to tell him that the work – a series of giant photographs of riot scenes coupled with a collage of various strange images – no longer existed.

"Theo set fire to it all," I told Arnold.

"Fuckoff," drawled Theo.

"Well, whatever…" said Arnold, and he seemed uncomfortable. "I'm in touch with a gallery, a resurgent independent firm fronted by a man called Brian Cavendish. Brian's a character who has very specific ideas on the kind of art he wants to patronise. Basically he's looking for something which will promote his new business," he told me, "and I think that what you two do will match his requirements. I want to put you in touch with Gallery 21, let you see what they are looking to do and have a chat about what you see happening in your ... futures."

Theo snorted again but I ignored him. I was in a good mood because I was leaving, so a sense of new purpose was happily lifting my spirits. Arnold's proposition was the best, if not the only one I'd had since leaving college, I would have been mad to refuse him.

"Gallery 21? Doesn't ring any bells."

"That's what they call themselves, though they don't actually have a gallery as such – not yet anyway. What they do is promote and sell exhibitions to established venues like the Hayward, the Tate, Whitechapel, Southwark and so on. What I want to do is show them your portfolio and talk with them about where you feel your work comes from, what it says, and where it's going. A project like Brian's is only as good as the art it has on show, and having seen your work, Jason, I really feel that what you and Theo have to offer is exactly what G21 are looking for. Of course the final decision is not mine to make. It's down to yourselves if you want to look and see what they can offer you, and down to Brian should he wish to promote your work."

"Well what d'you think, JJ?" rumbled Theo. "You reckon this might be the making of our brilliant careers or just some new fucking rip off?"

I stared at him, wishing that I could snap him out of his crap, and then wondered why I should even bother.

"Fine," I said to Arnold. "Let's do it. Who knows? We've got nothing to lose, have we, Theo?"

"No, mate. Nothing at all."

3.10

"I'm surprised you're talking to me," said Harriet. "Now you've got *other things* on your mind."

Damn she could be hurtful when she wanted.

"Sorry. I've been busy," I said. "Setting this thing up at the Dreadnought with Jhavesh's cousin."

"The quiet one?"

"Yeah he's quiet. But you should hear him with the guys at the gallery. The contractors so much as dare put a TV up in the wrong place and he comes down hard on them."

"He cares about the project," said Harriet, looking at her phone, then spinning her thumb over the screen as she tapped out a text. "So are you going to credit him in your art thing? Cut him in?"

I shook my head. "Brian won't allow it. Anyway to be honest he's only building the thing, the concept is still mine right?"

"Whatever. Anyway. Bus's here. Be seeing you."

A double decker clattered to the bus stop, and when its doors hissed open Harriet jumped on it. She flashed her Oyster and the doors flapped shut. I watched the bus move into the High Street traffic and saw her through the windows, making her way towards the stairs. She hadn't looked at me throughout that entire exchange and she didn't even look back as the bus rattled away.

Surprised you're talking to me, she had said. *Other things on your mind...*

"Shit," I swore.

She was jealous wasn't she?

3.11

"So... Liselle Duchamps," Arnold was saying over the phone, calling me up as I'd walked in through the door of my house. "I've got your request for an extension of her contract. I thought you said this thing was finished?"

"I'm taking a few extra shots while I've got her. Arnold, she's beautiful," I told him. "She's just everything you want in a model."

"So when are you getting married?"

I grinned. Feeling almost like a schoolboy.

"You're fucking her right?" he asked me, just as Bella swooped in past my legs, almost tripping me up.

"No!"

"Something wrong with you then," he said. "If I was your age again I'd be up her hole like a horny rabbit."

"What?"

"Or are you still gay? You've done gay right?"

I told him off for being crass, but then that was Arnold all over. High-brow and elitist one minute, and a brutish animal the next.

In truth, Liselle and I had sex pretty much every time she came round. A couple of times we filmed ourselves at it – the first time purely by accident when I'd left the camera rolling on its tripod. Afterwards we got a bit more adventurous.

One night I'd wondered about playing it through the TVs – this was before the thing was ready to go to the Dreadnought. So I loaded up the video file when I was alone, transferring from the Mac to the Windows laptop running the system, and I watched Liselle and me making love against different backgrounds.

I loved every minute I spent with her. When I was with Liselle, nothing else mattered.

So one night, I decided I was taking down The Wall.

It was a big moment, a big decision, but Harriet had been right when she'd said I was obsessed with the Camden Killer. So I took it all down, every last newspaper clipping, every photo, every report, every speculation printed off a rumour-site. I couldn't quite summon the courage to take it all outside and start burning it, that would have been too much I mean first steps first, right? Don't run before you learn to walk.

About the best I could manage was stuffing it all into one of many already-overflowing cardboard boxes hiding in the cupboard under the stairs, locking the door and hanging up the key.

Eventually I even stopped sneaking a look at the tweets and forum notifications on my phone. It took a little longer to exorcise the nightmares of Stephen's corpse but eventually his ruined face receded into the depths.

Sitting downstairs in the front room one night, listening to some Pharrell Williams stuff on the hi-fi, Liselle said to me: "You know what you need?"

"What?"

"You need a Christmas tree in here. I think your house needs lightening up. I think *you* need lightening up."

"Two reasons why not," I said to her.

"Number one?"

"Number one is I don't do Christmas."

"Really? And the second reason?"

"Second reason is I don't do Christmas."

"That's the same reason twice."

"It's worth repeating."

"Oh my God!" She said something in French. Sounded unpleasant and if the look in her eye was anything to go by I didn't need a translator.

Harriet had tried this on me too; couple of years ago she'd even gone so far as to buy me a Christmas tree, install it fully decorated in my front room, and then march me in with a blindfold going: "Ta-daaaa!" when she whipped it off.

It lasted two days before I threw it in a skip.

"Christmas is for families," I said to Liselle.

"And you have no family?"

"Not to speak of."

"I thought you had a sister."

"Where did you hear that?"

"You told me."

"Did I?" wasn't sure but it didn't matter. "Jenny's ill," I said. Which reminded me, I had to ring the hospital still.

"What's wrong with her?" Liselle asked.

"It's complicated."

Later, I tried ringing the hospital. Phone rang for ages and eventually a bloke picked up. It was late. Well after 10pm but the guy sounded wired and breathless, like he'd just been having sex or sniffing a line of coke. Maybe both.

"Can I speak to Doctor Pandghani," I asked.

"Doctor Pan? Oh my god now there's a blast from the past. He's not here. Hasn't lived here for a while. You a doctor?"

"No. No..." I was confused. "My name is Jason Jones. Doctor Pandghani was my sister's consultant."

"Ah. I see. Sorry. Well, maybe you'd be better off ringing the hospital in the morning and talking to reception. I'm sure they'd put you through to someone."

"Isn't this the hospital?"

"No," said the guy. "Doctor Pan used to stay with the family. We gave him this number to use for himself. Used to get plenty of calls soon after he left but it's been ... well it's been about a year since the last one."

"Sorry," I said.

"Not your fault," the guy said kindly, then wished me a good day and put the phone down.

I guess it had been a while since I last saw Jenny.

Obviously too long.

I checked the contact in my mobile. Seemed I had three numbers stored for 'The Hospital' and the priority dial-out number was this residential one, different to the number to the actual hospital.

I guessed I ought to try one of the other numbers but even as my thumb hovered over it my thoughts flew back to the last time I'd been there...

3.12

St Cecilia's Hospital was a brutal-looking building in the rain, a ten-minute taxi ride from Swindon station.

Jenny was on the sixth floor, in the Primrose Ward common room. This was a vast, open space divided by tall bookshelves. The carpet was deep blue, the colour of a placid, blue sea. Tables, chairs and potted plants floated upon it like islands, between which sailed Doctor Pandghani's lost-at-sea patients.

A woman sitting in a corner was playing with some plastic cups, banging them together loudly. Another guy stared out of a window, rocking slightly on his heels and making baby noises. I caught snippets of insane conversation from all around me.

I always felt unsettled in here, but Doctor Pandghani revelled in it. I could see his face lighting up as he walked the carpet like an Indian messiah amongst them.

At the far end Jenny was reading a picture book.

"Jason!" she squealed, leaping up from her chair, dropping the book to the carpet. She threw her arms around my neck and hugged me tightly. "Jason Jason Jason!"

I hugged her back, just as tightly, and lifted her off her feet while tears flooded my eyes and a lump in my throat made it ache. I couldn't let go of her. Didn't want to.

"I've missed you so much, little brother!"

Holding my hand she led me across the room to a quiet corner just behind a bookcase. We sat at a table set next to a rain-spattered window. The black metal steps of a fire escape were just outside, and I realised that the window was an emergency exit. I wondered what might happen if Jenny took it. Where would it lead her?

I sighed and turned to take a good look at my sister.

Her hair, though touched with grey, bounced around her neck and shoulders, occasionally revealing remnants of scars at her hairline and throat as though to remind us both of the breakdown, and of the suicide attempts which had accompanied her illness.

"Are you working again?" she asked me.

I wasn't, and I told her so.

"You need to work, Jason. It's your livelihood. Your art is your job. I saw that thing you did with St Leonard. It was on the news."

"The Pierrot?"

She nodded. "It was massive. Taller than the gallery!"

"And dripping with oil," I told her. "Which wasn't intentional."

"Maybe not. But hovering outside Tate Modern, it looked amazing. Your stuff still causes a sensation, Jason. Same as your St Rita and your St David."

I smiled. Held her hand across the table.

She said. "Maybe you should do something on St Cecilia."

I shook my head. "No. I've had enough of the saints. Moving on now to other things."

"Do you know what she's a patron of?"

"Musicians," I answered, "music... usually."

"That makes sense," she said. "There's a giant violin outside the front of the hospital. At least I think it's a violin. Could be a cello I guess. But why music? Do you know? Can you tell me?"

"She sang to God as she died. Something like that. Listen, Jenny-"

"Did it take her long to die?"

I nodded my head, then immediately wished I hadn't.

"How long?" Jenny asked.

"A few days."

"How did she die?"

I didn't answer.

"Jason?"

I looked through the window, staring down at the rooftops, at the waterfalls bouncing and tumbling off the fire escape steps.

"Jason, you can tell me. I'm not going to freak out."

Really? I looked right at her. Sometimes she could be so rational I wondered why she was here.

"Why are you so interested?" I asked her.

"Do you remember what you used to say about God?" she asked me quietly.

"I used to say all kinds of stuff. Not sure I believe any of it now."

It was growing ever darker outside, as though the world itself was drawing to a miserable end.

Jenny leaned forward and gripped my hand hard. "You said that God lived in a great castle, as big as the Universe. You told me he was buried inside a dungeon which was in a maze, way below the castle's lowest cellars. It was completely dark, you said, so dark that God couldn't see any part of his body, not even his hands when he held them up before his face. You said that God had forgotten what he looked like, that perhaps he had forgotten what everything looked like - all the birds in the sky and the fish in the sea, all the animals in the whole wide world and all the people too. You said he had forgotten who he was and what he had done. You said he was alone, and that he had forgotten he was alone.

"I will always remember that, JJ," Jenny said staring into my eyes. "In my darkest moments," she whispered, "I know exactly how it feels to be God. And if the saints felt that way too, then I know that I'm not alone."

I massaged her hands affectionately, pleased to feel that she was putting on weight again. During her worst period at the Novak Institute, she had weighed less than six stone.

"They tried to take her head off," I told her, clearing my throat. "The Romans, that is. After her husband and brother were killed for being Christians they wanted to behead Cecilia too. They hacked at her neck and made a mess but they couldn't sever the head."

Jenny's reaction was slight, a flicker of shadow across her face.

"The story goes that she didn't die until she received the Sacrament of the Holy Communion. And when that happened she started singing to God in such a beautiful voice that all her family were brought to tears."

After a moment, Jenny said, "I wonder if God heard her singing. And if he did, down in his dungeon, would he have known what it was?"

"Jenny," I began, "that's just something I said when I was younger... It's just... stuff."

"Do you believe it?" she asked me.

"No. Not anymore."

"You don't believe in God then?"

I shrugged.

"I believe there is a God, Jason, a God responsible for all of this."

"All of what?" I asked.

"This! The world, people, suffering, war, everything! He needs to wake up right now, JJ, and take control back. Maybe the saints were trying to do that in their own ways, or grab His attention. Maybe Saint Cecilia for all her beautiful voice didn't sing loud enough to reach Him." Then she looked at me. "If you don't believe in God, why are you so obsessed with the Saints?"

"The Saints were people," I answered. "Just people. But they went through extraordinary suffering and persecution. It – "

She cut me off. Bored of the subject already she started on something else.

"I've got a visitor," she said, in a low, conspiratorial voice.

My heart kicked. "A visitor?"

She put a finger to her lips. "Shush. Don't tell anyone."

"Who is it?" I whispered back.

"It's a man from the TV," she answered.

"A journalist? Jenny!"

"No. Not a journalist. I mean it's a man from *inside* the TV. It could be James."

My heart sank rapidly. "Jenny–" I croaked, but I couldn't go on. This was too painful

She leaned forward and kissed my forehead. "Shush," she whispered, her breath slightly sour. "I've dragged our secrets through Hell and back, and they're here to stay." She tapped the side of her scarred forehead with a shaking finger. "They're going nowhere."

Thunder rolled over Swindon.

I was still shaking like the little brother I always was. She was shaking too, and a tear shot suddenly down her face.

She held my face with her hand but still I was shaking, tears falling down my cheeks, some running over the back of her hand. There, at the hospital in Swindon as thunder rolled across the dark sky and it rained like Hell on Earth, I felt as though we were teetering on the lip of an abyss. The two of us. Ready to fall.

3.13

The phone was in my hand. It was the morning after I'd tried ringing Doctor Pandghani.

This time however I'd checked through the other numbers and pulled up the actual hospital number. Now I just needed to press 'call' and I'd be through to hospital reception.

Trouble was I couldn't do it. I knew what they'd say: "Take your sister in, at least over Christmas."

I … I couldn't. It was too painful. Every time I saw Jenny these days I broke into pieces. She brought everything back and I couldn't…

I was scared.

And I hated myself for being such a coward.

This was my *sister*... For whom I would do anything!

But... that was the heart of the problem. Wasn't it?

3.14

I was working on some photographs on the Mac; combining backgrounds, playing around with some of the stuff I'd shot with Liselle. It was dark in the studio. The only light came from the MacBook's retina screen and I was so engrossed I didn't hear Liselle coming in.

I felt her hands sliding around my neck from behind and down around my chest. Her breath was hot in my left ear.

"So..." she purred. "*This* is the famous exhibition?"

On the desk, lying next to the Mac, was the pamphlet that Arnold had given me weeks earlier. One of Liselle's arms reached forward and picked it up.

"Huh? Yeah yeah. That's Brian's Great Vision," I mumbled.

In the light of the Mac the cover art looked sinister, slightly disturbing. I'd never seen it that way before.

"What is it?" Liselle asked. "Looks like a woman in pain. Is it art?" She sat on the edge of the desk, her black-stockinged thighs close to my face.

I snatched the pamphlet off her. Leaned back in my chair. Looked it over.

"I did that," I told her.

"You did?" She kicked off her shoes, then placed a foot on my thigh, pressing down hard, nuzzling her toes forward.

"Sure," I said, deliberately not reacting to the foot. "It's a print from a thing I made years ago."

"It is pornographic," she purred, pressing her foot down so hard on my thigh that it actually hurt. "You bad man."

"It's *erotic*," I said.

"No." She opened her legs, ever so slightly, just enough to allow her short skirt to stretch tight and reveal a hint of underwear. "It is pornographic. There is a difference."

"Really? And you know that, do you?"

"I'm French," she said, and I felt her toes nudging the base of my balls. "I know about erotic."

I grabbed her foot and pulled it onto my cock.

"What about this?" I said. "Erotic, or pornographic?"

I moved like I was slowly fucking her foot.

The face she made as she worked her toes around my balls could have graced an entire hard drive of porn.

I dropped her foot, I stood quickly and moved between her legs.

She lifted her face to mine and I ducked into her neck: wisps of hair in my face, smell of perfume.

"Excuse me," I said. I reached round and flicked on the desktop light just behind her backside.

She recoiled, blinking in the light as I fell back into my chair.

"That's better," I said, casually.

It took her a moment, then: "You bastard tease!" she shouted, and threw the pamphlet at me.

Laughing I rescued the pamphlet. "Careful!" I said. "It's been through the wars!"

It really had been too, not that Liselle cared since she was busy feigning disgust at my tease, but the thing was dog-eared and falling apart, having been used as a mat for cups of tea and coffee, wine and vodka in the few weeks I'd had it. I think I'd even used it to mop up some of the cat's milk when Harriet had 'accidentally' dropped a tin of Liselle's special tea from the cupboard onto the cat's dishes. (oops!" she'd said, not entirely convincingly). Tea leaves, cat biscuits and milk everywhere and the only thing to hand? This fucking pamphlet with my art on it.

"It's *St Rita in the Crib*," I told Liselle, putting it back on the desktop.

Her face was a picture of pure blonde disgust. "What?"

"The picture of the woman on the pamphlet."

"I never heard of a 'Saint Rita'. You made her up."

"She was a nun."

"Pfft…"

And then she grabbed me and we did it on the desk, noisily and frantically, banging against the wall as everything, even the MacBook, slid off it and crashed to the wooden floor. Luckily the damn things are near-indestructible.

Later that night, Liselle broke it to me that she was going back home to France for the holidays.

"Do you still want to see me?" she asked.

"No," I said. "We're pretty much done. I've got everything I need from you."

"That's not what I meant."

We were standing in the lantern at the top of the house, holding hands like figures in a bell jar. The moon was fat and bright and full. Rising just a few degrees above the silhouette of St Leonard's Church it seemed to burn away the orange London light-haze, filling the sky with vivid silver strata.

Tonight was my last professional night with Liselle. Even the extended contract Arnold had sorted out had expired nearly three days ago.

"Are you coming back?" I asked her, holding both her hands tightly.

"If you want me to."

She stood in the middle of the small space and by god she was beautiful. She was shining. A modern-day Galadriel exuding unearthly, radiant beauty in the metropolitan moonlight.

"It's a Yes," I said before she could melt away, never to be seen again. "Yes I want you to come back. I want to see you again."

I pulled her hands towards me, and I leaned forward and I kissed her.

3.15

"Mate, you look happy," Jhavesh said when I collared him at the market a couple of days later. He was outside his Transit van still selling CDs, DVDs and now video games. There was tinsel sellotaped around his crates of stock and Slade's *So Here it is Merry Christmas* blasted out of his giant speakers. Jhavesh loved Christmas, mostly because he made a small fortune round this time of year.

He was also wearing a Santa hat.

"Where's Harriet?" I asked him. "Her stall's not there."

"She ain't been here all week, mate."

"What? Really? You're kidding."

"You're worried about her?"

I thought about it, then said, "Nah." Maybe a bit too nonchalant.

He saw through it straight away.

"Harriet can look after herself, man. She's cool."

I smiled at him in thanks. "Maybe."

Jhavesh threw away his fag – which meant he was serious – and put a hand on my arm to stop me walking away. "Listen, man," he said. "She ain't been killed by no nutter."

"I never said she had."

"It's in your face. Same look you had when we come out of your lock up that night."

Flashback: Stephen in the lock up.

"Mate," said Jhavesh. "There's bad people around but you got to get on with life right? Just 'cos someone got Stephen it don't mean to say he's got Harriet too. OK?"

"OK."

"Cool."

The Christmas lights in the high street didn't do anything to lift the sense of dread and fear I was feeling any more than Jhavesh's words of wisdom, and it got worse as the days went on.

I kept thinking about Harriet. Seriously now... *where the fuck was she?*

And Stephen... sack-mask face with crosses for eyes, and paintbrushes stuck in his body.

And I kept thinking: *what if I'm next?*

Talk about paranoia.

For a little while, with my work and Liselle, I'd been distracted and it had felt good. But now that the *Castle Mechanics* installation was out of my house and Liselle was off home in just a few days, it all started piling into me again.

Whenever I went out I was sure I was being followed. Whenever I was indoors I felt as though I was being watched. I couldn't shake it off. Kept thinking I could see someone inside my house when the lights went off, or standing in the churchyard looking up at my windows.

Then it got worse. I had dreams that Harriet was walking through my bedroom, drenched in blood.

Didn't help when Bella suddenly woke me up by yowling at something when she'd been asleep on my bed one night.

"Fuck's sake!" I hissed at her, and booted her off.

She fled the bedroom, no doubt embarrassed. Didn't help my heart-rate though. I pulled the covers over my head like a little kid awake in the dark.

Next morning I found Bella sprawled dead in the kitchen, half way to her cat-flap, and then I *knew* that someone had been in my house.

3.16

Liselle poked her face through my letterbox.

"JJ!" she called. "Come on, I know you're home."

Eventually I opened the door, and from somewhere within the cream-coloured woolly hat and scarf combo covering her head, I heard: "Oh my god you smell – of fish, cigarettes and dog biscuits."

"I haven't been –"

"Look I've brought you a tree!"

She smiled the whitest smile I've ever seen, and then lifted her arm to point with her mittens at the Christmas tree balanced on the steps behind her. Then the smiled vanished. "What's wrong?"

"Doesn't matter."

"No no. Jason, come on. Don't hide from me now."

"Bella's dead," I told her, but I guessed there was more to it than just that.

"Bella...?"

"The cat. My cat?"

She put a hand to her mouth and her eyes widened. "Oh my god! How?"

"Poisoned." I stared at her.

"*Poisoned?*"

"Maybe you'd better go," I said.

"Jason? No I didn't ... what? You think *I* poisoned your cat?"

"What? No... I never said –"

"Why would I do such a thing?"

"I never said you did, I just –"

"I don't understand. Your cat? I would never hurt your cat!"

"Liselle, for Christ sake..." I rubbed my temple. "Just... just go."

She looked at me as though I'd slapped her.

"Go?"

"Yes. Please just..."

"You want me to *leave*?" she said, stepping back. "Leave now?"

"Yes, I think it's best."

"Is that what you want?"

And then I snapped. "For Christ's sake yes. Just ... *go*!" I yelled at her. "Take your fucking Christmas tree and go!"

3.17

In the middle of the night I heard my phone ping with a notification of something or other. It hadn't woken me up, but strangely I was awake for it.

Harriet?

It was a text from Sh1tPolice, my Twitter pal. It was an actual text too, not a tweet. It said:

> Hey JJ. I got something for you. Check out <u>tinyurl.872ty</u>. regards, Sh1tPolice

"How the hell did you get my number?" I wondered out loud.

I got up and padded into the studio to power-up my MacBook.

Whilst it booted I scoured through my phone, looking for traces of Harriet. I thought if she'd taken off somewhere then she'd be there by now, Spain or the Maldives or whatever, and there'd be a clutch of Instagram photos splashed over my phone, telling everyone what a great time she was having. But there'd been nothing posted by her for over a week, and that was the thing because it really wasn't like Harriet to cut herself off so completely.

Unless she really had taken the first flight out of Stansted…

The MacBook was up and running. I typed the URL into Safari but nothing happened. Just the 'waiting' icon in the middle of the screen.

Then I heard something, someone in the house. Downstairs, moving around.

Not my imagination this time.

Because the sound came again.

There was a baseball bat around here somewhere. Maybe the present from Stephen would come in useful after all.

3.18

I crept downstairs in bare feet.

My heart was racing so hard it was going to choke me.

At the bottom now, facing the front door. Weird light filtering through the stained glass rectangle right above the lintel, everything else dark.

Slowly I turned and walked down the hall towards the kitchen. My eyes scanned the corridor, fingers flexing around the shaft of the baseball bat. Any fucker who wants to have a go is going to get it right in the face, I was thinking.

The house was silent as a tomb, the length of the hall rendered in shades of grey.

Nothing here.

My paranoia again, playing tricks. "Get a grip, JJ," I whispered, and reached out for the light switch.

A shadow detached itself from the wall and slid into my field of vision.

Shit!

I swung the bat but missed. Lost my balance. The shadow turned quickly and two arms shot out, grabbed me and slammed me up against the wall. A hand gripped my throat, choking me, whilst the other hand landed a killing punch into my stomach.

I felt sick.

I collapsed, out of breath, and dropped the baseball bat. Then whoever it was grabbed me, pulled me up by the collar of my T-shirt and threw me into the wall again. I saw a man dressed in black with a balaclava on his face.

I struggled, twisting in his grip but the guy was strong.

Time to get dirty.

I raked up the phlegm from the bottom of my throat and spat it at him, quickly following up with a vicious head-butt that connected hard with his face. He let go and stepped back but the bridge of my nose was crying with pain. There was something under his balaclava that was hard as wood.

Where was the baseball bat?

There, just on the floor. If I could reach it...

I cried out as a terrific pain exploded in the base of my spine. Fucker had kicked me in the back and I fell, face first into the carpet. I clawed forward with my fingers, reaching for the bat.

Then his boots walked into view.

He leaned down and picked up the bat.

My eyes tracked upwards, watching him inspect it. He smacked it against his palm a couple of times. Meaningfully.

"Who the fuck are you?" I gasped.

His voice was muffled when he spoke. "Don't you know?" He stepped forward, the sole of his boot crushing the fingers on my right hand. I wasn't going to scream.

Christ it hurt!

"Do you want to know how it feels? To be a victim?"

Was that a rhetorical question?

"Get off my hand," I gasped. "Take the mask off and let's just have it out. You and me, you *fucker*!"

The pressure on my fingers increased and I screamed out.

"Tough talk for someone who's about to get a baseball bat in the skull," he said, sounding angry inside the balaclava.

"*What do you want?*"

"Screaming's a good start," he snapped. "Do it again."

He increased the pressure of his boot on my fingers. I bit my lip. Squeezed my eyes shut and breathed hard through my nose.

Then he released me and said, "Get up!"

I snapped my hand back. Hugged it to my chest.

I knew that voice.

But before I could say anything he lashed out with the bat. I saw it in the corner of my eye and instinct took over. I rolled over and scrabbled away, clumsily climbing to my feet, gripping the doorframe to haul myself upright.

But he was fast. He adjusted quickly, raised his swing and the blow landed in one of my kidneys. I screamed again.

"Good!" he cried. "That's good, JJ! Great fucking scream!"

"Fuck you!"

I went at him. Primitive, brutal and desperate I lunged and then clawed at his face. Caught off guard he stepped back, but I stayed on him, slamming my hand up at his face. The balaclava came off in my hand to reveal a black oval reflecting my own bloodied face back at me, distorted like the back of a spoon.

Another mask. Some kind of reflective plastic, hard as glass.

He raised the bat but I grabbed his arm and forced it back.

We grappled desperately, breathing hard, and then blue lights flashed through the stained glass above the front door.

Police?

He let go of the bat. Swung me round and slammed my face into the wall.

I remember I slipped to the floor, as though the power had gone from my legs. I managed to turn as I fell and the last thing I saw was the bat swinging at my head.

I raised my arms for protection but the bat still connected with the side of my skull. There was a flash of intense, painful, explosive light and then everything went black.

3.19

"It was Theo!" I told Arnold.

"What?"

"I'm sure of it! It was him!"

"Jason, you've had a shock. For Christ's sake don't tell the police!"

"What? That my one-time best mate broke into my house and kicked the shit out of me last night? Why wouldn't I tell them that?"

"Jason."

But I went on. I wasn't letting up.

I was in casualty, getting the cuts in my face stitched and my nose fixed. Arnold had come round first thing in the morning and insisted on bringing me to the hospital when he saw the state of me.

"It was him," I said. "Wearing some kind of fucking mask like a mirror."

"So you didn't actually see his face?"

"I didn't need to see his face. I know him. I know how he fights. We've had fights before remember?"

Liselle came in. "Hey," she said. "You OK?" Arnold had called her up and he'd told her where I was.

I nodded, reached out a hand with bruised, swollen fingers. Tried to smile. "Sure," I said. "Nothing I can't handle. Look... about what I said. I'm sorry. I'm a dick."

"The police are here," she told me, kissing my fingers. "They want to talk to you."

Waste of time.

"Did you recognise him?" they asked me.

"No," I said. "He was wearing a mask. A balaclava."

The Q&A went on for a few minutes and nothing came of it. When they were gone the nurse finished dressing my face and I was free to go.

Arnold checked his phone for the *n*th time. "Gotta go," he said. "You look after yourself. No more fights!"

"I need some food," I said, walking out with Liselle half an hour later. "Come on, let's go find a café."

"You're taking this very well," she said. "Are you sure you're OK?"

I wasn't, not really. Inside I was angry and full of hate, and humiliation that I'd lost the fight so badly. It wasn't often I felt like a victim and it made me feel sick and weak and angry.

3.20

When Theo and I opened our first and only combined show with G21 it was a big success. Even though we'd already fallen out with each other and I was living somewhere else, we worked together as well as we had in the old days, pouring our creative vision into the modest collection of new works commissioned for the show.

We didn't get rich from it but we did all right, enough for me to move out of the shithole flat in Kilburn and put a hefty deposit down on this place in Camden.

The centrepiece of the G21 show hung in the foyer of the Southwark Gallery for the whole twenty days. It was an enormous skeleton, like a demon rendered in rust-coloured metal we'd called *Monsters & Gods*. It was actually a human figure but you had to look really hard to see that, and it was supposed to be in great pain. TV screens hung from the demon at various angles, and running through them were uncompromising shots from Nazi extermination camps and gulags, stills of skinny people thrown into mass graves, tanks rumbling through wastelands.

We showed riots from the news, football violence on the terraces, the faces of children who had died at the hands of others, horrors in the Gaza Strip. We showed footage from the Gulf War, infra-red images taken by cameras in jet planes as they bombed targets in Iraq. We showed people being executed in Serbia, we showed images of famine and civil war in Africa, kids armed with Uzis and machetes, and we showed some footage from 9/11. To tie it all in we showed the bombings of Nagasaki and Hiroshima at the end of World War II. Little Boy and Fat Man, a blossoming release of all the destructive energy that mankind held in store for our bleak future.

Some people liked it, some people hated it, but at least everyone who saw it had an opinion, and it served its purpose by creating enough publicity that people flocked to see what else Gallery 21 had to offer.

There was a party on our wrap night. Neither of us being into tuxedos and cocktails we didn't want to be there, but Arnold had insisted. "If either of you two want a shot at the big time then put your pride to one side right now and make sure you turn up. Don't forget to smile," he'd said.

At the party, when *Monsters & Gods* was being removed piece by piece, a journalist had asked us what the thing was supposed to represent.

"What does it fucking look like, prick?" Theo had said to him.

The journalist, stupidly believing Theo's hard-man image to be a trendy front, made the mistake of remarking that it looked like a big metal insect with tellies on it and he couldn't see the point.

Theo was about to punch him when I stepped in.

"It's significant of an idea," I told the journalist, "that being the atrocity of which the human race is capable. The monsters and the gods are ourselves, we are our very own demon and deity."

The journalist wrote this down. He made a face and then he said to me, "Isn't it an idea that has been done to the death? Since the Second World War there have been countless representations of Apocalypse, isn't it something which we are now desensitised towards and feel a little sick of seeing? Surely from a new talent we ought to be seeing new ideas and new images, not the rehash of themes which have been explored in the past with greater maturity and depth than this thing here?"

"You smart-arse little —"

I cut Theo off, saying to the journalist. "I take your point, but the Apocalypse is something we constantly need to remind ourselves of, especially as we approach a new era of history."

He said, "Why?"

"Because maybe we are beginning to forget. Maybe, like you say, we are becoming a little desensitised to it. That's a thing that should never happen. In order to survive our future we need to be able to come to terms with the potential monster within us all, we need to relearn how to value life."

Theo interrupted me. "Bollocks, JJ," he said. "That isn't what this is about at all."

The journalist looked interested. "Oh?"

"It's about the self-annihilation of the entire human race," he explained, "by suicide, execution, jihad, genocide and ethnic cleansing. It's about the choice not to submit to propaganda which tells us how precious life is. How can it be? If life meant so much to us, if your life and the lives of others were so precious, then all these things we're looking at here would never have happened. There's conflict in all corners of the globe, and the biggest conflicts come from points of difference. Differences in ideology, in race, in gender. So maybe the only way to get rid of conflict is to get rid of difference. Right? That's what all this stuff in this room is about and if you don't get that then go find another fucking job. The Nazis had the right idea — there's only room for one race on this planet, one ideology that does away with conflict through difference. Call it evil if you want but in reality it's just a form of evolution…"

He was talking so loudly that others in the room, people enjoying canapés and champagne, were starting to stare, in particular Arnold and Brian who were in deep conversation with an Arabian guy. Everybody was there by personal invitation and it didn't do to be seen arguing with journalists who had the power to make or break the future of Gallery 21.

I was losing my patience as Theo went on: "... I want to turn galleries into gas chambers and suicide halls!" he announced grandly. "And let people come here from all walks of life who do not want to live. Everyone can watch as we put to death all the misfits: the unfulfilled homosexual man, the battered woman, the cripple, the useless waste, the shit of society and the inbred elite. One victim after another. We could turn death into our art," he said, "and anyone who wants to can contribute to the ultimate evolution of humanity, our final solution – "

I punched him, clear and simple. I knocked him backwards and laid into him, venting the hatred I felt for him through my fists.

He responded vigorously, his punches fast and hard. We threw each other up against sculptures and stands that fell apart under our weight. Nobody dared jump in. The room strobed with camera flashes, and journalists scribbled frantically in their notebooks. I was in a frenzy, my head reeling, pounding with adrenalin. It was all noise, and blood and pain.

"You feel it, JJ?" Theo screamed, laughing as blood from his shattered nose poured down the crisp, formal white shirt under his tux. "Hey? Is this what it feels like? Come on, JJ, come on and kill me! Fuck knows I don't want to live!"

I just went at him. Pounded his stupid fucking face as hard as I could. It was two bony boys in the playground again, and here, just the same as all those years ago, I wanted to kill Theo as much as I'd wanted to kill James with my bare bloody hands.

A couple of bouncers tore us away from each other. The fight had lasted for less than a minute, but in that time my relationship with Theo had come to a terminal end.

Arnold said to me afterwards, "Good move, Jason. You've just launched your artistic career in the most dramatic way possible, now all you have to do is stick to it."

3.21

So where was he? Where was Theo Collins now, because I wanted to know!

If he was fucking me about, trying to wind me up by following me down the high street, playing his mind games – well that was one thing. But if he was going to walk right into my house with the sole intention of breaking my face then I wanted it out with him. The fucker had crossed a line, literally the line across my fucking doorstep and I wanted him to know full on that it wasn't welcome. So what if he'd been booted out of *The Odyssey Exhibition*. Grow up. Fucking move on.

I didn't want to tell Arnold I was looking for him so back home I Googled him, looking for something in all the links that might just give me a place to start.

"Gotcha!"

I found his website and from there an address: Studio 10b, Chalk Farm. It was off Steeles Road, in a little mews that looked like it needed some work spent on it. Ironic that he'd been so close to me all this time and I never knew it.

Clicking through his website I found some photos of his recent art: Dark things, twisted visions full of fire and hatred. Monsters screaming in the dark. Gods descending into paralytic fear. Jesus, Theo's vision was apocalyptic, it was Chaos incarnate, a state of unstoppable collapse.

Just like my head right now.

I copied and pasted the address of his studio into Google Maps on my phone and went to get my coat.

Let's see how he'd feel when I turned up on *his* doorstep unannounced.

3.22

It took me less than an hour that afternoon to walk up to Chalk Farm. I turned a corner off the high street and suddenly there I was, looking at the dilapidated archway leading into Steeles Road Mews.

Beyond the archway was a small apron of tarmac, lined on three sides by grim, terraced cottages. As I walked into the mews, first the noises of the high street, and then even the faint crunch of my footsteps, faded into insignificance a long way behind me. The snow, falling from a TV-grey sky, brought down a silence thick as a blanket.

A brass plate on the main door of a cottage at the back of the mews told me that this was Studio 10b. I pressed the buzzer on an intercom and tensed.

Nothing.

I even knocked.

Still nothing.

So I walked up to one of the windows, cupped my hands on the glass and peered through. On the other side of the window I saw a woman hanging from the ceiling in a clear plastic sack.

"Shit!"

No.

Hold on.

I looked in again.

What the hell was wrong with me? The woman was a mannequin. Right? Difficult to see properly through the plastic. There was some kind of dark liquid in the sack with her. I thought it was blood.

"Hello?" said a girl's voice from behind me. "Can I help you?"

I spun round at the voice and the girl facing me suddenly looked shocked, taking a step backwards.

She was late teens, maybe early twenties, and she was carrying a Pret's coffee in one gloved hand, a paper lunch bag in the other. There was a woolly hat on her head with tasselled flaps covering her ears. She looked cute, but scared, and I guess I probably looked like some kind of vagrant with my long hair down over the shoulders of my coat and my face swollen and full of bruises. I hadn't shaved for a few days either.

"I'm looking for Theo," I said to her, smiling in what I hoped was a friendly way. "He works here doesn't he?"

"Have you been here before?" she asked.

"No," I answered.

She stepped a bit closer. "You look familiar," she said. Then she sniffed on a cold, seeming to reset her approach by doing so. "Theo's not here," she told me, flashing a very cute smile. "Hasn't been here for..." she made a face while she thought about it, her freckled nose wrinkling, steam escaping from her lips when she spoke. "Couple of weeks I think. Yeah. About that. Only me here for now, minding the fort between the classes. Are you here for a class? You're a bit early."

I smiled wider. Seemed to be working as she looked more comfortable now.

"Maybe," I said. "I mean I was thinking about it. What's your name?"

"Sam. Are you an artist an'all, then?"

"Fraid so."

"Thought as much. You all look like tramps these days. Have you seen what's in there?"

"Just looking through the window."

"It's 'orrible," she told me.

"I saw a mannequin swinging from a rope."

"That ain't the half of it," she said. "I don't like to be in there in my own but I got to prep for Nugent's class. He's on in an hour."

"Can I have a look?" I asked. "Keep you company while you get your stuff together."

She studied me. I kept smiling, and then she relented with another smile of her own.

"Don't touch nothing will you?" she asked.

Sam gave me her coffee cup to hold as she fished for her keys.

3.23

The cottages were just a façade. Inside, all the connecting walls had been removed so that the entire space was fully open plan with brick-clad pillars supporting the beamed roof. Hanging from the beams, stretching the whole length of the studio, were more of these grotesque mannequins.

And that wasn't all.

Spread out over the studio floor were other dummies arranged in bizarre, frozen tableaux. I saw half-dressed women splayed across wrought-iron bedframes, legs broken and stretched impossibly wide. Other mannequins stood rigid, wearing masks with lipstick faces crudely drawn over them; some had had their heads or limbs replaced with kitchen utensils, blood dark at the joints, painted scars painstakingly detailed. They all posed in almost surreal, awkward positions; dead bodies arranged in ways designed to shock and disturb.

On one wall, an audience of mute faces stared out: beautifully painted, highly lacquered deathmasks, Pierrots, Harlequins and insect-heads. Must have been about fifty of them taking up half the back wall.

Another wall was covered in patterned circles: colourful peace signs, the Chinese yin-yang, swastikas, mandalas and Anarchy 'A's. The wall was a riot of colour and would have looked great if it hadn't been for the fact that the entire thing had words of hate sprayed over it.

"Jesus..." I whispered, walking through as Sam threw the keys on her desk and fired up her computer. "Who wrecked your mural?"

"They did that themselves," said Sam.

"What?"

"I know. Crazy right? They spent months working on their circles, and then they went and wrote that rubbish over it all."

I walked up to one of the hanging mannequins. Took a sniff on something sharp, tangy and slightly putrid coming from it.

Smelled like... "Christ. Is it real blood?"

"Horrible ain't it?" Sam called from the desk. "They call it Murderous Art, or Murder as Art or something... I think it's disgusting... I hate being stuck in here with this lot."

I nodded, and walked the through this abattoir of a gallery.

"And Theo did all of this?"

"Theo?" Sam barked. "No. Told you I ain't seen him for ages. But it was his idea. Him, Nugent and Sal anyway with their classes. Trouble is we do pottery for old ladies. Used to be a good earner until all this started. Now the numbers are down. The old dears won't come here while all this is around. I tried telling Nugent but he wants the guys to stick with this. Reckons there's a ... a ... sightghost? A sightghast?"

"Zeitgeist," I said

"Yeah. Whatever that means. He says murder's a big thing in art." Her face wrinkled and she sneezed, fished out a tissue and blew her nose.

"Murder's always been big in art," I whispered, walking between the hanging, translucent bodybags. The plastic was pressed right up tight against the mannequins inside them. Couldn't see much through the blood, just the impression of limbs, breasts, hair...

A face...

"Shit," I said.

I felt a sudden, real sickening horror.

I turned to Sam at the desk and her face collapsed when she looked at me. "What is it?" she asked, seeming very small.

"I'm bringing it down." I said.

"What?!"

"I'm bringing it down!"

"You can't," Sam hissed. "He'll go mental."

I pulled on the bodybag but it wasn't moving. The rope binding it to the roofbeam was too strong. It didn't feel like a mannequin in my arms. The body was hard inside the bag, but not hard like shop-dummy plastic.

I swore and ran towards Sam's desk as she stood rooted to the spot. Had to be a pair of scissors somewhere on the desk.

"Scissors! A knife! Something!" I snapped.

"Eh?"

"Come on, I want to open the bags!"

"You can't! You don't know what he's like, he'll kill me!"

"You don't like this anymore than I do, Sam. And you don't have to work here. Come on help me out."

I could see her face change as she made her decision to help. "Sculpting knives," she said, pointed down the studio. "On those tables."

I left the desk and ran into the studio. There was an island of worktables down towards the back. Full of all kinds of stuff: brushes, pallets, sculpting knives and chisels. I snatched up a five-inch blade and ran back towards the body bag I'd been trying to release.

Grabbing the thick plastic with one hand I pulled it closer to me. Stared up at the face of the thing lolling inside and took a deep gulp of air.

Then I lifted the point of the knife up to the plastic with my other hand.

"Shouldn't be doing this..." said Sam.

"But what if she's not a dummy?"

I stabbed the knifepoint right into the plastic sack and then I drew the blade down through it, opening it right up.

Blood sluiced out and limbs tumbled and clattered to the floor.

Sam gave a little scream behind me.

I looked at the heap of body parts. Still just a mannequin!

So I went for another. Sliced it open and kicked aside the dummy limbs that fell from the sack. I ran at the next one and attacked it with the sculpting knife. The blood poured onto my face, soaked my coat and my hands as I went from one hanging, plastic chrysalis to another mumbling Harriet's name under my breath, then roaring loudly, "Where is she? *Where is she?*"

Covered in stinking blood I opened up another, and another. I attacked them all and not a single one of them was Harriet.

Sam was back at her desk. She snatched her keys up and ran through the door.

There was no point going after her.

I went through them all, slicing open the body bags one by one in a mad frenzy of action and rage. They were all just dummies. Just plastic body parts and fake blood.

133

I'd fooled myself into thinking this was real. You couldn't use real blood. The stink and decay would be intolerable within hours. So maybe it was just a smelling agent, making me think it was real, and I'd reacted in the most animalistic way possible. Tricked by the art, the environment, the graffiti and the hate and terror that filled the studio.

"Bastard!" I hissed, and then … then I trashed the place. I swept everything to the floor and kept on going until I heard sirens from outside.

Covered in fake blood, I ran from the studio.

3.24

Murderous Art?

Dark thoughts began to boil and something I'd never considered, never even thought of, would never *ever* have thought of before that night, before recent events had taken shape, began to coalesce on the inner surface of my mind.

It started with that age-old question: *What if?*

What if Theo Collins was… What if he was…

What if…?

Was it so unlikely? It wouldn't be the first time that artists had taken serial killers as inspiration for their work. I'd done it myself, but maybe Theo was taking it one stage further. As Sam had said, not Murderous Art but Murder *As* Art.

Once back home I raced down to the cupboard under the stairs, opened up the box of stuff on the Camden Killer and pulled it all out. I spread it out in the hall and in this new light I thought I could see new patterns emerging. Terrifyingly, it all started to make sense. Because *what if* Theo Collins *was* the Camden Killer?

Later, standing in the shower, I found myself staring down at the patterns of soap and water marbling the tray whilst every inch of my body was pummelled by needles of heat. I stood with my hands flat against the shower door, head down, thinking everything through. I went over in my mind, over and over again, every single one of the murderer's kills. The steam that filled every inch of atmosphere became a three-dimensional canvas, externalising the bizarre details of each murder: the roses in the stomach of Rachael Clarke, the nail in her head, the flaying of old Judge Grace. The girl swinging from Blackfriars Bridge wearing a jewel-encrusted deathmask. I thought about Stephen in my lock up wearing a sackcloth mask and I wondered who was going to be next.

Lifting my head I looked through the steam and saw the shadows of my face partially reflected in the door.

Me?

Could I be next? If Theo was the Camden Killer was he coming for me?

Was that why he'd come into my house the other night?

3.25

Less than an hour later I was back on Twitter, using the MacBook instead of my phone.

Hey... @Sh1tPolice. U there..?

@Sh1tPolice: Yo. JJX. Wassup?

I checked out ur link. Has CK got a thing against gays?

@Sh1tPolice: You think he's a homophobe?

I think he's right wing...

@Sh1tPolice: Xtreme?

just an idea

@Sh1tPolice: Rachael Clarke was Jewish.

Old Judge Grace???

It was a while before he came back to me. A few others joined the conversation but no one had anything useful to add.

@Sh1tPolice: tinyurl.gomorrah/jjx. Go now.

I clicked on the link and a page started loading. Anti-virus notifications popped up on the MacBook's screen, warning me of attempted intrusions. The text shifted and jostled with other elements as the page tried to load. Every component of the webpage refusing to settle down.

I tabbed back to Twitter.

What is this? Computer doesn't like it.

@Sh1tPolice: not a public page. yet. something I'm working on. Is it loading?

I noticed he'd deleted the tweet with the link.

@Sh1tPolice: read first then msg me via the page. allow cookies. Trust me.

I went back to the tab with the troublesome page and allowed the cookies. McAfee told me that this was on my head if it went tits up and fucked my MacBook but at least the page loaded.

"Holy shit…"

It was Sh1tPolice's blog. A catalogue of the Camden Killer's crimes. Each murder was described in forensic detail and there were pictures. I felt ill looking at them.

At the top of the page was a hyperlink. It simply said JJX.

I clicked on it and a piece of software started downloading. It only took a few seconds to install, no restart required and when it finished there was a green monster icon in the bottom left corner of my screen. A speech bubble popped out of the monster's head and text appeared inside it:

Shouldn't discuss this on Twitter. That stuffs all public domain.
BTW click here and we can chat 1-1.

I clicked '*here*' and then another monster, this one bright red and with comedy tentacles growing out of his face, split off from the original. An empty speech bubble popped out of the red monster's head and I clicked on it to write:

You've taken over my computer…

A new speech bubble popped out of the original green monster's head. The little monster jumped about a bit and his boggle eyes rolled as the bubble filled with text. Cute.

No. Don't worry. It's just an instant messenger app.
You can uninstall it whenever you want. It's not invasive. I promise

The monster grinned and blew a kiss. Tiny love hearts fluttered away from it like balloons. I laughed nonetheless.

Is this your page?

A work in progress…

It's nasty. Where'd you get all this stuff?

Need to know only. It's not a live webpage. Yet…

Seriously… how do you know I'm not a 10-yr old kid?

Then your mum needs to install family web protection

Funny. Are you police?

Thought you wanted info on CK, not me? You think he's right wing...

I think he killed a friend of mine

Oh... Sorry. Shit... that's heavy. You want to tell...?

My friend was gay.

Old Judge Grace was gay. If your friend was also gay and CK killed him then that's two homosexual victims. But the others were women of different ages. Police are saying there's no clear sexual orientation evident in the killings.

Is that true?

None of the victims have been sexually molested as far as anyone can see.

That's unusual for a serial killer ... right?

It's rare, but not unknown. It means that sex is not a motivating factor in the killings.

So what is? What's driving this guy to kill?

We don't know.

We?

Figure of speech. I mean we generally.

So what if he's extreme right wing? Hates jews, hates gays... etc...

Nazi's tend to be more outspoken. Fascism is an ideology rather than an isolationist obsession.

Huh?? My spellcheck doesn't recognise that word!

LOL! That's Apple for you! Ideologists want to convert the masses, spread their message, make bold statements that enforce their point of view. Serial killers generally work alone or with one accomplice usually, but not always, a lover. Nobody else sees the world the way that they do. Their belief hierarchy, the rationale for their actions, is usually intrinsic to a single dysfunctional personality.

Long words! Basically you're saying ideologists kill en-masse, serial killers are more focussed. Their targets are individuals and they tend to choose them thoughtfully. But they still want to be known right? They want a degree of infamy.

Not always, but I think you're right. I guess CK could be a failed fascist - but I'm sure that's an oxymoron.

Or a tautology…

Now who's using long words??

So Maybe not a fascist. Maybe he just wants to be a celebrity.

That's not as crazy as you might think. To be honest I was wondering the same. I make the point on these pages. We live in a world of celebrity worship, right? Doesn't everybody want to win the X-factor or Big Brother? Celebrity culture is rife. Maybe CK failed too many auditions.

So why is Simon Cowell still alive?

Seriously don't joke about it. Think about Mark Chapman. How do you become a bigger celebrity than John Lennon? You kill John Lennon… Whatever the motive, at the end of the day this guy is dangerous and he needs to be stopped. Right now the police have no idea where to look. They've done all the usual things, looked in all the right places, and examined all the tracks. But they have nothing of substance that can tell them who this fucker is. Not even a profile. My opinion is that they need to throw the rule-book out of the window because this guy has broken the rules. New rules need to be written up for the 21st Century serial murderer.

He killed my friend… I'm certain of it…

You OK..?

I paused… fingers hovering over the keys.

I'm fine. But I need to know who this guy is…

Hey. Keep the app on your Mac. You don't need to revisit this page to message me. If you get any ideas, want to ask me any questions, just click the monster right? Or text me. You got my number from the text I sent you.

Sure. Thanks. BTW – where did you get my number from?

The usual places. Your friend. How was he… presented? You don't have to answer…

It's fine. He was tied to a post and stuck through with paintbrushes. They stuck out of his body like the arrows on St Sebastian the Martyr.

St Sebastian?

Look it up: Famous image of a saint. Patron saint of soldiers, archers and athletes. Something of a gay icon too…

Police looking into it?

Allegedly.

"Oh shit..." I said, staring at the words in the last couple of speech bubbles still on screen. In particular the words 'Gay icon' and then just 'icon'.

I remembered a time when we'd been to the National: Theo, Nugent Fry, Lucy, myself and a bunch of others. Same night we'd played the A-Z drinking game and ended up getting maudlin on the South Bank of the Thames at something-o-clock in the morning. Nugent heaving his guts into the river, Theo kicking off about his dad. Before that point, before we'd even started drinking, we'd been in the National Gallery. We'd all agreed to meet in front of Antonio Pollaiuolo's gigantic altarpiece *The Martyrdom of St Sebastian*. Theo had already had a few drinks before he got there and was already waxing lyrical about the gay subtext of the painting: "Look at that fucker with his big red arse pointing right out so the old priest can stand just here and whip out his cock. He'd be giving himself a good old wank, looking up at that poor naked fucker as he gets it going. I wonder how many priests and bishops had to wipe their cum off that paint over the years."

We were thrown out: chucked onto the steps and told we were lucky they didn't call the police.

Theo dared them to do it and we all laughed our nuts off.

But it isn't a laughing matter right? Because now I was thinking about Stephen, in the lock up and fuck me I'd even made the connection when I'd found his body. St Sebastian has been a homosexual icon since the Renaissance, Stephen was gay and the imagery had to have been deliberate – tied to a post and shot through with arrows, or paintbrushes in his case. The only thing was that St Sebastian didn't wear a mask, whereas Stephen had had this sackcloth thing put over his head.

But was that for the iconography, or just the shock value of pulling it off and finding out who it was? If you didn't know your art or your religion then there'd be little significance to the paintbrushes. So was the Killer leaving *me* messages?

The reveal of the face beneath Stephen's sack-cloth mask wouldn't matter to anyone who didn't know him. It was in my lock up. *My* lock up. So it had always been intended that I would be the one who found the body. Further proof that he was coming for me.

Theo had a thing about homosexuals right? The final solution he announced at the G21 opening.

It was Theo all right. I was convinced.

3.26

"Thanks for seeing me," I said to DI Hershey as she met me at the busy reception desk at Kentish Town police station.

"Come through," she said sweetly, and led me through one security door after another to a grey-walled room deep in the heart of the station. She pulled over a chair that had been up against a wall, put it near a flimsy, metal desk and told me to sit.

The room was nasty. A dull, grey soulless void.

I looked at the posters on the walls warning against drug abuse and violence, each one with the ruined face of a model dressed up like a victim or a hoodie thug. Each poster had a telephone number and a website URL in dramatic font screaming out like a B-movie legend.

They were all fake. The abused women and the hoodies were models, the posters designed by an agency. Fonts carefully chosen.

DS Burrows walked in and closed the door behind him.

"Sorry I'm late," he said, then cleared his throat as he sat next to Hershey and put some papers on the table between us.

"So. Jason. You've got some information?" began Hershey.

"I don't know if it's information as such," I told them. "It's an idea. A theory."

"Jesus…" muttered Burrows. "Another one."

"On the Camden Killer," I said. "About his motive."

Burrows gave out a sigh, glancing at his watch.

"Go on," prompted Hershey. She adjusted the collar of a white blouse she was wearing under her red sweater, then folded her arms on the table top, supporting her bosom.

I leaned across the table and put my bruised hands together, the tips of my fingers linking up.

"Look," I began, "you haven't released the full details about the condition of the Camden Killer's bodies have you?"

They stared at me.

"But there's a lot of speculation," I continued. "And there's a kind of common agreement, at least online, that Rachael Clarke was found dead with a hundred red roses packed into her stomach and a six-inch nail in her forehead."

I left a pause but neither of them filled it. Burrows made some notes. Not many. He was probably writing 'timewaster' on his notepad.

But I continued. "There was another killing attributed to the Killer," I said. "An old man called Benjamin Grace. He was a judge and his body was flayed and left on a park bench on Hampstead Heath. In some reports it says that the old man's skin was pinned to the bench. His son was also a judge and there were pictures of him scattered around the corpse. Is this true?"

"We're not at liberty to divulge any details – " began Burrows, but Hershey lifted a hand and nodded.

"That's true," she told me. "The reports are correct: his skin had been pinned to the bench like upholstery. And yes it was covered in photographs of the man's son, who is still alive by the way."

I nodded. "And Rachael Clarke?"

"All true," Hershey replied. "Just like you said. Red roses in her stomach, six-inch nail in her forehead, driven right into her brain."

I sat back and let out a sigh. So here was the thing. I was about to let them know my big revelation, the thing which had been going through my mind since I'd reawakened all the stuff I'd gathered on the Camden Killer. And sitting here right now it all sounded ridiculous.

"And the Killer is still at large?" I asked. I think I was stalling for time.

Hershey nodded, her blue eyes big and round, almost popping out of her forehead.

"Any leads?" I asked.

"Of course we have leads," said Burrows defensively. "You think we've been sitting on our arses all this time?"

Hershey lifted her hand again and Burrows' mouth snapped shut. "What've you got for us, Jason?" Hershey asked, leaning forward like a viper.

I reached into my coat pocket and produced an envelope full of prints I had run off that morning. I spread them out on the desk, picked one out and turned it towards them.

"What's this?" asked Burrows, peering forward.

"It's a painting," I told him. "By Gerard David. He was a Dutch painter from the fifteenth century and this is from one of two paintings that were commissioned from him by Bruges City Hall."

Burrows looked at the painting, then at me, then at Hershey.

"Sorry," he said. "Am I missing something?"

"Look at it," I said to them. "Tell me what you see."

They both leaned over the printout.

The painting showed a naked old man lying on a wooden table set out in the street. An array of fine, Dutch gentlemen in Renaissance garb stood around the table while the naked man was in the process of being undressed from his skin. Literally. His left leg was held in the air by a surgeon with a knife between his teeth who was peeling away the skin from the old man's shin as though he was removing a boot. Another surgeon, on his knees in the foreground, was carefully cutting an incision along the old man's right arm. Yet another surgeon, this one standing at the old man's head like a barber, had cut a line down the old man's breast and was starting to peel aside two flaps of skin from his ribs. The surgeons appeared methodical and unemotional, and the sheer, clinical, ordinariness of their gruesome street surgery made the horror seem that much worse.

The old man on the table could do nothing. His face was a frozen scream.

In the background, a younger man sat on a throne-like chair holding court with other fine gentlemen. The throne was draped in a pale cloth.

"The painting is called *The Flaying of Sisamnes*," I said. "Sisamness was a corrupt judge who operated in Persia in the pre-Christian era. David made the scene contemporary to his time to serve as a warning to all judges sitting in City Hall who might consider abusing their authority. It was common around fifteenth century Europe to have images of judgement adorning the Chambers of Justice."

"Should have something like this here," muttered Burrows.

"Jim!" snapped Hershey.

"The younger man on the chair in the background is the son of Sisamnes," I said. "He was also a judge. A good one, I think."

Hershey seemed to be taking a closer interest, sliding the picture over the table with long fingers in need of a manicure. I guess she was starting to see where I was going with this.

"The chair," I said, "that the son is sitting on is draped in his father's skin. That's not a cloth."

I slid another picture across the table.

Burrows picked it up. "Who's this?" he asked.

"Santa Rita da Cascia," I told him. "Saint Rita."

"Didn't know there was a Saint Rita."

"She was a nun who became the patron saint of improbable and lost causes. Especially abused wives and grieving women. It wouldn't hurt to have her face hanging on your walls," I said. "She was married at twelve and her husband was a bastard who kicked the shit out of her daily. Story goes that he started up a blood feud with this other family and it got nasty. Eventually Rita converted him. He mended his ways and became a better man. A real switch-around only it was too late. He was stabbed to death by a member of the feuding family. Rita loved her husband and she spent a long time grieving. Just a few years later both her sons died. Natural causes. Afterwards she went and joined the convent of Saint Mary Magdalene. They didn't want to let her in at first because she wasn't..."

Their faces were glazing over so I sped things up a bit. "Anyway," I said, "the story goes that one day, when Rita was praying , kneeling down in front of a statue of Christ in the convent, a thorn fell off the statue's crown and embedded itself deep in her forehead."

I tapped my own forehead with a finger, right in the middle about an inch above my nose, where Racheal Clarke had been impaled.

"The wound never healed," I said. "It persisted. It grew septic and she suffered with it for the rest of her life. It also stank, and the other nuns kept their distance."

I watched as Burrows, now looking serious, passed the picture to his colleague.

"When she eventually died in the convent," I said, "the stench from the wound was said to have miraculously changed. It became something else: the beautiful smell of roses." I left a silence before adding, "Saint Rita is depicted in art all over the world, always with a thorn and a wound in her forehead, and usually with bees, fig leaves or roses. Mostly the roses, which are brought to the table on her feast day, and which fill the shrines and churches in her name."

Hershey, now holding the picture of Saint Rita in his fingertips, looked across at me. "You said ... bees?"

I nodded. "There's another story about the day she was baptised as a baby," I told her. I pulled something else out of my coat pocket and handed it over. It was the pamphlet for Brian Cavendish's *Odyssey Exhibition*. On the cover, my own treatment of Saint Rita – a hollow-eyed, Giger-esque female with bees vomiting from her mouth.

Hershey's reaction was one of distaste.

"Apparently," I said, "a swarm of bees came to her cot. Some of the bees flew down and crawled over her face. They entered her mouth, and then they exited without causing baby Rita any harm."

Hershey put the paper down on the table, and then stared at me. Jim Burrows looked pale.

"Symbols," I said. "They're important in art, and not just religious art. I think they're also important to the Camden Killer."

Burrows looked at me. "You think our serial killer's what? *An artist?*" he looked like he was going to laugh.

That was exactly what I thought. But I said nothing for the moment. As soon as I gave them Theo's name then that was it. No going back. These guys would swoop down on him with everything at their disposal. Which was fine, if he was the Killer.

But if he wasn't…

Hershey said, "All right, Jason. Give us a minute will you?"

3.27

They came back into the room about half an hour later. Sat back down in front of me across the table.

"Tea?" Burrows stood a polystyrene cup of tea on the table.

Hershey cleared her throat and shuffled on her chair. She moved her hair behind her ears then leaned forward, hands together.

She had a bunch of documents in a folder.

"What I'm going to tell you now does not leave this room, Jason," she said.

"Ok," I whispered, shaking. I took a sip of the tea hoping it might calm my nerves a bit. I guess that was the idea. I didn't bother with the packets of sugar Burrows tossed onto the tabletop.

"If the press or anyone else gets wind of this, we'll know it came from you. So… there's a lot of trust in this room right now. It's about the latest victim, the one we're calling number four." She exchanged a glance with Burrows and I got the impression that he was not in agreement with the boss on this one.

I cleared my throat. There hadn't been much on number four, apart from the basic report in the press I remember reading in *The Mirror* back at the market. "The girl found in the church," I said. "Locked room?"

"A twelve year old girl," said Hershey. "Wrapped in clingfilm plastic. She was left in a locked room filled with rose petals in the Church of St Mary Magdalene down near Albany Street Station, which is where me and Jim are normally based."

Hershey pulled a photograph from the document folder and slid it towards me across the table. I wasn't sure I wanted to look, so I didn't. Not yet.

"Take a look," Hershey said to me, her big eyes never leaving my face.

I looked down. Saw a picture of a girl exploding with colour.

The girl was wearing an elaborate mask. It was patterned with diamonds. Big cheeks, small red lips. Looked like some kind of baby, or a cherub.

Hershey said, "When we pulled that thing off her we found that the girl's mouth was full of… full of dead bees." She paused. For the first time showing something which might resemble a genuine emotion. "I won't show you the photograph. But I've seen some things in my time, Jason. A lot of dead kids battered and broken, molested, even beheaded. I have to look at images worse than this more times than I ever see pictures of my own kids on our holidays. But this was ... something else. We couldn't figure out why she was locked in the room. It didn't seem like there was any reason for it. Other than theatre," she finished.

She stared right at me. Lips pressed together.

"What you said," interjected Burrows calmly. "The convent your Saint Rita went to..."

I nodded. "St Mary Magdelene," I confirmed. Same as the church. But there was more, and the locked room scenario made sense. "Saint Rita was refused entry to the convent when she first applied to them," I explained. "One morning the sisters found Rita inside one of the rooms. When they asked how she could have got in without a key, given that the convent had been locked up for the night, she told them she'd been transported there by Saint John the Baptist."

Hershey exhaled a long, loud sigh.

Then I said. "There's a thing about masks isn't there?"

Hershey glanced down at the document, pulled a few sheets of paper to one side of the folder.

"I mean – not on all the victims," I said, "but some of them at least. This young girl, the girl hanging from Blackfriars Bridge and Stephen Craine... He had a sackcloth mask on his head."

"Jason," interjected Burrows. "Stephen Craine was not a victim of the Camden Killer."

"So why were you two interviewing me afterwards then?" I shouted "Why not some other plods? You two are investigating the killings, so there must have been something in Stephen's case that made you think that his murder might be the work of the same guy."

"There was," Hershey said. "But we discounted it."

"But it fits the style of this nutter's kills!" I shouted.

"No!" Burrows snapped back. "It doesn't. I'm sorry, Jason, but your friend's murder was a homophobic killing." He looked straight at me. "Nothing more."

"He was stuck through with *paintbrushes*," I protested. "Tied to a fucking post with a sack over his head." Couldn't they see it? "Look," I said. "If there's any one of these murders which potentially isn't in the same vein as the others then it's the girl hanging from Blackfriars. She's a Harlequin or something similar from the *Commedia dell'Arte*, but the others are all decorated with iconography of the Saints. Stephen included."

"Bethany was the third one we found," said Hershey. "Prior to being hanged she had been stabbed in the throat with a long blade angled upwards that went right through to the back of her skull. It matched Rachael Clarke's deathblow exactly, and was certainly the same weapon. That's usually how we identify a single killer through multiple victims, Jason. That's usually the kind of thing we look for rather than ... artistic symbolism."

"But if your killer is an artist or at least someone with artistic pretensions than why wouldn't he use artistic iconography? Stephen's murder is outrageously iconographic."

"Nasty yes," admitted Burrows. "And theatrical. But sticking objects into a homosexual's body during the murder is a common–"

I scrabbled through the pictures, dug through them on the table and near-enough threw one of them right at him. "Here," I said. "Look at this and you tell me there's no link."

They scanned the picture of St Sebastian and Hershey swore, dropping the front for just a moment. "Another saint?" she asked.

"Yes," I told her. "Another saint."

"Why's he so hung up on the saints?"

Burrows answered. "Maybe he's a church-goer. Maybe he got kicked out of church. A priest?"

Hershey shook her head. "Saints are martyrs right?" she said. "And we all know what a martyr wants."

"You're both wrong," I said.

They looked at me.

"It's me," I told them. "The Camden Killer is tracking *my art*. I was the one who was obsessed with the Saints, and he's following them exactly."

"Care to clarify that?" asked Hershey.

"For... whatever reason..." I said, "the Camden Killer has latched onto my art. He's telling me that he knows me, so it's highly likely that I know him."

Hershey sighed, sat back in the chair and ran a hand through her hair. "What the hell. Why not? So where do we start looking for a psychopathic art lover, Jason?" she asked, not at all serious. "Where do we go with this and how many more martyrs and saints are we going to find on our streets?"

"Not many more," I answered. "But it doesn't mean it's over. After I'd finished with the Saints I moved onto Angels."

Burrows stared at me. "You a religious guy, Jason?"

"No," I told him. "I was just trying to subvert the iconography of historical pre-dispo…" I stopped in mid-sentence and shrugged. "What the fuck."

In the end it was the image of the twelve-year old girl that made up my mind. Nobody deserved that, least of all a child, and it was the thing that Hershey had said too, about seeing more pictures of dead children than her own kids on holidays. So she had kids. A husband? I wondered what they thought of her job, and the woman who returned home at whatever time of the day it finished.

"Studio 10b," I told them. "It's in Chalk Farm. Theo Collins runs an art class there and I took a look at it the other day. If you go there you'll find everything you need."

"Who's Theo Collins?" asked Hershey.

"He's the guy I think is the Camden Killer. You need to find him."

Burrows looked at me and frowned. "Studio 10b you said?" he asked. "Steeles Road Mews?"

I nodded.

"Interesting… There was a fire there a couple of nights ago," he explained. "The place burnt to the ground. When did you say you were there?"

3.28

Burrows slid his Beamer into Steeles Road Mews and parked up in the middle of the courtyard. The car stopped. We all got out, and walked towards the burned-out cottage façades.

"You weren't kidding," I said, hugging my chest against the mini-blizzard that had decided to spring up from nowhere. The wind whipped my hair over my face and I had to keep twisting it away as I scanned the Studio.

Where once there'd been a row of slightly rundown but nonetheless complete mews cottages, now there was nothing but burnt-out shells with sooty tongues staining the brickwork around empty, windowless frames. Police tape was all that secured the area and it flapped madly in the wind. There was nobody else here, no one to see it but us three.

We walked towards the building and Burrows shone a torch in through a couple of the window holes.

"Nothing in there now," he shouted.

Wrong.

I was standing next to him, looking in. "Let me borrow your torch."

The DI nodded at him and Burrows handed me his torch.

I took it, and pointed it through the blackened square hole that used to be a window. The circle of light swept through the ruin. It cut across falling snow, and picked out one last body bag which lay on the floor. It was wrapped in chains, and just before I pulled the torch away, it twitched.

"What?" I gasped.

Just my imagination?

No. It moved again.

Quickly I leapt inside, in through the window.

"Jason!" I heard Burrows shouting behind me.

It stank inside the building. Of burnt wood and old smoke. I stumbled over the bricks and timbers, trying not to lose my footing.

The body was in a dark place at the back of the floor and I approached it cautiously, memories of Stephen Craine flooding back to me.

So who was it going to be this time? Arnold? Jhavesh? Harriet?

Jesus don't let it be Harriet.

I hunkered down next to the body and looked it over.

The victim's hands had been tied to his sides and the bag had been wrapped around him from his elbows to his feet, exposing his head, his shoulders and upper arms. Chains criss-crossed the bag. It wasn't Harriet, she didn't have shoulders like that. These belonged to a man.

I shone the torch at the face and saw another mask. A plain white mask of stunning simplicity. Nothing on it but a pair of small blood-red lips at the mouth and a couple of black dots for eyes. There was a hole between the lips, providing an airflow.

Burrows was the first to join me.

"Go back, JJ," he said. "You shouldn't be here."

I stayed.

"Go back!" Burrows shouted.

My torch was pointing at the mask as Hershey came in behind us, picking her way over the rubble.

The victim in the mask was still alive

"Jim's right, Jason" her voice was urgent. No-nonsense. "Get back to the car. Jim, you take him. Radio this in."

Burrows took me by the elbow but I shrugged him off.

"I know who this is," I whispered.

I pointed my torch at the victim's right arm where a distinctive zigzag scar ran around it just below the shoulder.

"It's a man called Nugent Fry. We went to college together."

He was still alive and I found out later that he'd been pumped full of morphine.

He wasn't alive for long though.

"Let's get this mask off," Hershey said, when Nugent started making a choking noise like his airflow was restricted.

Too late I shouted. "No! No don't!"

Nugent screamed when Burrows pulled what was left of his face away, and within seconds he died.

3.29

I don't remember much about what happened straight after that. I remember police and ambulance blues whipping around the mews as I stood outside, shivering and smoking a cigarette. People in hi-vis jackets rushing to and fro.

Hershey came up at one point to talk to me. She asked me a bit about Nugent Fry and I told her all I knew, which wasn't much.

"I haven't seen him for years," I said, teeth chattering. "Since we were at college."

First Stephen, now Nugent. I hadn't known the other victims but I knew they were linked to me in some way.

Hershey got a car to take me home and once there I rescued a bottle of Highland Park single malt. Then I sat on the floor in the downstairs hall, hugged my knees up to my chin, and looked at all the stuff about the Camden Killer scattered around me.

So, if it was Theo, when was he going to make his next direct move on me?

Right now it felt like there was something dark sitting on my shoulder, chewing at my neck. The alcohol helped turn everything into a fudge and I thought if Theo came tonight then I didn't give a shit anymore. Let him do what he wanted. I'd abdicated all responsibility for this to the people who could now do something about it.

I wasn't really into drinking but that night I drank myself stupid, just like I had at Arnold's Scottish retreat. Difference was that this time I was on my own. Liselle tried calling me. Arnold tried calling me. So did Harish and so did Doctor Pandghani. He left a message on the landline, surprised that I'd been trying to get hold of him and if I ever wanted to I could call him back on this new number. I wanted to, but I couldn't talk to him. I couldn't talk to anyone.

So I spoke to no one and eventually I just fell asleep.

3.30

I woke up some time in the morning when I got a call from Harish. He sounded nervous. "JJ," he said. "At last! Listen up, we've got major problems with the TV thing, mate. You'd best come down and see this."

"I thought you said it was all sorted? Nothing to worry about…"

"You'd best come down."

Hershey and Burrows knocked round first. I let them in and they had a go at the state of me.

"Would you have a look through these names?" Hershey asked me. She sounded happy. She was even smiling as she handed me a sheet of paper with a list of names on it.

"Who are they?" I asked her.

"People who attended classes at Studio 10b. We can't locate this Theo Collins, yet, but is there anyone on this list whose name you recognise?"

I scanned through the names and my blood went cold.

"Well?" prompted Hershey.

"No," I told her, my throat dry. "Nothing. Theo should be easy to find."

"So help us out," she said. "Where is he likely to be if not at home?"

I shrugged. "Dunno," I mumbled.

Hershey snatched the list off me and put it back inside her coat pocket. She wasn't smiling anymore. "Worth a try. We might be back with more questions," she said. Then she barked at her lapdog, "Jim, come on."

Burrows flashed a grin at me as he walked past. "Be seeing you," he said. "Don't go anywhere."

I sat down in the kitchen. My hands were shaking.

I looked round for Bella but of course she wasn't here.

On the list of names had been one impossible name that I recognised, despite what I'd told Hershey. It *could* have been a coincidence. Maybe it was just some old lady who attended pottery lessons.

Jane Gordon.

Impossible.

My phone rang and made me jump, the sound of it cutting harshly into my thoughts. It was Harish again.

"I'm coming," I told him. "Leaving the house now."

With an effort I got my shit together and went to the Dreadnought, travelling down by tube and DLR. All the way there I still felt like I was being followed. Kept catching a glimpse of someone in a big coat as I turned a corner, walked past a shop window.

The police?

The Camden Killer?

I didn't know. Didn't know if it was real or just an expression of my increasing paranoia. Jane Gordon? How could the name on the list have been Jane Gordon?

The Dreadnought Gallery loomed like a stranded ship of the future over the wide concourse bisected by the Greenwich Meridian. I went in through the back door and soon I was walking into the space I'd been standing in with Brian Cavendish less than a couple of months earlier. It was strange being back there, surrounded by all the TVs and castle props that we'd been putting together in my house. It was the first time I'd seen the near-complete installation *in-situ* and it looked good.

However the screens were all blank.

I'd been expecting to see them working.

Harish met me. "Come and see," he said. "You ain't gonna like it." Then he said, "Mate. You don't look good."

"Just show me," I whispered, exhausted.

He led me to his laptop which sat on the floor inside the gigantic room, cables everywhere, and ran one of the video files that was to be used for the installation.

It was a recording of Liselle and me fucking each other in my studio. She was wearing soiled rags barely containing her breasts and I was up behind her, banging away.

"All right, mate," I said to him.

"What? Oh yeah. Sorry." He stopped the playback and the screen defaulted to the file list display. There were hundreds of video and image files banked up by the software that distributed them to the screens.

"Somehow," Harish said, "this movie clip of you and that girl is embedded in every video file."

It took a while for this to sink in, and he had to say it a few more times, each time with a little more explanation until I rubbed my face, brought myself back into the world and lamely said something like, "What? How?"

"I dunno, man. It might have been tampered with but you'd have to know what you was doing. I mean you could put in a trojan or summink that activated every time you used an application to open video files. So no matter what you played, it would switch to this, which is bad enough but what it does then is erase and replace the content of the old video file."

This was fucking with my head. "Are the original files still there?"

"They could be, somewhere, but I'm worried about running a search to check. I could do it from another PC but I wouldn't want that infected as well"

"Shit! I'll buy you another laptop," I said. "Just use it to check the video files. See if there's anything we can recover."

"It's only the prerecorded stuff," Harish said. "Running live images seems to be OK. But it could be doing shit in the background that I don't know about. That's why I turned the screens off."

"Let's get another computer. Run the files on clean software and see what we have."

So we did that. Literally walked into PC World and bought a new laptop which we used to search for remnants of the original video and run when we found them. We opened them on MediaPlayer, Quicktime and the pro-software that Harish had incorporated into his own thing running the installation. But we got the same thing every time. Just a ninety-second loop of me and Liselle fucking each other in my studio.

Harish sat back in his chair. "Sorry man. That's all of 'em. Bad news innit?"

"Fuck yeah…" I mean it wasn't the end of the world. We couldn't use the prerecords – all the stuff I'd spent weeks shooting – but hopefully we could still run live grabs and montages. It wouldn't be the same.

"Best not use that other computer to run the live stuff at the show," I said.

"It's cool, JJ. I can clean it out and re-install the software."

"Have we got time for that?"

"Mate it'll take a couple of hours. Half a day at most."

I left him to it with my head in a turmoil. All I could think was who the hell was pretending to be Jane Gordon?

3.31

I took a call from Brian Cavendish an hour or so later.

"Jason, it's Brian," he bellowed on the phone.

"I know. How's things?"

"I'm in New York and I'm hearing you're having problems," he said. "I'm hearing tall tales of pornography in my gallery. Is it true?"

"Just a hiccup, Brian. My computer guy can fix it."

"Hope so, JJ. You know me, I'm as *Avant-Garde* as the next man but I won't have porn at my show. You get that?"

"Yeah. Sure, Brian. It'll be fine. No porn."

"This is a serious exhibition, my friend, and I'm paying you a shitload of real cash so that you can deliver the goods. But if all you're going to do is show a reel of fucking and sucking then I will take a hammer and smash your bloody brains in. You understand? What you did at Lambeth was borderline, and maybe some people think you crossed that line. Not me. I think you stayed the right side of it. But only just. I don't mind you taking things out that far again, but do not cross over that line, Jason. Understand me? You do that and you're not only out of my Exhibition I'll make sure you are utterly finished. Get me?"

"Brian, with the greatest respect, you don't have to talk to me like–"

"Jason, I'm paying you four million fucking big ones for this show. Until we're finished on January the tenth, you, my friend, will be my bitch and I will speak to you however I damn well please."

"I'm not a child, Brian!"

"And I respect your resolve. But don't fuck with me."

"I'll sort it. I promise."

"That's all I'm asking."

I cut the call. Fuming with anger. Who the hell did he think he was?

3.32

Back home. Liselle was in the kitchen making some toast and I was in the front room drinking, trying to get Theo and Nugent out of my head. It was down to the police now, they could sort it. Nothing to do with me.

"Hey," said Liselle, shouting from the kitchen. "You want some toast?"

I hadn't eaten properly for days but I wasn't hungry. The landline was ringing but I let the answering machine take it. I poured out another drink and rubbed my eyes. *Snap out of this, JJ*, I was telling myself. *Just...*

"Mr Jones," the voice said. Thick Indian accent from the answering machine. "I understand you've been trying to call me. I'm going away in a couple of—"

I snatched up the phone.

"Doctor Pandghani. I'm sorry. It's Jason Jones."

"Ah! Mr Jones, hello sir. How are you? Looking forward to Christmas? How is Jenny?"

"How is she? I don't know. I was trying to ring you to find out. I didn't realise you weren't at the hospital anymore."

"I'm working in Bristol," he said. "A fabulous city but bloody cold right now. So what can I do for you? I assume it is regarding your sister?"

"Yes. Yes it is," I said to him, running a hand through my hair. "I just wanted to know, is she OK?"

"Is she OK? Is she back at the hospital? I'm very sorry if that's the case," he said. "I had every hope that she would make a decent recovery in your good care."

It took me a while to think through what he was saying to me. Sounded like there was some confusion.

"Stop. Stop, stop... What do you mean 'in my good care'?" I asked. "Jenny isn't with me."

Silence.

"Doctor?"

More silence. Then:.

"I'm so sorry, Mr Jones. What happened? Did she regress? Did she have to return to the hos —"

"Doctor Pandghani," I interrupted. "Jenny was never here. Not with me." I was finding it hard to speak. "Has she ... has she been discharged?" I asked him. "Is that what you're saying?"

"I believe so," he answered slowly. "Look, I might have got it wrong. My final recommendation was that she be discharged into your care and as far as I'm aware you came and collected her yourself—"

The lights in the house went out. The phone went dead.

"Hello? Hello, Doctor...?"

Nothing.

"Doctor!"

And then I heard a clatter from the kitchen. My first thought was that Bella was chasing a mouse across the kitchen sink but I remembered that Bella was dead. So what was it? There was only Liselle in the kitchen.

She screamed.

I got up and ran out, tensing for a fight. No baseball bat to hand but if someone was having a go at Liselle I'd fucking kill them.

In the corridor someone moved. A face covered with a balaclava, a man striding right towards me with confidence and purpose. Didn't care that I could see him.

"Motherfucker…" I whispered. So this is how he wanted it was it? Well come on then!

There was another man behind him, in the kitchen, and I caught the briefest glance of Liselle. Her face was swollen and split, a patchwork of bruises. Her eyes were closed up and raw. There was something stuffed in her mouth and her clothes were hanging off her. She was covered in blood.

The guy in the kitchen had one hand squeezed around her throat. There was a knife in it. His other hand was pulling at her top and he was pushing her out of view behind the door.

"Liselle!" I ran forward; went to push past the first guy but he was waiting for me.

He moved quickly and an explosive pain shattered the back of my skull as he hit me with something. I fell, crashing to the floor. He hit me again and then everything went black.

The Cottage

I arrived at the cottage near Helston, Cornwall, in a rented Transit van at around 8am. Reversed up the pitted, slightly overgrown driveway and then switched off the engine. I stepped out and took a walk back down to the driveway entrance.

Leaning against the centuries-old garden wall overgrown with rampant jasmine and honeysuckle, I lit a cigarette, took a look round and nodded in appreciation of the view.

It was a clear, sunny morning. One that promised a truly beautiful summer's day. To one side of the cottage a field of wild grass and flowers sloped down to a sudden clifftop. Beyond it, the sea stretched towards the horizon like the perfect mirror to a fresh, bright-blue sky, warming as the sun climbed ever higher. Bees hummed and birdsong rang through the cottage garden; even through the stink of my cigarette I could smell the fragrance of climbing roses, honeysuckle and magnolia blossom. Walking back into the garden I noticed how drops of dew clung to the spiky, purple stems and leaves of a huge, bushy lavender, and how they were disturbed into a sudden spray by the taking-off of a blackbird who'd been searching behind it for worms.

It was a scene that could have been painted by Claude Monet and hung in the Louvre.

Fuck that.

I was going to paint it.

I stamped my fag out, opened up the back doors of the Transit and took out the first tin of paint. The van was full of paint tins. All white.

I put some overalls on, pulled the ladders off the roof, switched on a portable radio and set to work.

It took me four hours to whitewash the outside of the cottage. Walls, doors and windows. By that time I was just dressed in a pair of old shorts; it was so hot I'd to abandon the overalls and I was covered in paint. I looked like some kind of tribal warrior.

I broke in through the back and used the rest of the paint on the inside of the cottage.

There were three rooms downstairs: a living room, a kitchen and a dining room. I covered everything in whitewash: sofa, chairs, TV, dining table and sideboard, kettle, coffee machine, cups, plates, sink, draining board.

I had something to eat, some sandwiches I'd made earlier which I ate on a bench in the lovely garden, then I went back inside the cottage and started on the upstairs rooms: the master bedroom, a second bedroom and a study.

Again, I painted everything. Including the beds.

By seven o'clock, eleven hours after I'd begun, my arms were hurting, ready to drop off. The sun was starting to sink, flooding the sky with a slight orange hue, tinting the white interior of the cottage nicely I thought through its newly-whitewashed window panes.

The study was the last room to be painted. It was full of books and magazines, hundreds of *Art Tabloids* in binders. I painted all of those. Took a lot of pleasure in drenching them with the cheap, white builders' paint. There was a desktop computer on his desk and I painted that too. Then I painted the desk.

There were some Celtic ornaments in the study, and these made me stop and think. The deep, warm shadows of the cottage interior bestowed a layer of beauty upon these objects of such ornate delicacy and intricacy that in the end I couldn't bring myself to ruin them with whitewash.

I told myself that it wasn't the fault of those long-dead craftspeople that the exquisite fruit of their labours had ended up in the hands of Hugh Donovan-Smith.

So I left them alone.

Just after 10pm I packed the empty tins, brushes and rollers into the van and drove off, my work done, a smile on my face.

A month later I was called to court, charged with criminal damage and forced into community service. I was virtually broke. But then some time into the sentence, an arty Texan couple commissioned me to do exactly the same to a property they'd purchased themselves in Cheshire.

They paid me half a million for it.

4

Deconstructivism

We tell ourselves that the Modern Artist has no place in Society. We say his services are not required and we turn away because we cannot understand what he so fervently wishes to tell us with his oblique installations, his oak tree glasses of water or his Neo-Pop pornography. We are embarrassed by him, and look to his ancestors for comfort – to Titian, and Rembrandt, Van Dyke and Van Gogh. But the truth is that society needs art, because without the modern artist testing and pushing our ways of seeing things, without him, without his work, without his need to enact our obsessions, then our own interactions with the world and our everyday thoughts and feelings remain abstract and unformed. And in this unexpressed, primal condition those raw spirits are dangerous.

The Art Tabloid. Issue 747. September 2001.
Editorial to the Death-Art Review Edition
Hugh Donovan-Smith.

4.1

The girl in the chair screamed, the sound of a young mind breaking down.

4.2

Earlier…
 "I want you to act frightened," I said. "To behave as though there really is no way out of this. Can you do it?"
 Bound to the chair at the centre of the room the wide-eyed girl nodded.
 I was still sculpting her when the gallery opened; adding a touch of shadow to her eyes, her cheekbones, retouching parts of the henna-pattern fake tattoo that spiralled across the left-hand side of her face and down her neck, her shoulder, all the way down to the fingertips on her left hand which gripped the arm of the chair tightly.
 "You sure you're OK?" I asked her, still rearranging her hair and clothes.
 She exhaled as I stood back. "I'm OK," she whispered. "It's just hot in here."
 "I'll get them to turn down the heating a bit. But let me know if at any time you're not comfortable with this."
 "As long as you're paying me, I'm fine."

I checked that the metal braces on her legs were strapped tight, and then I walked away, leaving her alone in the room.

Quarter of an hour later the doors opened, and the first of the gallery's viewers walked in. It was press day, and most of these people were journalists. The worst kind of audience, but necessary.

The lights went down. It was completely dark. I looked down from a windowed office overlooking the installation as the whistling, thunderous shriek of a passenger jet in flight started up in the pitch dark below. It was so loud it made the floor and windows of the room vibrate.

A spark of silver-grey light was struck like a match in the dark, and upon a cyclorama of screens surrounding the girl the first in a series of images flickered into life. They were all images of two towers standing side by side above a bustling modern metropolis. Just a normal sunny day in September.

The roaring scream of the jumbo jet grew louder, and within it a babble of voices started up, assembled from cellphone conversations, TV and radio broadcasts all around the world. All culled from that single moment on that single day in history.

The roar of the fated aircraft grew louder still.

4.3

The first thing I became aware of when I regained consciousness was the smell of gas. It got into me, right down into my beaten guts and I threw up. I couldn't stop it.

It wasn't easy, being sick whilst blindfolded and with my hands tied behind my back, but someone did help me. I felt hands on my shoulders. Not gentle hands, but they steered me into a position that made it easier to puke without it hurting so much. I was slapped on the back a few times and when the retching ceased a glass of water was pressed to my lips.

"Thank you," I gasped, "thank you thank you thank you…"

At which point I was left on the floor to the sounds of footsteps walking away.

I started gathering my breath, blowing chunks of snot from my nose, coughing roughly. Spitting bits of sick from my mouth.

I didn't dare to speak. I didn't know if I'd been abandoned or if I was being watched.

Plan was to stay quiet. Play dumb. Get my strength back.
Whoever it was had brought me here had picked the wrong person.
I wasn't a victim.
But the smell of gas… It was so strong…
I passed out again.

4.4

A Boeing 767-233ER carrying seventy-six passengers, eleven crewmembers, five al-Qaeda hijackers and about ten-thousand US gallons of jet fuel, slammed into the upper floors of the North Tower of the World Trade Center in New York City at 08:46 EDT on Tuesday September 11th 2001.

Just after 9am on the same day, United Airlines Flight 175, after dropping altitude at a rate of almost ten-thousand feet per minute, banked left into the South Tower and in that collision, on live television the world over, both the plane and the tower were transformed into a billowing column of fire and deadly, black smoke.

And so many people were inside it, dying as we all watched. Horrified.

I remembered thinking when I first saw the news reports at the time, what would it have been like to have been a passenger on one of those planes? For those who were passengers, and for those who were just starting a day's work at their office in the World Trade Center, what was that moment like when the plane hit the tower and disintegrated?

In a way it wasn't real. It *couldn't* be real. At the time, things like this just *did not happen.*

Like the rest of us on that day, the girl in the chair could do nothing but watch as people fell or took the awful decision to jump from the upper floors of those burning, ever-collapsing towers. Nor could she do anything when the towers broke down completely and tumbled into the streets of NYC.

At the time of the Lambeth installation, ten years to the day after 9/11, it was just a recording. But in a way that was worse, because as you watched it you still wanted it to change. You wanted the planes to miss, the passengers to overpower the hijackers and the planes to pull up at the last minute. Fuck, you'd even cheer to see Superman flying down from the clouds to take hold of the plane and pull it away. The thing you didn't want to see was what you knew had already happened.

And here it was, in the gallery, being replayed time and again on the massive screens surrounding the girl I'd paid to be tied to the chair and watch.

Her tears were real and so were mine. Even now, I can't watch the 9/11 attacks without feeling ... *something...*

4.5

"I've got a ni-deer," I told Arnold Evans, late one windy New Year's Eve, years ago. We were in Scotland. In his cottage or lodge or whatever you called it, near Kyle of Lochalsh. A small, two-story building composed of massive stone walls and a roof that smothered everything inside it.

It was just the two of us, warm inside while the elements raged outside. A log fire crackled deep inside a stone fireplace, its flickering light refracted into rainbow colours by the diamond-cut glass of our whisky-filled tumblers.

Over the top of my glass I peered, one eye closed, at Arnold. He was sprawled across a deep, leather armchair adjacent to the fire.

I was on the sofa, and we were both in formal dress shirts, bow-ties undone at the collar. Time was something-past-something in the morning.

"What is't?" asked Arnold.

"What?"

"Your idea," he said, rubbing between his eyes. "What .... what is it made of?"

"My idea?"

"M-hm."

It took a moment to assemble my thoughts. "You ever seen the film of *A Clockwork Orange?*"

He thought for a moment. "Stanley Kubrick's film?"

"Yes."

"No. I never seen him. Why would I want to? I know what it's about and I don't like the look of it. Why?"

"It was just an idea..." I took a sip of my malt. Had to think which one we were on now. Where was the bottle?

"You was thinking of doing Clockwork Oranges?" Arnold cut in. "How?"

"Dunno," I answered. "Just … maybe … like I could have someone in a room surrounded by tellies showing all kinds of … stuff."

"Boriiiiiing…" he sang cruelly.

"Was just an idea."

"Is a rubbish idea. Forget about it."

"I don't mean putting on nothing we don't see on the news or YouTube. You know… it's like we're all exposed to this shit every day anyway."

"Huh? What is this 'You Tube'?"

I shook my head. "Doesn't matter."

Then he sat bolt upright. "Whass the time, JJ? Is it Crissmas yet?"

"I suspect," I began, "that it has been Christmas for some hours already."

"Excellent! Murry-Crissmas!" Arnold offered, then downed his dram in one.

4.6

I was conscious – barely. I might have been drifting in and out of it for a while. It felt like I was coming out of a session under anaesthetic where confusion and disorientation reigned.

I could feel plastic straps wrapped tight around my wrists, binding my hands to the arms of a chair. They burned, cutting deep into my skin. Especially the right-hand one with the still-bruised fingers. It was a torment not being able to scratch it.

I was still blindfolded, so I couldn't see a thing. Had to rely on my other senses.

So I listened and I heard:

Boots scuffing on a concrete floor. People walking away. A chair (or a table?) being dragged over towards me. The strike of a match close by. The strong stink of the match was followed by the smell of a cigarette wafting past my nose.

Then gunshots, loud and sudden, made me jump. They ricocheted, and I heard horses galloping, hooves thumping dully over a landscape.

Dramatic music suddenly very loud, and someone close by laughing. It was a man, definitely. A real, smoky, throaty, growling laugh. More gunshots and ricochets: *pee-yowwn! pee-yowwnnn..!*

I heard earnest voices in-between the gunshots and dramatic music, and I sort of relaxed.

Somebody was watching TV. An old western or a Saturday morning serial from a bygone age.

I tried to speak but it was hard to find enough saliva to lubricate my cardboard tongue and sticky teeth.

"Hey..." I tried to say. "Hey... Please..."

More laughter. Louder this time.

I didn't give up. Kept working my tongue which felt swollen and ugly in my mouth. "Please..." I rasped. "I don't ... I don't know... who you are... But please ... a drink. That's all I'm asking..."

The laughter got louder the more I talked, and I pictured myself in some kind of Mexican jail, a set from a spaghetti western – which made no sense because I had to be still in London right"

"Please...?"

Laughter.

"A glass of water?"

More laughter. Louder. So I stopped talking.

As soon as I did, the laughter stopped.

The TV too, I realised.

Then I heard bootsteps again.

"Can you take this blindfold off?" I asked. "I mean, surely it doesn't matter right? If I see you? Maybe we can– Hey! What are you doing? Get off me! No... No! NO!"

A strong hand grabbed hold of my left wrist and pressed it down, hard into the arm of the chair.

I struggled. Breathing through my nose. "You shit! You fucker! You motherfucker! Don't you ... don't you fucking...! No! You're not... Fuck you, you're not..."

I felt something metal brush the back of my hand. It was cold and sharp. Unmistakeably, it was the flat edge of a knife blade.

I could *feel* the movement in the air: a quick up and down, down into my hand. Then a sudden, searing, white-hot pain bursting from the back of my hand as something was hammered through it and into the chair arm. One single hammer-like blow and it hurt like hellfire.

I screamed, unable to move the claws of my left hand.

Then there was a voice in my ear: "Shhhh...." It whispered. "SShhh... all done..."

And while I sat, bound to the chair, wondering how much blood I was losing, I heard the TV start up again. And the 'Mexican Guard', as I imagined him to be, lit up another cigarette and recommenced his laughter, watching whatever it was he was watching.

I didn't speak again unless I was spoken to.

4.7

Suicide bombers in Iraq. Refugees from Sudan. The War on Terror. George Bush and Tony Blair fighting the United Nations even before they sent soldiers to fight in Iraq. Weapons inspectors searching the deserts…

Image after image after image. We had seen them all before but never in a gallery in Lambeth.

Thing is, it didn't stop there. Without Theo to hold me back, without him saying "We don't need this" and with my recent successes, my reimagined Saints and Angels pushing me on, I really hadn't stopped. I'd opened Pandora's Box in Lambeth and everything I could find inside it I'd sent to the screens, no holds barred. *Modern Apocalypse*. That's what it said on their gallery invites, and that was what they got.

Napalm in the jungles of Vietnam. Screaming children running from a swarm of helicopters racing across a beach on fire. No Wagner here to make the whole thing ironic or rousing, just raw, unbridled horror. Like the human remains discovered in mass graves at a POW camp in Auschwitz. The black and white film slowly pans across the horror, revealing the true scale of Hitler's Final Solution to the eyes of Whitehall and Downing Street for the first time.

Skeletal wretches in Africa with flies on their faces, too weak to brush them away. Victims of civil war. Ordinary families caught up in a conflict between one War Chief who called himself President and another War Chief who wanted to replace him.

And all the while the Towers burned and people fell from the windows, tumbling head over heels to their deaths on live TV, arms outstretched, maybe hoping to fly like angels.

As I looked down from the darkened office I knew, with a cold knot twisting tighter in the pit of my stomach, watching the journalists and the girl in the chair down below, that I had crossed the line. This was as far as it was ever going to go and at that point I knew the public were never going to see this.

"Stop the show," I said to the gallery director standing next to me. Then louder: "Stop the show!"

Too late. The decision had already been taken out of my hands.

The girl in the chair screamed and I never forgot that sound.

4.8

"What is it with you and televisions, JJ?" Arnold asked me that night in his lodge.

I shook my head. "No," I answered.

"What?" He looked like I'd just rabbit-punched him on the nose. "No?"

"No…"

He stared at me. "No fucking what? What the fuck is 'no'?"

"Just… no…" I mumbled.

4.9

The next voice I hear belongs to my sister, Jenny.

"Shush," she whispers. "I've dragged our secrets to Hell and back and they're here to stay."

I see a doctor in my memories. Not Doctor Pandghani. This guy is gaunt and white, tall, thin, skeletal-looking. No, he's *ghoulish*. In my memory he's Peter Cushing in a white coat, peering into a flask of bubbling green liquid. In reality he was someone else but right now it's Peter Cushing I see and hear. "Why do you think your sister is so fixated on the common room television?" he asks me.

"You're the doctor," I reply. "So you tell me."

He calls up an image of Jenny on the CCTV. (They watch all the patients this way. Voyeurism in the name of medical science.) Jenny sits cross-legged on the floor in front of a TV screen filled with fizzing white noise. She looks like the little girl talking to the spirits in the film *Poltergeist*. Difference is that Jenny's ghosts are real. I know this because I've seen them too.

"The other patients no longer ask for control of their TV back," Peter Cushing tells me.

"At the Novak Institute they would have torn her away from it kicking and screaming," I tell him, wiping tears from my eyes. "And because of that they would have put her in a padded cell wearing a straitjacket."

"We don't do that here," Cushing says, turning away from the screen to check his bubbling flask. It was the reason I'd moved her to St Cecilia's, away from that fucking Bedlam up in Edinburgh.

Problem was, maybe they were too lax down here. Maybe Jenny had too much control. And now they'd lost her! Fucking idiots! How could they have let someone pretending to be me just walk her out of the fucking hospital? She could be fucking dead for all I knew and here I was tied to a fucking chair, blindfolded by someone who'd just stabbed a fucking knife into the back of my left hand!

When the delusions passed I heard a new voice and it chilled me to the bone.

4.10

"Jason…" she hissed.

I snapped my head round. Still groggy. Still in pain. Still blindfolded and still able to smell gas.

"*Jason!*"

Loud, but not too loud.

I couldn't speak. A gag was crammed into my mouth now, filling it up. All I could do was blow bubbles of snot from my nose.

The back of my left hand was just numb and I couldn't move my fingers. It felt like there was a plaster or some kind of dressing on it at least.

But I recognised the woman's voice. It was Liselle.

"Jason. Are you OK? Just nod if you are, please do something, please tell me you're OK."

She sounded terrified.

I nodded.

A victim again? Was I dreaming this? It couldn't be real could it? People didn't just get abducted from their homes, dragged out, tied up and stabbed did they?

And I thought about the Camden Killer working in the area. Taking people off the streets and killing them. Disembowelling them and leaving them for the police. Dressing up their bodies like works of art.

Works of art…

That had been the link I'd discovered. My great revelation. The girl with the flowers in her guts, the skinless body of the old Judge left on the bench on Hampstead Heath, Stephen in the lock up. And what about the girl with jewels in her face like a mask? A Pierrot or a Harlequin from the *Commedia dell'Arte*. Just like Nugent Fry whose face had been shoved in burning hot Plaster-of-Paris before the mask was grafted onto it.

Our serial killer was an artist.

So what was he going to do with me? Blindfolded. Gagged. Tied to a chair... just like the girl in my Lambeth installation.

What was he going to do?

"Jason, I'm scared," Liselle hissed. "There are two of them."

Made sense I guessed. It needed two people to create these things.

"They're not here. Not right now," she whispered. "They've left us alone. Can you move? We've got to get out of here."

I started panicking. Couldn't help myself. I tried to move my wrists but they were bound too tightly to the chair. I sat up and down again quickly and the chair moved, clomping on the floor loudly, too loudly. Sounded like it was a stone floor.

So where the hell was I?

"Jason!" Liselle hissed, her voice tight with fear. "Jason, don't. Don't move. They're coming back I can hear them."

But I panicked further. My left hand screamed with pain now.

"Jason, please don't. I don't know what they'll do to me."

What have they already done to her I asked myself?

I remembered her beaten face pushed out of sight in my kitchen by a man pulling at her clothes. Just a fleeting glimpse of savagery inflicted on someone so beautiful, who would never be the same again.

If I could have turned back the clock could I have saved her from this? I doubt it. I'd been too wrapped up in my own thoughts, drinking my way through a bottle.

I didn't care about myself anymore. Now that I knew Liselle was in this with me, maybe tied to a chair just the same, I had to get her out of here. Both of us if possible, but if she at least survived then my death, however it was dressed up, would mean something.

So I clomped the chair around and chewed on the gag doing my best to spit it from my mouth. It tasted vile, like the gas I could smell all around me. It was soaked with something, maybe a drug that kept me hovering between consciousness and deep, delusional sleep.

Looking back I think that was the source of the gas-smell: the gag stuffed in my mouth. And if I could spit it out, work my tongue and my teeth around it whilst at the same time pulling at the straps binding me to the chair then I could call for help. And maybe our abductors would come running to kill me but there was a chance, a slim chance, that someone else would hear me and come to our aid or call the police and tell them that they'd heard someone crying for help.

"*Jason, stop!*" Liselle hissed.

So for her safety I did.

The gag felt loose in my mouth and there was some give on the plastic at my wrists.

I'd leave it for now, pretend I was still unconscious, and when they left us the next time I'd spit out the gag, break my right hand free and whip the blindfold from my eyes. I'd quickly work myself free and then I'd rush over and help Liselle and the then two of us would run, hand in hand from wherever the hell we were to safety.

Except it didn't work out like that.

4.11

Civil war. Chemical weapons. People screaming in streets ravaged by rocket attacks and suicide bombs. You are different from us. We are right and you are wrong. Your God is false, ours is just, and if I hit the key on my mobile phone then it all goes off and me and everyone around me will become a martyr, a choir of saints ascending to Paradise or Heaven or whatever the fuck you want to call it. This is war. So kill them all. Just blow it all up. Unleash the Agents of Armageddon and let it all come crashing to a terminally destructive close.

Why not?

In a world where men could take teenage girls off the street and hide them in a cellar in an ordinary town, abusing them, defiling and debasing them, reducing their humanity to such an extent that those girls became nothing but objects, then why let it continue?

The sum total of humanity's horrors and depravities revolved around the girl tied to the chair in the form of news bulletins and cellphone videos, and when she screamed that hideous scream I knew that what I had done was add to the catalogue of atrocities I'd put in front of her.

Somewhere along the way, as an artist, I'd forgotten that this eighteen-year old model, this pretty girl tied to a chair in the name of art, my *Alex*, my Clockwork Orange, had a name, a career, a life. She was a person, not an object.

And now, I'd broken her.

"Stop the show!" I yelled to the gallery director.

Too late, down below us something was going on and the director was already running for the stairs.

"For God's sake!" someone on the exhibition floor cried. "Get her out of the chair!"

I remembered Arnold's words again, that night up in Scotland not quite a year before I went ahead with the installation at Lambeth: "It's a rubbish idea, JJ. Don't do it."

4.12

If the girl hadn't lied to the agency who'd put her forward when I asked them to find me someone who could do this, then I would have gone to jail. But she'd told them she was twenty-one, and she had neglected to tell the agency that flashing images had previously triggered seizures. The lawyer Arnold got me had dug all that out, and had pointed out that I'd made it perfectly clear, in writing, to the agencies I'd approached, exactly what would be required from a model for the installation. Therefore the agency was at fault. And in turn they blamed it on the girl because she'd lied to them and now her career as a model was over.

I got community service. I was blacklisted by the agencies and Hugh Donovan-Smith started his campaign of hatred against me.

Not long after that people started throwing shit over my wall. Sending me death threats, posting their hatred on Facebook, Twitter and Wordpress. Etcetera etcetera…

It was a bad idea and I should have listened to Arnold…

4.13

"It's him isn't it," said a quiet, gravelly voice close to me that could have been Theo's.

"Yes," said another voice, even quieter, sombre and thoughtful.

"And he attacked you?"

"Outside his house."

"Outside his house?" said the guy who could have been Theo. He tutted.

"Round the back. He came at me. Punched me to the ground and kicked the shit out of me."

"But you didn't go to the police?"

"No. I'd thrown a brick through his window."

"Oh…"

It was the guy I'd almost beat to death. If it hadn't been for Harriet maybe I would've done.

"Beth was your sister right?" said 'Theo'.

"She was."

"And here's the man who destroyed her."

Beth? Who the hell was Beth?

The two guys kept talking.

"So what should we do to him? What do you want to do now? It's your call."

There was a pause, and it dawned on me that Beth was the girl, the model from the Lambeth installation.

The kid answered.

"Burn him," he said quietly.

"Him?" said 'Theo'. "Or his girlfriend?"

"Her as well," said the kid. "But can I fuck her first? I want to fuck her."

Sometime later there were screams from Liselle far away.

4.14

Time passed. I just didn't know how much of it.

I didn't know if I was eating or not. I don't remember feeling hungry, but I knew they were keeping me drugged. Maybe that stopped me needing to eat. Maybe they were pumping some other kind of shit into me.

Had to get out of this. It was only going to end one way otherwise.

There was a moment when they took the gag out of my mouth and I coughed and hacked and spat. They left the blindfold on.

I thought they were going to let me talk but a few minutes later they shoved a new rag into my mouth, steeped in something which tasted sickly and sweet, and I passed out within seconds.

So it *was* the gag that was drugged, and it was this which was making me delirious.

It was like this for ... I don't know how long. Could have been days, could have been weeks. Maybe only hours or minutes. I stank of piss. I don't remember using the toilet or being taken to one. I never seemed to feel the need and maybe I was pissing myself when I was out.

Women haunted my dreams, calling out to me from deep tunnels into which leviathan steam trains and other dark engines half-hidden by fog disappeared. I jumped aboard one of the trains, riding alongside a man made entirely out of cogs. When I was deep enough into the tunnel I jumped down and searched along the edges, hearing voices from my childhood echoing around me:

"Mr Michael lives in the tunnel. He eats little children who go too far in…"

"Where is James anyway? Isn't he with you?"

"James? James who?"

"You're not making people up again are you, Jason?"

"Ha ha. Very funny."

"What's that?"

"Don't touch it…"

I walked towards the object and found it to be half a baby's head in a plastic bag. A cloud of black flies lifted away from it when I dislodged it with my stick.

"It's only a doll's head," I laughed.

Panic over right?

No.

Because right then, in my delirium, it really was a baby's head.

"Mr Michael doesn't eat the brains," the voices said. "He throws those bits out for the rats and flies."

Bodybags hanging in an artist's studio bursting open to spill blood and meat onto the floor.

I didn't know what they were tripping me out with but it opened all kinds of doors in my head. I saw so many things…

4.15

The gag was yanked from my mouth by fingers that stank of old cigarettes. Next they removed the blindfold and I sat blinking. Looking around.

The room was dark except for a few small points of light, one of which shone right at my face. I started making out some shapes in the room. I saw thick, stone columns holding up a shadowy, vaulted ceiling, monumental coffins, ages old, lined up against the walls. I guessed we were in a crypt or something.

In front of me, someone wearing a white mask sat on a chair. He sat still, as unmoving as a sculpture. Head cocked to one side.

The mask looked similar to the one I'd seen on Nugent Fry's body, a simple Pierrot; except that it was splashed with blood and inscribed with mathematical symbols. There was something slightly feminine about it, yet it was incredibly sinister.

Next to me was a table. Nothing on it but a small cube speaker.

A harsh voice bellowed from it suddenly, making me jump.

"Your name?" the voice demanded.

It took a while for my voice to come. "Jason Jones…" I gasped eventually.

"And what do you see?" asked the voice in the speaker. So not the guy in the mask sitting by the light then. I didn't recognise the voice. It was disguised by – what are those things called? – a vocoder or something.

"Excuse me?" I rasped. I'd never felt so weak.

"And what do you see?" the voice repeated in exactly the same way.

"I don't understand the question."

"And what do you see?"

"I see a man in a mask, sitting by a light in front of me."

"And what do you see?"

"I don't get it!" I shouted. "What do you fucking mean 'what do I see?' Fuck you! I won't play your game."

I was still tied to the chair so I couldn't lash out at the stupid fucking speaker and its stupid repeated question but I made moves towards it. Desperately. Pathetically. Like a crazy man.

"And what do you see?" it blasted out.

I stared at the motherfucker in the white mask.

"Who are you?" I spat.

The mask rose in the gloom as the man wearing it stood up.

The voice blared out again. "And what do you see?"

It took a while but eventually I looked down and saw my left hand, still tied to the chair.

In my head it had been a gory mess from having been stabbed. But now, in reality, in the glare of that spotlight facing me across the crypt, I could see that there was nothing wrong with it apart from some bruising around a surgical needle under a gauze stuck down with a plaster. A line curled out from the needle, a thin, plastic tube rising towards a clear bag of fluid suspended from a metal pole that that stood next to my chair.

They had me on a drip!

Then someone behind me threw a bag over my neck and tightened it at the neck with a drawstring.

I cursed whoever it was to Hell and left them in no mistake that if they ever let me go, I would kill them.

They used my head as a punch bag.

4.16

"How are you feeling?" Arnold asked me, months after the Lambeth debacle, and I'd finally started talking to people again.

"Fine," I told him, full of sarcasm. "I mean I'll never work again as an artist and everybody in the world hates me, but other than that I'm fine."

I remember him staring at me like he was going to kill me there and then.

"What?" I challenged. "What the fuck is wrong now?"

He said, "Why is it always about you, Jason? This thing happens and it's not about the lawsuit the gallery are facing, or the collapse of the modelling agency, or the end of the career which a young girl set her life on. No, it's all about *you*. Every time. 'The world hates me and I'm finished,' so sayeth Jason Jones end of fucking story."

He sounded so angry, but he was wrong. Because I did feel for the girl. To know that I caused her such distress killed me slowly every day and night. It tortured me to the point where I could hardly bare it; and I didn't know what to do – whether I should write to her and her family and apologise, send them some money, I didn't know. I was advised by Arnold's lawyers to leave it, to do nothing. Anything like that from me was an admission of guilt and my responsibility for the whole incident after I'd just paid them thousands of pounds to persuade a magistrate that I wasn't in any way responsible for this. So I did as they advised, which was nothing. No contact with the girl or anyone from her family no matter how many death threats I received in whatever shape or form.

"I was going to invite you up to Scotland," Arnold said to me.

"Again?"

"You're still my friend, Jason," he said. "And a good client. Most of the time."

"But I'm finished."

"No you're not," he said. "You just need a rest. Come up to the lodge again. Let's do Hogmanay this time."

"New Year?"

"Why not?"

So I did. And just like Christmas the year before, the evening ended with me and Arnold taking on a full bottle of single malt in the lodge after a late party at some baronial mansion in the middle of nowhere with kilts, pipes and dancing. At whatever o'clock it was, Arnold was sprawled on the armchair and I was again peering at the log fire through a crystal tumbler in my hand, watching the light split out into different wavelengths, tiny little rainbows dancing in the glass.

That was the thing about light, I remember thinking. Put it through a prism and it revealed its true colours. I wondered if there was an equivalent with people. What would you have to do with Arnold, for example, to make him reveal himself? What was his prism?

Actually with him it was easy. The guy was blubbing into his dram already and I remembered that he'd done this the year before. It was just that I'd forgotten about it until then.

"He was my son, Jason. Would have been about your age now."

I remember I nodded in sympathy, staring into the fire.

"My boy," Arnold sobbed – same as the year before. Same story. Same words, at least as far as I remembered them. "We used to come here for Christmas every year… We just used to argue. Two of us shut up in these old walls for a couple of days. Shooting during the day, drinking whisky by night …"

And then, the inevitable, "He was more his mum's boy than he was ever mine," and… "I gave him everything. Everything he wanted…"

Like a fucking script. Like I didn't have my own problems.

Shouldn't have come, I remember thinking. At the end of the day I didn't care much for Arnold or his dearly-departed son.

"… died when he was only twenty-one. Twenty-one, JJ. Think on that. So fuckin young."

I swallowed it back and drank my drink because my throat was so dry. The room was turning to amber liquid all around me and I felt as though I was in danger of drowning in bad memories.

I remembered being twenty-one. Not a good year for me. I remembered Jane Gordon: *Help me!*

There was a loud crack, like a jolt of electricity snapping through my arm. Looking down I saw that the glass I was holding had cracked and split open, cutting the palm of my right hand.

"Fuck me," I said, staring down at the blood welling up from the cut. I laughed nervously.

Arnold peered at it with one eye shut. "That was my best crystal, you bastard," was all he had to say before returning to his contemplation of the flames in the grate and sniffing and wiping his eyes.

I staggered to my feet and made my way to the bathroom feeling queasy. Memories I had been trying so hard to forget sped through my mind. On the giant steam train which carried them, faces stared out from brightly-lit windows: all the people I had known in the past and all of them dead. But it wasn't my fault, I kept thinking. *It wasn't my fault.*

I washed my hands in the basin, ignoring the contorted face in the mirror which hated me utterly. Never was good at reflections. Liselle had wondered why I had no mirrors in the house. Couldn't tell her it was because I hated looking at myself every fucking day of my life. When she stayed over, she always brought her own mirror.

And now… I'd lost her too…

4.17

Every time they took the blindfold off I was facing a guy in a mask. The mask was different each time but I was always in the crypt.

And they always set up this stupid speaker to fire questions at me:
"What do you want?"
"Fuckoff."
"What do you want?"
"Just let me go for Christ's sakes!"
"And what do you see?"
"I don't see anything!" I roared at them. "I don't see anything at all."

One day they played some music. It was a song by 'House of Pain' and it was their smash-hit *Jump Around*, a flashy, jingly-jangly hip-hop beat full of catchy samples. I always liked the record but not after this.

At the start of every bar there was a sampled scream in the tune, which was from a saxophone I think. Hard to tell.

The music was turned up loud, just not loud enough to disguise the screams I could hear behind it.

The blindfold was back on and the gag was back in my mouth.

The tune went on and on.

Within it I heard struggles. Bangs and clatters. "Stay still you fucking bitch!" and "No! Please!" and more screams.

Motherfuckers! I struggled to get out of the chair so I could help Liselle but the chair fell over, and with me still strapped into it I cracked my head on the floor. It hurt but I was so fired up I didn't care. I spat the gag from my mouth and I worked one hand loose, struggling, fighting the strap. It came free! I could hardly believe it!

I tore off the blindfold with my free hand and looked up to see a fist flashing towards my face.

It hit me hard in the side of the head and I saw stars. The drip stand clattered down next to me and all I could hear was that fucking song.

The guy in the mask pulled me upright, chair and all.

"Get the fuck off me!" I yelled.

He pressed my free hand hard into the chair arm, then smashed it down repeatedly when I struggled.

My wrist was ruined. I could hardly move it and so it was easy for him to tie it up. Once that was done, and still wearing the mask, he rescued the drip stand and planted it next to my chair. He inspected the bag but even I could see that the connection on the umbilical had come loose.

"Fuck it," he hissed, then turned on me, cocking his head again. "Time for a haircut!" he said, and it seemed like the volume of the music increased unbearably.

Fingers grabbed my head, pulled it back, and then someone shaved off my hair with an electric razor which tore it from its roots, all the while there were screams and that fucking song blared out, echoing around the crypt.

4.18

In Arnold's lodge that New Year's Eve I found some plasters in the bathroom cabinet. I stuck one on my hand, covering the livid line of blood his best crystal had opened in my flesh, and started out back downstairs.

But somehow I got sidetracked.

His bedroom door was open, and, initially thinking it was the room he'd put me in for the night, I walked in. My suitcase wasn't there, but an immaculate black suit hung suspended off the dido rail. Not my suit. Only one person I knew wore suits like this. Wore one every day in fact. Same suit? Surely not, he must have more than one suit.

Being drunk I wondered how many of these suits he had and so, in my pissed-up state, I opened up his wardrobe and looked inside.

There, confirming my suspicions, was a row of black suits and just as many crisp, white shirts.

"Ties," I muttered. What about his ties?

I leaned into the wardrobe, almost falling into it, and hunted the shelves at the side. I had expected my fingers to close on a neat row of rolled up silk ties, but instead they touched something cold, hard and metallic.

My fingers groped further, and my heart kicked when I realised what it had to be. I discovered a barrel, a weighty handle and a trigger. Pulling it out I saw that I was holding a heavy black handgun. A real one, not some fucking toy.

"Holy shit," I whispered. Then I heard a creak on the stairs. It was Arnold, on his way to bed, no doubt having woken up and realising I'd gone.

He was right outside the door, and there was nothing I could do but squeeze myself into the wardrobe and pull the door shut.

To be honest he was so drunk I could've stood right in front of him and he still wouldn't have seen me. He didn't turn the light on. He just walked towards his bed and when he was close enough to it he let gravity take hold. He landed on it, face down with a thump. A quick, ripping fart, and then he was snoring.

I was still holding the gun. Arnold had said he used to go shooting, so you'd expect him to have a gun in the cottage. But this wasn't a rifle or a shotgun. This was a proper handgun, like something the police might have.

Was Arnold a police?

No. I couldn't see it.

I came out of the wardrobe and looked over at him, snoring on top of his duvet, then I walked up to him and slowly lifted the gun in my good hand, my left hand, not my natural strong hand. I pointed it right at his head. Really close.

Was it loaded? Bullets inside it?

All I had to do was squeeze this trigger and that'd be the end of him. Right here, right now. *Blam*! Game over, Arnold. And he wouldn't even know.

I could see why some people got off on this kind of thing.

Holding the gun to his head, knowing that I could end this man's life right here and now in the half a second it would take to squeeze the trigger and unleash a single bullet to his brain, gave me a feeling of such power and control it was almost orgasmic.

My hand started to shake and I swore, told myself to get a grip. It wasn't funny.

Thing is... I couldn't pull the gun away...

I stood over him for a long time. Just holding the gun in my left hand. The world spinning through me at a thousand miles an hour.

The L-Shaped Ballroom

It's a weird ballroom because it's shaped like the letter L...

Throughout the world there are places that are locked in time: Landscapes commemorated for the bloody battles which changed the fate of a nation, buildings within whose walls some momentous decision was made or some charter was signed. Market squares in which a revolution came to a climax – one way or another.

And there are a thousand jail cells in which a thousand peacekeepers were executed, places in the desert known to hide the horrors of ancient genocides.

Even when they're long gone, pulled down, built-upon or buried in the sand, the echoes remain as long as people are there to remember.

And this L-shaped ballroom, in an old, big house long since burned to the ground, is one such place.

5

Nihilism

From my Father I inherited the seeds of madness.

Edvard Munch: Diaries
c1920

5.1

"Hey," said Jane Gordon to me on the phone. It was the middle of November 1999 and all the doom-merchants across the planet were telling us the world was going to end on December 31st. Come the Millennium all our infrastructure would be screwed as the computer clocks reset to zero, and that too could mean the End of All Things.

"Hey," I said. "How's it going?"

"Not good," Jane whispered, "if I'm honest."

"So ... what's up?"

There was a silence on the phone. I felt awkward.

Things had changed. I'd left Anglesey after finishing school in '96. Gone to work for a printing company in Liverpool where I thought I'd be able to exercise my artistic genes, or at the very least get a try out for LFC. Neither of those had worked out so instead I'd gone back to school: I'd enrolled at the Manchester School of Art and Media for a three-year diploma and had just started the final year that October.

"I want to come and see you," Jane said.

I thought about it. Then, "Sure…"

"Don't you want to see me?" she asked.

I cursed inwardly. Jane knew me too well; she knew the significance of every pause, every hesitation. "It's just that I'm busy, Jane. Coursework."

"I just want to talk to you."

"You can talk to me now can't you?"

"Not on the phone," she said after a pause.

"OK. When are you thinking of coming up?"

"This weekend? I've got a bus ticket."

"Fine. No worries. Let me know when your coach is due and I'll meet you."

5.2

So maybe I was a bit of a dick at the time but the old life at Llangefni seemed a long way off even then. When I'd moved to Liverpool, and then onto Manchester, Llangefni suddenly seemed remote and very small. A single town on a single island, isolated, enclosed and backwards. And despite the good times Jane brought with her whenever she came over to see me, she always somehow took me back there, spiritually if not in reality.

"Stay with me, Jane," I'd said to her, many times before. "You don't have to go back."

But she always went back and it hurt every time.

I'd had to learn the hard way how to live without her, and as I hadn't seen her for a while I was doing OK. Seemed like I was just getting the hang of it until she rang up that day.

So, come that Saturday afternoon she stepped off the coach, her legs clad in tight jeans and the heels on her shoes stabbing down at the steps. Her face was full of sunlight and fire, and I just wanted to run up to her and kiss her. I wanted to sweep her off her feet and hold onto her forever.

She smiled when she saw me. She knew exactly how I felt.

5.3

"This is Dougie," I said to Jane, introducing her to my housemates one by one. "And that's Kev."

They were on the Playstation. Eyes glued to the TV.

"Hi."

"Yo."

Jane sort of waved.

"Gareth's upstairs," I told her. "He might come down."

We went into the kitchen, which was a mess. I'd asked the guys to clean up but I don't think they'd moved off the sofa since I'd left them a couple of hours ago.

I found some cups. Washed them out and filled the kettle. As it boiled I remember I just stared at Jane. It was eight months since I'd last seen her. "You look… awesome," I said, probably lamely. Her cool, blue eyes stared right back. Chin straight. Snake torc at her neck gleaming in the kitchen's spotlights. "You're still wearing that?" I said. Again with the lameness.

She fingered it absently and her eyes looked around the kitchen. "Nice place…" she said.

We'd been fine on the bus through town, filling each other in on the details of our lives, and it was just bizarre that after everything we'd done together in the old days here we were now, standing in a shitty kitchen, struggling for conversation.

The kettle came to the boil and switched off. I poured out the tea.

"How's James getting on?" I asked her.

"He's passed all his flight examinations," she said.

Of course he would have, I thought wryly. At school he'd passed all his GCSEs with straight As – even though he'd probably only just made the minimum attendance requirement. So it made sense that he'd done the same in the Navy.

"He's on a carrier now somewhere out near the Gulf," Jane said.

"The Gulf? Jesus…"

"He's back home soon for a few weeks and then he's off again. I can't remember the dates but he'd love to see you."

I didn't really know what to say, or even what to feel. So I just said, "Has he still got the bike?" His dad had bought him a big old motorbike for passing his exams.

"He's took it with him so I guess so," she said.

Jane's accent seemed archaic, and I hated it.

"And … how's your job?" I asked her. "What was it? You're a bouncer?"

She laughed as I handed her the cup of tea. "Shut up! Can you imagine me as a bouncer?"

There was a voice at the door. "Who's bouncing on who?"

Jane turned on her heel.

Gareth was standing there. "Housemate number four," I said. "Jane, meet Gareth Evans."

He nodded. "All right?" he grunted.

Tall guy, Gareth. And big too. He worked out. Same Gareth Evans that Jane's brother had kicked the shit out of in town, years ago. Since then he'd never lost a fight – so he told me anyway. The guy was so full of shit you never knew when he was telling the truth. Still, he'd filled out for sure.

He was dressed in black sweat pants. No top. His chest and

shoulders were gleaming, probably from pumping weights in his room. Or wanking. He did a lot of that.

"Do I know you?" he asked, making his way to the fridge.

"I think I'd remember," said Jane, eyeing him up as he grabbed a carton of his special milk or yoghurt or whatever the fuck it was that made him strong. He nudged the fridge door shut with his elbow and padded barefoot through the kitchen, reaching into a cupboard near Jane for his special cup.

"Maybe I'm thinking of someone else," he growled, not looking at her.

Jane couldn't take her eyes off him.

"Plenty of girls look the way you do," he said, pulling out the cup.

Jane's expression grew hard. And as he poured the milk into the cup, Gareth finally met her gaze. "Sorry," he said harshly. "Didn't mean to offend you."

"Gareth Evans?" Jane said with half a smile, eyebrows arched. She stepped towards him and put her face close to his, lips parted as though she was going to kiss him. "*Very* common name," she whispered. "So maybe I was mistaken."

"Let's go upstairs," I said quickly. "Show you where you're sleeping."

Gareth leant against the counter, drinking his milk. He was grinning as I pushed past him.

"Dickhead!" I hissed, crushing his toes with the tread of my Doc Martens.

He yelped.

"So what does he do?" Jane asked when she came to my room and I dumped her holdall on the bed.

"Gareth? He's a film student. Dad's a fucking rich man so he's got no manners."

"I gets worse than that in the club," she answered. "I can handle him, don't worry."

She sat on the bed.

"So Jenny's still waitressing?" I asked, standing by the window.

Jane pulled her legs up and shuffled backwards to the wall like she was leaving a space for me on the bed. I stayed where I was.

"Yeah..." she said.

"What's up?" I asked.

She looked at me. "I'm worried about her, Jason. She's... not the same. I think she's ill."

5.4

I stared into my beer while the DJ played some techno version of *Fools Gold* by The Stone Roses. This wasn't the Haçienda, and although Britpop and the Madchester Scene were pretty much exhausted by 1999, this basement club, dark, smoky and filled with the stink of aftershave, Chanel and sweat, seemed to be clinging to those glory days like some kind of cultural leech. Ten quid on the door and it was packed. Gareth had got six of us in for free. Six because he'd picked up a girl from somewhere and this was who I'd been lumbered with. Dougie and Kev had vanished into the dark wall of sound and Gareth had spirited Jane away for a dance.

"I don't know this tune," said the girl. Can't remember her name. She pronounced tune like 'choon' and she was too young for us. Just a hip young thing looking for an anchor I guess. "What is it again?"

Her hand was on my leg.

I told her what it was and it didn't make any difference to the expression on her face. She still looked like she wanted to snog me.

"So what's your friend do again?" she asked.

She nodded over to where Gareth and Jane were jigging on the dance floor. I could only catch glimpses of them between the press of bodies but they seemed to be getting on.

Meanwhile I was stuck with this idiot.

I wasn't good in places like this.

"She works in a club," I said.

"I didn't mean her," said the girl, "I meant *him*."

"Film student," I told her. "Mostly as an excuse to fuck chicks like you on camera."

She recoiled and I laughed.

"I'm not kidding," I said. I wanted to offend her so she'd leave me alone, but I wasn't lying when I said to her: "His old man was married to a porn star and Gareth inherited the gene. Now his dad's rich and Gareth's addicted to porn. It's a dangerous combination and you'll find yourself being fucked all ways on video if you're not careful."

A new song came on. One I hadn't heard before. It was some kind of slow-beat techno trip-hop set against a hissing pop and crackle like the sound of a dusty old vinyl LP. I thought it was Massive Attack at first but it wasn't. It was a new thing called *Rushing* by Moby. The lights turned blue and low and the dance floor cleared, leaving behind only the few couples who were attached at the hips and the face, and who swayed and groped each other to this hypnotic, trance-like sound; including Jane and Gareth.

This girl I was with was staring at them, and maybe my expression was the same as hers because all I wanted to do right then was kill the both of them. Then I was grabbed by the face and this girl kissed me for all it was worth; hard and and wet, pushing herself onto me. I let her do it, hating every moment.

5.5

"You didn't tell me he used to go to our school," Jane said to me the following morning. "Bit of a coincidence that."

I shrugged, lighting up a joint I'd built yesterday, sitting up in bed next to her. Both of us butt-naked under the duvet.

"Not really," I said, gasping on the heat of the smoke. "Plenty of people from our school come here. Do you remember him?"

She shook her head. "No. You?"

"Nah." I lied. I passed her the joint and then I lay down on my back to exhale straight up like a chimney. Jane stayed sitting, so I was able to rest my face in the curve of her waist. My free hand slid under the duvet and found her knee. Squeezed it. "You seemed to be getting friendly with him last night," I said.

"So were you. With that girl I mean."

I grinned and looked up at her. "No one matches up to you, Jane."

"Likewise," she whispered. Then, after she took a toke on the joint she said, "That's half the problem though isn't it?"

She looked down at me like some kind of Goddess of Judgement. "What we had. What we used to do. Everything else just seems... ordinary."

It was true. What I'd left behind in Llangefni was something so strong and powerful that it was hard to live without it. Not impossible, but it made getting close to other people difficult.

I nodded. "Thought it'd be easier if I moved away," I admitted.

"It's not about the place though is it?" she said. "It's about the people, the four of us. The four J's..." she added.

I pulled my hand out of the duvet and slid it up her back, kneading her spine which caused her to arch it like a cat having a stretch.

She handed me the joint. "Keep it," she said. "I shouldn't be smoking."

I took it off her. "Still using the inhaler?" I asked.

"Sometimes."

"You ever think about that time?"

She nodded. "Always. Every time I close my eyes. And when I do… It's like I'm dying all over again."

"Shit…" I said. "I'm sorry…"

Then she moved round. She slid down the bed and turned onto her side to face me. Elbow on the pillow, hand supporting her cheekbone. Waves of blonde hair spilling over. She pulled the duvet up to cover her breasts but her shoulders stayed bare and the snake at her throat, eating its own tail, glinted at me.

"I want to ask you a question," she said.

I took a pull on the joint. "Go on."

"I'd prefer it if you had a clear head, Jay."

I took the hint, so I reached down the side of the bed and pulled up an ashtray I'd stolen from a pub.

"OK," I said. "It must be a very serious question."

"Do you love me?" she asked.

I carried on stubbing out the joint, inwardly stunned. Took a long time to make sure it was completely out…

"Hey!" she snapped. "Simple enough question, right?"

"I don't know."

I slowly leaned over with the ashtray and put it back on the floor, sliding it under the bed so I wouldn't step on it.

"You don't know that it's a simple question or you don't know that you love me?"

"Don't start playing word games."

"Well?"

"Do I *love* you?" I repeated, then turned to face her, mirroring her pose. "I think you're the most beautiful girl I've ever known. Without you, and James and Jenny I wouldn't be complete."

Her eyes narrowed. "You're saying you love the three of us?"

I nodded. "Yeah. Sure. Don't you? Remember what we used to say?" I asked her. "We used to say that we were all reflections of one person, one soul multiplied into infinity, like an image caught between two mirrors."

She turned onto her back and looked up at the ceiling. "I know what love is," she said, "and it's not that."

"Not what?"

"Not what you think it is. It isn't about what we did or what we could do again if the four of us ever got back together."

"That'd be explosive," I laughed, rolling onto my back.

I stroked the top of her thigh under the duvet, my little finger brushing against the soft mound of her sex.

She didn't push me away, but she did ignore the touch. Her eyes stared straight up and I thought they looked tearful. I took my hand away and wished I hadn't put the joint out.

"I remember the fire," she said quietly. "And I remember my mum screaming. Really screaming. Like something so primal from so deep inside her. It took a while to hear my name in that scream. I was in my room and smoke was coming in through the door. I remember sitting on my bed just looking at it. Watching it creep through the gaps, watching it curl and roll across the carpet like … like some kind of predator sniffing me out. It was a slow thing, but it was determined and unstoppable. It slipped inside me, pushed into my mouth and down into my lungs. It was in my eyes, my hair, even seeping through my skin. I took it all inside me, JJ. And it took its time killing me. No rush. It had to be done properly. But I let it begin to happen. I closed my eyes and in that moment I started to die."

She'd never told me this before. Maybe she'd never told anyone.

"I felt as though the smoke was somehow absorbing me into itself. The process would kill me I knew, but it didn't matter. I remember thinking that if I became part of the smoke then I could drift up and go anywhere. And next time, it'd be me that crept under the door to sniff out the weak and the old, the babies in their cots and the kids who couldn't run. I'd be the one snuffing out their lives and taking them into me."

"Jane," I said. "That's…"

"I don't know how long I'd been sitting there. It felt like forever – maybe it was only a few seconds but the pain in my chest was like knives in my lungs. My head was swimming, my thoughts drowning in an ocean of dark shapes. That was all I could see. The coughing seemed to be coming from someone else; and all the time, my Mum was fighting her way towards me, screaming my name over and over.

"The fire found me before she did. I hadn't thought about the fire. The smoke had been hiding it, fooling me like a whisper, a promise; but now I could hear it tearing through the house like a hunger coming right for me. It was evil, JJ. Fucking deadly. The door flew open and the fire burst right in, and I couldn't scream because I was so filled with smoke. It went for the ceiling, rolling over it like liquid, making beautiful, terrifying shapes. I could feel it pulling at me, sucking the air from the room. And it had me. I remember I curled up and hid my face and suddenly dying didn't seem like such a good idea. I just wanted my

Mum."

Jane wiped one eye with a forefinger, took a breath, then picked up the story again. "The next thing I knew I was in hospital. Mum was there, she was the first thing I saw, and it was like being born again. My eyes were blurred and they hurt almost as much as my lungs did, but I was sure, I was positive, that I saw a halo around Mum's head, a bright yellow glow that I thought was a display of her love for me, and she held me... so tight that it hurt, and I cried and she cried, and she ran her hands over and over and through my hair and she said my name again and again. 'My baby my baby my baby,' she cried and – "

Her voice stopped, ready to break.

I blinked back tears from my eyes as Jane took a long, shuddering breath. In a cracked voice she said, "I don't expect I'll ever love anyone as much as she loved me at that moment. She told me that if I'd died, then everything she was would have been dust and ash. So I guess we don't always realise what we mean to other people do we? I guess we don't always understand what something like love really is until moments like that."

I put my arm around her and she snuggled into my shoulder.

"I used to wonder if my mum had made a pact with the fire, just to keep me alive for her own sake." She was quiet for a bit, then she said, "But I thought... Well, I didn't expect to wake up alive. So when I did, and I saw my Mum, I felt like I was born again. And what I want to do now is break out and go see the world, use my borrowed time to *be* someone. I tried telling Jenny but she got angry. She won't leave the island but I have to. I can't be confined to just one place anymore. You know what that's like right?"

"You're fucked up, Jane," I said.

"Aren't we all?" she replied. "The four of us? We're getting like our parents. If we're fucked up then it's probably their fault."

I felt her hand under the duvet, her fingers closing around mine. Then I grabbed her waist and pulled her over on top of me with a roll. She reared up and then she slammed her hands down hard on my shoulders, leaned forward with her forehead against mine, her hair forming a golden cage around us.

"You OK?" I whispered, my lips touching hers.

She nodded, and kissed me as a tear dripped from her eyelashes onto my cheek. I held her tightly, as tightly as I could, and then slowly I moved up into her.

5.6

Later...

"I'm not kidding about the porn," I told Jane. "He's addicted to it."

"He doesn't look like he needs it," she said.

It was her last day in Manchester. The weather was windy, with the occasional burst of freezing sleet which made the day black, and I'd taken her shopping in the city centre. We crossed Deansgate, running between the traffic on the slick tarmac. She had a brolly and I was carrying her bags. Sharing the umbrella hadn't really worked.

"I think it goes beyond the porn," I said on the other side of the road. "He told me once he didn't care about actors faking it. He wanted to film what was real."

"So one day he'll make a good documentary."

"Just be careful with him, Jane. That's all I'm saying."

She turned into House of Fraser. Looked back at me as she shook out her brolly and pulled a cute face.

I followed her inside and she headed towards the perfume counters, ambling up to one of the concessions where a perfectly-sculpted young thing in a white coat smiled at her and enticed her into that realm where men fear to tread.

"I'll meet you in the café when you're ready," I said to her.

Jane walked into the café in House of Fraser carrying more bags. For my part I was dreading getting them home on the bus. Maybe I should treat her to a taxi, I was thinking. Trouble was I was skint.

I bought her a hot chocolate and a slice of carrot cake, grabbed myself another cappuccino and then we sat down at the table by the window and talked. It took a while for me to bring the conversation around to Jenny.

"You told me you were worried about her," I said.

She nodded, her eyes on a waitress with a ponytail who she seemed to have taken a shine to. "She's not right, Jason."

"So what's wrong with her?"

She looked back at me. "We share a house with two other girls: Carla and Emmeline. They're Christians."

"And that's a bad thing because...?"

"They're bloody fanatics," she hissed, leaning across the table. "And they want me out. I know they do."

"So leave. You said you wanted to."

"I do. But I'd be leaving Jenny with them. She won't leave the island,

Jason. She said she'd rather die."

"Better start from the top," I said to her.

So she told me about the crazy Christian girls she and my sister shared a house with.

"They frighten her with God," Jane said as she held her cup. The sun was breaking through, casting rainbows through the water droplets running down the tall windows we sat by.

"How could you frighten someone with God"

"You know what I mean," she said. "They talk about, you know, everlasting torment for the wicked and the perverse and all that shit. They go on about homosexuality being evil. They light candles and sit in front of Jesus night after night singing stupid bloody songs. They keep inviting her to church, telling her what a brilliant social life they have and what a wonderful life-changing experience finding God is."

I shook my head. "I can't see Jenny swallowing that."

"Don't be so sure. They're stronger than she is."

I scoffed.

"They have God on their side, JJ. They tell her he watches everything, that he infuses everything, that he's bloody well everywhere watching her. She's started obsessing over it. I don't think she believes them, but it's like they're trying to brainwash her, and I think they're telling her that I'm the bad influence."

"Really?"

"There's no need for sarcasm."

I thought about it, then said, "Maybe I should go home and speak with her."

"I don't think that's a good idea" Jane replied. "You'd probably make things worse."

"I don't see how."

"She's changed, Jason. I told you she's not the Jenny you used to know."

I felt cheated and angry. Why had she waited so long to tell me this?

I looked across into her pale blue eyes. They were staring right at me through the wet-curled platinum strands of her hair. I felt there was more to this. There was something she wasn't telling me.

"Have you fallen out with her?" I asked.

She took her hand away. "She's got a possessive personality," she said, then lifted her cup to her lips. It was a big, wide bowl of a cup and it hid most of her face from me.

I leaned across the table.

"And...?"

She put the cup down. "There's a guy at the club," she said. "Darren something. I know he wants to get off with me but he never will. But he gives me a lift home, right? Which is worth its weight in gold on a Friday night at four in the morning. Anyway, Jenny doesn't like this. She saw him bring me back one night. She'd been waiting up for me, twitching the bloody curtains. When she saw me get out of his car she walked right out into the street and lamped him one."

I laughed.

"Not funny, JJ!" Jane said. "I mean aside from the fact that it's my life and what the hell has it got to do with her anyway, she shouldn't have hit him. He was nothing. Probably never will be. He doesn't walk among the same stars we do, Jason; he's not you or Jenny or James so she has nothing to fear. He's useful, that's all. But ... she's getting worse. Now she wants to know everything, everywhere I've been, everyone I've seen. Jason, she comes out with these stories now and I'm really worried about what's going on inside her head. She sees monsters everywhere. She hears things and she wakes up on a night screaming or raging. She started on me one night, the night before I rang you. She just woke up, knocked on my door and when I opened it she flew at me. She said I wasn't me but some... I dunno, some fucking space-monkey or something in disguise."

"I've got to see her."

"No. Don't! I mean it. Your dad's with her and I think he wants to bring her home. If he needs you he'll give you a shout I'm certain." Jane put a trembling hand bisected by rainbows on my arm. "Don't go back, Jason. Stay here and I'll stay with you. This time I will, I mean it. I'm not going back."

She had no idea how many times I'd wanted her to say that.

"Jason," she said, holding my hand with both of hers. "Everything I own is in these bags and the holdall in your bedroom."

I sat back in the chair, letting go of her hands to run them through my hair. I had to look away for a moment, just take a good look at all the people in the café and the department store just getting on with their ordinary lives. Then I looked right at her.

"You're really not going back?" I said.

She nodded. Stared right at me. "I'm *dying* in that place!" she hissed, desperately. Then, calmly, measured and precisely, she said, "Jason, I love you. See? I said it. I've always wanted to say it because it's true. If it was you in that burning house, Jason, then I'd be the one screaming your name, coming to get you. And nothing, not even hell itself would stop me."

I swallowed, unable to take my eyes off her. Something rumbled in the distance, a train, an aeroplane, or maybe it was just the sound of something breaking down inside me.

Thing is, I knew Jane as well as she knew me. And just like she knew the significance of every pause or hesitation in my voice, so I knew the meaning of every twitch of her eyebrows, every one of her different ways of smiling, of touching and caressing my hands.

So all I remember thinking at that moment was that after all this time getting used to being without her, I was angry that she was treating me of all people the same as the guy who gave her a lift from the club on a Friday night, and right now I didn't want her living with me.

I'd moved on.

I smiled and took her hand, and she gripped my fingers tightly, making it seem like she was unwilling to let go.

5.7

"Jason," said Dougie when Jane and I bundled in through the front door of the house. "Yer dad's been on' phone, mate. Wants you to ring him."

Jane and I froze. Exchanged a glance.

Everyone froze. Even Gareth. It seemed like I was at the centre of a Universe on hold.

I dumped the shopping bags, sat on the stairs with the phone and rang the old man. "What's up?"

"Is your sister with you?" he asked.

"No."

"Shit. Has she called you at all? Any time in the last couple of days?"

"No. Dad? What's going on?"

He didn't want to tell me at first, didn't want me to worry, but eventually I got it out of him.

"Jenny hasn't been home a couple of nights is all. I'm sure she's fine but have you any idea where she might be, lad?"

"No."

"Is Jane with you?"

"Yes. She's here, she's fine."

There was a pause, then: "Thank God for that. Tell her we love her very much, right?"

I glanced up at Jane. She was standing in the dark hall like a ghost, her eyes locking onto me.

Dad was quiet for a short moment. "All right then, boyo," he said. "I'll be seeing you."

Then he put the phone down.

I shook my head and glanced up at Jane. "Jenny's missing," I told her.

Within half an hour I'd packed a Liverpool holdall full of overnight stuff and persuaded Kev to lend me his car. Jane was not happy with my decision to leave.

We were in my bedroom arguing.

"You don't have to go, Jason."

"I won't be long," I said. "I know where she'll be."

"So do I, so does anyone who knows us well enough, but she doesn't need you."

That was something I could not believe.

"It's not down to you to find her," Jane told me, pressing on with her cause, kneeling on my bed. "Whatever she does now has nothing to do with either you or me anymore."

I was upset by this. "That's not true."

"It *is* true!" Jane said, a pleading tone to her voice.

"You come with me then." I challenged her.

"No," she answered. "I told you I'm not going back."

"Not even for Jenny?" I shouted. "Don't you care what happens to her?"

"She doesn't need us."

There was something else. I knew it.

"It's a call for help," I said. "Jenny wants me to come to her." I tried to leave the room but Jane launched herself onto me, flying across the bed and grabbing my holdall.

"Jason, no!" she cried in exasperation.

"I'll only be gone one night, Jane," I said, peeling her fingers away from the bag. "You can stay here. You'll be fine with these guys until I get back." I wondered now who was the possessive one. More than ever I was certain that she was hiding something.

As I left the bedroom she called out after me, making a fool of herself. God only knew what the others made of it.

"Jason," she said, an edge of panic in her voice, "if you go to Jenny now then you lose me. I won't be here when you get back."

I paused, halfway down the stairs. "What are you saying?"

She came to stand at the top of the landing, looking down on me.

"It's either her or me," she said, her voice wavering.

"I'm not playing this game, Jane. No more. All right?"
"You think this is a game?"
"If it were you I'd do the same."
"Why?"
"Because I love her, Jane!"

Jane stopped in mid-word, her mouth open. She dropped to her backside on the top step looking worn and used, somehow lost.

"*Sorry*," I hissed. It hadn't meant to come out so brutally. It was just that emotions were running hot.

Shit, I had to go. Jane looked like she was going to either cry or burst into a rage and right then I couldn't handle either.

"Jenny's your fucking *sister*, Jason!" she shrieked. "You can't have her."

"Have her? It's not about having her! What are you talking about?"

Jane launched herself down the stairs at me, flying at me with her fists and nails swinging. It was all I could do to get her off me.

"Jane, don't – don't do this!" I said, trying to keep calm and she kicked and scratched and punched me into the living room. This was crazy. I'd never seen her like this.

Gareth came up behind her and pulled her off me easily.

With my hands trembling I fingered the line of blood she had drawn from my right cheek, and then I stared, almost in horror, at the pathetic creature being held in Gareth's giant arms.

Without a single word passing between the three of us I turned and left the house.

5.8

It was proper dark when I arrived at Llangefni nearly three hours later. Not quite a full moon hovering in the spaces between the tumbling clouds. The whole town was quiet except for the putter of a motorbike a few streets away.

I parked up Kev's battered Mini Metro in a decrepit, walled-off side-street. Climbed out, locked it, then ran quickly towards the break in the wall further down that opened onto the zig-zag platform of metal steps which led down to the sunken wood way below.

It grew even darker as I descended, and the trees around the steps grew thicker. Their leaves and branches both caressed and scratched my face and hands – *welcome back*, they seemed to say, *but don't leave it so long this time.*

The lower I went, the darker it became.

Didn't matter. I could have done this blindfolded, and after a while my eyes adjusted. By the time I reached the ground and set foot on the secret railway line, I could see clearly enough.

Nothing had changed. The tunnel mouth still gaped wide open, dark upon dark, a flash-reminder to me of the doll's head that might have been a baby's head, smashed open and infested with flies. Further on, the pitched angles of the old station house began to take form.

The entrance we used was at the back and slowly I made my way towards it, stepping across the thorns, nettles and brambles that grew there. I tried to be as quiet as possible so as not to alarm Jenny if she was inside, and I was sure she was; I was also sure that she was expecting me, despite what Jane had said.

The corrugated iron cover at the back door scraped across the ground no matter how quiet I tried to be when I pulled on it.

Inside, it was like a home from home. Everything was familiar. Obsolete train maps of Wales and Northern England and peeling, yellowed timetables still clung to the walls. The wooden floorboards still creaked in the dilapidated hallway and the stairs to the upper floor looked just as dangerous as they always had done.

"Jenny?" I hissed quietly, then louder: "Jenny! Are you here?"

There was no reply.

I searched the three rooms upstairs and in one of them I found her, curled up against the old stone fireplace. It looked as though she was just waking up, a fallen angel trapped in the angles between four walls.

"James?" she said sleepily. "Is that you?"

I laughed, relieved to find her. "Was that who you were expecting?" I said, walking towards her.

Jenny squinted, then looked up again. She seemed genuinely surprised when she saw me looking down on her. "Jason? What are you doing here?"

I knelt down beside her and took her hands in mine. She was cold and trembling, a lot thinner than I remembered. She seemed grateful for my touch. She'd had her hair cut wild again. Pixie-style, long at the front, short at the back.

"I've come to find you. Dad rang me and said you'd gone missing. I didn't tell him you'd be here." I stroked her hair away from her eyes. "What is it? What's wrong?"

"Nothing's wrong."

"Something is," I said. "Jenny?"

"Just kiss me, James," she said, throwing herself onto me.

"I'm not J—"

She pushed her mouth onto mine and kissed me. After an initial confusion I kissed her back hungrily, responding with warm passion. She put her hand down the front of my jeans, kissed my neck and pulled open my jacket with her free hand.

I slid a hand into her blouse and squeezed as much of her breasts as I could, feeling her nipples like familiar friends responding to my touch.

"I've missed you, Jenny."

"I've missed you too, JJ," she told me, face deep in my neck. "But just now, be James for me will you?"

There was an old mattress on the floor. Gently, we eased our bodies onto it and fully removed our clothes. "I'll be James if you want me to be," I answered.

I kissed my way down her body, down the inside of her legs, tasting and teasing with my tongue. I stayed there a while, hearing her quickening gasps of pleasure from above. We built a rhythm, and I savoured the taste and the texture of every part of her loins.

I moved upwards slowly, playing my tongue across her belly, sucking on her hips while my hands explored all those places I knew she liked. My tongue travelled further upwards, tracing her ribs and the soft skin just beneath her breasts. I felt her thigh rising to meet my balls and I pushed hard against it. Then I came up to her fully. I took her face in both hands and kissed her deeply.

We carried on like this for a while, reacquainting ourselves with each other's bodies and pressure points, taking turns to take charge; and when the time came for me to slide inside her it felt like the most beautiful moment of my life.

We made love slowly, tenderly. Lifting into each other as fully as we could. But it still didn't feel that we were close enough. I wanted her to merge with me, for us to become a single, beautiful being right here and now and I wanted it to last forever. I wanted her to let me fly with her, to take me up and become a creature of the air like she was.

I didn't want the moment to end, but eventually I felt the pressure building in my loins. I kept it under control for as long as I could, teasing out the moment, letting it build and build, letting her squeeze me harder as she came and clawed at my hips.

Keep going, don't let it be over yet, please not yet.

We were nose to nose, mouth to mouth, breathing and gasping into each other's faces. We were moving together, harder and faster, not caring now who heard us and quickly, all too quickly and uncontrollably,

I felt the first jolt of semen spraying from the tip of my cock. A cry of intense, beautiful agony screamed from my throat, wild and unexpected, growing with each upward thrust of my body. She gripped me hard and dug her fingernails into my buttocks. Another jolt, followed by another, releasing a massive pressure that left me weak and giddy. She brought her nails up against the skin of my back, grabbed my hair and called out James's name. Legs spread with her feet flat on the ground she lifted herself up and begged him to fuck her harder, and then she screamed like a demon, her cries ringing around the old station house.

As always it was delicious, but this time, tonight, it seemed as though we had transcended

5.9

Afterwards, I sat back against the wall, my sister in my arms under thick blankets.

I heard a motorbike screaming through the streets above us. It was harsh and way too loud, upsetting the moment slightly, but that was kids I guessed. Besides, once it was gone it was gone and then it seemed as though the whole world was silent.

After a long, dozy half-hour I said to Jenny, "Will you tell me what you're doing here?"

She didn't answer.

"Jenny?" I prompted. "Why'd you run away? What happened?"

There was a moment's pause in her voice. "Something I saw," she answered.

"Something you saw? What?"

"I can't tell you," she whispered as I felt a shudder spasm through her warm body.

I considered my next question. "What about James?" I challenged. "Would you have told him?"

"Yes."

Well at least she was honest. Didn't make it hurt any less. "Why him and not me?" I said it in a cruder tone than I'd meant to, but the emotion I felt was raw.

Jenny drew away from me and reached around for her clothes.

I gripped her arm.

"Get off me!" She wrenched her arm out from under me and pulled free of the blankets. "Sick of people holding me back," she muttered.

"Even James?" I said. "You thought I was James when I first came in. You were waiting for him right?"

"I thought he'd come."

"He's miles away!" I shouted. "Flying warplanes in the Gulf."

"Is that what *she* told you?"

I stared at her silhouette. Stunned. Jane wouldn't lie to me. She wasn't a liar.

"He's here, Jason," she said. "He came back."

"He's home?"

"No. Not as such. He's prowling around the island. On leave for a couple of months before they sail back to the Middle East. But I've seen him a few times the last couple of weeks."

"Does Jane know about this?"

She nodded. "Yeah she knows he's back. He came to see me. She found us. He didn't want to speak to her so she ran to you instead."

I held my head in my hands. "She lied to me. I bloody knew it! I knew something was going on!"

Jenny came round with some of her clothes in her hands. She knelt in front of me and I felt her hands on my cheeks. Her face was right in front of mine. "Go home," she said. "Go back to Jane and keep her with you. Look after her. She's vulnerable."

"*She's* vulnerable? What about you?"

"I don't need looking after." She stood, and pulled on her jeans in the dark. "I don't know what stories Jane's been filling your head with," she said, "but I can look after myself."

"She said you were trying to keep her here."

Jenny laughed as she dressed. "I've been trying to get her to leave."

I wasn't having any of this. "Enough of the crap, Jenny. What's really going on? You wouldn't run away for nothing and neither would Jane."

She reached down for her the ghost of her bra. "You shouldn't have come back."

"I heard you were missing," I snapped. "I wanted to find you."

She snorted. "Really?"

"Yes really! I love you, Jenny. I always have done. I've only ever loved you. No one else."

Clasping the bra behind her back she said, "Listen. Take your pretty face back to Manchester and don't come back here. Ever. If you need me I'll find you."

There was a lump in my throat. "No," I said. "I'm not going until you tell me what's going on. Why you're here, why James is 'prowling' the island, why Jane thinks you're in trouble and why you waited here for James to come and fuck you!"

She shook her head. "No. You don't. Trust me on this."

"Stop trying to protect me! After everything we seen and done? Just tell me."

She looked at me through the dark. There was a long silence and then: "It'll change you," she said. "It'll change everything you think you know."

"I can handle it," I told her. But I was worried then.

"All right. Since you insist, big boy, but don't say I didn't warn you. Get dressed and sit down. I'll tell you a bed-time story."

5.10

"I haven't been getting on with mum," Jenny began. "We've been arguing for years but recently it got worse. And then, last week... I wanted her to stop seeing Adam – you know they've been seeing each other right?"

"Adam...?"

"Adam Gordon," Jenny said.

"*Jane's dad?*" I hissed.

"Don't tell me you didn't know!"

"I didn't! Jesus, when did that start?"

Jenny sighed, long and hard. "If you can't handle that, Jason, then there's no—"

"I can handle it!" I interrupted. "I just ... I just didn't know about it that's all. Jesus. Mum and Adam?"

"It's so fucking obvious," Jenny said. "I can't believe you never saw it, but I guess you never were any good at reading people. I wonder if you're autistic you know..."

"I'm not autistic. Carry on."

"You might be."

"I'm not!"

"You should see someone. They could help you find ways to empathise with others and read people better."

"Jenny. I'm not autistic. I don't need fucking help. I just want to understand what's been going on here while I've been away."

"It's probably my fault."

"What did Mum say?" I asked, bringing it back on track. "Did you confront her?"

"I told her I wanted her to stop seeing him. I said if she didn't then I'd tell Dad everything."

It's what I would have done. "So what happened then? What did she say?"

"Nothing. She just laughed at me."

"She laughed at you?"

"And then she asked me if I knew where Dad was right now. She said something like, 'The wonderful Eve Gordon and that fabulous husband of mine? What do you think they're doing this very minute? Maybe you two dykes should take a look outside your weird little world once in a while and—'"

"You two?" I interrupted.

"Jane was with me," Jenny explained. "Mum knew we were having sex together in our flat and she didn't approve of it. It was because of that we were having this argument. And Mum never liked Jane."

"I know."

"Sure. Anyway she said Dad was a freak and she said to Jane that Eve was a monster, which Jane didn't like. So then she flew into one."

"Jane did?"

"Yes. Jane dotes on her Mum. Won't have anyone saying anything bad about her."

I thought back to what Jane had told me, about the fire, about her Mum.

"So Jane starts having a go, and then Mum said something like: 'If they're not in hospital again, they might be at home. And if you're quick enough you might just catch them at it.'"

"What? So ... Dad and Eve?"

"Yeah. I'll admit even I never saw that one. Anyway Jane was so angry. I never seen her like that. I always thought she was the calm one."

"You'd be surprised..."

"So me and her went round to her mum and dad's house. We used her key to get in the back door. They'd actually changed the locks on the front one. Anyway as soon as we were in the house we knew something was wrong. We could hear them banging away upstairs, but there was something ... different about it..."

She paused. Didn't sound like she was going to continue.

"Jenny," I pressed her. "Tell me."

"Wasn't like the kind of stuff you normally hear. This was like animals rutting, noises of pain. I could see Jane was scared, and to be honest so was I. First off we thought Eve was being raped. You know the smell blood gives off?" she asked me suddenly. "Sort of... I don't know… It's like, it triggers something inside of you when you smell it."

I think I knew what she meant…

"The whole house *stank* of blood and sex," she said. "Or it stank of something, or it made us both *feel* something. We went up to the bathroom and there they were."

"Dad and Eve?" I said.

"Dad and Eve Gordon. Our Dad, and Jane's mum. Only … "

She stopped again, and when she restarted her voice was shaking. "The bathroom was covered in blood, and so was Dad and Eve. They roared at each other. And their faces… Jason, they was wearing collars round their necks and each one was pulling the other one tight, like they was strangling each other. They were like animals. And then Dad grabs Eve. He slams her up against the tiles and her back – oh my God – her back was ripped to shreds. And not just her but him as well. Arms, legs, their arses, covered in scars and sliced red raw. Dad pushes her face into the wall and as if that wasn't enough he starts putting his fingers into her wounds and Eve starts screaming like I never heard before.

"Then Eve throws him off her. She turns and grabs his collar, putting her fingers under it, right into his throat, forcing him down into the tub and he's like choking. His eyes are literally popping and it was just…"

"And they didn't see you?" I said, filling the silence she'd left.

"I think we could have been standing right in front of them and they wouldn't have seen us," she said. "We just stood at the door, and most of what we saw was in the mirror. Big bathroom remember? And it was all steamy. We just stood there, Jane and me holding hands and I felt sick.

"Then Jane turned and ran, and when I caught up with her outside the house she was all shaking and angry, like someone drunk spoiling for a fight. I couldn't calm her down. She got worse. Then she started blaming our Dad, said that he had made her mum do this stuff and that we should call the police and say he was raping her. But it wasn't like that, Jason! They were both in it *together*! This was what they did, this was how they had sex together, and Mum and Adam knew it.

"So Jane ran off. Told me to stay away from her. Me and all my fucked up family she said. I couldn't let her go off on her own, and I was worried she might tell the cops so I followed her. She walked home and I followed her all the way like a bloody stalker. Then back at the house we just had a big fight. Both of us were in shock, but Jane was just enraged. And then I got angry as well and between the two of us… Jason, we damn near destroyed the house. Did she tell you we live with these two girls?"

"A couple of Christians, she said."

"God knows what they were thinking of it all. They tried coming between us but Jane just flew at one of them. I had to pull her off and then she started on me and it was all I could do to stop her. Jason, I tell you now, when she flies off the handle she just snaps. And I think she could kill someone. She could've killed that girl. Emily I think her name was, or something like that."

"Emmeline," I said.

"Was that her name? I dunno. She spent more time with them than I ever did."

"That wasn't what she told me."

"Look. You need to help her, Jason. You shouldn't be here with me, I can look after myself. I don't know what I'm gonna do about Mum and Dad but I'm thinking I'll just leave them at it and what'll be will be. I don't like it, and it makes me sick. I know what we do, and what we've done together – well, maybe some people wouldn't like that either and they'd get all judgemental. But this was different. And after I saw that, I started to feel for our Mum. Because if that's what she's had to live with for God knows how many years, then that's hard on anyone. And the same for Adam."

"Unless they do the same…"

"I don't think they do. But look. You need to go, Little Brother. Get away from here and don't come back. It's all lies here and they'll pull you in. You need to look after yourself and you need to look after Jane. She loves you, Jason. She loves you now maybe more than her Mum, and that's saying something. But all that feeling she had for her Mum is now pinned on you. So you can't be coming back here for the likes of me. Understand?"

Yeah I understood, except maybe it was too late. I'd misread Jane completely. Thought she was playing games with me…

"I'm going to talk to Dad," I said.

"No!" snapped Jenny. "Jesus, don't do that!"

Then, quieter and with a hand on my arm she repeated it. "It'll make no difference. Whatever goes on between the four of them, leave them to it. We can't change them and they don't give a shit about us. You know that. Not even Mum. You need to get back to Jane before she does something stupid, Jason. I mean it."

She was right.

"What about you? You said you could handle it but you can't stay here can you? Not now."

She said, "I thought James would come to me. He said he would, before he left. If ever I wanted him I was to think about him and he would come and find me." Then she said, "I'll be all right I promise. Go home, Jason. Go back to your friends and keep Jane safe. There's nothing here for you anymore. There's nothing for any of us. That thing we all had? It's long gone now."

5.11

I started driving back.

Got as far as Conwy before I pulled over into a layby and hit the steering wheel hard with the palms of my hands. I got out, walked up and down the roadside. Bought some fags from a garage half a mile away and even went for a walk along the shitty beach in the dark in an effort to clear my head.

I got back in the car; drove some more but I couldn't concentrate. I had to swerve and brake suddenly more times than I cared to, so eventually I pulled in at a services somewhere, grabbed a Burger King and passed the remainder of the night asleep in the car. When I woke up I wondered about turning back and confronting my Dad and having it out with him. What Jenny had told me... Was it true?

I was going to ask Jane. As soon as I got back to the digs I'd ask her, draw it out of her and apologise for being a dick, for misreading her so completely. If this was all true then yeah, Jane needed me, and I'd left her for my sister.

But when I got back, she'd left.

"She's gone with Gareth," Kev told me eventually. I'd had to slam him up against the wall and prise it out of him.

"Where? Where've they gone?"

"I dunno, mate. I don't! Honest! I promise you!"

I stormed up to Gareth's room. Bust open the door and ransacked it, looking for anything that might tell me where he'd taken her.

"He's got to come back for college," I said as Kev hovered in the doorway rubbing his throat.

"I don't think so, mate. He said he was going for good. I kinda got the feeling he'd jacked it all in."

I pushed past him.

"Now where are you going?" he shouted.

I banged on Dougie's door. "Dougie!"

"He's gone with them," Kev explained.

"*What?*"

"Well. He went with them some of the way at least. He might have gone home. He's been bricking these exams since we started back."

Gareth had left some of his stuff behind and Kev and I went through it all.

"Dirty bastard…" I heard Kev whisper behind me.

He'd found a stash of mini digital video cassette tapes and was loading them up into an Hitachi DV camcorder to have a look at what was on them.

"He's been filming us," he said.

"What? How?"

Looking at the videos we were able to figure out where the little cameras had been stashed in our rooms, Dougie's as well. And later I found the tape which had recorded the conversations and arguments I'd had with Jane. I played them back with the camcorder plugged into the TV downstairs, and when I heard Jane tell me the story of the fire again I got angry, at her and at myself and especially at Gareth.

"He took advantage of her."

"But you weren't here, mate," said Kev. "I'm sorry but that's how it was. She was in a state when you went off, sobbed into his arms and stayed with him all night. By lunchtime they'd gone."

"By lunchtime? And you didn't know?"

Kev shrugged. "I didn't get up till I heard 'em leaving."

I've still got the tape, it's somewhere at home, but I've got nothing to play it on now. Old technology.

For nights after I'd found it I just watched it over and again in the house.

Looking at her face.

The girl in the TV.

Gone.

5.12

"Do you remember me?" hissed this vocoder-disguised voice in my ear. Different mask this time, like Darth Vader; all black and metallic with a thing over the mouth and nose. Big glass eyes like an insect.

"No!" I yelled back. "Fuckoff!"

"What *do* you remember?"

"Nothing! I don't know what the *fuck* you're talking about."

"I'm talking about that night, you idiot!" screamed the voice. "Tell me what you remember so that I know I didn't just fucking dream it up."

Remember?

"My Dad," I gasped. "I remember my Dad."

"Your *Dad?*"

Yeah... my Dad...

5.13

The twenty-three-and-a-half-thousand-strong crowd at Huddersfield Town's Alfred McAlpine stadium, or at least the seven-thousand or so away-supporters packed in at the John Smith's Stand, screamed and roared like a single entity. The other lot, the home crowd, were quiet because they were beaten.

But the noise of the Liverpool supporters was awesome and the sense of union that I felt inside that sea of sound, that I shared with these thousands of others around me, was tribal.

I was no longer an individual. I lived for the crowd, I *was* the crowd, its voice was my voice and I sang, I shouted, I roared and I swore with it in perfect synch.

And it was an epic game.

Despite having all the chances in the first half, Huddersfield Town were one-nil down to Liverpool going into half time. They'd come out strong from the break, desperate to get an equaliser. A couple of times it looked like they were going to do it because they were still getting all the chances. But Liverpool were too strong, and when Titi Camara the first goal-scorer crossed the ball the full width of the pitch to Hamman, who dummied it to Matteo, I knew it was all over for the Town. You could sense it, feel it in the air that Matteo was going to score. And he did. He smashed that ball through the goalie and into the back of their net. To be fair to the Town, they played well. They gave us a good run and they had all the chances. But they weren't able to convert them into anything worthwhile and the Liverpool goals were clinical.

It was an awesome game, and I knew I'd never forget it. It just had that epic quality. And as the Liverpool anthem *You'll Never Walk Alone* resounded around the Alfred McAlpine I felt as though I was floating inside an exquisite bubble of time that would last forever.

5.14

"Fucking diabolical the chances they had!" said Dad in *The Horse And Carriage* later. "Westerveld? Fucking crap goalie. If it wasn't for Stevie Gerrard getting in the bloody way all the time they could have had four or five bloody goals on us and then we'd be royally fucked. Wasn't like that back in the day. Fucking hell! Still, who's next? Blackburn Rovers? Piece of bloody cake that at home, eh? It's gonna be good for us this year, JJ, I can feel it in me bones!"

He swung me a pint over from the bar.

"Quick quick quick!" he urged. "Grab it!"

I took it off him. "What's up?" I asked him.

"Me arm! Ouch! Bugger!"

I took the pint away and watched him stretch out his left arm as we squeezed our way through the packed pub, finding a bit of space near a window. So what was this? A raw wound from one of his sex games with Eve Gordon?

Going to the football was the only thing I'd ever done with my Dad. And we hadn't been for a couple of years. The previous year I'd got us both tickets to the fourth round FA Cup tie with Man United but Dad wouldn't come because he didn't want to set foot in Old Trafford. As it happens we lost that game anyway so he would've hated it.

But looking at him that night, as a man fired up by the victory of the team he'd supported all his life, wearing his red scarf and his stupid dustman's overcoat, looking at his greying hair and his deep-cragged face, his ice-grey eyes burning with emotion, I couldn't believe… I could *not believe*, what Jenny had told me just a few weeks earlier.

"What did you do to your arm?" I asked him.

"Eh? Oh. I dunno. No idea. Bloody hell though what about that lad's goal. What a fucking cracker that was, JJ. Eh?" he crashed his glass against mine in a toast, took a swig and then put it on a broad window ledge next to us. Rubbing his arm he decided he wanted to give me a history lesson. "Still…" he said, "the side ain't what it used to be, JJ. Now back in my day Liverpool was the undisputed kings…"

I interrupted him. "Tell me about Eve Gordon, Dad," I demanded.

Fuck the football. I hadn't been able to get this shit Jenny had told me out of my head and I was still pissed off that Jane had run out on me with Gareth bloody Evans.

The old man just stared at me, his eyes turning hard.

Eventually he seemed to come to a decision. He stopped fucking with his arm and then he smiled, reached out for his pint, and said, "Why don't *you* tell *me*, son?" before he took a sip.

"Me?" I started. "You're the one who's been fucking her!"

He kind of nodded, raised his eyebrows as if to say 'Fair play' or something, and then he put his pint back on the ledge. He wiped his lips then said, "Been fucking her for a long old time, Jason. Just as your mum's been having it away with Ad–"

Someone barged into him, knocking him against the wall and he swore.

I'd sort of noticed that the pub had started getting rowdy, but had been so wrapped up inside my own head that it hadn't meant anything.

My Dad wasn't an idiot, and he knew the signs. So, with a well-practiced move he whipped off his LFC scarf, stashed it in a pocket of his coat, and with his other hand he took one last, enormous slug of his beer. Then he made a move. "Come on," he said, abandoning his pint. "We're off."

5.15

Outside in the freezing Yorkshire evening, Dad walked quickly and determinedly along the road, pulling me with him. Breath steaming from his mouth.

Others were doing the same, heading quickly for the train station and looking over their shoulders nervously. The air was filled with danger and anticipation. "Don't know why they put it so far away from the bloody ground," he said, almost gritting his teeth.

Looked like his arm was really bad. He couldn't leave it alone.

"Still hurting?" I said.

"As it happens… yes!" he snapped.

"Anything to do with Eve?"

"What? Oh… You're bringing that up again is it?" He walked on. "You've had this on your mind all day which is why you been such a moody tart right? Listen, son, I been in love with your mum all my adult life. But I been in love with Eve Gordon even longer. And don't you bloody start giving me lectures on who to keep company with because I *know*," he said, turning to stab at me with his finger, "I know what you lot been up to, don't think I don't."

He was out of breath. Walking too quickly, talking too fast.

I didn't give a shit. I pressed him on it. "But it's not just sex with her is it? Jenny told me what she saw you both doing. Dad, she saw you and Jane was with her."

"Jane as well? So what did they see?" He was sweating. "Eh? What.... *Shit*.... What *exactly* did they see? Me and Eve Gordon having sex? Well so fucking what? I'm sorry Jane saw us but you're not kids anymore and I'm not the slightest bit sorry if it upsets the cosy little love-fest you lot got going on."

Now I poked him in his bad arm, hoping I'd got to a fresh wound. "Cutting each other with knives," I said. "Strangling each other with dog collars in the bathtub for Chrissakes!"

Blue lights flashed and sirens were wailing now. Fights were breaking out in the streets and the police were jumping in.

"You've no right to lecture me," Dad hissed. We both walked quickly towards the train station. He was sweating hard so I stepped up the pace. Then I turned on him, pointing at him. Blaming him.

"They *saw* you at it. It's why Jane ran, Dad."

"She ran away from *you*, you fucking..." Dad's face screwed up in pain. "Aw! Aw.... *Shit*... Christ alm... *Bollocks*!"

And then with a horrific scream the bastard collapsed.

I took a step backwards, my head roaring with noise. *What the fuck?* "...... Dad!"

I froze. I didn't know what to do. Didn't know what was going on.

People gave us a wide berth at first, and then gradually a few became more concerned.

On the ground, his teeth clenched, Dad screamed again. Now he was clutching his chest instead of his arm and I realised what he was going through.

I fell down next to him. Quickly I pulled open the collar of his coat, ripping the buttons off it. "Dad…"

Split flew from his lips as he spluttered, gasping for air, trying to speak.

I tore his shirt open.

"*Dad*!"

His hands turned to claws and he was dead in five minutes.

5.16

"So... Which one are you?"

That was Laurence, Uncle Larry, Dad's brother. He'd been staring at me during Dad's wake back at the house. I'd been watching him across the grave all through the funeral and I'd noticed that when his eyes landed on Eve, who'd been standing right next to me, so close that our arms were touching, then his expression had filled with what I took to be a look of absolute contempt.

So *he knew*, I remember thinking. He knew that Eve and my dad had been having this affair. I wondered if anyone else in the family knew about it. Maybe they did and maybe that was why they'd all stayed away for so many years.

Aside from Uncle Larry, I didn't recognise any of the other relatives who'd crawled up to Anglesey to see my Dad off.

"Jason," I answered him soberly.

Uncle Larry peered up at me with eyes that for one moment looked frighteningly just like my Dad's. "I'm sorry," he said. He put his whisky down on a table and then put both his hands around mine. "I'm so... so sorry."

I nodded, wishing at that moment that I knew Uncle Larry better. This was Dad's brother, I was thinking. These two had grown up together, climbed trees, swam in lakes, gone to school, gone to parties, shagged girls...

I didn't know what to say to him.

There was a scream from somewhere in the house. A woman shrieking with rage. I heard a glass smashing against a wall and then an almighty clatter as a table full of food was overturned in anger.

"Jenny..." I whispered.

Larry turned and swore.

"Get her out of here!" shouted Mum as I saw Adam struggling with Jenny. "Get her *out*!"

"You bastards!" Jenny screamed. "Bastards the lot of you!"

I went over to give Adam a hand because I was certain she'd be too much for him and anyway it was possible I might have been able to calm her down.

"Keep her away from us, Jason. All right?" Adam said, once Jenny was safely outside the house. He went back inside.

Outside Jenny was fuming. Pacing the driveway. Tearing at her hair with clawlike fingers ready to rip someone's face off.

"Hey," I whispered. "Let's go."

She wiped her hair away from her eyes. "*Bastards!*" she hissed. "Fuck the lot of them."

"Jenny."

"Where are you taking me?" she demanded suddenly, throwing me off her.

I lifted my hands up like a man in surrender while she stared at me strangely, searching my face for some kind of clue.

"Let's just go back to your house eh?" I suggested.

"Suits me," she spat, Then she turned and shouted back at the house. "I'm never coming back here again!"

5.17

Jenny's house was a Victorian holiday townhouse. Big and old, and in need of repair inside and out, it was screened from Glenhwfa Road by a bank of ancient trees that pressed right up against the windows. It was a sunny winter's day but it didn't seem like any of that light was getting into the house, and it was freezing cold in the hallway.

There was a payphone in the hall, next to the stairs.

"Don't touch the phone," she snapped as she started up them.

"I wasn't going to."

"Come on up."

Two out of the three upstairs rooms belonged to Jenny. Her bedroom was a cluttered mess just like it had been at home, with magazines, dinner plates, tea cups and clothes scattered around like she just didn't care. It smelled a bit too, and I said maybe she ought to clean it up.

"I might do," she said, untying the black cravat at her collar.

I decided to change the subject. "When was the last time you saw Uncle Larry?" I asked her.

"Years ago. When I was fifteen I think. He kept eyeing me up the dirty bastard."

"I remember," I said, sitting down on her bed.

"I've never liked him." She took off her smart black cardigan and threw a piece of paper at me. "Here," she said. "Look at this. Came this morning."

"What is it?"

"Read it."

She stepped out of her skirt, unbuttoned her white blouse and announced that she was going for a shower.

Alone in her bedroom I read with astonishment what turned out to be a letter from Jane:

Dear Jenny,
I hope everything's going OK for you. I miss you, you know x
Me and Gareth have been in Scotland, living in this enormous old mansion near a place called Balloch – which is near a gorgeous loch! Honestly it's just beautiful!
Jenny, you wouldn't believe this place. It's awesome!!! There are thirty-one bedrooms on two floors. Thirty-one bedrooms!!! I mean, who's going to use them all? Actually they smell a bit and everything inside them is covered in old sheets. Gareth says his dad comes over now and then from the States but I've never met him yet. And there's this old housekeeper called Mrs Flace who comes in every few days to clear up all our pizza boxes lol! But really there's only the two of us.
Anyway I've got to tell you about this enormous L-shaped ballroom on the ground floor which is where I'm sat writing this. It's got really tall windows with seats in them and a huge chandelier and all these dusty old paintings on the walls. The main hall on the west wing takes your breath away it's so huge, and it looks gorgeous when lit by the sunset. Also there are games rooms, dining rooms, a real-life banqueting hall and a bunch of kitchens and larders round the back. There are wings and turrets and towers and probably lots of secret passageways no doubt. Even an old chapel filled up with gardening equipment. Maybe this is what Jason had in mind when him and James built that stupid castle years ago.
But it's not all olde worlde!!
The basement's been converted into a hi-tech video suite, because like I said to you Gareth is studying film, and it's full of complicated-looking control boards and TV screens and stuff which must have cost a fortune, but of course, money means nothing to Gareth. Or at least his mum and dad. All right for some eh? I'm trying to persuade Gareth to let you visit. He's all right you know. You'd like him. I think coming here was the right thing to do in the end and I'm sorry about JJ.
So what about you? How are things? Have you seen Jason recently? Tell him I miss him too and that I'm sorry. Again!
I've been trying to ring mum and dad but nobody ever seems to be in.
I miss you, Jenny. More than I thought I would and I'm sorry.
All my Love,
Jane xxx'

So that's where she was.

I'd heard of this wonderful house Gareth lived in when he went to stay with his mum – his *real* mum, not his stepmum, but I'd thought it was just another figment of his deranged imagination, I hadn't believed for a moment that it actually existed.

And what about all this hi-tech equipment inside the house? This video suite in the basement? Was it true? I started thinking about Gareth's obsession with TV sex and his pornstar stepmum. I wondered if he and Jane had filmed anything there.

Probably. Undoubtedly.

"Have you seen any of her movies?" Kev had asked Gareth once.

"I've seen 'em all. Want to borrow some?"

"Na, man. That's your mum."

"Don't you think it's weird though?" I'd asked him, "Watching your mum get fucked all ways by these big-dick dudes?"

He didn't think so.

He'd said, "I just used to wonder why everyone else could fuck her and I couldn't. Anyway it's all just acting isn't it? I ain't interested in that. I want the real shit." His dad had put all this stuff in the giant house, and had paid for him to go to college and study film, and all Gareth wanted to do was film people having sex.

Jenny was still in the shower.

I thought I might tidy her room up a bit, so I moved some underwear off the bed and hung her suit up in the wardrobe. When I opened a drawer on a chest near the window I found a notepad on top of it, in which Jenny had started to write a reply to Jane's letter. I picked it up and started reading.

"Shit…" I whispered.

What the hell was this?

I read it again.

Watch out for the monster in the water, Jane…

she'd written.

You've got to blind it to be sure…

It was difficult to read because it was full of drawings of monsters and tormented faces, and the writing sprawled across it in all directions both in pencil and in pen. So I read the thing in snapshots.

When it can't see you it goes mad … The only way to blind it is to throw wet sawdust into its eyes…. Be careful because usually it will have a knife to protect its babies and it might lash out so you have to watch for that … also watch for any change in the way it moves its lips … You can't fight it because it is stronger than you Jane. You will need to be careful and so when you begin to run you should do so with your right foot forward first because the monster will probably have two left feet so you will have a head start.... I think it comes from the whales have you heard them singing? Thousands of them in the ocean where it's so dark they can't see their children...

It went on but I couldn't make sense of it. I put it back.

I heard the shower stop rattling in the bathroom, so I went down into the kitchen to make us a cup of tea. All this stuff was going round in my head and I wonder now how the hell I'd managed to keep it together. Seemed like everyone else was falling apart and I was the one who had to stay strong for them.

Jenny came down wearing her black dressing gown. "Tea," she said, watching what I was doing as she towelled her hair. "Good idea. You found everything? Here." She grabbed a tin of sugar which I'd never have found, and pulled a pint of milk from the fridge.

"Your housemates not in?" I asked.

"Yeah, Carla's in," she said. "Don't know where Emms is though."

"You get on with them OK? You know their names now."

She shrugged as I spooned a sugar into her tea. "We have our moments," she said. "I think they'd prefer it if I moved out."

"Is it down to them though?"

"No. But the landlord seems to like them. He stays with them most of the day when he comes over. They're probably fucking him sideways," she said.

"I thought they were Christians?"

"Sure. But I think they cherry-pick which parts of the Bible they want to stick to."

I laughed, and gave her the tea I'd made.

We went back upstairs carrying a packet of biscuits, sat in her room and ate them with our tea. "Do you ever wonder where the water comes from?" Jenny asked me suddenly.

"No."

"What about the TV?" she asked, nodding at the tiny portable sitting on a tabletop. A crude face had been drawn on the glass in what I thought was lipstick. X's for eyes, straight line of a mouth. "Who controls that?"

"Hey," I said. "You OK?"

She stared at me. "Not really," she said in trembling voice. "I don't..."

I took the tea off her, put it on a tabletop, and held her close to me, drew her right into my shoulder.

"It's been a shit day," I said. "Lots to take in."

I felt her head nodding in my shoulder. "How long are you staying?" she asked me putting her arms right around me.

"As long as you need me to," I answered.

She laughed. "No," she said. "You're off the hook. I have my Protector."

I raised an eyebrow and made out I was curious, but actually I was starting to feel jealous. "Really? Who's that?"

She frowned at me, like the answer should have been obvious. "It's James," she told me.

"James?"

She grabbed her tea and took a sip. "Yup," she said.

"But I thought he was …"

"He's here now, Jason!" she whispered with a smile. "He's my Protector. He looks out for me." She paused, drawing circles on the bedcovers with a finger. "To be honest," she said, "I think he's ill." She tapped the side of her forehead. "Up here. Mental like. He came to see me the other week when I was at work in the tea shop. Turned up in his leathers. Bike parked right outside." She looked straight at me, sunshine beaming out of her smile. "He looked *really* sexy."

I smiled too, but I wasn't sure what to feel. This didn't sound right.

"He took me to the station house," she went on, "and I thought we were going to have a good time, but then he just started asking me all these questions."

I hadn't expected that. "What kind of questions?" I asked her.

"He wanted to know if he was normal."

Typical James Gordon. Me me me. All the time.

"Anyway," she continued, "long story short I kissed him. One thing led to another and before we both knew what was going on, we started having sex."

"So now you and James… "

She was shaking her head and my voice tailed off.

"He couldn't do it, JJ," she said. "I wanted him, and he wanted me, but he just couldn't do it. He came out of me all limp. I told him it didn't matter but he said it did, said it just proved that he wasn't normal. 'I've always wanted you,' he told me. Ever since he first saw me, apparently. So I told him to just do it. I wanted him to fuck me. But he wouldn't, said he couldn't. He started getting dressed and was muttering under his breath. He got angry and slapped me across the face."

"What?"

"Don't worry," she said. "He was more hurt than I was. In fact he burst into tears, broke down in front of me. On his knees all pathetic as I got dressed again. I told him he was a gay, nothing more or less, and that it was fine. I had no problem with it but he did. Maybe it's because he's in the Navy or whatever it is and he's proper realised what he is. I told him that being gay was all right but he couldn't accept it. No matter what I said," continued Jenny, "he wouldn't come round." She shrugged. "I'll take him away from all this, one day. For now, though, he looks after me."

Something about the way she said this made me shudder. Was James really her protector? Didn't sound like it. But she needed one, that was for sure.

"Come back to Manchester with me," I said.

"Brother and sister?" she said, holding my hand and feigning shock.

"I didn't mean like that!"

"So what did you mean?"

I didn't answer.

She said. "You mean we should be like 'normal people'? Like every brother and sister? It'd never work. We wouldn't keep our hands off each other." She patted my knee. "Anyway, we've already had this conversation, JJ. And people would find out," she said. "They always do."

"Jenny, you can't stay here, it's driving you mad. This town is too small for you and besides that our whole damned family is ... *fucked*."

She stroked my face. "I can't go with you," she said. "It's too late." Then she kissed me on the cheek. "You'd better go."

I hugged her before I went. Couldn't let go.

"Go back to the house," she whispered, stroking the back of my head. "Do the family thing. You're good at that."

I laughed and wiped my eyes as I pulled away from her. "That doesn't say much for the rest of us does it?"

5.18

I left Jenny's house and walked the back way over the slushy fields that would take me to the top of Greenfield Avenue. And no matter how wet my boots were getting I didn't want to go through town – had no idea who I might meet and have to have an awkward conversation with.

I wanted some time on my own to think about stuff, and decide what I was going to do next. Would I go back to Manchester? Six months left and then I'd get my diploma – provided I passed the exams. But what good was it anyway? What the hell was I going to do with it afterwards? Everything I was dedicating my time to seemed shallow and pointless on this day.

Halfway up the hill I took a detour, tromping down the path which led to the tiny chapel in the grounds of which Dad had been laid to rest. I wanted another look at his grave, alone, and the walk would do me good. The white December sun was sinking into a dark wall of cold air gusting in from the sea. It was pulling in a brutal wind into the land. Already the trees up the hill were looking restless.

Eve Gordon, a vision in black-and-white against the stark, agitated landscape, was on her knees beside the new headstone, looking like she wanted to dig up the earth and jump into the box with my Dad.

If it was anyone else I would've turned around and left them to it.

"Hey," I said softly, walking up to her. "You OK?"

Eve had nothing on her but the dress she'd been wearing this morning so I took my coat off and knelt down next to her to put it round her shoulders.

She pulled at it with tiny, grasping fingers, pulling the furry collar over her neck so that her jet-black hair bunched up around it. Shivering, she whispered, "Thank you," so quietly I barely heard it.

"Some Christmas eh?" I said stupidly.

And then my voice caught in my throat. I couldn't help it. Everything I'd kept in for the whole of the day was released and I sobbed like a child next her.

The next thing I knew, Eve had her arm around me. I was pulled into the coat with her and I was crying into her delicately-perfumed neck.

5.19

Eve Gordon.

I always felt like there was a charge building in the air between us whenever I was in the same room as her. Like static build-up before a thunderstorm pricking up the hairs on my skin.

On the day of my Dad's funeral I was closer to her than I had ever been in my life.

5.20

The windstorm picked up quickly as Eve and I walked home from the grave. By the time I stood at the front door of her house it was blasting into our faces.

"Come in," she said.

I didn't hesitate.

The house was cold inside. The windows rattled as I searched for the central heating control, cranked up the thermostat and waited for the boiler to fire up.

I stayed with Eve the for the rest of the afternoon. Made her something to eat and made her some coffee. She shouldn't be here by herself, I thought, not tonight. So I stayed with her. Just sitting on her sofa, drinking tea at first, then something a bit stronger as the evening progressed. I said I'd go out and bring us back some fish and chips.

"You get some if you want to," she said.

But actually, I wasn't hungry. The thought of food just made me feel ill.

As darkness smothered the house and the wind encircled it like a protective dragon, Eve told me stories about herself and my Dad from long ago. She told me that they'd been childhood sweethearts in the late Sixties, then right through the Seventies. Sudden images of violent sex games in the bathroom flashed into my head as she spoke.

I kept them to myself. Curled up next to her on the sofa it didn't seem right to ask her about them.

But... It was still clear that she and my Dad had been proper lovers, and I hoped that the extreme stuff Jenny had told me wasn't true. I couldn't spoil my image of Eve because I think, right from an early age, I'd never been able to take my eyes off her.

She was beautiful. Like Jane but with hair as dark as the winter's night on the hills outside. Eve had porcelain-white skin and vivid emerald eyes with slightly upswept eyebrows. Her high cheekbones, and her wide mouth filled with straight white teeth made me think of her as someone who was ... I don't know... It sounds strange, and 'arty' and all that, but there was something almost alien – no, not alien. *Ethereal?*

In my mind Eve embodied the Earth and every element of nature in a perfect vessel. The storm of wind and rain sweeping the streets and the fields outside, the shadows shielding the house, even the winter itself seemed like it could have been some kind of sublimation of her spirit.

She was tall. She was confident and assured. Even here, right now after crying her eyes out all day, there was an air of untouchability about her. I could understand exactly what my Dad had seen in Eve and if it had caught hold of him the way it had me then I could almost forgive him.

But I wondered what she had ever seen in him.

Poor old Dad…

Shit. It had been a long and heavy day, and I wasn't able to stay awake much beyond nine o'clock.

I fell asleep on the sofa, and sometime later Eve woke me up. "You can sleep in Jamie's old room," she said, her voice full of whispering breaths, her gaze somehow distant and ghostly.

I went up and crashed out on James' bed.

Bad dreams followed.

In them I remember I couldn't decide who I was - whether I was Jason or James, or even if I was really Jane. I dreamed of having sex with Gareth, of dancing with him in an L-shaped ballroom while a musical troupe of goat-headed skeletons played a funeral march on violins and cellos. An unseen Loch Ness Monster brushed clumsily past the windows outside, shuffling forward on its two left feet. I saw snakes swallowing their own tails, twisting around my dad's heart, squeezing the life out of it, squeezing it until it burst like a bag of blood which was found at the back of terrifying railway tunnel, a baby's head in a plastic bag infested with flies…

5.21

I awoke in the morning to crisp, cold sunlight streaming through unfamiliar curtains. It took a while to remember that I was in James' old bedroom.

There were no posters on the walls, no old toys under the bed. I knew he didn't live here anymore, but even while he had there was never any of the usual stuff a teenager might stick in his room. James had never been into music, or sport, or girls. He had a passion for motorbikes and aircraft and I knew he'd subscribed to a few magazines when he was younger, but there was nothing here to show that.

Dressed in my undies I checked the time, then padded out towards the bathroom, desperate for a piss.

Eve passed me on the landing. "Morning," she smiled. "Grab a shower if you want. Clean towels in there."

I nodded mutely and made my way into the bathroom.

It was only when I was mid-stream it occurred to me that this was the same bathroom Jenny believed she had witnessed Eve's extreme sex scene with my Dad.

Nothing I could see on first glance apart from clean, white tiles on the walls and a clean tub. And when I finished my piss, and ran the shower and looked closer, investigating the lines of grout between the tiles, there was nothing I could see that might have looked like dried blood.

I thought about it while I showered. If my Dad had a dodgy heart would he really have been participating in violent, sado-masochistic sex? Or was it doing all that which had given him a dodgy heart? Maybe one day Eve had squeezed him too tightly, or cut him too deep. I wished Jane were here, then I could have asked her what she had seen.

My Dad had told me that he'd known Eve longer than he had my Mum, and from what Eve had told me last night, it sounded like they really had been in love with each other. Both sets of parents had known each other since before any of them was married.

So what had gone wrong, I wondered? If they'd effectively swapped partners now, why hadn't they married the right ones when they were younger?

I hadn't planned on staying long. I didn't want to intrude on Eve and besides I wanted to get away from this fucked-up place. Truthfully, I just wanted to be back in Manchester. Back at college getting involved with this semester's art project.

And interviewing for a new housemate.

Kev wanted a girl to move in – not that he knew any, but he had an ideal: A girl who was into Playstation, drank Carlsberg, ate Doritos by the bucket and who could stay up all night watching martial arts films. "If she's got big tits and likes to walk around the house in her underwear then that's a bonus," he'd said to me. "But honestly, if she ticks those other boxes then I'll be happy."

With a big towel wrapped round my waist and legs, and rubbing another one over my hair, I passed Eve's bedroom.

She was perched on the bed, wearing a dressing gown with her legs folded up in a tight 'V' shape. All around her on the bed were photographs pulled from shoeboxes. She looked up at me when I walked past.

"Hey. Sorry, Jason," she said. "I'll make you some breakfast. I was coming down honestly."

"No, it's fine," I said, hovering by the door as I towelled my hair.

"I'll do it. What's this? Old photos?"

"Yeah!" she said, and sniffed with a tissue to her nose. "Yeah, do you want to see?"

"No no. You carry on."

"Come in," she said. "Have a look. There are photos of your dad here."

I stepped forward… hesitated…

"I won't eat you," she breathed, and her face split into the widest smile I'd ever seen, revealing her big teeth, straight and shining white. This proper Eve Gordon smile reminded me so much of Jane that I couldn't resist it. I walked in and she made some space on the bed for me to sit on.

It was then that I noticed her legs properly. They were heavily scarred. The skin below her knees was tough like tree-bark. They were burn scars, I guessed, from the fire years ago.

Sudden image of Eve Gordon battling to save Jane with her legs on fire.

She covered them over with a flick of her gown. "Here you go. Check this one out," she said, handing me a picture of two blonde-haired children wearing red shorts and nothing else. Both of them were smiling at the camera and their outstretched hands proudly displayed the shells they had found on the beach behind them.

"Who's this?" I asked, thinking it was Jane and James.

Eve turned and looked at it. "That's you and James."

I was surprised. "Are you sure?"

She nodded and picked up another photograph. "This is Jane, same age. Two and a half, maybe three years old."

Jane was on the same beach, standing in front of a proud-looking Adam and Eve. She had the same golden locks as me and James at that age, but her face was frozen in a perfect scowl.

"She had a temper that day," Eve explained. "You won't remember it but you and James used to gang up and pick on her. This is before we moved away from Anglesey."

I shook my head and put the picture down, letting my eyes wander over others.

Mostly they were pictures of the four of us as children, either with or without our parents at various locations. The Gordons' house in Barnstaple, where they lived for a couple of years before returning to Anglesey, looked like a nice place.

"I don't remember any of this," I said.

"You were too young, Jay," she said. "Doesn't seem like so long ago to me but it's a lifetime to you."

"I've never seen any pictures of your house down there till now."

"Really? It was a nice house but I don't miss it."

"You don't?"

She shook her head. "Life's too short for …"

She stopped herself and produced the tissue again. She'd been worrying it ragged and there was hardly anything left of it.

"I was going to say regrets," she said.

Then she put a hand on my thigh and squeezed it, looking me right in the eye. "Don't ever live to regret the things you wish you'd done," she said. "Just go out and do them. Make things happen. Change the world if you must."

I nodded mutely.

She took her hand away. "It was me," she said. "All my fault. We moved to Barnstaple to get away from here, and we moved back because I couldn't handle being so far away from your Dad."

She might as well have knocked me on the head.

But at least she was being frank about it.

"You loved him right?" I said.

She nodded. "Like you'd never believe," she said.

"So… what about Adam?" I asked, biting down on a growing anger. "Why did you marry him and not my Dad?"

"My fault again," she whispered, and a tear shot down her cheek. "I loved your Dad but I wanted Adam. I treated Davy badly. Sometimes it's easy to do that to the ones you love. You start to take them for granted – or maybe that's just me. Adam and Ally were good friends, and I got in with them. Davy just tagged along but when I started pulling Adam away from your Mum, then she and your Dad kind of got it together."

I was shaking my head. I didn't know what to say.

"Times were different then, JJ," Eve said. "You can't understand it. We'd grown up during a big revolution, one that even sleepy Anglesey was caught up in. Our parents thought everything was going to be different and they'd brought us up to be 'free spirits'. They'd thought there'd be no more wars, no more governments laying down laws that didn't work, no more society based on greed and wealth. No more unnecessary marriages. Didn't turn out that way but even the darkest days of the Seventies didn't stop them believing, and telling us how it was going to be."

I'd never known my grandparents. Never met them.

"But there are some laws you just can't break," Eve finished with a whisper.

I picked up a black and white picture of my mum when she was pregnant, I assumed, with Jenny.

"Ally was so beautiful," Eve said, looking at the photo, "and she wanted a different life. She wanted to live on an island but I don't think Anglesey was what she had in mind." She laughed. "I was so jealous of her." She took the photograph off me and studied it closely, running her thumb over the face of my Mum.

"I wanted a baby," she said, "but it wasn't going to happen – at least, it didn't look like it would. Adam wanted me to go for tests but I went mad at him. Nearly killed him when I screamed that I didn't want some crackpot quack poking around inside my body. It wasn't like it is nowadays," she said. "Fertility treatment was dangerous back then."

"But you had twins," I said, and then: "Were James and Jane–" I stopped, feeling awkward. "Were they ... from the treatment?" I asked tentatively.

She looked surprised, and then she laughed. "No," she said. "No." She stroked my hair, kissed me lightly on the forehead and said, "No," again. "I didn't have the treatment. Adam couldn't force me to because he was too scared of me. He used to go running to Alison whenever I threatened to kill him - which I did a lot. Poor, idiot man. He looked pretty, but he never had much brains."

Shadows seemed to pass through her eyes and I thought back to what Jenny had told me. Maybe I could just see it, I was thinking, just starting to glimpse how powerful and darkly subversive Eve really was. Despite the fact that these revelations were rocking my world, I still found her totally magnetic. I guess I hadn't been the only one to have felt like this in her presence.

"Look here," she said suddenly, brightly, showing me a photograph of four young people who liked their shirt collars wide and their jeans flared. Or at least three of them did. "Davy wasn't really into the scene as much as Adam, Ally and I were. He was a little bit older and he was trying to fit in."

Both Eve and my Mum looked absolutely gorgeous, it had to be said. My Mum, with her blonde hair down to her waist, with a pattern of plaits and thin ribbons twisted up in it looked amazingly like Jenny: same build, same expression and everything. It was uncanny. Eve was thinner and taller. She was wearing an outfit that showed off a lot of slender hip and belly. She looked so sexually alive, so much like Jane that I just wanted to step into that photograph and fuck her right there. "You look great," I said. "You all do."

Except my Dad, I thought. He looked a bit of a dick.

Adam looked good too, even with the moustache and the little circular specs. He'd clearly worked out in those days. His open shirt revealed an amazing, well-muscled chest.

But as for Eve and my Mum... they looked *sublime*. I thought that if you changed the hair around, then you could easily have had Jenny and Jane instead.

"We were twenty-one there, I think," she said. "So about your age right? Adam and Ally had finished at Uni, and we had all announced then that we were getting married."

Suddenly it clicked. I guess it had taken a while.

"Adam's my dad isn't he?" I said.

Even though she said nothing, the expression in her jewel-like eyes was all the confirmation I needed.

"Bloody hell," I sighed, feeling light-headed and slightly sick. "That's why James and I are so alike. In those days you were all having it away with each other." I stared at her. "So, James and Jane..." I said, my brain racing and pounding in my skull, "...they're my half brother and sister."

I stood up, paced the bedroom and walked to the window. The street looked so ordinary, but who knew what was going on behind the Christmas decorations and twitching net curtains?

"Davy brought you up, Jason. As far as you're concerned he is – was – your Dad."

"Eve, just... just..." Then I turned and looked at her. "Fuck it!" I shouted.

I had to get away from there. As far away as possible, as quickly as possible.

I stormed into James' room. Got dressed and left the house, with Eve on the bed surrounded by all her old photographs. I went back home and with barely a word to my Mum – or Adam who I couldn't even look at – I grabbed my things and left, vowing to all that burned in Fucking Hell that I would never, *never* go back.

5.22

When I returned to Manchester I knuckled down and cracked on with things for that final half-year. Never did get a female housemate, never did get another housemate full stop and I've no idea what happened to Kev when college finished. No idea where he is now.

For four or five months I shut myself off from the old life, and every time thoughts and memories surfaced of James, Jane, or Jenny, my Mum, Dad (either of them) or even Gareth Evans, I pulled them down and shut them away in a big old box deep inside my head. Locked it and pushed it away, hid it in a very dark place.

Me and James ... *half-brothers*? After all this time?

I didn't know how to deal with it. Did he? Did James know?

The only one who refused to go in the box was Eve Gordon. I couldn't stop her haunting me at night. Her face, her alien eyes, her big white smile. It was like she had a hold over me that I couldn't fight, didn't want to fight. It got to the stage where I was jerking off to her. Used to imagine her scarred legs astride my cock while I tugged it and squeezed my balls. I imagined her bending right over me, holding my face with both her hands, lips pressing onto mine. My cock was so deep inside her we were truly locked together, and while she breathed heavily into my face her dark hair would spill around me and then she'd arch upwards in orgasm, eyes closed, mouth wide open, pushing down on my chest with her hands while squeezing my cock inside her, squeezing her thighs together and dragging her fingernails down my belly. Then I'd look up at her small breasts pressed together between her arms and I would come so hard I'd almost pass out.

Jesus...

I never returned any phonecalls from Mum, not even when she begged me to ring her back on the answering machine. She left messages, and it was only through those that I kept up to speed with what was going on in Llangefni. She got into the habit of talking to the answering machine like she knew I'd be sat next to it, listening. She'd spin out the entire tape and when she was done I'd delete it.

"I love you so much," she'd say. And my only thought in return was that it was too late for her to say that now because I didn't want anything to do with her.

When the exams were done and college was finished, Kev moved out and for a week or two I was alone in Manchester.

The only thing I remember about that time was when I sat on the floor, silently crying my eyes out as I listened to one final message from my mum playing out over the answering machine.

"Pick up the phone, Jason," Mum sobbed. "Please...?"

She had just told me how Eve Gordon had taken a bus to the Iron Forest in Powys, climbed a small mountain with a cliff-face, and jumped off it.

"She was still my friend..." Mum cried. "Davy, and now Eve... I know what they did but… Jason, please talk to me… I can't bear it, I know you're there…"

I couldn't do it.

I sat waiting for Mum to put the phone down, fists in my hair, sobbing quietly, shaking from head to toe.

Later, I imagined how Eve Gordon's suicide must have looked to anyone watching it, and in that way I was able to deal with what she'd done because it made perfect sense. And instead of grieving for her, I celebrated her.

I painted her suicide over and over again. It was one of the first things I did at the LCA, an Expressionistic portrayal of desperation and tragedy, a lone woman filled with the spirit of the world re-joining it. I wanted to show that by diving into the landscape, Eve Gordon had somehow found her way back into the Earth.

It was a powerful image that characterised most of my art for the first year at the LCA. The tutors told me that while it was competent enough, it was massively derivative. I wasn't Edvard Munch, they told me, and his famous work *The Scream* was so well-known that anything remotely resembling it would be considered immature. They challenged me to look at things from other perspectives and to explore 'my inner darkness' in a different way. They wanted me to look at how art captures moments, ideas, points of departure and transition, offering up new meanings and ways of seeing. So I did all that, and eventually I 'got it'. Only then I went too far and they tried to haul me back. Talk about contradictions.

I had a hard time of it that first year at the London College. It was a big move for me and it was completely different to Manchester. In addition I was angry and moody and I had no friends. I argued with the tutors and if it hadn't been for Theo Collins then I'd probably have jacked it in before the first year was over. I'd decided that I didn't need college and I should have gone it alone after Manchester. Who were these fucking idiots to tell me that my art was derivative?

5.23

"Theo…" I croaked, in a voice almost too painful to use. "It is you isn't it?"

There was no response.

I was back under the blindfold. Still strapped to the chair by my wrists. They hadn't bothered with the gag for a while, maybe because I'd given up shouting and raging against them. My voice was so weak it was barely a whisper. "Look. Whatever it is you want… Just tell me…"

Still nothing.

"Whatever you want, Theo…" I gasped.

Suddenly the blindfold was ripped off.

A bright light burned right into my face and I had to look away, force my head to turn in another direction where purple spots danced in the dark. Eventually it stopped hurting and through squinted eyes I was able to make out a spotlight on a tripod. There was a hood over the light, like a photographer's set up. Was he taking pictures of me?

Maybe.

An arc of D-SLR cameras on tripods faced me.

What the fuck?

I tried moving.

No good. Still tied to this *fucking chair*!!

I looked down at my wrists. They were ringed with bracelets of bruises and sores, swollen and angry under the biting plastic straps that held them tight against the arms of the chair. The catheter from the intravenous drip was still attached to my left hand but it didn't look good. The gauze holding it down was stained yellow and red.

Someone moved in front of me and I snapped my head up.

A face eclipsed the light and stared at me blankly. My heartrate increased. I could feel the muscle pounding like it wanted to burst out of my ribcage and flee.

The face was a mask, different to the previous one I'd seen, and it was absolutely terrifying. The eyes were hollow and splashed with red paint or blood. It look like the kind of mask a madman would have designed. I had to struggle to keep my breathing under control. My bowels felt loose and ready to give.

I'm not a victim… I'm not a victim… I'm not a victim…

Kept repeating it to myself like a mental mantra, getting my heartrate and my breathing back under control.

I'm not a fucking victim!

The guy wearing the mask was dressed in black. He bent down at me and cocked that terrifying face to one side. After a while he turned and walked behind the spotlight. A moment later he came back, wheeling something forward. It took me a while to realise it was a metal trolley about a metre high. A portable TV sat on top of it, while on the shelf beneath squatted the silver and black brick of an ancient VHS video recorder.

He stood next to the trolley, then reached up and pulled off the mask.

A new face grinned at me: Rugged. Bearded. Pierced at the nose, lips and eyebrows. Hair shaved very close to a pitted, tattooed scalp that glowed like a moon lit from behind by the spotlight.

"Hello, mate," Theo growled softly, his eyes looking into mine like he was searching for something.

"Fucker…" I whispered. Don't know if he heard me. "I knew it was you."

He sniffed, casually, then pulled over a folding chair. Set it down opposite me with a clatter, then he disappeared again. When he came back into the light he was holding a small, plastic cup full of water.

"Here." He handed me the cup.

My hands were tied. I indicated this with a glance down in the hope he'd cut me free.

Wasn't going to happen.

"Can't do that," he whispered, leaning forward with the cup. "But let me help you. There you go… Careful."

The water burned like acid. I coughed, choked and spat most of it out.

"Weird," said Theo as I hacked and dribbled down my front. "I've been looking after you as well."

"Looking after me?" I gasped

"Maybe it's psychosomatic."

"Let me go, Theo," I croaked.

He snapped into the real world and shook his head. "What? No. But it's nearly over for you. Not long now."

Calmly he placed the water on the floor next to the chair, wiped his mouth with the back of his hand and then stood up. He began checking the cameras, one by one.

I was dripping with sweat, tense with fear. The gas smell was still drifting around and it was freezing cold.

"Where's Liselle?" I asked him.

"Liselle? Why would you ask about her when you're the one in trouble?"

"Why d'you think?"

"You're worried about her?"

"Yes."

"Interesting."

"Interesting?"

"Interesting yes. Why are you so concerned – Oh… Oh shit. Yeah.

You was in love and all that. Sorry, mate. I forgot. Shame... I'm sorry," he said, pausing in his camera work. "Honestly I am. I didn't think my friend was going to be so brutal with her. But if it's any consolation–"

He seemed to freeze.

I stared at him. "*What?*"

He turned away from the cameras, walked towards me. Stopped and looked up. I realised he was looking at something or someone behind me. Above my head.

"You remember the model at Lambeth right?" he said, suddenly energetically. "Her name was Beth; *Bethany*. You know – the one *you* tied into a chair and put in front of all that shit in the gallery? Few years ago now so you'd think people would have forgotten but no, not her brother. He's been pissed off at you ever since the day she screamed."

He rubbed his nostrils with a finger, thoughtfully, then turned and pointed at me.

"Luckily for you though, I sorted him out."

"Sorted him out?"

"Yeah, mate. He's been stalking you, writing shit about you on the internet. Poor fucker's got a shrine to you in his flat. You should see it, it's genuinely impressive." He tapped the side of his head. "Between you and me I think the guy was OCD. Scary. But anyway, he'd pinned up all these reviews of your art, cut out pictures from arty magazines and exhibition flyers, interviews you've done, pictures of you ad infinitum. He knows you, mate – at least he thinks he does. Because here's the interesting thing: He knows the media construction of Jason Jones, not the man himself. Interesting that ain't it? All the stuff you put online, all the stuff you write in your blogs, all your online subscriptions, all your likes and dislikes; all this accumulated data and it all constructs a new persona, an alternative Jason Jones that tracks the real you in real time. A virtual doppelganger," he whispered, "that does the stuff you do except it ain't you. It's a shadow that creeps along the timeline of your life growing in strength and body the more shit you feed it until, as far as anyone is concerned, it becomes more real to people than you are right here and now. And *that's* the guy this idiot was so obsessed with."

He sniffed again and returned to his cameras, talking as he did so.

"Problem was that he had no balls. He couldn't find it in himself to confront the real you, the Actual You. I mean he wanted to. He planned how he was going to kill you night after night, day after day. But when it came to it he couldn't do it. For one thing he's not a very strong guy. He started taking Karate lessons and I told him he had to go to the gym and start bulking himself up a bit. He did, but he couldn't keep it going, no stamina. I thought he lacked commitment, motivation. Either way he just wasn't driven enough. So the guy fucked around with you for a while, throwing carrier bags full of shit over your garden wall, writing stuff on your fence, even dressing up like you at one point – like I said, a bit OCD. He camped out in that church so he could smoke pot and dream about killing you while you slept. But it was all a fantasy. He would never actually do it. Until, one day, his sister died."

The floor seemed to vanish beneath me.

"She disappeared for a week," he explained, twisting the focussing ring on one of his cameras. "And the next time anyone saw her she was hanging from a lamppost on Blackfriars Bridge. Naked except for the costume jewels stitched in her skin and the mask on her face. Gruesome, sick to look at but in a way … kinda beautiful," he breathed. "A bit sexy."

"No…"

"That was her, JJ. The girl *you* destroyed at the gallery in Lambeth. Bethany-Jane Swann. Bet you didn't even know right? Bet you didn't remember her name until you overheard us talking the other day." He shrugged. "What the fuck, why would you? I never remember their names. Pay them a fee and send them on their way, just like you should have done with wossername."

Liselle.

"Anyway. I told him you'd done it and finally he was driven to do something. He was like 'galvanised' into action." He did the thing with the fingers. "It was like he woke up and smelled your blood. So off he went, determined this time he was gonna do you. He had a knife and everything but he still fucked it up. He failed."

"I beat him up," I said.

"Yup. You kicked the living daylights out of him," Theo laughed. "You're a hard fighter, mate. You fight to the death, I know that. But he didn't. Why would he? To him all artists are gay and in his world gay equals soft. Except your gay friend, he wasn't soft either was he? He was a nutcase like you."

"Stephen?"

"That's the name! See? Just like you I forget the names. Stephen Craine that was it."

"You killed him?"

Nothing.

"Theo!"

He turned away from his cameras and walked right up to me. Bent low with his hands on the arms of the chair. Then he whispered, "No. I didn't kill him."

"I don't believe you."

"I don't give a fuck what you believe."

"You don't like gays."

"Says who?"

"I know you."

"No. You don't. Like you I have my own virtual doppelganger, my very own cybertwin: a fascist who thinks deformed babies should be put into a vat of acid at birth. He shares my name, but he ain't me."

"You're insane."

"I am what I am, JJ. But what about you?"

"What about me? I don't hide from anybody."

"Oh… really?" He put his hands on mine and gripped my fingers. Looked right at me, and in a sincere, earnest voice, he said, "Well, you and I both know that ain't true don't we?"

"Do we?"

He looked like he was struggling with something.

"No more games," I croaked. "Just tell me what's killing you, Theo."

"Killing me?" he snapped, then there was a moment where his ruined eyes flickered across my face, trying to read me, I thought. "You wanna know… All right… I'll tell you exactly what's *killing me*. In my head there are … things. Really scary, dark *things*. They're made of sound, and the sound is made of screams. The things have body but it's difficult to make them out because all I can see are the shadows they make when they move. Not a graceful movement, though it ought to be. They're thrashing like prehistoric sharks in a primordial sea. I know they're there because they affect everything, disturb every current of thought and action that flows around them. Worse, they poison my thoughts, colour it in with their own horrors. Twisted, dangerous animals; that's what's in my head. That's what's killing me. Thoughts bubbling like hot poison, raw fucking evil and I cannot – *cannot*! – get them out of my *fucking head*!"

So this was him was it? Constructed personality my arse. The guy was crazy. "I don't…"

"Don't tell me you don't remember!" he hissed suddenly. His face was in mine and he was breathing hard through his nose, barely containing himself. "Because you put them there, Jason! *You!* Understand?"

"No. I don't understand," I hissed, my throat raw and burning. I was eyeballing him. "So tell me."

He leaned in so that his face was close to mine now. Reminded me of the night he came to my room years ago, right after his dad had died.

"Remember, Jason," he said, "just… remember that day and tell me how it looked to you because I can't … I can't live with it!"

"That day? What day? I don't know what –"

"The day that changed me, Jason. The single day that filled my head with these demons that I *can't tear out*." His big hand suddenly shot out and his giant, dirty fingers grabbed me by the chin. Eyes blazing, he spat one single word right at me:

"*Balloch!*"

My heart skipped rapidly through a lifetime of missed beats.

"Let go of me," I croaked.

He did.

"And get me out of this chair."

"Can't do that," he said.

"You want the truth?"

He stood up and took a couple of paces backwards, still looking at me.

"*Halle-fucking-lujah!*" he breathed. Then: "Yes. That's exactly what I want. But you're staying in the chair until you finish."

All right. If that's how he wanted to play it. "Just one question first," I said to him. "Then I'll tell you."

His eyes narrowed.

I said, "Do you think you're the only one carrying these things in your head?"

"You see them too?"

"They've always been with me, Theo. Even before that day."

"And that's the truth?"

I nodded.

"And what we saw," he whispered. "What we did. It was real? Not a fantasy of death like this poor idiot behind you."

Behind me?

I struggled to turn but strapped into the chair I couldn't do it.

"Let me show you." Theo lunged forward, grinning. "I was gonna save this till after but there's no harm you seeing it now I suppose." He grabbed the chair by its arms and heaved it round, careful not to knock over the stand that held the IV drip next to me.

Then, suddenly, I was facing it.

"Oh…!"

Fully illuminated by the photographer's light now behind me, nailed to the wall and stretched out like Christ on the cross, was a guy with a gaping hole in his stomach. His innards splayed out from it like a starburst.

"It's brother Sean," whispered Theo in my ear. Then I sensed him stepping right away. "Like I said to you, he didn't have the stomach for it."

I stared at the corpse before me as the room or the crypt or whatever the hell it was exploded with multiple light-gun flashes and the thunderous roar of shutter clicks from the cameras behind me.

When it was done, Theo switched off the big light and the room went completely dark. But the after-image of the corpse was seared indelibly onto the backs of my eyelids.

"You won't forget this one right?" Theo said from the darkness. "So now it's your turn, JJ. You tell me the truth. Tell me in your own words what happened at Balloch. Come on," he said, and I heard him pulling his chair round and sitting on it. "Cos me and Sean are all ears."

J?

"So you're James, right?"

"No. I'm Jason."

"You're *Jason?*"

"Right. And this is my sister Jenny."

"I see. And you're ... *Jane*. This is going to be trouble. I'm never going to remember all your names. You'll have to have badges."

"Our names are easy. They all begin with a J."

"No. That makes it harder. Three of you at least. Well, never mind. Wasn't there supposed to be four of you? I've got four in my book. Who's missing? James. Where's James?"

"James? There isn't a James."

"But I have his name in my book."

"Sorry. That's our little joke. There isn't a James. We just make him up when we need someone else to balance things out."

"You really are going to be trouble you three. Well, never mind. Better collect your kit. Have any of you done rock-climbing before?"

6

Primitivism

Was it Albert Camus who said that murderers were only rarely found among artists? Whether that's true or not I'll tell you now that in my experience most artists are deceitful, lying bastards who possess an incredible talent for nothing but utter destruction. If they don't then frankly I'm not interested.

Laying the Foundations of Gallery21
Brian Cavendish.
Movers and Shakers of the Art World. Chicago 1999.

6.1

The colossal mansion, a few miles northwest of the Scottish town of Balloch was like something from a nightmare.
Later, it became exactly that.

The day Theo and I first saw it, it was raining hard. We'd been driving ahead of a terrific storm sweeping eastwards across Scotland, and when we got to Balloch we were right in the thick of it.
At about the same latitude as Moscow the town was a tourist trap, although in this weather I couldn't see much to write home about. I think the main reason it was so popular was because it was right on the southern tip of Loch Lomond and the cruise boats all left from here. Anyhow we drove through it, then out over the swollen River Leven, and on into the Scottish National Park where it was wild and raw.
I had the map and Theo was driving. Neither of us had spoken during the last hour and the mood was grim and fearful. I think we both knew that whatever happened today our lives were going to change. We pressed on, crossing unsafe bridges over frothing waterways and through near-flooded lanes lined with scrawny, windswept trees, any one of which threatened to blow over and crush the car.
"There," said Theo, nodding ahead at the dark monstrosity that stood out on the low hills ahead of us.
A few minutes later we drove past signs warning us that we were trespassing onto private property and that our approach was being watched on CCTV.
As we progressed up the long driveway the house grew larger. A great, black castle of centuries-old stone.

6.2

Antonio Pollaiuolo's gigantic altarpiece, *The Martyrdom of St Sebastian,* hung pride of place in the Renaissance section of the National Gallery. Theo, drunk already, had started waxing lyrical about the gay subtext of the painting. "…. I wonder how many priests and bishops had to wipe their cum off that paint over the years."

Later, I sat on the South Bank of the Thames next to Theo. Smoking a cigarette while Nugent Fry chucked into the River.
"JJ," Theo said, his voice a croak.
"What?"
"You OK?"
I shrugged.
"Still thinking about that letter from your mum?"
I nodded. It had arrived this morning.
"Don't worry," he said. "I'll take you up there tomorrow. OK?"

I can play this out in my head over and over and nothing changes.
We meet in the gallery.
We get thrown out.
We walk down to Embankment as selected on the London A-Z and we all get blind drunk.
Later on, Nugent is sick and Theo starts talking about having wanted to kill his dad most of his life…

… "Used to kick seven tons of shit out of me twice daily."
"And you're a better man for it eh?"
"No, mate. I hated it. He made me want to kill him. I used to lie awake on a night, my face hot and bruised, and so wet with tears … I used to dream up different ways of killing him, all the detail – what I would do, what I would say. One day was all I would need with him, J, just one fucking day. I would take him apart, bit by bit by bit. I'd tie him down in a chair and bleed him slowly, and somehow I would break him."
"Shit. That's grim."
"Pipe dreams. Fact is I'm frightened of the old cunt. He could look at me and I'd literally piss in my pants I was so scared."
"Sorry, man."
"Cars…The great escape. Except they're not. Know why?"
"Na."

"Because *he* makes the cars."

"Your dad?"

"Yup. He's in there, in the metal, in the petrol as it burns through the engine, in the smell of the seats and the oil and the paint and the rubber. He's in every component, every single piece of that car and every car, and no matter what I think I'd like to do to him, he'd always be in the car, laughing at me, calling me a useless piece of shit."

"Does this mean you won't drive me to Anglesey, mate?"

"It's fine, JJ. I'll take you up to Anglesey. Don't worry about it."

The next day, we drove up to Anglesey

He should have said 'no', but every time I remember this thing and these words that were said, it's always the same. It only ever plays out one way and it always ends with Theo saying:

"It's fine, JJ. I'll take you up to Anglesey. Don't worry about it."

He should have said 'no'. I wish he'd said 'no'…

6.3

"Jesus, it's fucking miles away!" Theo cursed as we headed across the north coast of Wales, still a good two hours away from my old life.

I didn't say anything. I was too busy going through what Mum had told me in her letter. I had it with me, alongside copies of the official documents explaining how and why Jenny had been sectioned.

"I'm not complaining," he said. "It's just that I didn't realise it was so far away."

"You didn't have to do this," I told him. "I could've got the train."

"Sure," he said. "But we're mates right. Best buddies, brothers in arms and all that? This is what mates do, Jason, so get used to it. You and me? Mates for life." He was grinning widely and I couldn't help smiling myself. He was good company and I appreciated what he was doing. And the fact was I wanted him with me. I'd maneuvered him into this because I didn't want to do this thing on my own.

He leaned forward suddenly. "Music!" he demanded, and switched on the cassette player.

The sounds of Moby's album *Play* flowed through the car and instantly I was back in that smoky underground club in Manchester. I saw Gareth Evans and Jane Gordon swaying on the dance floor, UV light playing over their shadowed forms.

The first few tracks played to the gloomy clouds gathering ahead of us, and I listened almost reverently as the tarmac of the A55 was swallowed beneath the wheels of Theo's Peugeot. By the time track four crackled out of the speakers I was in a world of my own...

6.4

The hospital was in Holyhead, way beyond Llangefni. We parked up and got out of the car. Theo stretched his arms and legs theatrically, muttered something again about it being a long drive he'd never do again mates-or-not, and then looked me straight in the eye.

"You OK with this?" he asked me.

I was lighting up another cigarette. I'd smoked loads in the car and felt like I needed one more before I went inside.

"No," I told him, trying to laugh.

"Thought so," he said. "I'll come in with you."

I nodded, then puffed smoke and crushed the cigarette under my shoe. "I'll be fine," I said. "And I appreciate it."

I clapped him on the shoulders, smiled, and walked into the hospital. It took me a while to find Jenny, even though I had instructions of where to go in Mum's letter and all the documentation, but eventually I got there.

"What have you done?" I said, running to where Jenny sat on a chair next to a bed. She stood, we hugged, and then I pulled back and looked at her face. It was gaunt and bruised. Her right eye was swollen up and her lip was cut. I noticed that there were stitched cuts criss-crossing both her arms.

"I've been a bad girl," she said, smiling as she hugged me again, her lips under my right ear. "I went for those two bitches downstairs and apparently that makes me crazy."

"Jenny," I began.

"*She's in the TV, JJ,*" she hissed, now digging her fingers into my shoulder-blades. "Back at my house! Go find her!"

Someone shouted my name behind me. "Jason?"

When I turned I saw mum and Adam walking into the room.

Jenny was gripping my arms hard. "They don't know," she whispered emphatically, her face in my hair. "They think I'm crazy but it's true. I've *seen* her."

"Jenny, you're scaring me," I whispered.

Mum and Adam were closer. A nurse was with them.

"You've got to rescue her," Jenny said urgently.

"Who?"

"Jane," she squeaked, her eyes filling with tears. "You've got to help her, JJ. He's put her inside the TV."

I was too scared to listen to this, too shocked to understand what she was saying.

Mum put her hand on my shoulder and made me jump. I turned. "Glad you made it," she said, her face full of tears and I knew she wanted to hug me.

"Jason!" Jenny shrieked, not letting me go.

At once the nurse with mum rushed forward and tried to extricate Jenny's hand from mine, calling loudly for assistance. Her fingernails dug into my skin and it hurt.

Jenny's eyes locked with mine and she didn't seem to care now who heard her. "She's in the television, JJ! She's inside the screen I saw her!"

Another nurse appeared, and between the two of them they released Jenny's hold on me. I fell backwards, right into Adam.

Jenny screamed.

They tried to sedate her but she wasn't having it. She kicked, screamed, punched and clawed at the nurses.

"Jenny!" I cried, terrified by what was going on, unable to believe that any of this was real.

I tried to step forward to help her but Adam grabbed me from behind and held me back. "Let me go, you shit!" I yelled.

"Jason, leave her," he said.

Mum was watching quietly, her face white and blank and streaked with running tears.

I threw Adam off and leapt at the nurses holding Jenny down on the bed. Jenny grabbed me with both arms around my neck and I tried to lift her up to take her away from it all, but then someone pulled her away from me, dragged her across the bed and someone else grabbed me from behind. I turned and saw Theo.

"Hey…" he said, his eyes wide and blue, comforting.

"I can't leave her here," I sobbed.

Jenny stared at me and yelled out, "She's in there, JJ. Back at my house. Get her out before it's too late."

Both my mum and Adam stepped back as three male nurses appeared and pushed us all out of Jenny's room. Casting a glance at Mum I saw that she was shaking. All those phonecalls she'd made when

I was at Manchester, all the times I'd sat on the floor listening to her voice as she spoke into my answering machine, it all burst in a flood of emotion and right then what I wanted to do was hold her and say I was sorry and have her tell me it would all be OK.

Too late. Mum flung herself into Adam's arms and started sobbing. Neither of them looked at me.

"Come on, mate," whispered Theo, steering me away. "Let's get some air."

A moment outside in the hospital car park where I fumed, smoked another cigarette, and then made a decision. "We need to go to her house," I told Theo.

He nodded. "Okay."

6.5

"Anyone in?" I asked, knocking on the front door of Jenny's house again.

"Can't see anyone…" Theo was peering in through the windows, hands cupped against the glass, eyes between them.

"Let's go round the back."

I had to clamber over a high, wooden gate to get to the back of the house and I cut my hands from doing it. However, once over I opened the gate for Theo and then the two of us walked round to the back garden.

"Wow…" whispered Theo. "Look at all this shit."

It was getting late and the sun was sinking, turning the sky pink. Ethereal shafts of orange and green speared the trees crowding the rain-soaked, overgrown garden. It was thick with nettles, brambles, tangles of ivy and all kinds of wildflowers. In-between the growth were these statues of angels and fairies. Some were damaged, some had fallen over and succumbed to the creeping wildlife, and some were upright, posed, peeking through the grass.

"Creepy," muttered Theo.

Extending from the back of the house was an ancient conservatory. The glass was old and dirty and the frame was wood rather than UPVC, so it was easy to force the door – even if it took half the frame with it and rattled the whole structure.

We walked in, me first, through the hot greenhouse and then through a pair of French doors into a stuffy lounge. Where the light seeped into the lounge it illuminated floating motes of dust that stilled the air. There was a dark grey, three-seat sofa in the room, a couple of armchairs, a bookshelf and a TV in a cabinet

"Hot in here," said Theo.

I looked at the TV, my mouth dry. Whatever had thrown Jenny screaming off the edge of the world of reason, it wouldn't be down here. I remembered the letters I'd seen in her room the last time I was here.

"Let's go upstairs," I said to Theo.

We exited the lounge, walked down the hall and turned onto the old wooden staircase next to the payphone.

A dark-haired girl sat in the gloom half-way up the stairs.

"Jesus!" Theo put a hand to his heart. "Scared the fucking life out of me!"

The girl was staring into space, not looking at anything around her. Seemed to take a while before she saw me, creeping up towards her gently, my hand outstretched.

She gasped and shuffled up a step, drawing her legs up into her arms.

"Carla?" I whispered.

She shook her head and I had to remember what the other girl was called.

"Emmeline…"

She cocked her head to one side in a feral kind of way. "Who are you?" she whispered.

The girl was traumatised, like something had snapped inside her. So even though my nerves were jangling I tried to play it steady and gentle.

"My name is Jason," I said. "I'm … Jenny's brother. I've come to pick up some of her things and take them to her. Can I do that?"

"Jenny?" she said. "Bitch! Is she in jail?"

"No," I answered. "She's in hospital."

"She should be killed for what she did to Carla."

"What did she do?"

"They had a fight. Jenny won. I didn't realise people could hurt each other so much."

"Are you OK?" I knelt on the step in front of her, then reached out to brush her hair away from her eyes.

She recoiled and shuffled away from me.

"Get off me!" she cried. Then, "Just get your sister's things and go. Don't come back."

6.6

Jenny's room was a mess. Worse than before. Most of the wallpaper had been torn off and strips of it littered the floor. The new blank spaces on the plaster had been drawn on, scribbled over. Cartoon faces with 'x's for eyes and giant monsters shared wall-space with Jenny's random writings. I didn't bother reading them. Didn't want to, but Theo seemed fascinated by it. He lingered, taking it all in, muttering to himself.

Jenny had pulled the mattress off her bed at some point and leaned it up against one of the walls. It looked like she might have been living under that. Most of her clothes seemed to be in there, and there were cups and dinner plates nearby. The black and white TV was parked in front of her mattress shelter, wired up to a VHS recorder. A bunch of videotapes were stacked up around it, no more than four high and a couple of the stacks had fallen over. There was a tape in the machine, its spine sticking out from the loading slot.

I hunkered down and picked up some of the tapes while Theo looked around the room, taking it all in.

The videos were horror movies. Ones I'd never heard of with crazy B-movie titles and lurid covers.

I took the tape out of the machine and looked it over, wondering what Jenny had last been watching. This one was different. It was a BASF Gold 180-minute tape with a sticker on the spine saying simply: *Balloch 22/7*

Theo came over. "What's this?" he asked.

I showed it to him.

"What's Balloch?" He sat down on the floor, next to me.

"Balloch is a place," I told Theo, remembering Jane's letter. "A big house up in Scotland belonging to an old housemate of mine who ran off to live there halfway through his final year. Jane went with him."

He nodded. "Sounds complicated," he said.

"Jenny said Jane was in the TV," I told him. "This would be the tape she watched last."

There were other tapes in padded Jiffy bags nearby. They had my Manchester address on, crossed out and replaced with this one which I'd left the landlord as a forwarding address meaning to change it once I got myself sorted in London. I'd forgotten to update him though, so Jenny had been receiving all this stuff which was meant for me.

So what was it?

I hit 'Play' and the picture came right in.

On the TV was a room. Sunshine filled it. The camera was high up in a corner of the room and it overlooked a large bed.

There was a shape on a bed.

Turned out to be Jane.

She was naked, bruised and she wasn't moving.

The camera zoomed into her face. Her left eye looked up at the ceiling. The right eye was missing, replaced by a bloodied, scarred mess.

I hit 'stop' and stood up. Walked away with a hand over my mouth.

"What's up?" asked Theo.

I leant against the wall trying not to be sick.

"Hey," he said. "JJ. I don't get it."

It wasn't real, was it? They were making a film. Jane's eye was just make-up.

I took a breath, gathered myself together. Called myself an idiot.

No wonder Jenny had reacted. I mean it was easy to misinterpret things right?

"Sorry," I said, and walked back to the TV.

Theo pressed play again, and after a few more seconds Dougie's terrified face filled the screen like an audition reel for *The Blair Witch Project*. I'd forgotten about Dougie, forgotten that he'd disappeared the same time as Gareth and Jane.

"Jason," said Dougie, hunched in a dark room, his voice barely a whisper. "Jason, you have to come up here. He's crazy and if this doesn't stop he's going to kill her. The stuff on this tape… It's real, man. *It's fucking real.*"

6.7

Back on the chair. In the crypt.

Theo had pulled his chair round and put it down between me and the corpse outstretched on the wall. He sat on it back-to-front and crossed his arms over the back of it.

"That wasn't all of it though was it?" he whispered, his chin down in his elbows.

"No," I answered.

"And it *was* real," he said, matter-of-factly. "It wasn't make-up, it wasn't an act. He'd actually cut her eye out."

That wasn't all he'd done. Gareth hadn't started with Jane's eye and he hadn't stopped with it either. The tape had showed much more than Jane just lying docile and half-blinded on a bed.

I felt sick all over again. I'd always tried to hide those memories far away and for the most part it had worked. Theo obviously couldn't, so the events that had played out in Balloch all those years ago had been eating at him ever since.

"Gareth didn't want acting," I whispered. "He only wanted to film what was real."

Theo nodded.

"And what we did when we found him," he said. "That was real too."

"Yeah," I nodded.

6.8

The storm was in full swing when we got to the house and it was difficult to see much beyond the thrashing wiper blades of the car and its puny headlamps.

Theo was struggling. His face was pressed almost against the windscreen, touching the wheel with his chin as he slowly steered down the long drive to the house.

Suddenly he swung the wheel hard. There was a horrible crack and the car jolted. "Shit!" he cursed.

Lightning flashed, illuminating the silhouette of the great baronial pile. I saw towers rising from steeply-pitched, heavy-looking rooftops. Thinking back on it they were probably just chimneys but at the time they looked like towers to me: giant, black fingers of stone reaching up to the mass of cloud. Felt like I was in a horror movie.

"What did we hit?" I asked.

I opened my door and stepped out into the deluge, soaked instantly.

Thunder split the sky. Sounded like a rock the size of a mountain was being rent open.

"Fuck me," I hissed, walking round to the front of the car.

There was a motorbike parked close by. Theo had swung the wheel to avoid hitting it and had driven straight into a decorative stone wall as high as my waist. The wall stretched across the front of the house, broken by a set of steps that led up to the front door. I bent down and picked up a stone gargoyle or dragon that had been knocked off its perch by the impact. I inspected it in the car's broken headlamp, turning over the stone in my hands.

Theo got out and sprinted round to the front of the car, holding the tails of his jacket over his head only to expose the back of his shirt to the rain.

"Come on," he said. "Don't fuck about."

I put the gargoyle back on its perch and joined Theo as he ran up the steps to the doorway. Looking up, it seemed to me as though the whole house was moving through the rain, like something alive, as though the stone it was built from was full of enormous power. It was so black, so dark. It seemed to be screaming.

And in my head I saw Jane. Somewhere inside it.

Come on, said the rain, energising me. *She's in there. He is in there! Do what you came here to do!*

I didn't know what to do at the door. Ring the bell? Smash it down? The latter wasn't an option. The door was solid and huge.

There was a crash of glass from my left. I stepped back from the porch and saw Theo smashing out glass from a tall window to one side of the door.

"What the hell are you doing?" I shouted at him.

"You don't think he'll just come to the door do you?" he said, knocking jagged edges out of the frame, covering his hands with his jacket.

"It's alarmed!"

He looked around and I pointed at an alarm box flashing up above. Fucking idiot.

"It's broken," he said. "Look I know these alarms. When they flash like that it means there's a fault."

"So someone's on their way to fix it," I shouted.

He looked at me and grinned. "In this weather? Come on."

He climbed in through the window and I followed him inside, soaked through to the skin.

6.9

We were in a large room. No surprises there since I expected the rooms to be huge. But the scale was immense; you could have put the house I grew up in inside this room. The ceiling was high up and dark, and the walls stretched away into the darkness like blank canvases. Furniture was covered in pale sheets.

Behind us the storm blew through the broken window.

It was freezing in here, and my boots clomped loudly on the wooden floor.

I found a door at the far end and opened it.

Theo joined me and we stepped into a wide reception hall.

I remember the layout vividly; the architecture mapped onto my nightmares for years afterwards.

There was a grand staircase which flowed down to the hall, its wide, curved steps spilling over the flagstones. We were facing the steep side of the staircase, the wooden balustrade curving up and away towards a giant stained-glass rose window high up where the staircase split left and right. Down here at the bottom the front door was to my right. To my left the area became a corridor as it disappeared underneath the staircase and into the house. The walls were panelled with dark wood.

"Gareth!" I called out, my voice echoing. "*Gareth*!"

Theo nudged me and told me to shush. I didn't. I wanted Gareth to face me, and then I would kill him.

"Hey!" said Theo, and he pointed down the corridor from which direction a grey-blue, flickering light played across the walls.

Fighting my nerves, thinking only of what I was going to do to Gareth Evans but terrified what I might find of Jane, I followed Theo down the corridor towards the flickering light.

We came to an open door cut into the wood panelling on my left. There was a narrow set of steps leading downwards beyond it. The grey-blue light was coming from down there.

I took a step forward but Theo caught my elbow.

"What are you going to do?" he asked me.

I was shaking. "I'm going to kill him. Why?"

"Seriously, Jason!" he hissed. "Don't be stupid. Find Jane and we'll call the police."

I shrugged him off.

"That isn't what you said when you saw the tape."

He stared at me and I couldn't read him.

I turned away and walked down the stairs, deliberately building my anger, finding the rage and fuelling it by remembering what we had seen on the rest of the tape:

Jane, drugged and dopey, was dancing with Gareth, if you could call it that. It was like a man dancing with a ragdoll. Waltzing around an L-shaped ballroom lit like a nightclub to the sounds of The Prodigy's *Firestarter*. Jane was blindfolded, and when Gareth leaned her against a wall and kissed her, he took the blindfold off and I saw that both her eyes had gone.

He's crazy, Dougie had said... *and if this doesn't stop he's going to kill her!*

By the time I got to the bottom of the narrow flight of steps I was ready to murder the first person I saw with my bare hands.

However. It looked like someone had beaten me to it.

6.10

Litres of blood covered the slate flagstones in the room at the bottom of the stairs.

The body was strapped into a chair, tied up with cables.

Face slumped down, clothes soaked through with blood.

Everything was covered in blood. Everything sticking and stinking like a butcher's storeroom. The smell was meaty. Rank.

"Oh … oh shit!" Theo gagged.

I felt like my feet weren't touching the ground. My head was buzzing and not in a good way.

Grimly, I lifted the corpse's head. There wasn't much left of the face so it was difficult to recognise who it was. Took me a while to realise it was Dougie. He'd been stabbed plenty of times.

I let the head flop back down and took a look around. This must have been the room Jane had written about in her letters to Jenny, the 'hi-tech video suite' I assumed. Video cassettes littered the place and it looked like someone had gone mad in here. They'd all been smashed up. There were bits of plastic and streamers of tangled brown tape everywhere.

Banked up against one of the walls was some kind of control desk covered in sliders, buttons and dials. It looked like it had been ripped from the cockpit of a Concorde or something. Above the desk there was an array of twelve monitor screens built into the wall. Only three of them were active; two were showing images from around the house but one of them was playing back the image of a single face.

Jane.

There was a time code at the bottom of the screen, slightly warped by noise bars. There was no sound, but her cracked, bruised lips were moving.

Help me… she seemed to be saying, I was sure of it.

Her destroyed eyes held the screen and I remembered how blue they used to be. I remembered how you could lose yourself in them like dangerous waters. Her head was bald and scarred, and I remembered her platinum blonde hair. The touch of it. How soft it was and how it ran like water through my fingers. I remembered it falling around me like a cage of light.

Help me...

Gareth strode into view. He was naked, erect, and what he did next was just ... horrific.

"*Where is he?*" I roared. "Where the *fuck* is he!"

I turned and kicked the chair holding Dougie's body. It wheeled down the room, crashed into a pile of tapes, spun into the wall and tipped over; and the stupid fucking corpse fell to the floor. Still held by the cable tying him down he sort of dangled.

A knife slid free. It had been stuck somewhere in Dougie's body. It was sticky with blood and gore but I picked it up and then I turned to leave the room with it. Something else was happening on the screen. Theo was staring at it in horror.

I don't want to think about it. I don't want to see it. I can't...

I didn't realise at the time that the image of Jane was on playback. Right then I thought it was live and that I could still rescue her.

Theo was blocking my way out.

"Move!" I snapped.

He didn't resist. I shoved past him, stumbled up the stairs and ran into the house proper. I stood in the reception hall, right in the middle, turning on the spot as the dimensions of the house reeled around me dizzyingly. I lifted my head up to the ceiling and screamed his name out: "*Gareth!*"

The knife was red hot in my hand, like a burning iron. It had tasted death already and through me it would taste it again.

Upstairs, the knife was saying. *Take me upstairs. That's where he is the fucking monster!*

6.11

Theo faced me from the back of his chair. "When you ran off looking for Gareth," he said quietly, "I stayed in the room with that body. The recording of Jane's death played itself out on the TV over and over again, and each time it started up I thought it would end differently, like this time maybe he wouldn't kill her, or maybe this time she would fight back and kill him instead. But the tape always ended the same way before it rewound and began again."

He looked distraught.

"Do you remember it, JJ?" he asked, his voice thick with emotion. "You saw the rest of the tape. What did you see?"

I closed my eyes tightly. "No. I don't want to see!"

"Remember what you saw. *Face it*!"

I remembered...

Gareth took Jane's hand. The camera panned out as he pulled her to her feet. They were ... they were dancing again. This time for the last time. No sound. Just the pictures, the images caught on tape. In the pulsing UV light of the L-shaped ballroom, Gareth moved Jane gently to the side. He cupped the back of her head in one giant hand and turned her face into the wall.

First he kissed the top of her head, pulling it towards him gently, like a lover. Then he smashed her face into the wall viciously. Once. Twice. Three times. And then... and then she... she slipped down.

Dead.

She was dead.

Here in the crypt I was sick. I moved my head to the side and expelled the poison that had been buried deep down inside me for all these years. It exploded out of my mouth uncontrollably, violently, painfully. Took a long time and afterwards I was numb.

"Sorry..." I spluttered. I don't know why. My whole body was shaking. I couldn't control it no matter how many deep breaths I took.

"You OK?" Theo asked, gently.

I looked up at him.

"All right," he said. "Dumb question."

"Just get me out of this chair," I gasped, my voice thick and stupid.

"And then what?"

"What?"

"I mean 'and then what?'. What are you going to do, if I let you out of the chair?"

"What do you *think* I'm going to do? I'm not in any... any fit state for much am I?"

"Guess not," he said. "But you're a deceiver, Jason Jones. You're a dark and very violent man."

"I'm not going to do anything."

"Hmm. I don't believe you. You see, I saw you on the live monitors. I saw you running through the house, and I saw what you did when you found him."

6.12

The house wasn't deserted, not quite.

Gareth *was* in there.

But it took me a long time to find him because most of the rooms I barged into screaming his name were empty, covered in dust sheets.

Eventually I found him, only it wasn't what I was expecting.

He was in a room in a kind of tower. A door opened when I pushed it and I walked up a spiralling stone staircase, the kind you got in a castle. I think this house had been designed to resemble a castle in some ways. I had no idea how old it was, or whether or not it followed the rules of any particular style or design, but I think the castle motif had been important to whoever had built it.

At the top of the stairs there was a door which opened into a room with circular walls covered by thick, red drapes. The ceiling was crisscrossed by wooden beams and a rope dangled from one of them.

There wasn't much else in the room, just a chair in the centre with a small, round table next to it. On the table was a lamp glowing with pale, yellow light.

A naked man sat on the chair and the place smelled of human shit.

There was a sack over the man's head. It had a crude face drawn on it: a sad mouth and two 'x's for eyes, one bigger than the other.

A rope, which dangled from one of the ceiling beams, had been looped into a noose and slung around the naked man's neck.

I could feel and hear my blood pulsing, pounding in my ears as I walked forward. I don't really know what I was feeling. Rage, hideous anger, revulsion, sickness – all those things. Maybe more besides. It didn't feel real, but it was. It was happening. All this *happened*.

I walked quickly towards the figure on the chair. I remember flexing my fingers around the knife as I reached out with the other hand and grabbed the sack.

I yanked it off, tugging it up and away just as I would do with Stephen Craine years later, but here with real intent to do damage to whatever was beneath it.

I didn't need to. The face under the sackcloth had been beaten. Badly.

Bruised, swollen eyes looked at me in terror. The mouth gasped like a fish out of water, just a couple of teeth left in the bloodied maw, bits of them, sharp fragments, stuck in his lips and cheeks.

The rest of the figure was emaciated. Starved, beaten. Tortured.

Both his hands were crooked. Only three fingers remained on each hand and they were broken. His right hand still had a thumb but the left had been properly destroyed.

I stood back in horror. The blood in my head was hissing, rushing like a riptide across an ocean. I felt as though my entire brain, my whole way of looking at the world, was being rewritten by some fast-moving biological machine-code.

"Gareth…"

And just as I wondered who had done this to him, a figure stepped out of the drapes, doing up his fly.

"Jason," said a familiar voice. "I thought you'd never find us."

I glanced up and stared at the tall, rugged man in the black leather biker's trousers and black, short-sleeved shirt.

It had been years since I'd last seen him but his face was instantly recognisable.

He looks like me, a voice screamed inside me. But then he would, wouldn't he? He was my half-brother after all. We shared the same father.

"James," I said.

He smiled. "Good to see you, mate. And welcome to my brave new world."

6.13

James Gordon stepped towards me but I moved back, keeping my distance. Gareth was whimpering, gurgling like an infant on the chair between us.

"So … is that a knife in your hand or are you just pleased to see me?" James said with a toothy grin.

"What have you done?"

"What have *I* done?" He sounded genuinely surprised and I guess it was a stupid question. But the fact is my brain was doing weird shit. It was chaos inside my head, literally a burning fugue of chaos as it tried desperately, I guess, to process and reconcile what I was seeing and hearing.

"Isn't it obvious?" he said. "I'm doing exactly what you came here to do. Right? Unless you just popped up for tea and cakes. With a bloodied knife in your hands."

It was hard even breathing.

"What do you think?" he asked Gareth, pushing at the man's

shoulder playfully. "Do you think JJ's a bit dim?"

Gareth didn't respond.

James looked at me apologetically.

"He hasn't got a tongue anymore," he said, looking around. "It's … well it's on the floor somewhere. That smell? It's his tongue, his fingers…" He shrugged. "All the other bits I cut off. I forget where I put them all."

"When … when did you get here?" I asked him, croaking.

"About a week ago," he answered. "So not long, really."

And then I remembered the bike outside the house. It was his.

"I came in much the same as you did," he said. "Except I cut the alarms first. They still haven't sent anyone round." He laughed. "Useless fuckers. It wouldn't have mattered anyway," he said. "I'd have had to kill the engineer, so it was just as well they didn't."

"You killed Dougie…" I whispered.

"Yes. Yes I did. Couple of days ago now. Actually with that very knife," he said, nodding down at it. "Which, by the way, will have your fingerprints all over it. So you should take it with you when you leave."

"Leave?" I whispered.

"Unless you want to stay here," he said, "with me and this thing?"

The look of disgust on James' face was clearly visible.

"Where's Jane?" I asked.

"You know what?" James answered in a slightly strangled, almost hysterical tone. "This fucker still hasn't told me." He put a hand on Gareth's head and ruffled it through his hair almost affectionately. I heard Gareth breathing hard through his shattered nose. "Give him his dues, he's held onto that single piece of information to the last and now he'll take it to his own grave. If I give him one, that is."

James looked at me.

"To be honest," he said, "I'm not so good at this as he was. I'm not experienced in torturing people. And I made the mistake of telling him he was going to die. Funny that. Once I'd said it to him he began to take the pain. It was an extraordinary thing to witness. He took it all, as though it didn't matter anymore."

"And Dougie?" I asked. "Did you torture him as well?"

James was still stroking Gareth's hair.

"No no," he said. "I just stabbed him a few times. Well… not entirely true. I guess before that I *sort of* tortured him."

"You made him watch," I said, after a while. "Downstairs the tape is still showing Jane…"

"It's what you would have done right?" James grinned. "Yeah. I tied him to the chair in that room and I put Jane's murder on a loop so he could sit and watch it and hopefully, wracked with guilt and remorse, *he* would tell me what they'd done with her body. At first he refused to watch it so I cut his eyelids off, although it turned out that was a mistake because then he wouldn't stop bleeding and the blood covered his eyes plus the knife had sort of *slipped* so he couldn't see much of anything…" He blew out his cheeks affecting exasperation. "I'm not much of a surgeon and I cut away more than I should have. So in the end I had to kill him because his *fucking screaming* was doing my head in."

"And … what do you do now?" I asked him. "Where does all this go from here?" I was shaking and it was hard to speak.

James let Gareth's hair alone with a shove and then he faced me, arching an eyebrow. "Well," he said, "that kind of depends on you."

"Me?"

He nodded, then walked towards me. As he moved he fished around the back of his trousers with one hand like he was tucking his shirt in.

"What are you going to do with that knife?" he asked.

I looked down at the knife in my hand, then up at James.

"You wanted to kill him, right?" he asked.

I couldn't answer.

"Come on, JJ. You saw the same tapes I watched with Jenny. You saw what he did to Jane, and you heard wosissname – fuckwit downstairs pleading with you to come and save her. So you came up here. You broke into the house, you took this knife without a second thought from the dead body of someone you once drank beer and shared a house with and you went screaming through the house, calling this fucker out. I could hear you from way up here. So, what would you have done, JJ," he whispered, now close to me, "if I wasn't here? Huh?"

I didn't answer. I couldn't. I hadn't had a plan. I'd just thought…

James said, "Let's say you came barging in, angry, like really fucking angry, full of the most intense kind of rage, and you saw Gareth – not like he is now – but fit and strong like he used to be and ready to defend himself. Maybe even expecting you. What would you be doing right now?"

I looked at the crippled, emaciated figure on the chair and tried to superimpose the frame of a much bigger man on top of it.

"Would you really have killed him?" James asked. "Do you think you would really, truly have killed him? In cold blood?"

Yes, I wanted to say. *Yes I would have killed him.*

But I couldn't say it, I didn't say it. I hadn't even brought anything up here to kill him with.

James sighed, and then produced a handgun from the back of his trousers. It was an ugly-looking, black plastic thing; square, angular, but with some contours moulded into the grip.

"Maybe," he said, "Gareth would have killed you instead. He would have heard you coming and he would have known exactly why you were here. He tortured, sexually abused, mutilated and then killed your girlfriend... my ... my *sist–* "

For the first time, James' voice broke. He gathered it in, controlling his own rage.

"Bollocks!" he swore. "I told myself I wasn't gonna do this."

And then he kind of exploded.

"*He* would have been ready for you, Jason," he snapped. "You would have turned a corner and he would have shot you in the head. *Bang*! Game over just like that. Let me show you. Let's role-play this."

He turned to Gareth and undid the straps holding his right hand to the chair arm. Then, and I could hardly believe what I was seeing, he offered Gareth the gun, handle first.

"Here," he said to the figure gently. "Take this."

The man's wrecked eyes furrowed.

"Take it!" James roared.

Then he said, "For fucks sake do I have to do every fucking thing myself?"

Angrily he lifted Gareth's right hand, the one that still had the thumb, and pressed the gun into it. He curled the thumb and the fingers around the compact handle, and even put Gareth's forefinger into the trigger guard.

"This," James was saying as he worked, "is a Glock19. You know what that is?"

"It's a gun," I answered soberly. What the hell was he doing?

He laughed. "Yeah it's a fucking gun. Jesus. To be a bit more specific it's a compact semi-automatic pistol, loaded with nine-nineteen parabellums. Hollowpoints, they're called, expand when they enter a target to cause a mushroom-shaped point of impact. OK?" He paused, stepping back but keeping his eyes on Gareth, then said, "Mad to think that people are paid salaries to design and build something which has the sole purpose of ripping out a person's insides and killing them... Can you imagine the corporate execs at Glock – product managers, sales managers, marketing managers, directors etcetera etcetera – sitting around a table in a meeting room watching a PowerPoint presentation detailing the gun's USPs, the sales forecasts and potential markets using bar charts and Clip-Art? Crazy-fucking-crazy."

Gareth now had hold of the Glock in his three fingers and thumb. His face was contorted by extreme pain and his arm wobbled as he tried to keep hold of the weapon.

With a rare flash of humour, and in a mock German accent, James said, "Und here ve have ze Glock19 vich is variant of ze Glock17. As you vill see it is shorter, more compact, yet compatible viz all ze ballistics vich ze 17 uses. Ze primary markets are law enforcement, private military und crazy-assed mozzerfokkers who like to kill pretty girls." He looked over his shoulder back at me. "Not my gun, JJ," James said, back to his characteristic self. "I'd get shot if I had this. No, it's his. Fucking room full of weapons downstairs: Rifles, shotguns, pistols. He had this on him. All loaded up and ready to go. If you look around the house you'll see hundreds of bullet-holes in the walls where he'd been practising. So yeah... I think he fucking knew you were coming. He was waiting for you. And I think both you and I know that he doesn't like to kill straight away. So maybe, and here's what I think would have happened if it wasn't for me getting up here first, I think you would be the one sitting in this chair right now. You reckon?"

By now James was standing next to me. He tugged his shirt straight and stared at Gareth.

"Well, he's here now and you have your gun back," he said to Gareth, loudly like he was talking to a child. "OK? You, my friend, have control. Now all you have to do is shoot. Three bullets left in the mag. One's enough to kill me with if you get your aim right."

I stared in horror.

"Come on," whispered James dangerously. "Right at me."

Gareth's hands were so destroyed he could barely manage to hold the thing. Tears streamed from his eyes and I could only imagine what was going on inside his head as he willed strength into his broken fingers.

But he managed it. Shakily, slowly, Gareth lifted his arm to point the gun at James, who grinned.

I swallowed. Dangerous games.

They eyeballed each other and the moment seemed long and tense. I didn't dare move.

And then slowly, with pain clear on his face, Gareth nudged his arm sideways to point the gun at me.

"Interesting," James said, matter-of-factly. He turned to look at me and his expression was one I knew well enough as concealed rage and disappointment. "He must really hate you, JJ," he said tightly. "Either that or he's making a really big mistake."

"James. This isn't funny…"

There was no mistake. The gun was pointing right at me and there was a determined look in what was left of Gareth's eyes. I wanted to run.

I made to move but I felt James' hand grip my arm. "Stay!" he hissed.

Then, to Gareth he said, "Actually, before you do anything… let me tell you something about my sister first, OK? She is… *was* beautiful. You remember that right? To coin a cliché she had her whole life in front of her. But here's the thing, and Jason will back me up on this. Thing is that Jane nearly died when she was eleven. That was my fault. I set fire to the house and I didn't realise she was in it." He sort of laughed, then controlled himself and continued. "But, thankfully she survived. And anyone looking at her life story might think, if there was a God, that He only gave her that second breath of life for *you*. For *your* sake. Because *you* are the one who took it."

James was breathing hard, his brow darkening. He wiped spit away from his lips with the back of his hand.

Gareth's face was a rictus of pain and effort, and with horror I realised he'd been squeezing the trigger as hard as he could for some time and it was still pointing at me.

It wasn't going to happen. He couldn't shoot.

"Can't you do it?" James roared at him. "Come on, you weak piece of shit, you fucking piss-ant cock-sucking kiddie-fucker! Shoot him! Shoot me! Shoot one of us and get the fuck over it! You think it hurts? You think your hand hurts because you don't have enough fingers to hold a gun? At least you have a gun. I've given you a chance so fucking use it, it's more than you ever gave my sister, you shit you fucking coward you fucking weak, pissy fucking cunt. Jane would have killed *you* without a second thought if you'd given her the same chance but you never did. You controlled her. You took away *everything* that made her beautiful. Left her nothing, not even human and what I'm doing for you now is a fucking mercy because you can get over the pain in your hands you can move away from it and squeeze the trigger and fucking shoot! Come on, you wanker! Shoot! *Shoot!*"

Gareth's finger, broken thought it was, seemed to be at last coming down on the trigger. He started squealing, his mouth moving. Tears fell from his eyes and snot bubbled from his nostrils.

"James," I whispered, "let him – "

"Fuck this!"

Before I knew what was going on James moved. He whipped round and snatched the knife right out of my hand. Then he walked quickly towards Gareth, marching up the line of fire. "Three seconds before I reach you!" he shouted. "Better shoot now because if you don't I'm going to stab you in the face."

Gareth was panicking. His arm was shaking as he tried to track James with the weapon but his crooked fingers could not put enough pressure on the trigger. Baby noises issued from his throat.

"Two!" shouted James.

Gareth was gasping.

"One!"

He panicked. Pissed himself.

"Game over, fuckwit!" snapped James.

He knocked the gun out of Gareth's hand and it went skittering across the floor. Then he stabbed him once in the face. Hard. With all his strength behind it. The knife went deep into Gareth's eye releasing a jolting spurt of thick, red blood from the socket.

Gareth screamed, or maybe that it was in my head. I don't know, I didn't know anything anymore. This was just…

James yanked the knife out, releasing more blood. "She had a *name*!" James screamed.

He slammed the knife down into Gareth's stomach on the word 'name'.

"She had a *life*!"

James stabbed him again, and again, and again…

He kept on stabbing him and the blood spurted out, covering the both of them. He was quick with the knife, brutal, vicious, totally inhuman. And Gareth was suddenly nothing. Not a man, not a person, not *anything* after just a few seconds as James went at him.

I stood there and watched his life blink out, and I did nothing.

Maybe I could have grabbed James and stopped him, but I didn't. I was too stunned. Too shocked by the speed of this.

And it was because I wanted Gareth to die; I wanted that cunt dead after what he had done to Jane. No one like him had the right to take away a life that had so much more worth than his. Jane was special, she was like me, like James, like Jenny. She was elemental, a whispering strand of the universe made real on this Earth and this shit had taken her and instead of using her beauty to better himself he had used it to fuel his own depravity. And for that, for everything he had done to her, he deserved to fucking die.

He deserved it!

But to see it like this... To be in the same room...

Eventually James stepped back and wiped his mouth with the back of his arm.

He dropped the knife and then his fingers hung limp, deep red and dripping.

The knife was just as gory.

I retched. I held my stomach.

I saw a door, and I ran for it.

"Jason!" James called after me. "Come back here! *Jason!*"

6.14

The door opened out onto the roof of the house.

Apart from the wedge of light spilling from the door it was pitch black and still raining, though not as violently as before.

I staggered on, and then fell against a low wall a couple of metres from the door. I leaned over and vomited over the edge. It hurt. Every surge twisting my stomach into tighter and tighter knots.

6.15

There was silence between me and Theo in the crypt. Fact was I'd buried this down so deep it hurt to bring it all back. It was a poisoned memory.

"Get me out of here..." I sobbed.

He stared at me from the back of his own chair.

"I said get me the fuck out of here!" I roared at him. "You've played your game! And you win! All right? You fucking win!"

He ran his thumb and forefinger around his mouth in thought.

Then he said. "No."

"No?"

"Exactly that. I said no. I'm not going to 'get you the fuck out' because I saw it," he said to me. "I was watching from downstairs. On one of those tiny little TV screens. I saw what you did."

"Just get me off this chair!"

"No," he said.

I stared at him in pain and disbelief. "Why?" I cried out. "What did I do to you, Theo?"

"We'll come to that," he said quietly. "For now though, just tell me what happened next. You went to get some air?"

"James came out after me," I answered. "He wanted to know what I was going to do."

6.16

"I don't know," I whispered to James. "I don't know what I'm going to do."

He stood there like a blood-soaked demon in the rain, his posture tense, his body quivering with barely controlled energy.

"You shouldn't have come," he said angrily.

I turned my back on him and leaned again over the wall, letting the rain hammer me down. I was shivering and not just because of the cold.

"You came steaming up here in a rage but the fact is you wouldn't have done anything," James snapped. "You had no plan. You just drove up here on impulse and the fact is Gareth would have killed you."

Maybe he was right.

"So in a way," he said, coming over to stand next to me, "I saved your life."

"What the fuck are you on?" I hissed at him. "You just … *killed a man*! Two men!"

I started retching again but nothing came out.

"Don't play the saint with me, you fucker!" he barked while I struggled to keep my body under control. "Fact is you wanted to kill him just as much as I did. The only difference is that *I made it happen*. So it's me the police will be looking for, not you. You get away from this with your life intact."

I snorted. "How can you say that…?" My dad was dead, Eve was dead; Jane was dead, Jenny was sectioned and now James was … what was he exactly?

I felt his hand on my arm. He swung me round to look at him. "Hey!" he barked. "This is me. All right? Your fucking guardian angel."

"Shut up."

"Take control, JJ," he hissed. "For once in your life, take control."

I shrugged him off and backed away.

"I was told you were in the Gulf," I said, leaning over the wall again.

"I was," he answered. "I was stationed on a carrier the size of a small town flying sorties over the sea and into the desert when I was told to.

Protecting UN weapons inspectors and enforcing the no-fly zone. Dodging ground-to-air missiles and doing whatever I was told to. Did my nine months and came back here. To *this*," he snorted. "Should have stayed on."

He moved next to me. "There'll be another war out there," he said, and leant his elbows on the wall, looking out into the darkness. "So maybe I'll have to go back." Then he shook his head, mumbling under his breath, "George Bush is on a mission, and it won't be long before the whole thing in Iraq kicks off."

I wanted to pull my head away from what had just happened and take a breath, so I let him talk about his oncoming war.

But then he said, "I saw you with her, you know."

"What?"

"In the station house with Jenny. You were fucking her but she was calling my name."

My heart kicked.

He shrugged. "Well... maybe you did me a favour. I don't know."

The night I left Jane alone in Manchester. The night we fought, when she kicked and screamed and begged me not to go. When she told me that I'd lose her if she went, and when she told me she loved me. When she forced me to choose between her and my sister.

At the time I'd thought she was using every means of coercion possible and I'd hated her for it. She'd made me feel worthless.

But it had been the last time I'd seen her alive and now...

"You got there just ahead of me," James continued. "I walked in and you were already me: For one night only you fucked your sister pretending to be me." His voice had started to sound dangerous and I knew the signs. It meant he was liable to lash out at any moment.

I breathed out, steadying my nerves. This night wouldn't go on forever. Sooner or later the sun would come up and one way or another all this would be over.

"Did you need her that much?" he asked. "More than you needed *my* sister?"

I didn't answer.

"Just think," he said tightly, "If you'd stayed with Jane that night she'd never have gone off with Gareth and she'd never have been brought here, she wouldn't have died and you and I wouldn't be having this conversation here and now in this fucking rain. Funny how things turn out right?"

Warning bells rang in my head.

He said, "Why didn't you stop me?"

"What?"

"When I stabbed him just now. Why didn't you stop me?"

I was wondering the same myself.

"I'll tell you why," he said. "It's because we're the same, you and me. The same person divided. Difference is you sit in college painting your pictures, dreaming shit up but essentially doing fuck all. I mean sure you came up here to do some damage who wouldn't? But you didn't have a plan did you?"

"We're not the same."

"That's where you're wrong. We're two sides of the same coin. And you need me. Like tonight right? Think about it. If I wasn't here you'd be a dead man right now. At best." He paused, then said, "*I*, on the other hand, I had a plan. I fully intended to humiliate, dehumanise and then kill that sorry motherfucker whereas all you probably wanted to do was shout at him. I bet you didn't even call the police. Am I right? I hope I'm right. If I see the merest hint of a flashing blue light out there then I'm gonna throw you over this wall. You're a dreamer, Jason. A fantasist."

I rounded on him then. "You don't know me!"

"Wrong!" he retorted. "You're my brother, Jason. I know you as well as myself. We are the same like it or not," he went on. "The only difference is that I'm dead inside and you fucked your sister! When you became me, when you took that moment away from me you took my soul away. I rode down to the island with nothing but Jenny on my mind for the whole trip. The months I was stationed in the Gulf all I could think about was her and thinking about her was the only thing that kept me going, that kept me sane. I promised that when I got back I'd find her and fix the thing between us because I knew that she wanted me as much as I wanted her. It was like destiny! Nothing could stop us being together. And when I got there, what did I see? Huh? What did I *hear*? You fucking her while she called my name! You took her away from me, Jason. The same night you made a decision to abandon Jane to your depraved friend in there!"

"So this is all my fault?"

"You know it is!" he spat. "*That* is why you're here. It's guilt. Eating you up!"

I turned on James quickly and I punched him hard in the jaw with all the strength I still had.

He wasn't expecting it and in truth neither was I. He fell back and nursed his split lip.

Then he looked right at me. "You see?" he growled. "We *are* the same."

I swallowed, waiting for the retaliation. Balled my fists.

Here it came.

He rushed me but I was ready for it. I sidestepped and smashed him between the shoulders as he went past. He fell, his face hitting the wall, and for a moment I thought it was all over.

No chance.

He moved quickly, getting to his feet.

"That's all you get," he said, and then he spun round and launched himself at me, raining controlled blows from left and right, knocking me back into the wall of the tower. My vision went. My balance went. And suddenly I was doubling over, spitting blood.

I felt him grab hold of my hair and lift up my head. He must have had a bunch of it in his fist.

He leaned down, his face right next to mine.

"And you know what? I always fucking hated you, JJ," he spat.

"Feeling's mutual," I breathed. And I rammed his stomach with my head, knocking him backwards.

My turn now and I didn't care if he was combat-trained or whatever. We were two bony boys in the playground again, fighting to win. Punching each other hard and fast. Scrapping. Using elbows as well as fists, aiming for the places where we would cause real damage, real pain. No fucking around.

He elbowed me in the chest, turned and kicked me with the heel of his boot. I hit the wall with my back and felt something crack.

"You better finish this…" I gasped, slipping on my feet as one hand clutched at my stomach, "because the fact is I've been planning your death since the first night you stayed with us… You remember that… right?" I gasped, wincing with pain. "The night you set fire to your house… The night you almost killed Jane so don't … don't lecture me about guilt!"

He screamed like a monster in the rain and he came right at me. Punching. Again and again and again. The world went dark. I spat and coughed blood. I struggled to breathe when he wrapped his arm tight around my throat and squeezed.

This is it, I was thinking. This is it. Now I don't have to worry about the morning. I don't have to worry about tomorrow and what happens next because now there will never be a tomorrow. Not for me.

James was enraged. He was screaming.

I felt my eyes bursting and my lungs pleading for air. Each laboured beat of my heart struck my insides like a hammerblow.

Any second now and it'll all be over. Come on *come on!*

He let me go.

I collapsed onto the wet rooftop.

He grabbed me by the neck of my T-shirt, hauled me up onto my feet and smashed my back against the parapet.

"Finish it," I gasped.

He put his face close to mine.

"No," he hissed into my face. "You don't get out of jail that easily. Not this time."

He let go and I collapsed. I rolled over and over, shivering with pain and cold. I sobbed like a child, hoping that the rain would wash me away, dissolve me into the roof of that fucking house and leave nothing behind.

Truth is he was right. If only I'd stayed with Jane that night in Manchester. That was all I kept thinking about. If I'd stayed then she'd still be alive and all our lives might still have had some worth.

I stayed there for – I don't know how long – seemed like forever. But at some point I coughed, spat, sat up and staggered to my feet. Made my way towards the wall at the edge of the roof thinking I'd throw myself off, dive into the geometry of pitched rooftops and chimneys spread out like a demonic landscape below me.

But something was wrong.

I think I could smell the smoke before I saw the fire. I scanned the building and there it was: a ribbon of bright, orange flame burning through the seams of the house way below, between the lower rooftops, blistering and blossoming through cracks in the slate.

So instead of diving off the roof, I walked back to the doorway and re-entered the room in the tower.

"Oh Christ," I gasped.

There was one more horror to face.

6.17

Gareth's corpse was now hanging from the ceiling, dangling from the noose that had been thrown around his neck. The chair he'd been strapped into had been kicked over and the rope had been hoisted up and anchored into a tie-back for one of the red drapes that encircled the room.

James was slumped against the far wall. He had the Glock in one hand and a cigarette in the other. His face looked how mine felt.

"The house is on fire," I said, and my voice sounded strange: choked and high-pitched. I didn't know how much more of this I could take.

"Doesn't matter," James muttered. He sounded calm. Sober. His eyes were staring into the middle distance.

I staggered across the room and sat down next to him. It hurt.

"You walked away," I said. "You should have finished me."

"What? So I could make this easy for you?" he sneered. "Fuck you." Then: "You should go," he said. "I'll tidy this shit up. Keep you out of it. I promise you."

Smoke was starting to creep under the interior doorway. In some way I didn't care about that. James definitely didn't. He seemed oblivious to it.

He said, "You came alone right? I mean, you'd be an idiot to drag anyone else into this mess."

I nodded, suddenly remembering Theo downstairs – if he was still there.

"Just me," I told him.

James nodded and he dangled the gun on one finger from its trigger guard. He sighed. A long breath out. Shaking. Coughing.

"He could have killed us both you know," I said.

James shook his head. "The thing about Glocks," he said, "is that they have this three-way safety feature. Each stage of the firing process is an independent mechanism that triggers the release of the next stage. The first part of it is in the trigger." He turned the gun over and over in his hands. Showed me the trigger, which was more complicated than I'd realised. Plastic petals overlapped each other within the guard. "There's a secondary lever built into the mechanism," he said, and I could see it. "When you pull it, it activates the trigger bar and moves a steel rod up from the firing pin channel inside the weapon. The third part is a drop safety that only releases after the first two mechanisms have been actioned. So it's unlikely to go off by accident. It also means you have to pull the trigger pretty hard to fire the gun. Here, you try."

"No." I shook my head. Coughed. The smoke was really coming in now, obscuring the ceiling of room with a darkening haze. I got to my feet, still coughing. "We need to go," I said.

A low, booming wind howled eerily through the house. Was it my imagination or was the floor getting hot?

"Fair enough," James said. He stood suddenly, planted the cigarette in his mouth, then he turned and aimed the gun at the dangling Gareth. Arm high and steady.

The gun went off and my ears split. At the same time, Gareth's body bucked, jolted on the end of its rope as a chunk of flesh was blasted away from the shoulder to hit the wall behind it.

James made a disappointed face, like he'd missed his target, and the swinging body slowed.

"Fact is, JJ," he said, walking towards the body. "He'd never have been able to fire this thing. Not with his broken hands. He still tried though didn't he?"

"You're sick," I gasped.

"Now you're just being judgemental," he said.

There was a noise below us like a thundercrack, like something under the floor had split. I moved to the edge of the room holding my hand over my mouth and nose. James was at the other end, standing next to his trophy, spinning it round to face him.

"James!" I urged, aware of the fire.

"Interesting though, that he pointed the gun at you," he said matter-of-factly. "Why do you suppose that might be?"

"Is that a serious question? Look, let's do the psychoanalysis later. We need to go."

He shrugged. "Just wondering what you did in the past to make him hate you so much," he said.

"I've no idea."

James nodded. "That's your problem right there," he said. "Fact is you don't see what effect you have on other people. You don't know how destructive you are. And yet you have it all, mate. You have the looks, you get the girls, people think you're fucking brilliant. But you're a dangerous man."

"You're the one who killed him," I said, starting to cough. "Not me."

Then he said, "Did I ever tell you about the Zero-sum Equation?"

"James? We *really* need to get out of here."

"I was going to call it Equation Zero but that sounded too much like a military operation. The Zero-sum Equation," he said, "is where two or more sets of numbers added together equal zero."

I just stared at him, wondering what the fuck was in his mind. He sounded ridiculously calm and rational.

"Like minus one and plus one," he said. "You get it? But the sums can be much more complex than that."

I didn't answer. I was looking at the exit into the house wondering if it was safe on the other side of the door.

"It's a kind of annihilation," he continued, "like a meeting of matter and anti-matter. A natural, long-burning fuse that runs up the backbone of the universe; hotter, brighter, faster the closer we get to the end of creation. A countdown to zero reflected in every macro-cosmic event and microscopic element that makes it up."

The floor was burning. I was sure of it now.

There was a sickly petrol smell in the air.

"Certain things cancel each other out," he said, "and the great thing is that you can actually apply it to people – people like us: you, me, Jenny, Jane and our parents."

I looked at him.

He said, "Your Dad plus my Mum equals Zero."

"Look, James," I said. "Just…" I stopped. Fact was I didn't know what to say. My head hurt. I felt sick all over again, and I was so tired of this I just wanted to disappear. "Don't," I said, lamely.

"Don't what?" he said dangerously. "You know the truth right? About you and me?"

I nodded. "Your mum told me," I said.

"She *told* you?" He looked surprised.

"Day of my dad's funeral. I spent the night in your room."

I regretted saying it the moment I'd said it.

"You were in my room?" he hissed. Then, explosively, he shouted, "Once again! You. Stepping into my life! Fuck me, Jason!"

"It was just your bedroom," I hissed. "Get over it! Now come on, *we need to go*!"

He wasn't going anywhere. "What did she tell you?" he shouted.

I put my hands to my face and pressed down hard on my eyes. I'm going, I thought. If he wants to stay here and burn then fine but I was out of here.

"What did she tell you, Jason?"

I was aware of the gun at my head before I saw it. I opened my eyes and when I pulled my hands away from my face I saw the ugly, square barrel of the Glock, the hole in the middle of it dirty, black, and somehow vast like I could disappear into it.

"She said Adam was my Dad," I answered him. "Seemed he'd been fucking my Mum for longer than we ever knew. You going to shoot me now?"

The gun disappeared.

"*I* knew," he said. "For as long as I can remember my Mum used to talk about Davy like he was some kind of god. Like Dad didn't exist, like he didn't even matter or like he was just some kind of… lesser species than she and Davy belonged to. I remember when my Mum pushed for us to move back to Anglesey and how when we got there it was like she became alive again."

He was ranting, tripping over his words.

"They should have been together," I said. "I don't know why they didn't do it."

Then James froze.

He was staring at me like I was an idiot. Then he started laughing.

"She didn't tell you everything then did she?"

"What?"

Smoke was billowing in now, blowing up from cracks in the floorboards, eating up the air in the room.

"James…" I said, filling up with dread as he stepped into the middle of the room and made the gun dance and twirl in his fingers.

I hugged the wall and crabbed around towards the door.

He was still laughing.

"So you don't know why, if my Mum and your 'Dad' couldn't stay away from each other, why they never got married? *Really*?"

I shook my head, but I guess it was dawning on me then, when I thought about it.

I guess it was obvious.

"They were *brother and sister*, Jason," he said. "It might have been all fucking 'Hey man, peace and love' when they were at it but there are some laws you can't break and incest is one of them no matter how fucking liberal you are. Your mum and Adam already had a thing going, so Eve and Davy engineered this bizarre four-way relationship so that Eve got exactly what she wanted. Except children. My 'mum' thought she couldn't have children so when yours gave birth to twins one of them went to Eve, passed off as her own. I don't know how they managed it but that's what they did and you and me, and Jenny and Jane – and even those four fuckers themselves have been paying the price ever since!"

"Twins?" I gasped. I was staring at him in shock.

James' face was burning red.

"Yes mate," he said. "You, and me… We're not *half*-brothers. It isn't like Adam fucked your mum and they had you the same time as Eve had me. We're *brothers*, actual, proper, real-life brothers. Adam is *our* Dad, and your mum, Alison, is *our* mother. Eve was never my Mum and Davy was never your Dad. It's all a big fucking lie, my friend."

I stared at him. "We're *twins*?" I said, choking, unable to breathe.

"It's the Zero-sum Equation, Jay. Everything cancels itself out and the components of the universe grind towards a terminal solution."

At which point a great hole in the floor opened up with a terrific cracking sound and a fountain of sheer heat filled with black smoke and thousands of burning sparks exploded upwards like a geyser.

6.18

At that moment my world changed. The horizons fell away and everything that defined my being burned like the house. Everything I thought I knew was wrong and my brain raced as I tried to refit everything into this new order. James had backed off, hiding his face from the fire that had exploded up through the floor.

Streamers of flame had caught onto the drapes and now they were starting to burn. Flames ripped through them fiercely, howling like something alive while Gareth's body swung from its rope. And even while the fire took hold James still talked endlessly, insanely.

Jane, he shouted through the flames, was the daughter of Eve and the man I always thought of as my dad. The man who had collapsed and died in a street after a football game. The man I never knew. Apparently Jane was an accident. It couldn't happen, and yet it had. Eve had thought she would never be able to have children and then Jane was born a year after me and James. Adam was put down as the father on her birth certificate because that made sense. It was allowed.

But in reality, if James was to be believed, then she was actually the product of an incestuous relationship...

And yet... she'd been so perfect...

Past tense. Because now she was dead. Killed by the fucker who swung from his rope, ready to be cooked and burned by the blaze heating up the room to an inferno.

James believed in patterns. Mathematical patterns that repeated themselves in the DNA of the universe, by which he meant us. He was insane, crazier than Jenny, and he believed that Gareth was an agent of the universe acting against the abhorrent creation of Jane Gordon. "So now there's an imbalance," he yelled as the drapes fell in burning tatters behind him. "But it makes sense right? She dies, so I have to die."

"James..." I began. "James, just... stop talking. Listen to yourself." *And get the fuck out*, I was thinking.

Another thundercrack, and when I looked up I saw that the fire was eating up the ceiling crossbeams. One or two of them were full-on burning: bright, orange, crackling rectangles of flame, spitting embers, ready to collapse.

"You need to go," he shouted, pointing the gun at me. "You need to get in your car, drive to somewhere far away and dump it. Don't let it be found. Take the train back and let things play out here. It's a way out, Jason. Take it!"

"Come with me," I coughed, standing by the door.

"I just fucking killed a man!" James roared. "I'm not going back. I can't!"

One of the crossbeams collapsed. The heat in the room intensified and the air was sucked in by the fire which seemed to burst with a new sense of rage and purpose now. I covered my eyes from the blistering heat with the crook of my elbow. The heat was unbearable and the smoke was killing me, scouring out my lungs and my throat. The sheer energy of it was terrifying.

When I lifted my arm away I saw James, almost obscured by the fire. The beam holding Gareth was still in place but he, the body, was burning now, flames crackling around his feet and at his fingertips. James stood next to it, reaching out.

"James. No."

"*Go!*" he screamed.

And then the flames leapt onto him, transferring easily from Gareth's burning corpse. He collapsed backward and there was nothing, nothing I could do but get the hell out of there.

I heard a sickening crump as what was left of him hit the floor, and then I ran.

6.19

I remember pulling the door open and racing out – heading down the smoke-filled tower stairwell, through another door and onto a landing where the acrid smell of burning carpet fibres and paintwork stung my lungs. I lumbered forward, coughing, spluttering, fighting the urge to be sick with the need to survive.

I found my way eventually to the grand staircase which led down to the entrance lobby. But there was no way out that way. The entire lobby was a field of flame racing forward to devour the staircase. The door to the outside world was wide open behind it, promising freedom but in actuality it was fuelling the fire with fresh atmosphere. It was tempting but I'd never make it.

So I went back up the staircase, heading left instead of right. The giant, stained-glass rose window at the top of the staircase exploded inwards, showering the place with glass. But I was past it, racing through the smoke across another landing towards another wing of the house. I burst into a room, a large, dark space with a wall of windows at the far side. I ran to a window and frantically searched for a catch, trying to lift it. It wouldn't open. It was locked.

There was furniture in the room, all covered in white sheets just waiting for the fire to reach this far. I whipped off a sheet and found a chair. Picked it up. Ran back to the window and threw it at the glass.

The glass and the frame shattered. Rain blasted through and I climbed up, squeezed through the frame and jumped down onto a wide ledge.

I caught my breath. Coughed. Looked down through eyes that stung like crazy.

It didn't look so bad from here. There was a terrace below the ledge which I reckoned I could drop down to without injuring myself too much. So I sat on the ledge and dangled my feet over, and then I dropped. Hit the ground hard and felt my knees give way. It hurt but I got back to my feet and raced to the edge of the terrace where a stone balustrade decorated with a rank of gargoyles and demons overlooked the ground floor.

I was at the front of the house and the whole scene was lit up by the light from the burning building. Through the lashing rain I saw Theo, racing for his car.

"Theo!" I screamed, my voice destroyed by the smoke. "*Theo!*"

Didn't sound like he'd heard me.

He opened the door of the car and jumped into the driver's position. Then I heard him gunning the engine.

"Shit!"

Gathering myself up I gripped the stone balustrade and swung my legs up and over.

The car engine roared into life and then I jumped, hitting another terrace lower down just as hard as the previous one.

My legs were shaking so badly I could hardly stand, but I got the strength from somewhere. I ran down the steps faster than I should have been able to and I literally threw myself onto Theo's car bonnet.

He looked at me through the windscreen, his wipers going crazy, and his expression was one of absolute horror.

I didn't wait. I peeled myself off the bonnet and wrenched open the passenger door. I threw myself in and slammed it shut behind me.

Theo was frozen at the wheel. Still as a statue. Pale.

I looked at him with water pouring down my face from my soaked hair. "What are you waiting for?" I cried in a cracked, sore voice spitting rainwater. "Drive!"

He slammed the car into reverse, zoomed backward quickly, changed into first before the car had even stopped and then put his foot down. The car wheeled away from the house, spraying gravel with a roar.

"North," I gasped. "Head north."

6.20

Sometime later it was the end of a new day. The sun was low, a fat orange melting into the hazy North Sea and we stared at it from the clifftops of a long-forgotten, secluded inlet high up on the northeast coast.

We waited until it was dark again, and then the two of us pushed Theo's ancient Peugeot off the cliff. It impacted the rocks below and fell, crashing, into the angry waves. Theo stared at it for longer than me and I wondered what was going on inside his head. This had been difficult for both us but I wondered at that moment whether Theo was pushing his own ghosts off the clifftop. His dad, perhaps, who used to make the cars.

When it was done we turned away, picked up our rucksacks, and began the long hike over the hills back to the nearest town. The first leg of our long journey home.

We dreaded the moment the police would come for us, but as the days, months and years stretched on, they never did.

And I never looked back.

Turns out that James had always intended to burn the house down. He'd dumped a petrol can in the kitchen. Maybe it had been filled from his motorbike's tank or maybe he'd brought it with him separately. We'd never know, but anyway Theo had found it and set the place going.

"I thought it was best," he said to me as we tromped over the Scottish landscape, just a couple of hikers caught out by bad weather and lucky to be alive. "What I saw..." He couldn't finish.

"It stays with us, Theo," I said. "It goes no further."

"But what do we do after this?" he asked.

"We go back to college," I answered. "We pick up our lives and we carry on."

"Can't do that," he said.

"You have to, mate. Lock this away in a dark place and throw away the key. If you can't bury what you saw it'll destroy you. It'll destroy the both of us."

It wasn't that easy but the routine of college worked for me. I thought at the time it had with Theo too, but in retrospect I can see that he never fully sealed up the cracks in his bad memories, and over time the cracks began to split and widen and all the stuff he'd walled away leaked out.

The Broken Woman

Once upon a time, a Broken Woman wanted to disappear. She didn't want to be in pain any longer and she didn't want to fight a losing battle with nurses and doctors who came to try and kill her each day. *One day I will disappear completely*, she promised herself, *I will leave this dark universe, all its storms and its pain behind.*

The problem was that her dark universe existed all the time she was there to perceive it, and whilst she perceived it, it was always there. So, no matter where her mind took her, her universe always followed; and this included the daily terrors the nurses brought with them.

The Broken Woman began to think very hard how she could be rid of it.

If I stop seeing things, if I stop being me, maybe then this place will disappear.
She tried it.

Using all her willpower to change the way her head worked, she tried it. And for a while the acts of Not Seeing Anything and Not Being Me worked. She put her thoughts and her feelings into the seed of a new universe full of light and colour and nurtured that instead, watching it grow daily as she populated it with all the things that brought her joy. However, it was too fragile. The dark universe caught up with her and, wrathful, it destroyed this new place utterly, reinstalling itself as the only universe that was meaningful and real to the Broken Woman.

This wasted effort had exhausted her, and the ease with which she had lost the thing of beauty had destroyed her hope. What else could she try? There was nothing. The dark universe was too strong. Oblivion seemed the only place left for her now and she called out to that constantly, heartbreakingly, curling up into a ball and wishing herself into Nothingness whenever she was able.

It didn't work. Oblivion refused to hear her desperate pleas and every day, the nurses still came. Every day they tied her up and they stuck her with needles. If she was lucky they'd dump her back in bed when they were finished. If she wasn't so lucky, they'd put her in the room with the padded walls and no matter how much she raged and ranted and swore at them, it was only when the drugs calmed her down that they let her out. And that was only so they could repeat the process tomorrow.

The Broken Woman realised that she couldn't get out of here on her own. She needed help.

One day, right out of the blue, her famous brother appeared. When he saw the pain in her eyes, and the bruises and cuts decorating her body, he was wracked with deep sorrow. Without a word he took her away from the dark universe and put her somewhere new.

This new place was good, and in it her hope returned.

Gradually, light entered her world and a new reality flowered around her.

It seemed too good to be true. *Is this new place real?* she wondered.

The brother told her to forget about the old place because right now she was the most important person in her life: here, now and forever. This new reality needed her to perceive it if it was to grow, and if it thrived then maybe in return it would mend her. "You," the brother said, "are the most important person in your universe. Without you to see it, it means nothing."

"If that's true," she asked him, sounding unsure, "does it mean that I can be whoever I want to be? That I can do whatever I want?"

At which point the brother took her hands in his and kissed them. He looked up into her eyes, and said, "Yes! You don't have to be this person, Jenny. They'll make you better here, and then one day we can walk out together."

From then on, whenever he came to visit, she was happy. Soon, the old dark universe of pain and torment was a distant memory, and then, eventually... Nothing.

The Broken Woman began to feel less broken.

However, the famous brother visited less. Months would go by before he would walk across the blue carpet with a smile on his face and tears in his eyes, and very soon the Broken Woman wondered whether or not she had been deluding herself. Maybe she had no brother?

There was a television in the new place and she used to watch it with the other patients. One day the TV began to show her images from her dark universe. The images were few at first, and they flashed by so quickly that she questioned whether or not she had seen them. Then, after a while, the images would stay, pinned onto the TV screen, and no matter what she did – change the channels, turn the TV off – they stuck around, fading in their own time, not when she wanted them to.

At first she tried to ignore it, and when that didn't work she tried to fight it. It was strong. It was coming. She couldn't ignore it. The only thing to do was smash the TV. And that seemed to work. The dark universe wasn't coming back that way.

She kept this to herself. She told no one. The new doctor asked her but she didn't tell him why she had smashed the TV. Maybe she could tell her brother, she wondered. What brother? Where was he? Had he even been real?

It worried her that she could even ask herself that question.

But soon, it didn't matter. His place was taken by someone else, another man who came to see her and who promised to take her away.

Pleasingly, he saw her often and his promises were good.

One day he took the Broken Woman's hand and led her away, out of the hospital into a place where she could truly be herself. And not even her famous brother knew what had happened until she had fully vanished from the world.

7

Solipsism

They're stick men, devoid of humanity's trappings, stripped-down utterly to the freezing core of Being. They wander amongst the teeming crowds and infernal heat of our cities without direction or purpose. Predator? Prey? No. I say they are victims. Like all of us. Homeless, abused and utterly lost within the Hyperrealities of the modern world.

New Reflections on the Statuettes, Figures and Paintings of Alberto Giacometti
Theo Collins.
The LCA Student Review, Jan 2003

7.1

There was a deep silence between me and Theo. I broke it by saying to him, quietly and slowly, "Now, you've had your moment. Get me out of this chair. Let me help you."

He looked at me. Frowned.

"You want to help me?" he whispered.

"If I can," I said, and it felt like I was getting through to him. So I continued, softly, persuasively, "Yes. If you want me to. All you have to do is—"

"You are in no position to help me!"

His voice echoed around the crypt, filling the shadows, bringing them to life.

He gathered his rage. Pulled it in. He breathed deeply and exhaled, then faced me, pointing with a meaty finger. "You said there was someone else in that room with you." he hissed. "Up at the house. Someone who was already there. Your fucking brother?"

Two could play at this.

"Yes, my fucking brother," I replied in pretty much the same tone.

And then it dawned on me what he'd actually said. So I eyeballed him. "You saw the whole thing. Right?"

"I saw it all," he said.

"So why …"

"The house had cameras on the closed circuit. I was fucking around with some of the controls and then I saw you, stabbing that kid in the chair like he was a piece of meat."

"No. Theo, that wasn't me. You know it wasn't me." I was feeling a kind of cold panic kicking in. "It was James who killed—"

"Yeah yeah – your brother, your 'evil twin'." He sniffed. Rubbed his nostrils. Then he said: "You're deluded, mate."

I was deluded? "What?"

"I kept the video tape," he told me, cutting right in before I could say anything else.

My heart froze. "You... you *what?*"

He said, "I recorded you. Onto a tape. More by accident than deliberate, if I'm being honest. Though once I realised what was happening I let it carry on. So it recorded everything. And as it was recording I watched the screen. I saw it all."

I could hardly believe what I was hearing.

"Part of me wanted to get the fuck out straight away, but another, stronger part of me wasn't able to leave. I don't know why that was. Maybe there's some kind of syndrome for it – stuck in a room with a dead body syndrome. Maybe it taps into the primal DNA, the animal inside us. Maybe I wanted ... I dunno. Anyways, I found the feed from the room you were in and it recorded onto a VHS and I kept the tape. I kept it in case the police ever came for me. I thought I could show them what happened. I sort of panicked, grabbed the tape, found the petrol can and then I ran. I wanted everything in that house to burn. You included. If you hadn't thrown yourself at the car I would have left you because at that moment I didn't care about you, after what I'd seen you do. But I kept the tape. The tape was my insurance if the police ever found out I was there."

I swallowed. Hard.

"Do you ... still have it?" I asked him slowly.

He nodded. Then I realised what the TV and the video machine were for. Panic set in. "Let me go, Theo. Then we can talk properly. There's no need for this. You've punished me now. All right?"

He stood up, kicked his chair away and turned on me. "You don't know what it was like in that room. With a rotting fucking corpse for company! Watching all that stuff on the screens." He paced the crypt. I watched him, not knowing what he was going to do or say next. It was clear I couldn't control him. Not while I was stuck in that bloody chair. "The thing is," he said eventually, "I know why you killed him. I saw what he did to your girlfriend and I would have wanted to do the same. I mean I was there to back you up, to help you. But wanting to kill someone, and actually doing it, are two totally different things. To most people. We should have called the police and shown them the tapes we found in your sister's flat. We could have let them sort it out. But we didn't. The both of us went up to Scotland, to this big fucking house, and we both wanted to kill him." He paused a moment. "The difference is that I bottled it and you went right ahead. You tortured and you killed that boy."

He wiped his mouth with the back of his hand. "We had no right to be there, to do what we thought we had to do – for you to do what you did."

"It was James!"

"Jason," he said as though he was talking to a small child, "there was no James. No evil twin. Like I said to you I kept the tape. I've watched it only a few times but each time I see it, it's the same thing: only you and Gareth in that room. And you kill him every time. No matter how I might want it to play out differently, it's always the same. I'll show it to you."

He grabbed hold of my chair and swung it round, scraping the feet over the flagstones.

"I don't want to watch it!" I shouted, releasing the full panic that had been building over the last couple of minutes.

"I just want you to see what I saw when I was in that room." He wheeled the TV trolley closer towards me and switched it on. "And then you'll see."

"No!" I cried. "Theo, it *wasn't me*!"

"Look, mate," he said, "I'm doing you a favour."

He studied a remote control in his hand. "Time for you to see what you really are," he said, and he pressed the remote.

The TV flickered into life, making new, grey shadows between the thick, stone columns. It was an old fashioned portable TV, similar to the one Jenny used to have in her room and it was only tuned into the video channel. Suddenly there it was, the room from the back of my mind. Until now it had been sealed away, but as I watched the thing unfold those seals burst apart and the contents spilled out.

I watched in revulsion as the horror unfolded frame by frame. I watched as James beat Gareth and I kept on watching until the moment he stabbed him. At which point it ended.

And Theo was right. If you believed the tape then there were only ever two people in the room. One of them was Gareth, and the other...

"He looked like me but it wasn't me," I said, voice thick, choking with horror. "I've known him since I was a boy, Theo. James was my brother and he went up there because he saw the tapes in Jenny's room before we did."

"There are no mirrors in your house, Jason," Theo said to me. "And I remember when we got home after this and tried to carry on with things, as if nothing had changed, that you got rid of them all in our house. Is that because you can't look at yourself? After what you did?"

Theo stood and switched off the TV. The picture receded to a little white dot centre-screen before fading out. "You brought me to this place, JJ."

"I didn't make you into a killer," I hissed at him. "You did that yourself!"

"I'm not a killer." He paused as I considered how to broach it. "I'll prove it to you," he said. "Time to end the deception, my own little fiction."

He came towards me and turned the chair back round so that I was looking again at the corpse stretched out on the wall of the crypt like Jesus on the cross.

"It's a dummy," he said, marching up to it and snapping off a plastic arm. "A dummy. 'Armless see?" He threw the thing to the floor. "You saw my studio, before you burned it down. And don't lie because I know you did. Sam called me, and from her description it could only have been you. But this is a dummy, just like the ones you tore down at Studio 10b."

I was horrified.

"Why?" I whispered.

Theo hunkered down next to my chair. He leaned right into my face. "I'm just trying to work this out of my head. Been trying to do it for years but I couldn't … But here's the thing: the process is…" He stopped. Thought about his words and started again. "The process of facing up to this thing gave my art the fuel it needed to be successful. Ironic eh?"

"You're mad, Theo…"

"The problem, is that the art also fuelled the thing itself, made it live and breathe inside me until it was chewing my head off and that," he said, "was hard to live with. So. Anyway. Long story short. It comes to this. You and me, here in this room. You know, I sincerely believe that everyone on this planet is capable of murder and torture. Most of us never do it, would never even consider it because the conditioning of civilised sensibilities and deeply-ingrained morality comes into play. But things happen, events take over and lives become suddenly dispensable. People become so easily de-humanised; laws change and morality goes out with the first bullet, the first gas attack, the first chemical bomb, the first nuclear warhead, and by the time the second one hits then civilised sensibilities are nothing but a distant memory. Two nuclear warheads in Japan at the end of the second world war. Two aeroplanes on 9/11. Two towers falling. Remember the installation we did which opened

Gallery21? Where we had the fight? Remember the horrors, the atrocities we exhibited in that piece? And your own installation at Lambeth, with Bethany in the chair surrounded by 9/11 and God knows what else. You tapped right into it. Even the thing you did for *The Odyssey Exhibition*, the *Castle Mechanics* piece with all the TVs… This was all you working stuff out of your head, you dealing with what you did in Balloch right? And this, all this," he indicated the crypt with a sweep of his hands, "this is all me, working it out of my system. I had to get you here, you see? I had to put you through this so that you would… understand and feel the weight of what you'd done."

No. I wasn't having this. Something didn't ring true. "You sabotaged my installation…" I said. "Am I right?"

"Me?"

"Makes sense. I might have done the same if the roles were reversed."

"You mean your TV Castle? No. I didn't. It was someone else who put the virus into your laptop and all your homemade porn. No, mate. Truth is I never even knew you were doing that gig until Hugh and Brian told me I was booted out of it. I remember the day. I went fucking mental."

"You wanted to kill me?"

He raised a finger. "Wanted to, yes," he said. "But you see I turned it into something positive. I saw the opportunity to finally push this thing out into the open between us."

I could have laughed. "You think this is something positive? You started planning this headfuck just because I got you replaced in an exhibition. Nothing else." I knew that wasn't entirely true, but I needed to get control somehow.

"It was the final straw, mate," Theo said, and maybe that was true. "The catalyst. And don't knock it down because this thing is not just any exhibition, JJ. It's a job worth four million pounds. What right did you have to ask Brian to tick me off his list?"

"Because your art is … sick!" I yelled at him. "It's depraved! You're a racist and a fucking Nazi!"

"You look like you believe yourself when you say that," he said, looking hurt. No, not hurt; disappointed.

But I pushed him. "Why not? It's what you put out to the world."

"No different from you, JJ."

"It's completely different."

"The only difference is that I faced the horror head-on. I wanted to understand it, to put myself in the same headspace as the people who did all that shit. Whereas you... you were already there. Instead of facing it down, you tried to ignore it, or maybe rationalise it. Maybe you were looking for... I was going to say forgiveness but that would mean you felt remorse for what you did. No, I think you were trying to pass off your dirty deed as something ordinary, something that was acceptable in the natural order of things. That's why you wrapped it all up in the shapes of saints and angels. But ... you see that's not you is it? You're no saint, just as I'm no fascist."

"You're still a murderer."

"You're not dead yet are you?"

"There was no sound on that tape," I said.

It seemed to throw him and he paused a moment. I thought I might have got through to him, but then he shrugged it off. "It doesn't matter."

"What I mean is, that if there was sound then you would have heard me talking to James."

"Ravings of a madman," Theo replied. "You invented him, this twin of yours, and I can't help you with that."

"You're deranged."

"Not me. I'm not crazy."

"Theo," I gasped, "this doesn't make sense. You holding me here, putting this thing in front of me. I know what you're saying but I don't buy it."

"It makes sense to me."

I stared at him as he played with his cameras. Why the dummy body? Why the show?

And then it dawned on me. I got it. Everything he'd said and done... Maybe part of it was true but the real answer, the real reason I was here... It was suddenly, blindingly obvious.

"You're an idiot," I said. "An absolute idiot, Theo."

He turned to look at me then, and stopped fiddling with his cameras.

"Are you back in the exhibition?" I asked him.

He frowned. "Thought that was obvious."

"And I'm out of it, right?"

"What are you getting at?"

I started laughing. I couldn't help it. Nothing was funny, but my head wasn't exactly in a good place and all that terror, and anxiety and trauma, it all came out in the laugh.

Theo didn't like it.

"What are you doing?" he asked. "What's so funny?"

"It isn't funny," I said. "But you've been played." Eventually I stopped laughing. "Who's behind this, Theo? Huh? Who persuaded you that bringing me here and fucking with me was a good idea? If you've had the tape all this time then we could have had this out years ago. But we didn't. You never talked about it, never confronted me with it. Why not? Did you talk to someone else is that it? And don't tell me this is all about getting booted out of *The Odyssey Exhibition* because it isn't the first time I've gazumped you – nor you me, for that matter. Big cash prize but so what? There'll be other opportunities. So who put you up to this? Who played you? Who sabotaged my material?"

"Nobody *played* me!" he hissed.

"I don't believe you. You've already said someone else was involved."

He smacked me hard across the face with the back of his hand and I spat blood.

"Harriet said I was obsessed with the Camden Killer," I gasped. "And she was right. Now you're using that obsession against me. But someone is using your trauma against you. You should tell me who it is. If you don't then it won't be good for you."

"Really?"

I nodded. "Really."

He scoffed. "Worse for you," he said.

"Maybe. But let me ask you this: why are the police looking for you?"

It was a gamble but it got a reaction. His body snapped up straight. He tried to recover but I knew I had him.

"They've been to your studio, your office. I'll make an educated guess that they've been to the Dreadnought and I know they've been to your house. And you're avoiding them. Why are they looking for you, do you think?"

"It doesn't matter," he snapped.

"Yes it does," I said, as calmly as I could except that I had to spit blood again. "I'll tell you: It's because they think you are the Camden Killer."

7.2

He was breathing hard. Staring at me.

"Why would they think that?"

"Aren't you? You told me you killed Bethany to motivate her brother into confronting me."

"I didn't kill her," he said. "I'm not the Camden Killer."
"You said you hung her from Blackfriars Bridge."
"I lied."
"You killed Stephen Craine. You killed Rachael Clarke and hammered a six-inch nail into her forehead! The old judge on the bench. You can't lie about those things, Theo!"
"I'm not a killer, Jason."
"You are."
"No!"
Theo ran his hands over his face, pacing within the circle of cameras.
"If you didn't kill that girl, who did?" I barked at him.
"I don't know," he replied.
"Tell me!"
"No! I – I don't know!"
Silence for a while as I thought it through. I remembered how scared he'd been in the house at Balloch, how he'd turned pale as a sheet and stayed in the basement room while I was the one who'd marched upstairs screaming Gareth's name burning white-hot with intentions of vengeance.

I guessed if anyone was a killer here, then fine, hands up it was me. He was right about that. And maybe he was right about his own sensibilities. If I gave him the benefit of doubt and accepted that his fascism was an elaborate act, then the question, no matter what he'd said, remained: why would he put me here? Why not just have it out with me? Because someone was feeding his trauma? It had to be. And if that someone was the *real* Camden Killer...

"You've been played," I said again. "We both have. Someone's covering his footprints killing those people and he's putting both of us in the frame, using our rivalry, twisting and blowing it up out of all proportion. It's not an accident I thought you were the Camden Killer, Theo. Someone pushed your buttons and made you do this. Breaking into my house for Christ's sake. The masks in your studio. Someone laid out the tracks for me, playing my obsessions. And those tracks led me conclusively to you."

Seemed like he was thinking about it. So I stirred him up some more.
"I've been helping the police," I told him. "Like I said, they think you're the Killer. That's why they're looking for you."
"You're lying, Jason."
"No. I'm not. Why would I lie?"
"It was just ... art!" He sounded worried. "A couple of projects me and Nugget were working on with the day classes. Sticking up a few

shop-window dummies in polybags filled with fake blood does not make me a murderer."

"Tell that to the cops. What do you think they'll do when they see what you've done here? If they came barging in right now and saw us like this, what do you think they'd see? Think about it."

He sort of laughed. Shook his head. Paced up and down anxiously.

"I've still got the tape," he said. "I'll show it to them."

Now I shook my head. I wanted to undermine the value of this thing that he had, this asset he'd been clinging onto all these years which had been destroying him. "I'll tell them we set it up, that it's another art work of bad taste, and maybe I'll tell them you tricked me into doing it, that you set me up. After all I'm the clear victim here. I'm the one tied to the chair with a fucking drip in my hand."

"They'll know the tape ain't art."

"Really? You think they'll know the difference now? When they see that thing on the wall? Besides, it's just a room on the tape. Could be anywhere. You can't prove that it's the house in Balloch. I mean, it's not like you took any establishing shots of the exterior is it?"

"I'm not the Camden Killer."

"I know," I said, gently, tired. "So who is? No more games."

He looked at me. Calmer now, and it seemed like he was on my side at last.

But then he shook his head.

"We can turn it around, Theo," I said quickly, realising I was losing him. "You and me. We can hunt this motherfucker down and– "

He snorted. "Kill him?" he interrupted.

"No," I said. "We'll go to the police."

"Too late for that," he said, and it was as though something had already broken inside him. He looked unstable. He was still a big guy and I was still strapped to the chair.

"What happened to Liselle?" I asked him gently, changing tack as he returned his attention to the cameras. He was taking the memory cards out of them and putting them in his pocket.

His face snapped up. Looked like he was going to say something. Then he cleared his throat and said, "Nothing. She's gone home."

I kind of knew it and I was relieved that she was OK, but it hurt nonetheless. "She was part of the act?"

He nodded. "I'd worked with her before. And when I found out she was with you… She didn't take much convincing."

"Fuck. And – and that guy Sean. Bethany's brother?"

"He was even easier to recruit. That part was just like I said. He'd been trying to find ways to get at you for years. Another life you destroyed, Jason. But he ran off after a few days with you here." He laughed again. "He lost his nerve when I brought the dummy in. Didn't like to see what he'd look like if he was butchered."

"So it was just a kind of *Trompe l'oeil*. Me, drugged and confused, looking at that thing... Why wouldn't I think it was a real corpse?"

"Indeed."

"All right," I said. "So now we've finished here. Nothing more to say. You're not going to tell me who put you up to this so you might as well let me go."

He stared at me.

"Not yet."

What the fuck? "Theo, there's nowhere left from here."

He was shaking. He was so stressed he might have done anything. As it happened he rubbed his face and then walked towards me with a determined look.

"I get where you're coming from, Jay. And I take my hat off to you for getting through it so far. But it ain't finished. Not yet."

"What are you doing?" I whispered.

"Bethany's brother works in a hospital," he said, checking the IV drip and stand. "He set all this up. There's a drug in here, I can't remember what they call it – oxypoxyhydrofuckingsomethingorother – but whatever the fuck, it makes you stupid. Increase the dosage and you go to sleep for a long old while. Increase it further and it kills you."

There was a rectangular green button on the box. It had a plus symbol embossed into it at one end and a minus symbol on the other. Theo pressed the plus symbol a few times and the number on the LCD above it went up in increments. There was a warning beep from the machine.

"Works in seconds this," he said. Then frowned. "I think that's right…"

Then he looked at me.

"I'm going now," he said. "Happy Christmas, Jason. Looks like you got what you deserved if not what you wanted. If you wake up, it won't be me looking down at you."

He walked away.

"Theo?" I called. "Theo!"

He disappeared into the darkness.

"Theo!" I screamed.

He was gone.

7.3

I tugged and I stamped, howled, heaved and screamed myself into a rage. I crashed the chair against the side-table, against the television on its trolley. I whirled and thrashed like some kind of caged animal smashing every part of the chair into anything close by to loosen it. The IV drip and its pole crashed to the floor and I kicked it away, yanking my hand so that the catheter ripped free. Damn it hurt! I pulled on the straps around my arms and wrists, almost like I was possessed. That hurt as well because these fucking plastic straps were almost impossible to –

Suddenly one hand was free. Ripped, bloodied and fizzing with pins and needles but free nonetheless. With it I tore at the strap on my other hand, stretching it, pulling at it until the fucker thinned out like tough spaghetti and I was able to scrape my hand out of it. Then I did for the straps around my ankles and when I was done I literally threw the fucking chair off me, into the cameras. Then I heaved up the TV and threw that at the fucking wall. And when that was done I picked up the video player and I destroyed that too. I smashed it again and again until it broke apart into a mass of circuit boards and bits of sharp metal. The cassette fell out. I picked that up and dug my fingers under the plastic protector to pull at the actual videotape. I tore it out, ripping at it when it snagged, scrunching it up, then pulling and twisting it in the hope of rendering it utterly useless.

The giant photographer's spotlight was still shining but I'd knocked it over. It shone up from the ground, throwing monstrous shadows at the vaulted ceiling.

I threw what remained of the videotape at the floor then stumbled around looking around for a way out. Breathing hard, my head buzzing. Unsteady on my feet I almost tripped over the spotlight's massive power transformer.

"Theo!" I called out. Dizzy with adrenaline or the drug? I didn't know but I had to keep it together, had to stay in control of my body.

Had to be a way out of here, somewhere…

I crashed into the array of cameras, some of which had already fallen to the ground. Had Theo taken the memory cards out all of them?

I thought he had. Was sure I'd seen him do it.

It didn't matter. I just had to get out. I couldn't be trapped down here forever now that I'd managed to get out of the chair. Also, the smell of gas was really strong and warning bells clamoured in my head.

Was he gassing me out? Was I supposed to sleep while he poisoned me with carbon monoxide or something?

I remembered reading somewhere that carbon monoxide didn't smell, and actually that natural gas didn't smell either. The smell was produced by an agent introduced into the supply by the companies piping it into your house, and it was done purely to warn you of a leak. Didn't know if that was really true but it didn't matter. I could smell gas and that couldn't be good.

How the hell was I going to get out of here? I couldn't remember which way Theo had gone and despite the light from the photographer's light, my head just couldn't map the room into any kind of order.

The light.

Had to be powered from somewhere right?

The TV too. There was no power down here probably so maybe …

Yes. A cable. Leading away from a giant transformer, a great big box into which everything had been plugged, and from that, snaking away…

I turned the fallen spotlight round to shine at the thick cable running over the flagstones, round a couple of columns and off to the right where everything disappeared into shadow.

An L-shaped crypt. How apt, I thought ironically.

I dropped the light, got on my hands and knees and felt for the cable, tracking it around the bend in the crypt, into the darkness.

I felt, more than I saw, a flight of wooden stairs leading upwards. Still tracking the cable with my hand I groped my way up like a blind man, knocking my shins on the steps until I reached a door kept open by the cable. From behind the door I heard the first sputtering sounds of a diesel generator.

Without another thought I pushed on the door and stumbled into a stone passage on the other side. It was so dark. The walls were thick, massive blocks of grey stone which felt as though they were closing in on me. I could feel a panic-attack starting up so I ran for it.

I made it to the far end of the corridor and when I stumbled out into a ruined church altar I realised exactly where I was. The smell of gas made sense now because it was mixed in with the stench of piss and putrefying timbers, as well as diesel exhaust spewing from the generator. The diesel was new but the rest of the stink was unmistakable. I'd walked past this place so many times, looked down on it from the windows at the top of my house.

I clawed through a hole in the shattered wall covered by a flimsy tarpaulin and a corrugated iron sheet, and when I emerged into a snow-covered churchyard I knew for certain where I'd been all this time.

I turned and walked backwards, hugging my arms around my chest, shivering, teeth-chattering, looking up at the dilapidated west-facing gable of St Leonard's Church.

I laughed under my breath with the irony of it.

St Leonard, the patron saint of prisoners; of whom it was said that if you repented your sins and prayed to him, then his spirit would set you free. Maybe ... Just maybe there was something in that...

My house was within walking distance.

All this time...

I turned and moved towards it, ambling through the snow and the timbers and poles that littered the ground.

I guessed it was mid-afternoon though it was difficult to be sure. The sky was dark and full of heavy cloud, meaning more snow was on the way most likely. Or maybe it was too cold to snow. Either way, it was dark enough and late enough for people in the houses to start putting their lights on.

I didn't expect to see a light on in my house. But there it was, the big, glass patio doors of the second floor studio fully lit.

And someone was up there, moving around.

I wrestled a metal pole up from the ground by the fence. A wicked-looking thing bent and split at the top. It felt like a good weapon, good enough to scare the shit out of someone anyway. I just hoped I didn't have to use it because I wasn't sure I felt strong enough, especially if the person in my house was Theo. Or his accomplice? Nonetheless, it was my fucking house and right now I'd had enough of being a victim...

7.4

Creeping in through the kitchen door, which was open, it felt like I'd never left home. The interior was so familiar on the one hand, yet on the other it felt completely alien. A place I hadn't been to for so long.

Or maybe it was just a couple of days?

I was still groggy and my legs moved slowly. My muscles ached. Everything was hurting and all I wanted to do was lie down and sleep. But I wasn't going to let anyone get away with breaking into my house again and if it was Theo, well... I wanted this finished, one way or another.

I could hear whoever it was moving around as I climbed the stairs to the second floor. I tensed my sore fingers around the pole, remembering right then that I had a baseball bat in the house somewhere. Fat lot of good that had ever been.

Second floor.

I crept up to the studio door, then I burst in with a screaming: "Yaaaaahhh!"

7.5

A guy in a baseball cap had been sitting with his back to the door, working at my MacBook.

When I burst in he jumped out of the chair, knocked it over and backed against the wall, his hands in the air.

"Whoa whoa whoa!" he cried. "It wasn't me, man! I didn't do noffin!" Then he got control of his eyes back. He stared at me. "JJ? Is that you, mate?"

What the fuck…?

"Jhavesh?" My hands were shaking. Everything was shaking. I thought I was going to drop the pole.

"Mate," he said, warily. "You look bad. What did you do to your face? Where you been?" Then, he said, "You gonna hit me? Please don't hit me. Can I put my hands down?"

I breathed out, walked forward and pointed the end of the pole at him. "What are you doing here? Why are you on my PC?"

"You gonna hit me though? It's fine but don't hit the face. Please?"

"Depends on what you're fucking doing here," I answered. "Mood I'm in I don't know what I'll do."

"Hey hey it's all cool, mate. Take it easy all right? I don't believe all this shit in the papers. I never read 'em anyway."

"Tell me right now what the fuck you're doing on my pc."

He said, "Strictly speakin? It ain't a PC. It's a Mac."

"Don't fuck around, Jhavesh. I really ain't in the mood for it."

He grinned and dropped his arms to his sides. "You said 'ain't'."

I didn't know whether to laugh or cry at that moment. State I was in, I could have done both.

"Are we good?" Jhavesh asked.

I lowered the pole. Shakily, I answered him. "Yeah… Yeah, mate. We're good."

Jhavesh grinned and I very nearly cried. Had to work hard to keep it down.

Then he relaxed and pulled his coat together. "Grab a seat, JJ," he said, as though nothing had happened. "Someone's been messing with your computer and it ain't nice."

7.6

"My cousin Hari," he said, when I crashed onto a sofa by the patio doors and he retook his seat at my desk, "don't like it when people get the better of him. Thing is that he thinks he's a real Harry Potter when it comes to IT and shit like that. So you know all that porn that got into your TV thing at the gallery? By the way, mate, big respect to you cos she was well-fit."

He turned to look at me and his grin vanished. He returned to the Mac quickly.

"Anyways," he went on. "Harish couldn't sleep at night cos he kept thinking 'bout how someone had managed to infiltrate his software with something so destructive. He knows a lot about worms and viruses and he knows what all the latest ones are, so anything that creeps up on him like this and he freaks out, man. He was like OCD wiv it. So he went back into the architecture of the system to run all the stuff and he pulled it apart, even the pre-written mods he plugged into his own thing. Took him a few days but he's that kind of guy."

My head was still buzzing. My eyelids closing. All I could see was Theo's big face, crazed, in front of me.

"Stay with me, mate," Jhavesh said. "I'll cut to the chase. Man, you look real bad… I think you should go see a doctor."

"Just… just carry on. But make it quick. You still haven't told me why you broke into my house."

"Mate, your house was open front and back. Anyone could have walked in here."

Which could have been true, I supposed.

"What day is it?" I asked Jhavesh sleepily.

"What? It's Tuesday," he said. "Anyway, long story short. Harish found the worm which overwrote all the video files and reckoned you must have downloaded something onto your Mac where the porn files, he reckoned, were stored. He asked me to come round and see you about it so that's what I did only you wasn't here. But your house was open."

"I don't get it," I said. "I didn't download anything."

"Yes you did," he told me. "I just found it. It's here look."

He picked up the Mac and brought it over to the sofa. Sat down next to me, then edged away with his nose wrinkling.

"I know, I smell of piss," I said. "Get over it."

On the screen of the MacBook a little green monster was dozing. A window of code, white scrolling text on a black background, took up one half of the screen. Images of the monster icon flashed past in the same window.

"Give me that." I took the MacBook off him and sat it on my lap. It was Sh1tPolice's instant messenger app.

"Mate. You were crazy letting this shit onto your computer. Even the kid on the street knows you don't let this kind of stuff into your laptop. This thing here has copied all your data files. All your passwords, all your personal shit. It has rewritten your registry and right now this thousand dollar machine is as much use to you a cardboard iPad. Or even a real one…"

His mobile rang. Sounded like a nightclub had opened its doors for a second before he answered it.

"Cuz!" he barked.

Then: "Yeah, man, I found it. JJ's wiv me innit. Right here… I know, bloody fool." He paused, listening. "Hold up."

He whipped the computer off me and then hammered at the keypad, mobile tucked between his beard and his shoulder.

His fingers moved fast and multiple right-clicks on the touchpad ensued. Windows I'd never seen before, full of dollar signs and hashtags, opened up on screen.

I was falling asleep.

He nudged me awake and I realised he'd put the phone down. "Stay wiv me, man," he said. "Right, I'm letting Harish into your MacBook, then he's gonna wake up that little fucker and try and trace it. He was saying it copied all your video files over to another computer somewhere via remote."

"Isn't that a lot of data though?" I said. "Wouldn't it have slowed the thing down while it was transferring?"

"Not much, mate," he said. "You're on lightning speed broadband so this thing just compressed the files, zipped them up and sent them over to whoever it is in no time. Hari reckons he's seen this thing before, just that your one is more sophisticated so it tripped him up. He told me journalists are using this shit to hack into celebrity laptops. You used to be able to do it via Facebook but that was a long time ago and they closed that route off. Google too but same thing. The only way this kind of worm can get onto your computer now is if you behave like a numpty and let someone you don't know install something like – oh I dunno –

an instant messenger app for example onto your platform."

"All right. I behaved badly. I was investigating things."

"The Camden Killer?"

"Uh-huh…"

"Mate, you need to get rid of that shit," he said in a low tone. For the first time since I'd known him, he sounded serious.

"What shit?"

"I saw it all spilling out of your broom cupboard. An you still got some up on your wall."

I shrugged. "Not yet. The fucker's still out there. He knows me, Jhavesh."

"Knows you?" He looked horrified.

"Stephen Craine?"

"No way! It was him?"

"No… never mind."

"Mate," he said, "have you … seen the papers?"

"Huh?"

"The papers."

"I haven't been – No. I haven't seen the papers."

"Well you should. I'll bring you one up."

"Why?"

"Cos they think you're him," he said.

"Who thinks I'm who?"

"Everyone, mate. It's been in the papers since yesterday. Your name, your picture and everything. You don't look much like that now, mind you. When did you get your hair cut?"

"What?"

"They think you're the Camden Killer, mate."

7.7

"Fuckoff," I said.

"It's true!"

"Me? Why?"

"I dunno. Something to do with art."

"Me? The Camden Killer?"

"I thought that was why you wasn't in. I thought you was in hiding. Oh my days! Look, mate, leave this with me and Harish. You get the fuck away from here and hide up some place."

"I'm not going anywhere."

"You need to, Jason. Before the police decide they're gonna come looking for you."

"Let them come," I said. "I'm not the Camden Killer. And if they thought I was then they'd have been here already."

"Maybe they have," he said. "Maybe that's why your door was wide open."

"What? And they left the laptop? The camera? They didn't take it away looking for evidence? No one's been in my house except you, right here and now."

"Don't say I didn't warn you," he muttered, clicking on the MacBook.

"Fuck this," I said. "I'm going for a sleep. Let yourself out and lock up behind you. Keys are … somewhere."

I stood up off the sofa and shuffled away. I reached the door and heard him shout, "Yo! We're in! JJ!"

"You sort it out, mate," I said, because frankly I didn't care. I just wanted sleep.

I walked onto the landing and went down a floor into my bedroom, which was in the room below the studio, a single, small window looking out over the back garden. The answerphone on the bedside table was flashing, telling me I had messages. My mobile was next to it.

So my computer was still here. My camera was still here, and my phone was still here. Yet my house had been open for a week? In Camden?

What was the world coming to?

I pulled open the bedside table drawer and found my wallet. I opened it up and checked that everything was in there. It was. I peeled through my Oyster card, credit cards, sixty pounds of cash. I put it in my coat pocket thinking that something was wrong. You didn't leave the doors of a house in North London open for a week and expect to find your wallet still where you left it. I couldn't think straight, I needed sleep.

The mobile was dead so I plugged it in to charge. Then I pressed the play button on the landline's base-station. While I listened to the messages I caught sight of some of Liselle's clothes and underwear scattered around the room. Had this all been here before Theo had barged in and dragged me into the church?

Or … had she been living here? Using the house as a base… which would make sense, I thought. Maybe they both had.

I crashed onto the bed, still in my coat, and listened to the messages whilst my eyes traced the cracks in the ceiling and quickly began to close.

The first voice I heard playing back on the answering machine as I drifted away was Arnold wondering where the hell I was, and that was followed by the thick, Indian accent which belonged to Doctor Pandghani. "Hello, Jason," he said.

My eyes opened wide.

"Excuse me for calling you again. But the last time we spoke you cut off." he went on. "Anyway you need to know that I am very concerned about your sister." Oh Christ! Jenny! I'd forgotten.

I'd been on the phone to Doctor Pan when Theo had attacked me and dragged me from the house.

His voice continued, "… as you have not called me and there is no sign of Jenny Jones as yet, I am afraid that I have had to call the police. If you did not discharge her from the hospital then somebody else did and–"

That was when the church exploded.

7.8

At first it was just a light outside the window: a flash as bright as a strip of daylight that lit up the bedroom.

My heart leapt into my mouth. *What the fuck?*

Then instinct gripped me. I grabbed the duvet and covered myself over with it. Rolling over, I wrapped myself up like a caterpillar and allowed my sideways motion to carry me over the bed and onto the floor the other side of it –

Just as a deafening blastwave punched through the house. It knocked in the windows and threw all the doors open. The whole structure quaked, rumbling with thunder. It was terrifying.

"Shit!"

Above me the bedroom window exploded inwards. My head was buried deep in the duvet and right under the bed, so I couldn't see what was happening but I could hear well enough.

The silence which followed it left me numbed. My ears rang, and then gradually the ringing faded and I became aware of the clamouring from outside of house alarms and car alarms.

I unravelled myself, wide awake but so tired it was unreal. The bed, the floor, even the walls, were covered with shards of glass. My boots crunched down on them as I walked towards the window and looked out.

"Holy… fuck…!"

It was an apocalyptic scene.

The church was gutted. Burning. Black smoke filled the atmosphere, billowing up from a roof that had been reduced to a monstrous, upturned ribcage. Initially the only thing I could think of was that maybe I was supposed to still be down there, and then, more rationally, I thought of someone else. Upstairs in the studio with that big, glass patio door leading out onto the back.

"Jhavesh!"

I raced up.

7.9

Jhavesh was curled up against the wall. The desk had been upended and the MacBook was on a floor covered with glass.

The air was choked with smoke and there was a chemical smell to it which made me gag as I stepped quickly towards him, slipping on debris.

Jhavesh stirred and gasped for air but it didn't look good. There was glass in his jacket, all down the back, and although it was a thick material it wasn't a suit of armour. I turned him gently onto his side, pulling him away from the wall. His face was peppered with bits of glass but far worse was the back of his head.

"Oh no," I said in a small voice. "No no…"

It was hot and sticky when I pulled my hand away.

His eyelids fluttered, and as he opened his mouth to speak he released a fat glob of blood from between his lips. The way his lungs were raking at the air made me think that they'd been punctured right through.

"You're good, mate," I said to him loudly. "It's all good. It ain't that bad. Just keep still."

I put his head down carefully on a cushion from the sofa, then I raced out of the room, down the stairs, back into my bedroom. I grabbed the phone and made to dial up 999 but it wasn't working. The electrics had gone. I found my mobile, scrabbling in my bedroom amongst the glass and wood splinters, but there was no charge, it hadn't been plugged in long enough.

"Fuck!" I roared, and I threw the thing at the wall where it clattered and broke.

Back upstairs. Quickly.

Jhavesh was gasping horribly and the cushion was darkening with his blood. "Oh fuck fuck fuck..!"

What about *his* phone?

Good idea, so where was it?

He'd put it on the desk, next to the MacBook so I crunched over and searched by the upturned desk frantically. Seemed like my own hands were bleeding, having picked up some glass from somewhere. Jhavesh was convulsing, making a retching sound, spasming because he couldn't get enough air into his lungs.

The phone was on the floor. I picked it up, dusted it down, swiped it on and stabbed the number nine.

It needed four digits and I realised it was a pass-code entry, not a dial-up screen.

"Fuck!" I roared.

Then Jhavesh made a sound that made me feel cold: an animalistic, guttural cry that rattled away to nothing.

My hand went to my mouth because I didn't know what I could do. I sat there, with the church burning behind me, sat there in the gloom and watched this man die and I couldn't call an ambulance because I didn't know the number to operate his fucking phone!

No. Hold on. It would still let me make emergency calls wouldn't it?

I swiped the screen again and breathed a sigh of relief when I saw the option to dial emergency calls only, so I pressed that and tapped out 999. I got straight through to an operator and I spewed it all out.

But the guy on the phone was good. He slowed me down, asked for my address and said the ambulance was on its way already. Then he asked some specific questions about Jhavesh's breathing, and could I see where the blood was coming from, and were his pupils dilated, and where did he live again, and who were his family and where would they be now. And I answered them all. All the operator's questions because I *knew* where Jhavesh lived, and I *knew* his mum and his dad and his two sisters; I could see them both smiling and flirting with me, and I could hear his dad's voice in my mind – stern and authoritative, his quirky humour so that you never knew if he was joking with you so he had to tell you he was messing you around: "You're always so serious, JJ" – and his mum shaking her head, telling her son he should grow up and get a proper job. I knew the answers to those questions because I realised right there and then that Jhavesh was my friend, a real friend, a true and proper friend, and I never knew it until now and now it was too late because there was no fucking way that the ambulance going to get here on time and he was going to die and there was nothing *nothing* I could do about that.

7.10

Then I heard the paramedics at the door shouting up the stairs. A loud, booming, "Hello! Mr Gordon?"

Yeah. I hadn't given the operator my real name. "They're here now," I said to the operator. And then, "Thank you."

I cut the call and shouted out: "Upstairs!" but it didn't sound loud enough amidst the chaos from outside, so I shouted again, by which time they were at the studio door.

Two of them barged right in, right past me and I edged back, getting to my feet, brushing glass from my coat. I noticed light from the MacBook's retina screen leaking through the lid.

Was it still working? Opening it up the screen looked like it had taken a hit but damn these things were indestructible.

"Mr Patel!" one of the paramedics shouted as they both ran in and hunkered down by Jhavesh. They brought torches with them. I hadn't realised how dark it was.

They didn't need me here.

I took up the MacBook and slipped out just as I heard one of them calling my fake name. So I continued downstairs and walked straight out of the house. Out through the front door and into the street.

I walked away quickly but steadily, and even though the road was filled with cars and police vans and people were taking snapshots and movies on their phones, no one saw me. I was invisible. Mr Nobody.

I walked right through them, even as police started herding people away, erecting barriers, pulling people out of their houses in case there was another explosion, even in the blue lights flashing on top of the cars and vans no one saw me. The armed police arrived before I got to the end of the road, more ambulances screamed into the street, and I figured that soon there'd be television crews and reporters and before you knew it this would be a big story. Explosions in London were Big Serious News.

And I just walked through it and away. The guy who, in the papers according to Jhavesh, had been recently identified as the Camden Killer.

7.11

Although Jhavesh had told me it was Tuesday, he hadn't told me it was the day before Christmas Eve. This was something I discovered later as I shambled down a fully decked-out Camden High Street and saw how busy it was. I hustled my way towards the Underground station where a couple of Santas paraded their collection buckets amongst the crowd to the Sally Army Band's rendition of *Once in Royal David's City*.

And it really was ultra-busy. Not that I planned on using it but the station was closed because of the security alert triggered by the church blast. Shivering kids, dressed up for their Christmas parties, were badgering the guys in Transport For London uniforms for info on when it was going to open again before disappointedly walking off towards Mornington Crescent or Kentish Town.

The tarmac was rammed. Packed with cars, buses, bikes and every other animated piece of metal that had ever been made in the history of the world. Didn't seem to be a space to walk between anything and I watched as a cyclist wobbled down, holding a hand against the railings at the side of the road to stop herself falling into the side of a bus. No doubt the police had shut down most of North London and diverted all the traffic along here. So now, beneath the Christmas lights strung over the road, horns blared, loud music pumped and drivers threw their hands up in anger at the antics of everyone else.

Not much to see in the way of Christmas spirit, I thought.

I was walking towards Kentish Town. Northwards. And it was hard going. Now that the adrenalin which had saved my life earlier was gone I felt more tired than ever, and it was all I could do to keep walking in a straight line.

It didn't matter. There were plenty of people like me in Camden and nobody ever paid any notice. Seemed that being an utter physical wreck, walking in diagonal lines in front of everybody and stinking of piss was the perfect disguise because people actively never saw you. Even the Santas turned away when I got close to them.

Christ my head was cold though. It was a real shock to feel an icy freeze on my naked scalp. I hated it. In some ways, the fact that he had cut my hair upset me the most. There was no getting away from it: Theo had utterly controlled me during the last week or however long I'd been stuck in that fucking church crypt.

I made it to Harriet's flat and I straightened myself up, leaned against the street door and rang up on the buzzer. There was no answer. It was purely on the off-chance that I thought she might have come home, but obviously she hadn't. I was about to leave when a good-looking couple in winter coats and scarves, both of them carrying a Starbucks each, said, "Excuse me," at the door and entered a passcode on the keypad which then buzzed to let them in.

I was too slow to catch their code.

"Hey," I said, stepping forward. "Do you know Harriet Brisley, in flat six?" My voice was fucked. Hadn't realised it until then I guess.

The smiles on the couple disappeared as quickly as their bodies into the hallway. They wanted to get away from me so much that they didn't wait around to let the door shut properly.

Fine by me.

I shoved my foot in to stop it, catching it about an inch before it shut. I waited a while, and then I walked in after them. Quietly, carefully and slowly.

It was gloomy inside. Energy-saving lightbulbs oozing a soft, honey-coloured glow on the beige décor.

Harriet's flat was on the top floor, in the attic space. It was easy enough to find because there was just one flat on each of the floors. When I made it up there however, I found that her door was locked and there was no answer.

I hadn't expected one so I broke in. It was easy enough, surprisingly. I shouldered the door and on the second go it sprang open and bits tinkled to the floor on the other side.

The place was a mess and at first I thought she'd been burgled. Even for Harriet this was a tip.

There was a three-seater sofa at the back of the room, strewn with clothes. A couple of armchairs, a television and a long, low coffee table. Boxes of stock, the stuff she sold on the market, were stacked in the corners, adding to the mess. She'd had to bring it home because she wasn't able to use my lock up in the end. Still, I thought she would have found somewhere for it.

"Harriet?" I called.

She wasn't home. She'd left. More than that she had abandoned her old life completely, just like she'd said she would: *You don't know me*, she'd said at the market. *You don't know the first thing about me.*

I checked through the flat to make sure she wasn't around. Most of the space was taken up with a lounge-cum-dining room with a kitchenette off to one side. Three dormer windows with deep ledges protruded from the pitch of the roof offering a landscape view of grey rooftops receding towards central London. Just off a short corridor running behind the kitchenette was a bathroom and a couple of bedrooms. She definitely wasn't here. Then I thought about how tired I was and I did the sensible thing. I moved one of the armchairs up against the broken door and wedged it shut. Then I stripped off and went for a shower.

I stayed in there a long while, letting the water sluice away the shit that had accumulated onto me in the last few weeks: all the dirt and the blood and whatever else was in there. The mental stuff might take longer...

Harriet's toiletries were still in the shower so I used them. I soaped down and carefully washed the hand which the IV tube had been stuck in, and my skinhead too, which felt strange and humiliating, and I began to feel sick as what I had been through was finally processed in my head.

I sat in the cubicle. Lifted my knees up to my face and buried my head between them with my hands over my head.

Some time later the water turned cold and that was probably the only reason I came out of the shower. I checked my face in the mirror, for the first time in a long time, and as I wiped away the steam from the glass I began to make out someone I didn't recognise. My eyes were wrecked, bloodshot whites ringed with black circles. Swollen and shiny. My lips were fat, cracked and cut, and my neck and shoulders were horrifically bruised. And on top of all that was my skinhead. I ran a hand over it. It was a badly-shaved fuzzy mess.

To be honest, I think I would have crossed the road if I'd seen a guy with a face like this walking towards me.

But I stared at the reflection, stared for a long while. Standing there, naked in Harriet's bathroom, in the steam, reacquainting myself with my self.

The past was the past now, and it didn't hurt anymore because no matter what Theo had said, I hadn't killed Gareth in the tower. James was not a figment of my imagination. I hadn't just made him up in my fevered attempts to reconcile what I went through in Balloch. He was real. He'd been my brother, my twin. Not an identical twin, but close enough so that people sometimes got us confused. Either way, he was dead. Well and truly dead, and the ghost of him, I think, was gone now. Destroying the videotape seemed to have achieved that exorcism for me.

No more saints and angels.

Just me: Jason Jones.

And Jenny. She was out there somewhere and I wasn't going to let her down. I'd known since I'd first spoken to Doctor Pan, before I'd been taken by Theo, that I'd have to find her.

But for now…

It was all I could do to stay awake long enough to make it to Harriet's bedroom.

I slept naked in her unmade bed, running into a dark world full of nightmares. Mixed-up memories, voices and images battered me around and screamed at me. A few times I woke up in a sweat. It was always dark and it turned out that a couple of times I hadn't woken up at all because I was in someone else's bed – in a vast, burning house in Balloch, fighting to the death with a man who looked just like me. And sometimes I was still in the crypt of St Leonard's Church, unable to move because I'd been drugged, so when the building exploded I went up with it.

Sweating. Almost feverish. Always in pain. I slept nonetheless.

I slept the rest of the night and through most of Christmas Eve.

7.12

First thing I sensed when I woke up properly, deciding that I'd spent enough time throwing myself around on Harriet's mattress, was the smell. It was like something had died in the flat. I got up and swung my legs out of the bed, then I padded into the living room.

Frosty sunlight shone through the dormer windows but it wasn't an early-morning sun. Turned out it was almost three o'clock in the afternoon.

I realised that the smell was coming from the pile of clothes I'd left in the middle of the floor before going for the shower. They needed to be incinerated.

I took another shower then stripped the bed down. Dressed only in a bath-towel I started looking around for some fresh clothes. I didn't really think Harriet would have any men's clothes lying about but you never knew. Some girls kept supplies in for their one-night stands. I just didn't know if Harriet was that sort of girl.

I opened her wardrobe.

Seemed she was exactly that kind of girl.

I took out some pants and a t-shirt. There was a pair of straight-cut Levis in there too, folded up on a shelf. They fit pretty well. No need for a belt and the leg length was just right. It wasn't until I put my hand in one of the pockets and pulled out a folded-up wine bar flyer that I realised these were my jeans.

I remembered the wine bar. The flyer was given out to passers-by on the high street, offering them a free cocktail on the opening night over a year ago. Harriet had scribbled her new mobile number on the flyer and given it to me so I could update my contact.

When I looked through the wardrobe I saw more of my clothes.

I sat at the breakfast bar separating the lounge from the kitchenette and turned the wine bar flyer over in my hands.

"Wish you were here…" I muttered.

Wished I hadn't kept her at arm's length.

There was a two-pint carton of milk in her fridge. It was unopened but way past its use-by date so I wasn't going to chance it. My body was wrecked enough. I ate some dry Cheerios and made myself a black Earl Grey. Although I usually made it from leaves in a teapot back at home, I knew she only kept these teabags in for me because she couldn't stand it herself.

I thought about her. "You don't know the first thing about me," she'd said.

Not true. Was it?

I knew she liked boybands and Cheerios and didn't believe in half the mystical shit she sold on her stall – apart from the tarot maybe. She seemed to think there was something in that because she'd offered to 'read my cards' for me – something I'd always refused. But that was all surface detail. So I pondered on what I knew about her and her family. I knew she had a sister called Penny who was some kind of corporate goddess in the city, and a mum who lived out in the sticks somewhere.

I knew she didn't want to stay in London.

What I didn't know was how much she 'liked' me.

There was a canvas up on her bedroom wall which I'd painted for her. A widescreen, abstract landscape of autumnal fog and dispersed lemon-coloured light. She'd told me she liked it and Harriet wasn't a woman who ever minced her words. If she hated something then she'd say so. But sometimes, if she liked something so much, she would say nothing. Deep down she was frightened of rejection, and she put up this spiky fence too often, hiding her real feelings behind it.

Also on her bedroom wall were some photographs. They were pinned into the plaster and there were hundreds of them. She looked good in the photos, her cheeky, elfin features vibrant and lively as she partied with mates at a club or blew a kiss from a beach in Spain with half her face hidden by enormous sunglasses. Seemed I was in some of them, in fact, now that I looked, I was in quite a lot of them. She'd snapped me in the street, at the market, even at home, most of them I clearly hadn't been aware of since I was turning away or reading the paper, smoking a cigarette whilst on the phone etc etc.

Anyone would have thought she'd been stalking me.

There was a dressing table below them and amongst all the toiletries and hair clips were more photographs of me, specifically of me and Liselle – again snapped without us being aware of it. In all these pictures she'd scratched out Liselle's face.

"Oh, Harriet," I muttered. "What have I done to you?"

7.13

The explosion at St Leonard's Church had been caused by a faulty gas main. At least, that was what the news reports were saying when I switched on the TV. They were filming from my street, interviewing my neighbours then cutting to aerial views of the ruin by helicopter. There was nothing about the Camden Killer.

I made myself some tomato soup as the TV news finished and a family film about training dragons came on. I watched it as I ate and it was hilarious, but I fell asleep half way through and didn't wake up until it was gone midnight.

Christmas day.

Trading Places was on the TV. Late night film. Dan Ackroyd was dressed as Santa, stealing food from a corporate Christmas party he should have been a guest at while Eddie Murphy, having taken his place as the firm's MD, nipped off to the toilets to smoke a joint.

Great film, and I watched for a while as it played out: Dan Ackroyd getting thrown onto the street after being caught planting a ridiculous amount of drugs in his successor's desk. Eddie Murphy overhearing the exchange in the toilets where the two old guys responsible for the switchover discussed their wager and the one who lost the bet paid the other guy his one dollar.

Funny how lives could be changed so rapidly when someone decided they were going to fuck you over.

The great thing about the film was how the victims turned their situation around and destroyed the two old guys by playing on their greed.

I switched the TV off and grabbed my MacBook. Maybe I could do the same?

There was eighteen percent battery left and no charger, but it was enough to get me onto the wi-fi of the guy who lived downstairs and dive onto the internet via his router. Idiot never changed his password.

First I went into the news pages and dug out more detail on the church. BBC News said there were twenty-eight people in hospital suffering from wounds inflicted by flying glass. A twenty-year old woman had lost an eye whilst 'a thirty-one-year old man was in St Mary's Hospital undergoing surgery for a head wound'. That had to be Jhavesh and I prayed to a God I'd never believed in that he was going to pull through.

I thought about calling the helpline number that had been set up but decided against it. I had no right to be concerned about Jhavesh or to interfere in his life.

Then I opened up stories on the Camden Killer, looking for the latest. And just as Jhavesh had said, there was my face.

It was a shock. A real blow to the stomach which took the wind out of me but there I was. At least, there was my old face, the one framed with long hair and bisected by a slightly ironic smile; it came from an old publicity shot which usually accompanied gallery programmes and stories on my art. It was at least six years old and looked nothing like my 'new' face.

Clicking through to the newspaper pages I saw it on the covers of the tabloids.

No one will recognise me, I said inwardly, forcing myself to stay calm.

I didn't read the reportage. There was no point.

Instead I clicked open Facebook and Twitter.

Still nothing from Harriet, and the Camden Killer (my saved search) wasn't showing in the top trends.

I clicked into the feed anyway and scrolled through the garbage.

@SarahBGoode: I'm worried there'll be another body for Christmas Day

@FatBelly666: Police are onto him..

@GordonHainesSmith: About time. Anyone really believe its that artist guy?

@Sh1tPolice: I think it is. Check out my blog http://goo.gl/d2qPJm

I stopped there.

Clicked on the link though with some trepidation given what Jhavesh had said about the messenger app I'd installed on the Mac.

Sh1tPolice's latest blog entry described how I'd worked with the police, going on to say:

This is not uncommon with serial killers who seek the double gratification of

both the kill and the chase. Although reason would assume the prime motivation for their assistance would be to throw the investigators off the scent, in some ways this behaviour also serves to reconcile the unnerving guilt that gnaws at a killer's conscience.

The comments expanded on this, and someone had written that true serial killers and psychotic personalities rarely showed any guilt for their subversive actions. It was more likely that 'helping the police' was a further illustration of the killer's need for control.

It went on.

So who was this Sh1tPolice? On the one hand there was a person here who seemed rational and able to put forward a persuasive and compelling, well-reasoned series of blog entries discussing the nature of the Camden Killer and his psychology, and other hand... I don't know. His last message to me was 'Got any pictures?' repeated ad infinitum when I'd told him about finding Stephen Craine's body. Could have been an error, a glitch in the instant messenger app, but it was precisely that which, according to Harish, had sabotaged my video files at the Dreadnought.

Nine percent battery left.

I opened up iCloud and emailed Harish, typing furiously:

Hey. How's it going? Look I hope Jhavesh is OK and I'll check in on him when I can. But I need your help, mate. I need to find this guy who put the app on my Mac. Jhavesh said you were working on tracing it? Any progress? Really appreciate your help, Harish. Happy Christmas btw

Maybe it was presumptive, maybe it was a tad trite, but I sent it anyway.

If anyone could help me track someone down in cyberspace then I thought he was my best bet.

I got rid of the trash as I waited for his reply. Who was I kidding? It was two-thirty on Christmas morning. Who'd be up at this hour?

There were some old emails from Brian Cavendish — one of them, sent a week ago, formally ended my contract with him regarding *The Odyssey Exhibition*. There was an attached pdf which he wanted me to read and sign but I didn't bother opening it. Following that were more emails demanding a response, and a final one from a solicitor saying that as I hadn't responded to repeated emails my contract with Gallery21 was terminated 'without prejudice' and all rights to appeal under the terms of the contract were waived.

I deleted it.

Ironically there was an email from 'Odyssey21.uk' advertising the exhibition itself. The email invited me to attend as a special guest, promising free canapés and cocktails and an exclusive tour of 'our latest installation by Theo Collins ahead of the public opening', which in itself promised an extravaganza of fireworks, street entertainment and live music. All I had to do was click on a link and either print out or save to my phone, an e-ticket to bring with me by 8pm on the night: December 31st.

Five percent battery.

I was about to shut down the Mac when an email pinged into my inbox.

It was Harish. Should've known he'd be awake.

> Hey JJ. It's cool, mate. I heard from Jav's mum and she says he's out of the worst. They operated on his thick skull and maybe they gave him some better brains whilst they was at it LOL! He's OK man.
> About this IM app....
> You shouldn't have installed it. I've never seen anything rip through a system like this. Don't give no one remote access to your computer. Unless its me of course!!! Haha!
> I don't know about tracing it. I can try. It came through a bunch of floating gateways stretching right across the world – usual suspects like China, Russia, India, the US etc etc. These things open up for limited times then shut down so you can't track them back to source once the dialogue has closed. But it aint impossible. Leave it with me. I like a challenge. Keep your head down, mate. I'll be in touch. Best. H.

I sent him a quick reply saying thanks and he sent another email back to me quickly.

> Just had a thought... The apps still on your Mac. I couldn't get rid of it but its quarantined. Harmless while it stays that way. If you got nothing to lose you could try messaging him. If he replies to you I can try tracing it while the dialogue is open. Cheers. H.

I replied:

> I'll give it a go. Are you on my computer now?

> Not right now but I can be. Where's your phone?

> Out of service...

> Ok. I'm going to email you some instructions which will give me remote access to your Mac. You trust me. OK?

> Go for it.

He sent his emails and I did what he asked. Within minutes the mouse arrow circled the screen, controlled by him. A 'notes' window appeared on screen and within it appeared the words:

> OK. I'm in. I've lifted the app out of quarantine so now you write him something. You need to charge up btw!!

A power level warning flashed up on screen. Less than three percent battery remained.

One last throw of the dice.

I took control of the trackpad and clicked on the sleeping green monster that had reappeared on screen. It woke up, immediately throwing a speech bubble full of symbols out of its mouth as though it was angry at having been disturbed.

I typed:

> Hey. Sh1tPolice. Are you out there? I need your help.

Then I waited. Seemed like forever, watching the screen, watching the battery indicator as it tried to turn off my wi-fi. I turned down the screen brightness in an effort to squeeze out the battery.

It was late wasn't it? Harish might have been awake because he was OCD but what about this guy?

Two percent left.

Nothing.

It wasn't going to work.

Suddenly the monster danced and split into two when a reply came in.

A speech bubble opened on the second monster and text appeared letter by letter, spelling, simply:

> JJ? Where are you?

I was about to reply when the Mac died on me.

Black screen.

I breathed out and sat back on the sofa. Had it been enough? Didn't matter. Harriet didn't have anything Apple so she wouldn't have a charger, and I wasn't going back home to get mine.

7.14

A loud, angry buzzing noise woke me up.

I'd fallen asleep on the sofa. Didn't know what time it was but there was sunlight in the room.

The buzzing sound came again. Harsh and grating.

It was the door entry.

But not for this flat. It came from the flat downstairs, directly beneath this one.

I felt a sudden tension. I don't know why but it probably saved my skin. I'd been in Harriet's flat for two nights and no one had come for me. Now I felt instinctively like my downtime had come to an end.

There were hurried footsteps on the stairs outside the door getting louder and closer.

I leapt off the sofa. Then I went round the back of it and heaved on it, pushing it towards the door. The armchair was still in place, wedging it shut, but the sofa would add weight to it.

Maybe I was being paranoid but I leaned in and listened at the door.

Whoever it was they were definitely coming up here. I was sure it couldn't be Harriet. The sound was big and hurried. Like Nazi jackboots, I thought.

I turned and ran back into the flat.

I grabbed my coat, the stinking one covered in blood and piss, figuring that no one would want to get too close to me wearing that. Then I ran into Harriet's bedroom. She liked woolly hats and there were a few of them lying around. I picked up a black one and jammed it down over my head.

I'd had some time to consider my escape route and although I'd hoped to go by the door, it seemed plan-B was now the only option.

Trouble was that plan-B was terrifying.

There was a loud shove on the door and the furniture I'd stacked up in front of it budged suddenly.

Shit!

I made for the window in the bedroom, then turned and ran quickly back to the lounge. I needed the MacBook. It was the only conceivable way I was ever going to stay in touch with Harish and find this guy who called himself Sh1tpolice.

I caught sight of a face in the gap of the door as someone tried to shove it open.

"Jason? It's Jim," said a familiar voice. "Jim Burrows. Come on, let us in. We need to talk to you."

And arrest me for murder? No chance.

I shoved the computer under my arm and ran back to the bedroom. The reason for this was because I'd discovered it was only the window in the flat that actually opened wide enough for me to climb out of.

I'd been formulating Plan-B since yesterday. Plan-A had been to leave the normal way but clearly that wasn't an option now.

So I climbed up onto the wide sill of the dormer window in the bedroom, slid my legs round and shoved the thing open. Immediately, ice-cold air and the noise of the city blasted me down. Even on Christmas Day it sounded busy.

It was a long way down.

"Jason!" shouted Burrows struggling at the door. "Jason, you can't go anywhere. Move this—"

There was a slate-grey ledge just outside the window. Easily wide enough for me to stand on. I leaned forward and slid out, feet first, holding onto the window frame with one hand, trying to keep my MacBook in the other. However, as soon as my feet touched the surface of the ledge, I fucking slipped.

I hadn't realised how icy it would be, which was stupid given how treacherous it was even on the street, but I slipped and I grabbed onto the sloping window frame with both hands for dear life, scrabbling to get myself a proper footing.

Dropping the MacBook in the process.

"Fuck!"

It slid down the ledge.

It hadn't fallen off totally. It was caught on some moss clumped in the guttering, half-on half-off. If I got down to my knees and reached forward I could probably get it.

Slowly, terrifyingly, I let go of the window-frame. Hunkered down and leaned out down the ledge, arm outstretched…

"Whoa!"

The whole of London seemed to tip upwards to meet me and I scrabbled back to safety, breathing quickly.

Try again…

I leaned forward again, this time more carefully.

Reached out with my fingers…

Touched the aluminium case, nudged it. And then the thing slipped off the roof completely, falling to the street.

Quickly my survival instinct kicked in and I pulled myself back to the window.

Fuck fuck fuck!

Ok. Forget the computer.

Fuck!

I'd find another way to catch up with Harish.

Fuck!

I turned my body around, away from the terrifying cityscape, to face the sloping outer wall of Harriet's flat and I looked along it left and right. If I went left then I would have to jump down to the street. Unless I could fly, or didn't mind hitting the ground like an egg, that wasn't an option. Going right seemed to offer at least a chance of getting over to the neighbouring block, and maybe there was a safer way down to the street there.

So I edged right, sidling along the face of the slope, desperately grabbing for any kind of handhold I could find – pipes, edges in the cladding, any kind of ridge or break in the surface.

Pigeons flapped away when I closed on them and my feet slipped more than once.

I was terrified. I'd never been frightened of heights until now. Any minute I could fall to my death and that would be the end of me. Like it had been for my MacBook.

Fuck!

The route took me past a couple more windows. When I reached the first one I looked inside to Harriet's living room.

There was nobody in the flat yet so I edged past it relatively confidently. But when I got to the second window I could see arms flailing through the gap as Burrows tried to get inside.

I slid past it carefully, as quickly as I could, trying not to slip.

The block was terraced, and the next building continued with the sloping attic-storey wall punctuated by dormer windows. I moved onto it, crossing from one building to the other as easily as Superman, hoping that the police would wait before they poked their heads out of Harriet's bedroom window, giving me enough time to get out of their line of sight.

Through one of the windows some people stared at me from their kitchenette, horrified, as though we were in some kind of farcical comedy sketch. It was all I could do to resist the urge to wave.

By now my fingers were freezing. In retrospect I'd never have been able to keep hold of the Mac, I needed both hands to navigate this bloody rooftop.

There was some brickwork to negotiate at the far side. It was like someone had built a wall at one end of the roof which reduced the ledge depth to about a couple of inches. I had to hug the edge of the wall and clamber around it precariously, putting the weight on my toes, leaning forward with my face in the bricks.

"Don't look down, don't look down…" I whispered to myself over and over, not looking down.

Definitely. Not. Looking down.

"Oh fuck. Oh fuck. Oh fuck…!"

I made it around the wall, turned and pressed my back to it. Gathered my breath and looked ahead.

Focus.

Ahead of me now was the next rooftop. The buildings weren't all the same. They were different heights, different styles, built or modified during different decades for different purposes. The rooftop I was now looking at was a whole storey lower and it didn't have the pitch of an attic. It was flat, square, rimmed by a low wall.

I could jump…

Yes, I could but – there was a gap.

It was less than a metre wide but it went down the full height of the building, a stupid little alley that was probably nothing more than a toilet for the homeless or a dumping ground for peoples' shit. Whatever it was I didn't want to fall down it.

But here's the thing: if I was on the ground I'd jump a metre easily. It wasn't too much of a stretch. But the drop here must have been about sixty or seventy feet and the wind was blowing brutally against me. Psychologically, it was a difficult jump.

Then, from the sky, I heard the sound of a chopper.

It might have just been a domestic helicopter taxiing over London, but given that the police had probably by now burst into Harriet's flat and my face was all over the papers, it was more likely one of theirs. Besides, even if it wasn't a police vehicle the pilot would probably radio in that he was looking down on some idiot stuck on the edge of the roof deciding whether or not he was going to jump.

The sound was louder now so…

Fuck it.

I jumped.

7.15

I hit the deck hard and tried to roll so that I didn't break my legs. I twisted my ankle, fell forward and put my hands out in front of me. The surface of the roof was hard and gritty and my hands got badly scraped, but at least nothing was broken.

I scrambled to my feet and ran, heading for what looked like an air-conditioning plant on the rooftop, a big, grey cube of metal covered in streaks of pigeon shit. From there I looked around and got my bearings.

The next roof along was a slight step-up from this one so shouldn't be too hard to get onto. Trouble was the chopper was circling. I could hear it getting louder, closer, and I imagined the police sitting in it, one of them looking out of the windows while he steered the chopper, the other one checking the feed from the onboard cameras, talking into the radio and advising the pilot where he needed to go.

I ran.

I ran as fast as I could, trying to keep in cover so that the chopper wouldn't see me. But I was exposed and easily noticeable. It wasn't often you found people racing along the rooftops of Kentish Town Road.

I clambered up the next rooftop and threaded my way through a nest of satellite dishes, accidentally knocking one or two of them. Looking over my shoulder I caught sight of the helicopter. It was high up against the grey clouds, a black and yellow wasp, circling.

Definitely the cops. And they might even have seen me now.

I kept low, shivering. I was so cold I reckoned they wouldn't even see me on their thermal cameras. Still, I didn't want to hang around.

The next rooftop was about two storeys higher, a sheer brick sidewall, so there was no chance of climbing that. Which meant I had only one option left, which was to go down.

I skittered to the edge and looked over.

Seemed my luck was in.

It'd be tricky, but I could do it.

The back side of the buildings was a criss-crossing network of access ladders, fire escapes, metallic box flues with great big fans in them, flat roofs and wide windowsills – with bars on the windows I found out as I clambered down from one level to the next. I used everything I could: hanging onto poles like a monkey, jumping from one ladder to another, pulling myself around the corners of walls even despite the pain in my shoulders. The angles were tight, it was narrow and dark and I was breathing hard. Looking behind me now there was no view of either Harriet's flat or the police helicopter.

I couldn't help smiling. They'd never find me in all this.

This complex of staggered rooftops was a thief's paradise, which probably accounted for the vicious spikes and razor wire, cement-embedded glass and security cameras I discovered on my way down. There was an alley at ground level which ran parallel to the high street. It stank, but it was only three or four metres below me now. Trouble was that I had to get across the razor wire on the edge of this last flat rooftop to be able to jump down to it.

I hunted around, hoping for a sheet of wood or metal the size of a door that I could plonk over the wire.

Nothing.

So I took off my coat and pressed it down over a section of wire, flattening it with my feet. "Thought this shit was illegal," I said to myself, as I turned and knelt on the coat. I turned around and slid my body over the ledge, stomach down, then hung from my fingertips. When I was ready I let go, pulling the coat down with me.

I heard and felt it rip as I landed. I tumbled backwards and crashed noisily into a wheelie bin.

"Whoa!"

When I picked myself up I had a look and saw that the razor wire had done its worst for the coat, tearing strips down the back like the slash from a monster's talons.

I put it back on regardless and headed out of the alley at a brisk walk. Seemed like I'd clambered down behind Iceland, McDonalds and the couple of shops sandwiched in-between them. I guess this is what had made it easy. It had the additional advantage of being closed on Christmas Day – so no one would have seen me on their CCTV and wouldn't until the shops re-opened in the morning for the Boxing Day rush – if they could be bothered to look at the footage.

Grinning at my cleverness I turned right at the bottom of the alley.

Straight into the car park for Kentish Town Police Station.

I almost froze.

Two dark-silver police cars were parked in a bay right next to the massive, century-old building in Holmes Road which bristled with CCTV clusters. This was a 24-7 station. Thanks to a public appeal a few ago, even at Christmas it didn't close.

I put my head down and continued walking. Round the car park, in front of the police station steps, and then onwards, down Holmes Road, away from the High Street.

Fuck me, I was shaking like a leaf.

I couldn't believe what I'd just done.

7.16

So how did anyone keep away from the police when they were hunting you down in a city on a terror alert, where every building was covered with CCTV cameras, and patrol cars swept the neighbourhoods twenty-four hours a day? How did you keep your head down when your face was on the cover of every major newspaper in the country? I wasn't an expert. I had no clandestine contacts I could meet up with who could score me a new passport and a ticket to France. The few friends I had were either in hospital, missing, dead or out to kill me. I hadn't seen Arnold for a while but I doubt he'd want to talk to me since getting kicked from *The Odyssey Exhibition* would have lost him his fee. Besides, it was Christmas. So he was most likely up at his lodge in Kyle of Lochalsh getting stupid drunk with some other fool willing to listen to his maudlin drivel.

As it grew dark I wandered down towards central London, banking primarily on not being recognised.

The picture in the paper was so unlike me now that it may as well have been someone else. Besides, I looked, smelled and felt like a vagrant, and there were so many of those on the streets that nobody looked too closely. The police might, I was thinking, if they were looking for me specifically and if they knew I was dressed like this, then they might just pay closer attention to the faces under the hoodies and the bodies in shop doorways. But the chances were that they were looking for any number of people homeless and lost in the city. Even here the police were spread too thinly and had a lot on their plates. Hershey and Burrows might have a team, but how many coppers was that realistically likely to be?

So I figured I needed to keep the vagrant look. To be honest I had no other choice.

I thought briefly about going home, but that wouldn't achieve anything. I'd never find out who Theo's partner was, I'd never find Sh1tPolice. I was convinced it was the same person, maybe it really was the Camden Killer. Yeah… the more I thought about it, wandering the streets, the more it seemed to make sense. There was too much of a connection between the theatre of the bodies, my art, and my clash with Theo to make it a coincidence.

However, unmasking the murderer wasn't so important to me. What mattered was why someone was fucking me over. If the same guy was the murderer then fine. But in either case the big question was why didn't he just come out and kill me? Why lead me to thinking the Camden Killer was Theo Collins? Was it to ensure that Theo would have enough reason to hate me? So much so that he'd be willing to torture me in a church crypt and leave me to die when it fucking exploded?

I was convinced that the guy had been playing us off, maybe so that we'd kill each other and cancel ourselves out of existence. James' Zero

Equation...

I could have been wrong about Sh1tPolice. Maybe he was just some lonely guy who spent too much time on his computer? But I didn't think so. If Hari was right, then this was the same guy who'd installed the virus which had seriously fucked up my *Castle Mechanics* piece, and that was main factor in my expulsion from *The Odyssey Exhibition*. In itself this made Sh1tPolice an ideal place to start and maybe to finish.

Trouble was that without my Mac I had no link to Harish, so I had nowhere to start looking.

Theo then.

Maybe I could get him to talk. Not that I'd been so successful in achieving this back at the crypt. But if he saw me walking up to him when he thought I was dead...?

It was all I had.

And then the Other Thing pinged into my thoughts like a new message alert, or a reminder notification with an urgent red flag attached.

It was that last message from Doctor Pandghani regarding Jenny: 'If she's not with you...'

So where was she?

Years ago I'd have dropped everything to go find her, and a big part of me wanted to right now. Her name was like a powerful singularity pulling me towards it. In the end I gave in to it, because Jenny was vulnerable and she was family and she was missing. Until I found a way to communicate with Harish I wouldn't know where to start with Sh1tPolice, but at least I knew where I could start looking for my sister.

7.17

There were plenty of homeless shelters around. I went to one in Islington and spoke to a lanky guy with a ginger beard who looked like he was on the wrong side of the desk.

He checked something on a computer when I gave him Jenny's name.

"Saint Cecilia's?" he said.

I nodded.

"Jenny Jones... Jenny Jones..." he mumbled while I tried to act casual. My fingers were tapping on the counter while behind me a group of girls were singing Christmas Carols. Loudly. Laughing their faces off.

Sounded like they'd been on the vodka all day.

"Welsh?" the guy asked.

"Yup."

"My sister married a Welshman," he said, clicking down his screen. "Lives in Barry now. You know it?"

I shook my head. "No."

He shrugged. Sang Paul McCartney's *Frog Chorus* under his beard for a moment: "Pommm-pom-pommmm...Ah!" His eyes widened.

"Found her," he said. "I think."

He swung the screen round to show me a picture of Jenny. It was years old but definitely her. Her eyes looked dark. Her face was scratched and gaunt, framed by thin black and grey hair.

"That's her!" I said, leaning over the desk.

He swung the screen back and clicked through some more detail.

"Yup, she's in London," he said. "Or she was... three weeks ago... Seems she checked in at a shelter in Hackney. Not one of ours but we all use the same CRM."

I had no idea what that meant. "Anything since then?" I asked.

He clicked his tongue. Hummed again, then shook his head. "Nope. There's an alert out for her though. If she's seen then we have to call the police. What did you say your name was again?"

"James Gordon," I answered.

He typed it in.

"And where do you live, Mr Gordon?"

"No fixed abode. Look, can you give me the address of the place in Hackney?"

"I doubt she'll be there..."

"I can ask around," I said. "I really need to find her."

"What's your connection with this woman?"

"I'm a family friend."

He stared at me hard.

"Look, she ran away from hospital and I've come to look for her."

"Says here she was discharged to another Jones. Jason Jones, her brother?"

He looked at me again, peering through his stupid glasses.

I stood up. "Thanks," I said, turning to leave.

"Hold on," he called. "You don't have the address."

"I'll find it," I called back.

The singing women were blocking my way out.

"Oi oi, pretty boy!" one of them shouted, throwing her arm round me and pressing her fat lips to my cheek. "No need to run off!"

I shrugged her off me and hurled myself at the door, almost falling outside into the cold.

Hackney, I thought. Couldn't be that many shelters in Hackney could there?

7.18

Turned out there were plenty.

I didn't find the one she'd been in but I stuck around one of the bigger shelters long enough to get some food. I had a conversation inside the place similar to the one in Islington with the glasses-guy, only this time they did a better job trying to keep hold of me.

When I walked quickly away from it, two uniformed police were climbing out of a car.

I didn't know for sure that the cops had been called in because of me but I wasn't going to take any chances. I turned away from them, pulled the woolly hat down over my brow and hurried into the night.

I'd have to think harder about what I did next.

7.19

It was dark now.

I was freezing cold and lost in North London. Getting nowhere.

I was hungry again, wishing I could have stayed in Harriet's flat where she had tinned food and a bed. I could have pretended that everything was normal.

For a while...

My head was pounding. My whole body sang with pain.

Throughout the day, blood had been leaking from the bruised wound on the back of my hand where Theo had inserted the drip catheter. My legs and my feet were sore and aching.

I guess I wasn't in any state, either physically or mentally, for a long walk up and down the London streets. But what other choice did I have? I felt like a hollow man stalking Christmas night. Some kind of vampire hunting the empty streets for signs of a lost, broken woman who probably wouldn't recognise me. I walked down to the snowy railway lines and canalsides because I wondered if there might even be a body.

Late at night the city settled down and the streets grew unnaturally quiet. It seemed to me as though every soul in London had moved on, leaving the city hand-in-hand without me. I'd always been something of an outsider I guess, but tonight it felt as though I truly was a figure who walked the metropolitan wilderness entirely alone.

Christmas night and no one around but me.

I sat for a rest in the recessed doorway of a closed Bengali restaurant, but ended up staying longer. The metal shutters were down on the giant front window but the shutter which should have closed off the doorway had only come halfway down, allowing me to get under it and grab some protection from the cold. I hadn't been there for long when a dark, near-silent Prius whispered down the road like the blade of a knife; reflections of streetlights reduced to sine-wave forms as they slid over its glossy paintwork. The car was crawling, the driver and a passenger looking left and right, checking the pavements. Police?

I drew my legs up tight and slunk into the shadow of the doorway.

Eventually I fell asleep, only to be awakened first by the stink and then the sight of someone's dick splashing the doorway shutter with piss. Faces of grinning idiots loomed either side of the dick's owner, laughing.

"Motherfucker!" I shouted, trying to scrabble from the spray but finding that the door at my back stopped me.

When he finished and zipped up, the guy hacked up from deep down in his throat and gobbed at me through the shutter.

The lads hooted, called abuse and rattled the shutters like a bunch of baboons, then they all walked off, laughing.

Not alone then after all.

7.20

The morning after came and I was hungry, cold and in pain. It felt like I'd fallen off a cliff overnight, and the heights of yesterday – where I had a mission, a purpose, something to focus on – were lost to me.

There was a constant, freezing lump in my chest which I couldn't shift. Shooting pains ran up my thighs and as for my hands, even shoving them deep into my pockets didn't make them any warmer. The abuse I'd suffered the last week or so was taking its toll, and sleeping out in the cold overnight hadn't helped.

I shuffled along the streets of East-Central London as Boxing Day ticked on and people starting repopulating the city: shop workers lifted the shutters on their windows and doors, van drivers stopped by to deliver boxes. Buses roared past me on the streets. A few at first, then more as the morning progressed. Cars, taxis, bicycles, scooters – more vans. Traffic building up as people hunted down the sales.

I shambled along with my head down, hoping that the wind would drop, or that the sun might just warm my blood a little more. Hoping that this was nothing more than a fucking nightmare I could wake up from.

I could barely walk straight. Barely think straight. Random thoughts rocketed through my head like out-of-control fireworks. Plans I made or tried to make fizzled away to nothing.

Jenny. Theo. Masks. Killer. Stephen. Gareth. James. Jane. Blood. Sex. Eve. Suicide. Death. Names, images, memories and mixed-up feelings freewheeled in my head like an unwanted word-association exercise, and I couldn't get any of them to stay still. I couldn't… focus…

I didn't even know that I'd fallen over. All I knew was that I just wanted to sit on the steps of Holborn Underground station for as long as I could and let the Earth continue to spin without me for a while.

7.21

"Come on, mate. Up you get. You can't stay here."

Fine by me.

The guy from the station didn't help me to my feet, he just squatted down in front of me and bellowed into my face to wake me up. When I struggled to stand, he rose and stepped back a bit.

I growled, trying to rub life into my legs.

"I don't want no trouble, fella," he said. "Christmas and all that."

"Happy fucking Christmas," I mumbled as I walked away from him, struggling up the steps, clinging to the railings.

The sleep seemed to have done me some good. Still hurting, but maybe I was able to manage it better. The cramp faded as I walked, replaced by a deep hunger exacerbated by the smell of a street vendor roasting chestnuts on a brazier.

It was dark now. Busy too. People were everywhere.

By some miracle I still had my wallet with me. Just on the off-chance I put my hand into the inside pocket of my coat and felt my fingers close upon its familiar, reassuring shape. I ducked around the side of a building, opened it up and found I still had my sixty-quid cash inside plus credit cards. Another night on the street would kill me, so there and then I decided I was going to spend tonight in the YMCA. There was one close by I was sure, at the roundabout on Tottenham Court Road: at the Centre Point tower – or close by it anyway. I didn't know if they charged for rooms, I didn't think they did but I'd be happy to 'donate' or whatever if they'd let me in.

Feeling relatively uplifted I continued walking as the atmosphere grew colder and darker quickly.

There was a coffee stall on the way down. I thought I'd kill for a cappuccino. I gave the guy on the stall some cash for a hot cheese and ham croissant, plus the coffee, and it tasted like the best thing in the world.

As I ate and drank on a bench in the street, it felt like my head was starting to work again.

If there was a bed at the YMCA, I was thinking, and I could get in, then my chances of figuring a way out of this shit would be greatly improved.

7.22

"I'm sorry, sir. We have no rooms available tonight."

"You're absolutely sure?"

The girl nodded. She was a slender, pretty, blonde thing despite the rash of red acne that covered her cheeks and her forehead. She sounded Polish, or Hungarian – something like that. I don't know. Foreign. European. She kept her distance behind the massive desk at the YMCA which I'd found over an NCP car park at the bottom of Tottenham Court Road.

"I'm very sure," she said.

I didn't know what to do.

"I need a place."

"Hmmm…" she looked like she wanted to say something. Eventually she did. "I can see if there are any rooms available at Errol Street."

"Where's that?" I asked.

"It's um… Islington?" she said.

I nodded. Smiled. "Please," I said.

She smiled back and reached for the phone. "What was your name again?" she asked me.

"James Gordon," I answered.

"Do you have any ID?"

I did, but not with James' name on it.

I was about to open my mouth and fumble some kind of lie when the girl lifted a finger to silence me. Seemed her call had been answered and she began to speak to someone.

"Uh-huh… Uh-huh…"

This went on for a while.

"Uh-huh…"

A few people came and went. Backpackers dumping keys in a slot on the high counter, and some vagrant looking worse than me shambling in off the street.

With one hand the girl behind the desk thrust out a sheet of paper. The vagrant guy grabbed it without a word and headed for the door to the stairs.

I looked back at the girl.

Up at the camera on the ceiling.

Then back at the girl.

Eventually she put the phone down.

Smiled at me.

"Well?" I asked her.

"Did you have any identification?" she asked me back.

"I was attacked and robbed in the street this morning," I said, having decided upon the lie and come to terms with it.

Her face was a picture of perfect sympathy and distress. Well practised.

"I'm so sorry to hear," she said.

"It's why I need a room. Just need to sort myself out."

"Have you told the police?"

I nodded. "And as soon as I can find somewhere to stay I can get back in touch with them, call my family, get some money and go home."

She was nodding her head, still looking sympathetic. Any minute now she was going to tell me there was no room at the inn.

"Do they have a room?" I asked her.

"No," she said.

My heart sank.

"You can try Union Street?" she said.

"What's that?"

"It's a hostel run by another charity. Sometimes we work together when it's busy."

"OK. Where is it?"

"Still in Islington. I will write down the directions."

"Will they have room? Can you phone them?"

"It's not a hotel," she said. "It's best you can go there? Just walk in and see what they can do."

I sighed. Exasperated and disappointed. But I couldn't do another night on the street so what choice did I have?

"It is the best thing," she told me. "But you will need to show them ID."

"I can't," I said tightly. "I just told you I was attacked and robbed in the street. They took my wallet and everything."

"Do you have a crime number?"

"Probably."

"Then you can try and say it to them you have been attacked." She shrugged. "Maybe they will let you in."

She gave me the address and some directions on a piece of paper.

I glanced at them as I walked out.

Straight up Tottenham Court Road, turn left past Kings Cross then another five or ten minutes north from there. Around forty minutes' walk in total and not really in Islington – closer to Camden I'd guess. Anyway I didn't go straight up TCR. I figured it was too busy; I'd been lucky that no one had recognised me but I didn't want to take unnecessary risks. So I went the alternative route, heading up the back streets which I knew reasonably well. It was still busy, but there was nowhere near the press of people as on the main road.

7.23

I was being followed. Same feeling I'd had weeks ago at home. I kept looking over my shoulder and although I couldn't see anyone, I knew they were there. So for the whole journey I was tense, ready for someone to jump out. No one did. So maybe it was just paranoia, my fucked-up head playing tricks on me.

The hostel at Union Street was a dump. It smelled worse than my coat and I could hear a screaming kid bawling his face off somewhere in the building. The guy on the desk didn't ask any real questions. Just took my name and a fake address on a piece of paper, then gave me a key to room 22.

"You're going to have to share. Is that OK?"

At first I wanted to say no, actually it wasn't ok. I wanted my own space.

But again, what choice did I have?

I'd passed a Premier Inn on the way up and I'd considered walking in there for a comfortable room and a guaranteed quiet night. But I was down to around fifty-quid cash in my wallet which wouldn't have been enough, even for a budget hotel in London, on Boxing Day night and I didn't want to use my credit cards. For all I knew the cops were waiting to track me down and as soon as I entered my PIN number they'd swoop right in and put me in cuffs.

Room 22 was on the third floor, up a narrow staircase carpeted with a liver-coloured, cigarette-burned shagpile that had seen much better days.

The place was a terraced townhouse; one of many in the street, and all of which were hotels promising quality accommodation and wi-fi for a cheap price but which in reality probably failed to deliver on all counts. The hostel's walls rattled as trains rumbled past, something which happened, so I found out, pretty much every minute of the night.

And that screaming kid didn't shut up either.

I knocked on the door before I opened it with the key. A young guy in a T-shirt and pants looked up as I walked in. He sat cross-legged on a tiny bed by a tiny window, which was open. He was stabbing at the keys on a tiny laptop plugged into the wall.

"Hey," he said, flicking a cigarette butt out the window.

"Hi," I answered, closing the door and walking in.

It was stifling hot. Two radiators in the tiny room whacking out heat.

The guy closed the window and then reached out a hand for me to shake. I guessed he was in his twenties, looked pretty fit and healthy. I wondered what he was doing in a place like this.

"Steve," he said as I shook his hand.

"Ja – James," I told him.

Two beds in the room. Mine was close to the door.

"You look shit, mate. What happened to you?" he asked, and I detected an accent. Australian maybe. Or New Zealand. I could never really tell the difference but I'm sure if I said he was one he'd tell me he was the other.

"Not much room in here," I said.

Steve grinned. "Even less now," he said jokingly. "Just kick my shit around if it gets in your way. But seriously, mate. You look like you need a doctor."

There was a massive rucksack next to the bed. I lifted it off and sat, then groaned and lay right back, head against the headboard, ankles dangling over the bottom.

"I'll be fine," I mumbled.

The springs dug into my back through the thin sheets and the entire frame creaked under my weight, but I didn't care. It was a bed. It was in a room, and it was fucking Heaven compared to last night's horror.

7.24

I awoke in the morning to the sound of trains screaming beneath the house, shaking the building hard.

Steve wasn't around but his rucksack was down at the bottom of his bed, so I guessed he hadn't gone for good.

The window was open slightly and beyond it delicate flakes of snow drifted downwards, collecting in the cracks of peeling paintwork on the rotten sill, melting if they floated too far into the room's volume of heat.

The corner of Steve's laptop was poking out the top of it.

Either he was an idiot leaving it behind in a place like this or he was very trusting.

Not that I'd steal it. It was no good to me.

My own laptop would have been, since I'd have been able to see whether Harish had emailed me concerning the trace on Sh1tPolice – if he'd managed to do it, that is. It was probably in pieces on a pavement in Kentish Town, or some chancer had nabbed what was left of it and sold it on eBay.

I sat there thinking about what I was going to do next, whether I was going to continue looking for Jenny and if so, where to pick up the trail.

The door behind me opened suddenly and Steve walked in carrying two Starbucks and a bag of pastries.

"You're awake!" he said, booting the door shut behind him.

His fingers were covered in spilled coffee.

He handed me one of the cups and shook the loose liquid off his hands. "Here you go, buddy. Got you a straight Americano."

I could have kissed him.

"Thanks," I croaked.

He sat down on his bed near the window. "I didn't know if you liked milk and sugar so…"

He fished a couple of raisin-filled pastries out of the bag, plus a lidded espresso cup of milk and a handful of sugar sachets.

I didn't normally take sugar but I felt I could do with the energy boost, so I emptied three of the sachets into the coffee and tipped in some of the milk.

"So you're a local guy?" Steve asked me.

"Kind of," I answered. "What about you?"

He grinned. "Just visiting."

"You could have found a better place to visit than here."

He shrugged. "Same as most places. All I need is a bed, wi-fi and easy access to an ethically-challenged chain of coffee shops, and I'm cool."

I laughed at that, and asked him a bit more on where he was from. Seemed he was Australian. He had some friends here and he'd spent some time with them over the last couple of weeks, but his friend's girlfriend had tried it on with him at a party they'd all been to on Christmas Eve and that had caused 'issues', as he put it.

"So I done the decent thing and left 'em to it. I was just chatting to the guy last night on Facebook when you came in. I think we're mates again but it sounds like all hell broke loose after I went," he laughed. "Who needs friends and family eh?"

"Tell me about it."

Steve told me he was off to Scotland for New Year. Had some friends up in Glasgow he'd arranged to catch up with. Train was leaving in ninety minutes or so from Euston.

"You could come with me," he said. "I'm sure you could still get a ticket."

I shook my head. "Thanks. But I need to stay in London," I told him. "I'm trying to find someone."

"Who's that?"

"My sister. She ran off a few weeks ago. Trouble is she's … she's been in hospital. She has a … a mental condition." I shrugged. "I don't know. They've told me all sorts over the years."

He nodded, his face a picture of empathy and I pretty much told him everything.

"She used to be in this place up in Edinburgh. It was called the Novak Institute after some fucking Nobel Prizewinner or something. I thought it'd be a good place since they advocated a course of treatment that had turned in real results for cases like hers. At least that's what they said at the time. The reality turned out to be nothing but an exercise in terror and control."

"How'd you mean?"

"They just put her on drugs which fucked around with her head. She was drowsy a lot of the time so they gave her more drugs to keep her awake. She was on three or four anquil tablets a day which suppressed her so-called 'deviant behaviour' but these worked her up, made her agitated, so she had to take some other shit which lessened the agitation but the end result was that she didn't know where she was from one moment to the next. She used to go wandering round the wards. She became listless and refused to eat, and when it was really bad she just curled up saying she wanted to disappear.

"It went on for years, as they tried different combinations of anti-psychotics, and anti-Parkinsonians to combat the side effects. Eventually she was being injected daily with something in a fuckoff massive needle jabbed into her arse. Got to the stage where, as the nurses approached her for the injections, she'd become violent. Two male nurses would have to hold her down by her arms and legs. They'd turn her over and because she was fighting so much they'd literally have to tear off her pants so that she could be injected."

"Jesus…"

"Less than an hour after each injection she'd be virtually comatose," I told him. "I hardly recognised her when I saw her, and I'm not sure she recognised me when it was really bad. It was difficult."

"I bet…"

She used to get these … spasms, and I'd seen video tapes of her in fits. I remember one doctor telling me that the fits were false, just her way of getting attention he said, and so to combat them he put her in a padded room wearing a strait-jacket."

"You're shitting me. They still do that?"

I nodded, remembering my big sister, reduced to a skeletal wretch with her arms tied together in front of her, throwing her body repeatedly from wall to wall, screaming with rage like a caged animal, then curling into a corner crying quietly.

"After a while, when she was let back into her bed, she shat herself whenever she saw the doctor, her way, he said, of defying him. But I knew it was because she was genuinely terrified. She used to write letters," I said, "which were addressed either to me, to our mum or dad, sometimes all three of us. It was impossible to tell what the letters said because the writing was tiny and messy, with whole sentences written on top of other sentences over and over again. She used to draw sometimes, in wax crayon, great big colourful Js on page after page of paper, each one surrounded by different motifs: flowers and jewelled animals, swirling wind-patterns, fish and water, thorns or barbed wire or smoke and fire. They began quite simple but she's quite artistic. So the

Js became more complex, more difficult to distinguish from the embellishments she made. In the end, just before I got her out of the Institute, the J itself would be broken up into pieces and scattered through the picture like a shattered mosaic. I'm no expert, but to me it was a sign that her mind was ready to give up and go out forever."

"And now she's run away?" said Steve.

I supped on the coffee, my hands shaking. "She's been in this other place for the last three years. Still on drugs but not so many. She had a good doctor but now she's out of there. They think she's with me but I haven't seen any sign of her."

"I'm sorry to hear that, buddy," Steve said.

I shrugged. "Thanks for listening," I said. "You don't need all this crap right?"

"We've all got baggage, mate," he told me. He nodded at his rucksack on the floor. "I'd like to think that was all I had, but there's plenty more of me back home. But look, if I can help you find her. If there's anything I can do – I mean I don't have to go to Scotland..."

"Yes you do," I said. "You've bought your ticket and you've a train to catch. But thanks. I really appreciate it."

He nodded. "Easy."

I couldn't help looking at this kid. Studying him and wondering why he was so... nice, so willing to help me. Was it genuine? Were people really so generous and without an agenda? I mean, if I'd seen someone looking like me walking into this room I'd have made my excuses and got the fuck out. But here he was, bringing me cups of coffee and offering help and tickets to Glasgow.

I'd pretty much finished the coffee by the time I'd stopped telling him about Jenny. I took a last gulp and then put the empty on a shelf which looked like it might collapse and pull half the rotten wall down with it. Thankfully it stayed put.

"Don't suppose there's a shower or something in this shithole is there?" I asked him.

He grinned and nodded. "Down the hall," he answered. "Good luck with it though. I hear the roaches are as big as dinner plates."

He grinned.

"Take this." He said, and fished out a tiny bottle of body wash robbed from a Marriott. He tossed it at me. "And this," he added, throwing me a towel.

"I'll bring it back."

"No drama," he said with a shrug.

I gave him a smile then picked up his towel and body wash. Left the room.

7.25

The shower was pretty bad. Just an attachment hooked up over a cracked bath in a room which didn't have a proper lock on it. It stank. They weren't exactly the size of dinner plates but there were roaches – and spiders and fuck knows what else hiding in the cracks. The mirror was smashed, the basin was hanging off the wall. But all I needed was the shower and even if just trickled out, it was water and it was red hot. Seemed like there was no shortage of hot water in this place.

I was thinking about what I'd told this Steve guy regarding Jenny; asking myself why I'd told him so much about something so personal. I'd never even told Harriet any of that, let alone a complete stranger. I couldn't change it now, the words were out.

But it had felt good, finally telling someone about all this stuff which had hidden inside me for so long, eating me away.

Jenny was so close to my heart it hurt every time I pictured her in that fucking place, and I was so glad I'd managed to get her out of there and into St Cecilia's. But now... now she was gone. Someone posing as me had taken her out of there and fuck knew where she was.

I wondered...

Wondered whether...

"Ah *shit*!"

I'd missed it! Missed the *fucking obvious*!

"Shit!"

Dripping wet I climbed out of the bath, grabbed the towel and wrapped it around my waist. I picked up my bundle of clothes and ran from the bathroom, racing barefoot down the landing, back towards the room.

I burst in. "Steve!" I shouted.

But the guy was gone.

"*Fuckit!*" His rucksack, his clothes, his bastard laptop. Gone. "Shit!"

I could have used it, I'd realised.

I could have asked him if he'd let me access my iCloud emails. It was a cloud right? A web-based email which meant that as long as I knew my password I could access emails from any computer, any internet browser, anywhere in the fucking world. I hadn't needed my MacBook at all.

I got dressed quickly. He'd said he was going to Euston to catch a train. Maybe I could find him before he boarded. Had to be time right? It couldn't have been ninety minutes since he'd come in with his Starbucks.

7.26

Train was gone.

I hadn't realised how much time had passed whilst we'd been talking, how long I'd been in the shower, or even how long it took me to get down to Euston and fight my way through the crowd so I could get a clear look at the departure boards. But the next train to Glasgow was over an hour away so I reckoned I'd missed Steve's train.

I hung around, asked someone in a uniform if a train had just left. "Twenty-one minutes ago to Glasgow Central," was the answer.

I guessed Steve must have been on it. There was no sign of him now.

The station was busy as people started making their way up-country in the Christmas break, catching up with friends and family etc. There were bodies and noise everywhere. Armed police skulked at the exits, watching.

Didn't feel to me like it was a good idea to hang around.

So I headed out with a group of people, keeping my head down – but not so that I'd look conspicuous. I hoped…

I couldn't believe I hadn't realised until now that I could have used Steve's laptop to access my iCloud. What an idiot. I'd spent the night and most of the morning with him. The guy had even asked me if he could help.

"Dickhead!" I called myself loudly, getting a few looks.

Never mind. Nothing I could do now except recommence my search for Jenny.

So I headed out of the station, back onto Euston Road, back into the falling snow and the press of people.

Then I had another brain-wave.

"Internet café," I said to myself.

If I could find one, then I could get onto my emails that way.

7.27

It took a while to find an internet cafe. Not so many around as I'd imagined since most places offered free wi-fi for people to bring in their own laptops and tablets to get connected, but I found one nonetheless. It was north from Euston, dangerously close to Camden, in a back street next to a bridge overlooking the artery of trainlines running down to the station.

I went in, ordered a tea and a sandwich from the Turkish guy behind the deli and took a seat at a counter near the steamed-up window. There were a couple of people inside, two kids with their eyes glued to a battered computer screen, one of them texting on her mobile, the other clicking through an ancient PC screwed into the countertop. Looked like all the hardware was nailed down. Even the crappy mouse on the terminal I sat at was tethered to the counter by a steel-wrapped cable restricting its movement.

The Turkish guy told me I'd have to purchase time online using a debit or credit card. He'd bring my sandwich over to me when it was ready.

I didn't want to use my cards but I had no choice. Besides, I only needed to check my emails and see if there was anything from Harish. So I shouldn't be here too long.

The PC was slow to load and it kept bombarding me with pop-ups urging me to join online gambling and social network sites I'd never heard of. I bought an hour using my Mastercard and kept an eye on the window in case my paranoia about the police tracking my spending turned out to be true.

Nothing yet.

Eyes back to the screen, and eventually iCloud loaded.

I took a breath.

Here goes…

Then I looked back at the steamy window. Nobody there but I was sure I'd seen someone hovering around. I still felt as though I was being watched. I took off the woolly hat and rubbed the back of my neck. It was still alien to me and right now it was tingling with unease.

I looked at the thirteen unread emails in front of me.

There were three from Harish. The first one sent over twenty-four hours ago, the most recent one this morning. I opened the earliest one first as the Turkish guy brought my lunch over. He put the plate and cup of tea on the counter, then just as he turned to leave I asked him, "Do you have a pen I can borrow? Please?"

He made a show of looking on the counter as though he expected to find one there, but eventually gave me the biro from his white shirt pocket. "You want to write as well?" he asked.

Good idea. "Yes, please," I answered, smiling at him.

He tore a couple of leaves from his order pad, said I could scribble on them.

"Thanks," I said as he left.

I read through the first email, copying the relevant details onto the pad:

> I got something, JJ
> So you might be in luck. Your mate was on a smartphone in North London when he last messaged you. The exchange he was using was in Caledonian Road but there was a packet of 4G metadata which carried a GPS geo-tag I tied down at N7 1UU, which is a bit further north. You can't normally track to postcodes but I got this app which maps coords to postcodes and its way cool. Pretty accurate. Don't tell the cops tho man!! LOL!

I tapped the postcode into Google Maps and the computer struggled. More fucking pop-ups slowing things down. Using Windows as well… which made me long for my Mac.

I split the screen and while Google Maps loaded – or failed to load – I read through the other emails from him. The last one I read was saying he'd pinged something or other, discovered something else and blah blah blah and this time got a totally different postcode.

> Don't know which one you should go on, mate – if any. This one's off in the East End. E13 9 something… That one I gave you yesterday… not sure if it's any good. They could both be foney. Turns out that first one is just some knackered old builders yard off Caledonian Road. I've attached a screen grab of both locations from Google streetview.

I exited Google maps, closed the browser completely, and waited for Harish's images to download instead. Slowly a 'knackered old builders yard' with a distinctive-looking tower standing amongst mountains of aggregate appeared on screen, then a random-looking warehouse in the middle of nowhere.

I asked the Turkish guy if there was a printer attached to these machines.

"It's ten pence a page," he told me.

I sent the images and the map of N7 to print, and whilst that was going on a new email notification floated up in the bottom right corner of the screen. Not from Harish, but from someone else: saintwalker449@gmail.com. I realised there'd been a few emails from him over the last day or so. An image was attached to this one and there was text in the message box saying simply:

Is this the face of the Camden Killer?

My heart kicked inside me.

What the fuck was this?

I stared at it for a while, then eventually I clicked to download the image hoping this piece of shit computer would let me do it. Maybe it was worn out by now because this image was downloading slower than the other two from Harish.

I took a bite of my sandwich in an effort to calm my frayed nerves, then my heart gave another, this time much harder, kick.

It was a large image file, achingly slow to load, but gradually it revealed itself from the top down. And when it was maybe a quarter of the way down I could see that it was a picture of me. A recent one. From the crypt of St Leonard's. Bald-headed, bruised and manic-looking, with what looked like a corpse on the wall behind me. You couldn't see that I was tied to the chair, or that the body behind me was a dummy. It just looked as though I was sitting in front of one of my trophies.

I cursed under my breath.

Then another email popped up from the same guy:

Seems the pictures of you in the papers are outdated. Don't worry. I'll send them this one instead. And btw, your sister says hi

I sat back as far as I could, staring at this bullshit. The single mouthful of sandwich felt as though it was lodged in my throat and the temperature in the café seemed to drop.

Motherfucker...

I felt sick and weak. All I did was stare at the picture, still loading, and read the text again.

...your sister says hi

No no no.

He didn't have Jenny. He couldn't...

I picked up the cup of tea but my hand was shaking so badly it was all I could do to stop it spilling.

In the corner of my eye I saw a police car slowing outside. Drifting past the window.

It moved on past the café but I wasn't taking chances.

Calmly, but with my heart now in my mouth, I put the cup down, closed iCloud and logged off the browser.

I shoved the sandwich into my coat pocket then I got up from the seat and headed towards the back of the café. I gave the guy his pen and pad back and slapped some cash down for the food. He handed me my printouts from the machine behind the counter, and as he checked the money I asked if he had a toilet I could use.

"Through the back," he said, which was what I was hoping he'd say.

If the police came in through the front, then I wouldn't be here.

I stuffed the printouts into my pocket and headed through a door. The toilet was down a flight of three steps. Off to the right was an exit, a door with a metal bar over it.

I took a breath and went for the exit, pushing down hard on the bar. I emerged into a yard full of crap. A couple of guys stood smoking, looking surprised, and one of them made a half-hearted move towards me as I climbed the back wall into an alley.

"Hey hey!" he called.

But I was over the wall by then, running down the alley, away from the café with a million thoughts whirling through my head.

7.28

Shit.

This was bad.

I was still shaking.

Come on, JJ. Hold it together. Keep calm.

Did that bastard really have Jenny? Why? What the hell had she done? She didn't deserve this.

"Fuck!" I cursed. Fuck fuck fuck!

No doubt about it now. Whoever this motherfucker was I had to find him. I had to hunt this bastard down and face him because if he wanted to take me out then I wanted him to look me in the eye when he tried.

So where to start? The postcode? Maybe.

N7 1UU or E13 something or other... the 'knackered old builders yard' or the warehouse? I guessed the yard was as good a place as any to start.

So where the hell was it? This yard?

Streets away from the café I leaned against a wall and pulled out the printouts. They were crumpled pretty badly since I'd hardly bothered to fold them properly, but at least I could see the tower and the warehouse.

Should be a third page... the map... the Google Maps printout. I checked all my pockets, turned the paper round ... "Shit!" Garbled text, no image and some random error codes. I wasn't going back to the café if the police were there.

So now what?

According to the street sign opposite me I was in NW1, which couldn't be too far away from N7. I couldn't be more than five or ten minutes away. I guess if I had a sat-nav or even my phone I could have entered the postcode and found the location quickly enough, but I had neither of these things. So I had to go by the street signs alone, which, in London at least, told you (sort of) where you were. I wasn't sure, but by my reckoning N7 had to be further north and slightly to the east.

I stuffed the pictures back into my inside pocket and set off along a street that became a bridge overlooking the railway. All the way over I kept my eyes and ears alert in case another police car swooped down on me.

The snow started falling faster. Tiny feathers of ice tumbling steadily downwards. It looked pretty but the temperature dropped rapidly and soon I was freezing cold. Streetlights were on already and we'd barely seen the back of lunchtime. It was maybe two o' clock at the latest.

I put my hands in my pockets and in one of them my fingers closed on the sandwich from the internet café. I felt I could eat it now, so I walked up to a wall overlooking a riverbed of railway lines far below and leaned over, eating and thinking, shivering, watching the carriages hurtle along in the snow.

Here, London was dominated by the architecture of the railways. Euston, Kings Cross and St Pancras; three massive train stations conjoined by cold, steel arteries that came together from every part of the country. Below me, it was like a city within a city. One that moved, that raced and pulsed so fast it operated on a different level to the slow, metallic grind of congested cars and buses that choked the roads.

I wasn't a train fan, an anorak or some kind of trainspotting nerd, but having lived in this part of London for so many years I had a respect for this network of metal that burrowed beneath and reached between the buildings and streets that surrounded it. It was always noisy, always alive always constant, always impersonal. It wasn't a thing that cared for the flesh and blood lives swarming around it.

When I'd eaten the sandwich I walked back to the high street proper. N7... N7 ... North Seven. Had to be around Haringey, or Islington. Somewhere like that. Not far from here, surely.

I peered closely at the map on the inside of a bus shelter and tried to read it in the gloom. People parted to let me through, but maybe that was more because I stank than through any real sense of politeness. Or maybe I was just being cynical.

Harish had said Caledonian Road on his email. Was that where the guy was operating from? Or had he just been visiting, sat in a bistro, picking at a chicken Caesar Salad as he typed out his inflammatory email on his laptop, iPad, phone or whatever?

Still, it was the only lead I had so I peered at the map in the bus shelter in an effort to locate it.

Good thing about bus shelter maps was that a big red arrow told you exactly where you were. Bad thing was that they divided the region up into transport zones rather than postcodes. However, Caledonian Road *was* on the map. A long road east of Camden that I knew reasonably well, and I knew that the further north you went along it, the more industrial it became; so I guessed it was possible there could be a derelict builders yard up there and maybe that was where this guy was hiding out.

It was a long walk from here though. Dare I jump on the bus?

No chance.

Buses were fitted with all kinds of smart surveillance devices. If you so much as looked at a bus these days your picture was logged with GCHQ, sent around the agencies and matched against known terrorist and serious-criminal profiles.

Ok, probably not quite so bad as that. But I wasn't taking chances. I'd been lucky so far but if this joker had sent my new picture to the police then it was only a matter of time before they caught up with me. This many cameras in London meant no one could stay hidden on the streets for long. So don't increase the chances of them finding me – stay off the bus.

I stayed off the buses.

As I walked I kept an eye on the streetsigns: Randolph Street, NW1. Algar Grove, still NW1. I kept heading east, through the mass of people and traffic, as the snow fell harder and the sky grew darker.

I turned into roads that went nowhere. Roads where shining glass and dull, redbrick office blocks sat next to ancient, concrete bunkers squatting behind high metal railings. I saw 'keep out' signs. Signs to reception. Commercial entrances and red-and-white striped traffic barriers. CCTV clusters and large, bottle-green road signs pointing to The North Circular and places like Barnsbury, Islington and Hackney.

I was feeling desperate, angry and lost.

After a good couple of hours of walking – my feet hurting, my face freezing – I found myself on a high street that wasn't quite so busy, and now it was properly dark. I figured it must have been about four or five o' clock. The wind had picked up. Snow was squalling around buildings and the freeze was even more intense. People moved around, chins down in their winter coats and scarves.

And yes, I *was* being followed. It wasn't my paranoia, not this time. Someone was on my tail and I wanted to know who and why. I was pretty sure it wasn't the police.

So I walked on, slowly. Headed across the road and turned a corner, slinking into the shadow of an office doorway to see who came up after me.

I almost pounced out on some guy in a big dark coat with his hands in his pocket who was first round the corner, and maybe I would have done if I hadn't seen Theo Collins right behind him, moving purposefully like he wanted to get in front of the guy.

I slipped out and shadowed him.

He must have heard me because suddenly he turned, froze for a second when he saw my face.

"Hey," I said. "You want to tell me what's going on? Why are you following me?"

He bolted suddenly, barging past the guy with the coat, almost knocking him off his feet.

"Theo!" I called, then I ran after him.

7.29

Theo was quick on his feet. He sped up the road, running like a man whose life depended on it. I wanted to have it out with him, this time a proper one-on-one, face-to-face without being tied into a chair.

It was hard to keep up with him though. Every bone, muscle and nerve inside me crashed and shrieked with pain, but the anger I felt was so powerful it drove me on, faster, stronger, forcing me to push myself to the limit so I could chase him down through the streets of North London.

Ahead of me Theo turned a corner. I was maybe a second behind him now. I turned the same corner and slipped on the ice. Gritters had been dusting the pavements all winter but I guess peoples' feet had spread it thin, and now a new layer of ice was bedding down. I stumbled, crashed against the wall of a building. Just about kept myself upright.

Theo was way ahead of me now, pushing people out of his way as he ran.

"Theo, wait!" I called, and threw myself back into the chase.

No good.

He raced along the street, almost dancing between cars and bikes blasting their horns.

He turned again: Left into a narrow side street.

I could hardly breathe. The air was freezing, drying out my mouth and nose. My heartbeat raced and my legs threatened to collapse. But still I ran, crossing the road and turning into the street.

It was dark down here and I slowed, stopped to catch some breath. I bent over, put my hands on my knees and spat sticky, cold saliva onto the pavement. Gasping I looked up and saw just a couple of streetlights highlighting the frosted details in a wall of converted millhouses: Blank, staring windows. Drainpipes and doorways. Cars parked nose to tail. Snow drifting down between them. The street terminated abruptly courtesy of a high-wire fence, and there was a shadow climbing it, lifting his legs up and over the top.

Had to be Theo.

"You got to be … kidding me…" I gasped as Theo dropped to his feet on the other side, glanced back at me for a second and then continued running.

I was drained.

I could have left it I guess. Would have been easier. But I had to have this out with him. So I got up and stumbled towards the fence. On the other side of it, a wasteland stretched vast and empty with Theo's giant frame picking his way through it. He wasn't running. He looked as knackered as I was.

With a massive effort I scaled the fence. Grunting as my breath left me, I dropped hard to the ground the other side of it and then set off after him.

Theo must have heard me. I saw him turn his head to look over his shoulder before he set off running again.

There were kids on bicycles playing about at one end of the wasteground. They turned in wide circles on their bikes, faces looking at the two of us in interest.

Ahead of me Theo disappeared.

He just … vanished. And I had no idea how.

I collapsed out of breath against a wall running at chin height along the far perimeter of the wasteground. I couldn't run anymore. I was beat.

Breathing hard I looked left, right, then over the wall and down.

"Jesus Christ…"

My senses were reeling.

I'd found myself, suddenly and vertiginously, overlooking a train depot far below. It was like looking down on the entrance to a subterranean city of shadow and ice, with train sheds and static carriages lit up by powerful floodlights. Down to my left I saw Theo clinging onto the wrong side of the wall, edging along it with nothing but the drop beneath his feet. Must have been a ledge or something but there was no way I was following him over.

Instead I raced along this side of it.

When I got to the same point on the wall I leaned over and looked down. There he was, crabbing along it like Lara Croft. I could see he was shivering, shaking, and I could hear him grunting with effort.

"Don't do this!" I called out to him. "Come on, mate. Let's just talk eh?"

He didn't acknowledge me. Constantly checking his slipping feet he continued to inch sideways.

"Theo!" I called.

Then he changed direction. Started going downwards.

At first I thought the shadows caused by the floodlights around the train sheds were playing complex illusions. He couldn't possibly be going down. But then I saw that he'd found a service ladder, and he was making his way to the ground via that. Or at least, he was hoping to.

Looked like he was stuck half way down it.

Suddenly a screaming, booming train shot out below him, making the wall shake. Eight long carriages slid quickly past in a river of light. Theo hugged the rungs of the ladder.

Seemed the wall was actually the top of a train tunnel.

And I could see that Theo's feet were only as high as the top of the tunnel arch; there the ladder stopped, and it didn't look to me as though there was anything connecting the ladder to the ground. Maybe there had been one day, maybe there used to be an inspection platform, a second ladder, or something else which allowed people access to the ground from here, but there wasn't anymore.

So unless he came back up, he was screwed.

Courtesy of the floodlights I could see that the mounts holding the ladder to the wall were coming away under Theo's weight.

"Theo, come up. You can't get down from there!"

I didn't know if he could hear me. Another train screamed below, this one heading into the tunnel, still filling the atmosphere with noise. I could see Theo looking anxiously around and then reaching out with a tentative leg to where there was a thin ledge of metal cladding on his left. He could probably reach it, I thought, but it was awkward.

The ladder moved. The top end jerked free of the bricks and Theo lost his position.

The ruler-thin ledge he had been reaching out for, his only possible escape, was now too far to reach and so he snatched back his leg hastily. The movement caused the ladder to fall even further away from the wall.

"Theo! It won't support your weight! Come up!"

He looked up at me, terrified.

He was saying something, yelling at me; but over the noise I only caught snatches, fragments of words.

"… your sister…" I heard.

"What have you done with her?" I screamed down at him. "Where is she?"

I leaned right over, screaming still: "Where is she?"

There was a new voice behind me. "Is he gonna kill himself, mister?" It was one of the kids, standing high on his bike pedals to look at Theo over the wall.

The others strained to get a better look.

Another train shot out from underneath the tunnel. Everything shook, and the ladder bent right back under Theo's weight.

Instinctively I reached out for it, my belly over the top of the wall. Theo reached out for my hand but then with a horrendous tearing sound the ladder just simply fell away from me.

"Fuck, man!" cried one of the boys, panic-stricken.

Theo's hand flapped in the air uselessly as he fell.

"Theo!" I screamed.

He hit the roof of one of the carriages, the train still spewing from the tunnel exit, and then bounced off it, flung away like a ragdoll.

The boys all swore and so did I.

"How can I get down there?" I asked the boys.

They were all shocked, but one of them managed to point right along the wall and told me that I could get down that way.

"Call 999!" I yelled at them. Kids always had mobiles right? "Police. Ambulance. Tell them what happened."

I ran along the wall and jumped a spiked gate which tore at my clothes, then headed quickly down unsafe, graffiti-ridden stone steps which zigzagged down, down down to a steep grass verge covered in litter. The grass verge itself led down to the train track, dark and choked with overgrown vegetation covered in snow. I hacked through it, making my way to where I thought Theo had fallen.

I saw him, a crumpled, broken shape lying in the snow, and I ran over.

"You fucking idiot!" I roared at him "Why did you run?"

He was lying face upwards. Holding his right arm in the air like he was touching something invisible.

"… didn't know how you'd react… after what I did…" he gasped. "You're a … dangerous man, JJ…"

I bent down. Looked him over.

"He's got Jenny," I said. "Where is she?"

His eyes narrowed and he made to move. He shook his head, croaked, "no…" then immediately howled with pain.

I stood, and turned on my heel, grabbing at my hair only to find the woolly hat covering my skinhead.

"Why?" I bellowed. "We used to be mates, Theo!"

He gasped something out.

He was in no position to answer.

Trains shot back and forth along the tracks.

"Truest thing… you ever said, JJ," he rasped suddenly.

I calmed down. Hunkered next to him. I wanted to check him over for damage but I wasn't an expert and even with the floodlights nearby, it was so dark down here that everything was a shadow against the snow.

"I got to find her, Theo," I said quietly. "Tell me where she is, mate, come on."

I heard sirens in the air, then I saw blue lights reflecting off the railings and from the high wall above us.

"… tower…" he said. Then coughed.

Tower? "What tower? Where?"

There were voices from above. I could hear the kids shouting and maybe they were looking over the wall, pointing us out to the police.

I remembered the picture in my pocket. Hastily I dug my hand in and pulled it out. Two pages: one with the tower, one with the warehouse. I tried my best to straighten the paper out and showed him the picture of the tower. The other one fell away from me and was whipped away by the wind.

"Is it here?" I hissed, desperate and angry. "Is this where he's holding my sister?"

Theo stared at the picture, then his eyes flicked up at me and he nodded his head. I put a hand on his face. "Thank you," I whispered.

I couldn't stay. Maybe I should have, but I didn't. I couldn't be here if the police were on their way.

"You'll be all right," I said under my breath, then folded the page away.

He put a hand on me, holding my arm.

"Let it go, JJ…" he gasped.

I shook my head. "I can't, mate," I whispered.

"He's changed her…"

Fuck me, I didn't want to hear this.

Close to tears I looked up at the high bridge wall Theo had fallen from, then back at the man himself. Was this all my fault, I wondered? Really? Was it because of me Theo was now lying here close to death?

The voices were louder. I heard the crackle and squawk of police radios and I saw torches bobbing at the top of the steps.

"I have to go," I said. Then: "Don't die on me, fuckwit."

I think he may have laughed, or tried to. There was a gasp of pain as I went, leaving him for the police or the paramedics or whoever was on their way down right now. I had to go. I had to find Jenny and the motherfucker who had her and if I was in a police cell answering questions I'd never find her alive I was sure of it.

And that was the place. He'd nodded his head. That builders yard in Caledonian Road was where I'd find Jenny and her abductor. And it had to be the Camden Killer. No doubt in my mind now that he was one and the same.

So I ran off, bobbing low along the railway embankment, stumbling through a landscape of overgrown weeds and wildflowers, not knowing whether Theo was alive or dead in my wake.

I felt like shit, leaving him there but what else could I have done? It was the right thing to do… Wasn't it?

7.30

I was dancing with Jane Gordon in an L-shaped ballroom. It was dark and the furniture was covered in ghostly, white sheets. Vast paintings of screaming horrors hung on the walls, each image a private Hell too terrible to look at.

Jane was light in my arms. A husk. Bald-headed and blind. I steered her towards the wall and lifted her sad, sightless face up in my hands. I gently turned her face around, and then with all my strength I slammed it into the wall. Once. Twice. Three times. The bones in her face splintered and cracked. Clouds of plaster dust exploded outwards and stayed in the air. She sagged in my arms, and eventually she died.

Elsewhere in the ballroom, elsewhere in the darkness, Stephen Craine's body hung. A sound resonated from his still, pale form stuck with sharpened paintbrushes. It was like a barely-audible tuning fork, ringing around the L-shaped ballroom. In some long-forgotten corner of the same room Gareth Evans, tied to a chair, thrashed and raged like a beast, but in perfect silence. His head, his features, were a blur. Theo Collins, wearing his terrifying white mask, its hollow eyes splashed with blood, stayed at my shoulder keeping just behind me, watching everything. His body was broken and screaming like a train.

"Hey…"

Someone was shaking me.

"Hello…? You OK?"

I sat up with a start, waking suddenly. First thing I smelled was my coat, and the first thing I saw was this guy's face smiling at me in the darkness.

"Sorry to wake you," he said. "Only you shouldn't be sleeping here."

He spoke in a considered, gentle tone.

I rubbed my face, struggling with the transition from horrific dream to horrific reality. I was on a bench, not even in a park. Just some grassy triangle off a parade of closed shops. After the encounter with Theo I'd been wandering; I vaguely remembered making my way towards here. I'd sat down on this bench and fallen asleep.

"If the police see you here, they'll arrest you or move you on," the guy said.

I nodded. Gathered my coat. Shivering so much that I had to fight my body just to get my hands doing what I wanted of them.

"Are you all right?" he asked.

"Sure," I croaked, then cleared my throat. The cold lump was still there.

I saw that the guy had a torch with him. He wore a 1970s-style parka with a furry hood which rustled at his arms when he moved them.

He thrust a leaflet out at me and I grabbed it off him. I couldn't even read it.

"It's the address for a shelter," he said calmly. "A food kitchen run by volunteers. It's not far. I'm afraid you won't be able to stay the night but you'll get some warm food inside you." He shrugged apologetically. "The least we can do," he said.

There was a silence between us for as moment, and then he nodded awkwardly and started walking away.

I called him back. "Wait!" I said.

He turned and I tried to stand. My legs were stiff and my feet were covered in blisters. But I made it.

"You – you could help me," I told him, teeth chattering. "I need to find... I need to find a p-postcode. I need to fffind where it is. My sister..."

"You have family close by?" he said.

"My ss-sister's mmm-issing," I answered, really struggling to speak. "I have to f-f-find her." I shoved my hands into my pockets one by one, looking for the photograph.

"She's on the streets?" he asked.

"I don't know," I said. "I have a ... postcode. If I could find it... then... then..." I went through every pocket.

He nodded. "OK. What's the postcode?"

The paper wasn't there. My pockets were empty. Even my wallet had gone.

I had to think. For some reason I couldn't get it into my head, couldn't remember the letters or the numbers.

"N..." I said, eventually.

I started to feel agitated. Anxious. They'd taken everything while I'd slept.

"N... N7!" I said. "N7... something UU. 1UU I think..."

"OK. Do you have the full address?"

I shook my head.

"I used to have a p-p-picture..."

The guy smiled. "Don't worry. I don't think it's so far," he said. "Go to the shelter, get some food, and one of the volunteers might be able help you."

He smiled more, if that was possible. Then he gave me directions to the shelter and walked away.

I watched him go, disappearing beyond the parade of shops to spread his charity further.

Useless fucker.

I stumbled away, memories of Theo Collins speeding through my mind like a train-crash. And no wallet, no picture of the builders yard.

Nothing.

7.31

I didn't know what time it was, only that it was late. In truth I didn't know what day it was either. By now the whole of this experience was one unending torment and thinking back on it I'm not sure whether I've even remembered the last few days in the right order. I remember I did find a soup kitchen though. I'm sure I did…

Afterwards I lay down on another bench and spent the rest of the night awake and shivering. The following day… I don't know. I had it in my mind that I needed to head back towards Caledonian Road and find this builder's yard with the tower. Trouble was I had no idea where I was now.

I remember walking. Lots of walking. I remember sitting down on the street, legs crossed. I remember money falling into my hands and I vaguely remember walking through a park…

Yes… that was it. I was up near Alexandra Palace. N22. I remember I walked through the park southbound. Came out on Muswell Hill which was in N10. I remembered wondering how the hell you could go from N22 to N10 in the time it took to walk through a fucking park. It must have been a bunch of sadistic bastards who'd first designated postcodes to the boroughs of London. They made no sense.

Later that night… at least I *think* it was that night, I walked into a McDonalds. I remember that. I remember it because I had some money, around five pounds in coinage, and I remember the delicious stink of Big Mac and fries when I walked inside; it was so strong that I could have died on the spot. People had been giving me money. Not much, but it was enough to buy a Big Mac and fries with.

It was busy and brightly-lit. I remember I sat in a corner and ate my burger and fries greedily, stuffing them into my face with dirty fingers whilst listening to the Christmas songs playing from the speakers in the ceiling. When I was finished I walked upstairs to the toilets, had a piss and washed my hands and face.

And I remember this…

I remember looking at my face in the mirror, hardly recognising the gaunt, ruined man staring back at me.

I looked like an animal, but not a healthy one. I looked like the kind of creature that needed rescuing by the RSPCA, a beaten, broken thing with dejection in its ruined eyes.

"I am not a victim," I told my reflection under clenched teeth. Then louder, and closer to the mirror. I wasn't frightened of the reflections now: "I am *not* a victim!" My nose pressing right against the mirror. My eyes to his eyes.

Someone came in. Then headed straight back out.

"*I am not a victim!*" I yelled at the mirror.

I left the restaurant to the sounds of John Lennon singing *War is Over* and headed back out into the freeze.

I shuffled on. Head down.

He's changed her... Theo had said.

What had he meant by that?

7.32

At some point I found Caledonian Road, and then a whole new feeling of fear ripped through me as I asked myself, could I really face this guy?

No choice.

I had to.

But if he was strong, if he was crazy, violent, what chance did I have? I was a wreck.

I figured it didn't matter.

If he'd already killed Jenny then there was nothing left for me to live for. Too many people who mattered to me now were dead or dying.

My dad, Jane Gordon, James... Eve... That whole family more or less wiped out.

Jhavesh and Theo in hospital at best.

Harriet gone.

Even my cat was dead.

So maybe, if this fucker killed me, maybe it was for the best.

The builders yard drifted into view.

Just like the photo I'd lost.

"Christ there it is..."

From the railway bridge on the high street I could see it just the other side of a train-cleaning depot which straddled the tracks below the bridge. The yard was lit by the depot's floodlights, not by its own, and I got the impression that most of it was invisible from here. Except for the tower, which I could see rising like a monolithic rectangle against the yellow glow of London's night sky.

I could probably get to it heading down a couple of side streets. It was late now and there was no one around. Just black cabs and the occasional night-bus. The Underground station was shut.

Maybe I should wait until morning.

Why? What would be the point?

Terrified, I pressed on.

This was it then. Right?

If he was in there, then this could well be my final hour.

7.33

I scaled the wire fence and dropped down the other side of it. Landed painfully in a world of grey and black.

I could see now that it was more than just a 'knackered old builders yard'. It was a real complex of industrial pre-fab buildings, and between them threaded train-tracks and mountains of aggregate covered in glittering ice-caps. Closure notices were everywhere.

The tower, as blank and monolithic as a tombstone, loomed over a colourless landscape. Dark, rectangular windows stared out from it like empty, soulless eyes. The face of the tower was just about illuminated by the floods from the train depot far below and out of sight. A scaffold of skeletal steps zig-zagged up its side.

Keeping low I darted along a winding track that had been carved out over the years by gargantuan vehicles: earth-movers, trucks, loaders, cranes. Etcetera, etcetera. The regular, repeated movement of caterpillar tracks and immense tyres had gouged out deep craters in the muddy ground that were now filled with ice.

Hold on. Someone was here.

There was a light on.

Up in the tower: a single yellow square of light in one of the dead-eye windows. Someone moved.

I ducked back down into the shadows, dislodging a pile of rusting metal bars, fixings and brackets that ran away from me with a loud clattering crash of metal.

"Shit!"

Suddenly a train raced along the mainline out of sight. Brakes shrieking and screaming, its diesel engine tore a hole in the world as it rocketed onwards. Eventually it faded, but I could still hear screaming.

My blood turned cold.

That was a woman – not a train.

For a moment I froze. Then I took a deep breath and reached down for a good-sized metal pole I could use as a weapon. I came out from behind the mountain and ran at the tower, which was where the scream was still coming from.

The bastard had seen me, he'd been waiting for me and now he was starting on Jenny.

This was it then, I guessed. Me and the killer, right here, right now, and nowhere to hide.

7.34

I ran up the steps, my boots pounding the metal, making the whole structure wobble and shake and ring like a tower of bells. Stealth didn't matter. He'd already seen me I was sure of it. And so the more noise I made, the more this fucker was going to dread the moment I burst through the door and swung for him.

At the last moment I thought: what if he swings for me first?

Too late. I couldn't back out now.

Just halfway up the tower I grabbed a door handle and yanked the thing open.

I burst in, prepared to fight off an attack from anyone waiting behind the door, ducking and steeling myself, quickly turning in a wide circle, my vicious-looking metal bar at the ready.

The screaming had stopped.

And there was no one here.

My heart was beating hard and fast.

I took a quick look around, letting my eyes adjust to the gloom.

The inside of the tower was hollow, a shaft that ran from top to bottom. Right at the top of it, the city glow struggled to illuminate much through a giant Toblerone of cracked, dirty, glass panes which formed a strip across the middle of the roof. Either side of the glass, great machines hung like spiders. Long chains dangled, reaching down, down, down into the shaft.

I was on a gallery that ran round the inside of the tower. I leaned over a metal railing and looked down into its depths. It felt like there was water down there. I couldn't see it, it was too dark, but I just got a taste of that damp chill in the air that you get in a room full of cold water.

As far as I could tell I was on the second of four galleries. There may have been more further below but if so they were shrouded in a Hellish gloom.

Stairs connected the galleries. Looking upwards, on the opposite side of the chamber, I saw a row of windows on a box that jutted straight out of the wall. Some kind of cantilevered office. Could he be in there?

There was light behind the windows, as though someone was moving around, passing in front of a torch.

It was the only significant light in the tower. Just enough for me to see my way around.

I was breathing hard. Aside from the occasional clink of a swaying chain and the odd whistle of wind through the structure, my breathing was the only sound I could clearly hear.

So he was in there was he? Sh1tPolice. AKA the Camden Killer. And somewhere in here, he had Jenny. Maybe she was in that office.

I came to the corner where the gallery met the adjacent wall and turned a sharp ninety-degree angle inward. If I kept going past the next corner, then climbed one more flight of steps, I'd be on the same level as that office.

My eyes were adjusting and I was able to see more of the interior of the tower, not that it was so great to look at. But there were details I hadn't been able to see before, like the metal wheels on the railings just outside the office box. Looked like they were connected by some mechanism to the dangling chains. There were cupboards and control boxes built into the walls, fire extinguishers, and even things like ancient posters: safety advice and warning notices. Then suddenly there was light.

Lots of light.

I ducked down instinctively.

The light came not from the roof or the office but from way below, a dull, yellow glow that crept slowly forward like some kind of sickly infection. It spread up the walls and infested the corners, eating away the shadows that had seemed so still and comfortable before its arrival. And with it came a sound. A rumbling, growling machine that sent echoes clattering around the interior of the tower.

I looked through the railings and saw the source of the light. It was coming from some kind of boat, a long, flat platform carrying cubes of garbage tied up with rope way down below. A barge driven by a solitary boatman standing aft at a waist-high pod, holding down a lever, a dead-man's switch. A yellow spotlight stood in front of him, shining forward into the gloom.

The barge's light illuminated large sacks hanging like pods on the ends of some of the chains, dangling close to the water. Difficult to see clearly but I thought they were probably counterweights or something, there to help lift containers up or down the shaft.

The barge passed on through, leaving behind it the thick stench of rotting refuse.

Then it was dark again.

So the tower was built over some kind of underground canal used by barges carrying landfill to the Thames. And maybe, when this place was active, the owners had used this hidden waterway to transport the stuff they stored here.

My eyes had to readjust when the light had gone, and when I felt I could see again I pushed away from the railings and continued towards the office block jutting from the wall.

I ran up the steps to the next level, then to the door in the side of the block.

It was ajar, opening inwards. I lifted the metal bar in my right hand and kicked in the door. It swung wildly and I stormed in, ready to smash it down on the first head I looked at.

And there she was, sitting cross-legged on a black swivel chair. Hands resting under her thighs.

Her face was cast down, so all I saw was the silhouetted oval of a scarred skinhead, until she lifted her eyes and looked at me with a dark but delighted expression from her heavily made-up eyes.

I'd been this close to smashing her brains in with the bar.

"Hello, Jason," she said.

It was all I could do to croak her name.

"Jenny?"

7.35

The light in the office came from the floor, from a giant bulb in a portable, metal cage. It sprayed harsh, white light into the office; so bright even through its cage that it showed up every patch of dirt, every stain, every scratch on the windows, making them fully opaque. A thick cable snaked away from the light towards the back of the office, where black, plastic binbags bulged and split, sharing space with newspapers and magazines, plates, food wrappers, boxes, cardboard cups, packets and cartons.

It stank in here. Much worse than the contents of the barge. Much worse than me.

Jenny had shaved her hair down to a dark fuzz; it made her gaunt face more striking, her eyes fiercer and her bones more defined. Her body was lean, willowy, and she wore a baggy t-shirt streaked with some kind of dark, splash pattern; looked like the designer had slung a couple of paintbrushes at it and left it at that. A pair of dirty, stained jeans covered her legs, but her feet were bare, covered in filth.

"I thought you weren't coming," she said in a whispering, cracked voice full of relief.

I stepped forward, my senses on fire.

"It – it took a while," I said, full of emotions. I held it together, forcing my head to stay rational and clear. It was so hot in here. It didn't seem real and I was sweating. "Let's go," I said, "before he gets back."

"He won't be long." She jumped off the chair, and there was something… I don't know, feral, I think, about her movement. "He told me you were coming days ago," she said, then frowned. "I think it was days. It's hard to tell. What's that for?"

"It's a pole I'm going to beat the fucker's head in with." Strong words but my voice wasn't strong at all.

I felt her hand like a claw on my arm, holding me back for a second. "You can't hurt him," she said, looking right into my face. "I mean it," she hissed. "You're a wreck, JJ. Look at you. What have you been doing?"

I couldn't speak. The best thing was to get out of here. We could talk afterwards, when my head was straight.

"Let's go," I croaked. *Jenny was alive!*

I was glad to get out of the office. With my sister behind me I walked quickly back into the main shaft of the tower, down the steps and along the metal gallery that led around the interior wall. I still had the metal pole in one hand, my sister's bony fingers found the other, and as we walked together all kinds of thoughts and emotions swirled around the insides of my head. I couldn't put them into words at the time. I couldn't articulate anything and I'm not sure I can now. If I had to paint what I was feeling at that moment, it would be an angry explosion of red and yellow on a canvas the size of the Shard, shot through with bolts of searing, jagged forks of energy slicing the image into razor sharp fragments. If I was sculpting, then I'd be constructing the most beautiful piece of symmetry then hurling it at the wall.

"I'm sorry I took so long to find you," I said.

She squeezed my hand. "It's OK," she whispered. "I knew you would eventually. It was just a matter of time."

"But if I hadn't heard you screaming…"

"It wasn't my scream," she said. "Must have been one of the others. They do that sometimes."

My head was full of noise, as though something was trying to push through all the crap that seemed to be swirling around inside it.

Jenny was still talking. She said, "When you think they're dead they suddenly surprise you with a scream. It can make you jump. And what I think it is, why it sometimes takes days — I mean they usually scream like animals when they first come here — but they quieten down — and I think it's because their brain sort of shuts down for a bit, like it's trying to process all this new information and come to terms with what's probably going to happen to them. Then suddenly: 'Aaaaaaaaaaahhhhh!'" she screamed, the sound ringing around the interior. "Days later and usually only the once, as though something, some kind of realisation, some kind of horror, hits them suddenly."

She said it so matter-of-factly that I started shaking, wondering how long she'd been here and what could this guy have subjected her to?

"I'm sorry I left you alone for so long, Jenny," I said. "I'm so sorry."

"Shush…" she whispered, stroking my arm tenderly. "It doesn't matter right? We're together again. And we don't need him."

We turned the gallery, walking along the wall I'd come in by. The door to the outside, to the fresh air of London, was along here somewhere. Just a few steps away.

"Who is he, Jenny?" I asked. "Do you know him?"

"Yes," she answered. "It's Gareth from school. You remember him? Gareth Evans?"

I shook my head in the manner of a nurse debunking the delusions of a patient. "Jenny. It can't be him."

Never mind. Let's get out first, I was thinking. Let's just both get a long way from here and then we could talk. I didn't know where we could go. I thought that going to the police now was the best option, get Jenny in front of Burrows and Hershey and let her tell her story.

She was alive!

But I felt her pulling back on my hand.

"Don't you believe me? It is him, Jason. I swear it!"

Like a petulant dog who suddenly didn't want to move she tugged me back. And then she let go of my hand so I stopped and turned to face her. From way down below, the distant rumble of another barge started rising. A moment later the dull, yellow light began to drift upwards into the tower. It caught her face, and I saw the remains of a woman I used to know staring back at me like a stranger. The emotion of it choked me. This was my sister. And I'd neglected her for so long … long enough for some nutcase to seduce her and pull her away from me.

"He told me what happened, JJ," she said.

"What do you mean?"

"He told me what happened at Balloch, at the house where Jane died. He told me how he killed her, and he told me where he buried her. How would he know all that if it wasn't him?"

I felt like… I don't know… like I'd been punched in the stomach so hard I felt sick. Or like I was falling backwards into the interior of the tower, down towards the sickly yellow barge-light but never reaching it because suddenly the tower was so much taller and so vast.

Where he'd buried her?

"Jenny, no. Look it – it can't be Gareth," I said. "Gareth died. The same time as Jamie died. In the fire."

She was shaking her head, her eyes fierce, growing brighter in the barge-light.

"Jamie shot him," she told me, "but he didn't die. He got out."

No… it was impossible. Gareth was utterly dead. No tricks.

The interior was now fully illuminated as the barge trundled through. Jenny's gaunt face glowed with that dirty, yellow light and I could see her more clearly now. It was a face devoid of any kind of empathy, and for a fleeting second I was back in the chair in front of one of Theo's deathmasks.

A surge of sheer terror ripped through me.

"Jenny, listen…" I began, my voice wavering.

She pushed me away with surprising strength.

"He isn't dead!" she snapped. "He's coming back here soon, and then you'll see. You'll see for yourself."

"And then he'll kill me," I said.

"What makes you think that?"

"Isn't it what he wants?"

The interior settled back into darkness, but it was much deeper than before. The skylight up on the roof was purple and the wind hummed and rattled through the skin of the tower.

"Do you ever think you're somebody special, JJ?" she asked me in the dark.

I didn't answer.

"I do," she said, "and you should too, because you are. You and me, Jason, we're not the sort of people who wander the world like animals, like cattle moving from one milking shed to another, chewing like idiots on the same grass in the same field day after day. You and me, we change people, Jason. We transform them."

I was shaking my head.

"You changed Gareth Evans," she said. "You made his life different. Same with Jane. Same with Jamie. You changed them all. And you changed me too."

I couldn't speak.

"And Adam, and Eve, and Mum and Dad," she went on, speaking softly, lyrically. Seductively. Almost like she always used to do. "Everyone who's known you has had their lives transformed, which makes you a very special kind of artist."

A scream split the air suddenly.

It was short and sharp and full of terror, a lifetime of hopeless fear condensed into a single moment in time. It came from below us.

Jenny moved to the edge of the railing. Looked over.

"She won't die quickly this one," she said. "I think it's the same one you heard earlier."

Again, as though it was the most natural thing to say.

"Do you want so see?"

"See what?" I whispered.

She ran back along the gallery, pulling a tiny pentorch out of her jeans pocket. "It's so dark," she said, shining the torch. "Give me a hand." She was running back towards the office.

"Where are you going?" I shouted. "Jenny?"

We had to get out of here.

I looked at the door to the outside world.

Just metres away…

Then I looked back at Jenny racing around the gallery, and I went after her.

7.36

I caught her up by one of the wheels connected to the side of the railings. The door to the office was open and the light from the giant bulb inside it sprayed out. Jenny was swinging the wheel round and one of the chains was rising upward with a great clanking sound, the gears in the roof grinding laboriously. She must have had hidden strength somewhere because she was pulling on that wheel like an expert. Sinews and muscles stood out on her arms and her expression was locked in a grimace of concentrated effort.

The chain screamed and clanked upwards. It took a couple of minutes and I watched as one of the pods which I'd taken to be counterweights was heaved up towards the railing. My head was spinning, and so was the pod.

Something was moving inside it.

Sounds came out of it.

Human sounds.

Whimpering, panicked breathing.

I saw movement on the surface of its skin as though something was trying to kick and elbow its way out. A horrible realisation began to dawn on me, one that I should have grasped as soon as I saw Jenny sitting cross-legged in the office but which I hadn't wanted to believe.

She was alive and hadn't been tied up…

The pod was actually a sack, like some kind of tarpaulin suspended by ropes attached to a hook at the end of the chain. I could just about see a figure inside it, curled up, moving, kicking.

"She's fierce is this one," said Jenny, straining on the wheel. "You remember Donna Llewellyn from years ago?"

"You've got … Donna in there?"

She looked at me like I was an idiot, an expression that reminded me of the old Jenny Jones.

"In here? No."

"Then who…?"

"I was only asking if you remembered her, when you caught her at the old station house back home? She had spirit, some kind of fight in her when she first came upstairs, remember? She was a strong girl but she broke easily. There was a moment where she gave up. Like a rabbit that knows it can't fight the fox anymore. You could see it in her eyes. You ever wonder what happened to her?"

I couldn't answer. I was staring into the sack as it came closer to the railing.

"Gareth looked her up for me," Jenny said. "She got married and had a kid. Just the one. She moved out of Llangefni and started her little family. And then the kid died. Eighteen months old in suspicious circumstances. She went to court and tried to prove that the kid died from cot death. But nobody believed her, and so she went to prison for murder. Two years later they let her out with an apology – seems they got it wrong. Her own child though, Jason. Did she kill it? I think she did. I think she realised one day that she had the power to end the kid's life and she did it."

I stared at her. Shaking from head to foot.

"Reminds me of our mum and dad," she went on. "They never cared about us, only themselves. We could have done anything – we *did* do anything. Anything we liked. And as a result we became powerful. You and me, Jason. Like I said we are agents of change. We make people different. We transform them. We made Donna Llewellyn into a woman who took the life of her own child. That's real power isn't it?"

The sack was now just below the railing and Jenny stopped the wheel. She threw a lever next to it and locked it off. The sack swung slowly on the end of the chain and the figure inside it began to whimper.

Jenny shook her arms loose.

The whimpering turned to a wailing noise, almost sub-human. Full of fear.

"But this one won't break," she continued, shouting above the noise. "I tried everything and she still fights. And that's what I have to break before I transform her."

Sitting there... cross-legged on the chair, hands under her legs.
She was alive and she wasn't tied up...

"Bring her up," I said slowly, quietly, past the knot in my throat and the sickness in my belly, "I'll help you. I'll break her."

Jenny smiled widely. "I knew you would!" she enthused. "I knew it all this time! I said to Gareth we should bring you in but he said no. We even had a fight about it."

She went back to the wheel, unlocked it and heaved it round. It was slow, clearly difficult. She was struggling.

Then it slipped and she threw the lever, locking it.

The sack swung wildly below us.

"Here, let me," I said. I put down my metal bar and took the wheel. I threw the lever, unlocking the mechanism, and started to turn the wheel clockwise.

Overhead the chain slipped through the gears in the machine in the roof and the sack rose another couple of feet. When it was high enough, I locked the wheel off again and reached out.

7.37

The sack swayed on the end of its chain and Jenny helped me bring it in. There was a pole to one side like a boat-hook which she used to snare the sack and haul it over to the railings.

She looked like she'd done this a few times.

"I tried looking after you, JJ," she said as we heaved together. "I watched you for a while, thought I could protect you. It seemed like you were having a bad time of it, especially with that bitch French model. I followed her round for a week, watched her working in the studios of that other guy with the scars on his arm."

She meant Nugent Fry.

"I couldn't kill her. Gareth wouldn't let me."

"But you killed Nugent though, right?" I almost choked on the words. It was all I could do to try and put on a mask of calm.

She nodded as we lowered the sack onto the gallery.

"I had to put one of them out," she said. "They'd have hurt you otherwise. Did you see what they were doing in that studio?"

"Yes. That was good," I said. "Did you burn it down?"

She smiled again, evidently pleased with herself. "I even enrolled as a student. I used Jane Gordon's name. Gareth didn't know and when he found out he went crazy. I got friendly with Nugent though, and one night I drugged him and covered his face in Plaster-of-Paris. I set fire to the studios and put him in there before the fire crews arrived." Her smile was even wider now. "I was going to paint his new face but there wasn't time. Not like the others. Bet you didn't realise I was such a good artist myself right?"

I felt sick.

"I… I saw your work…" I said, fighting to stop my stomach from rising. "The girl on Blackfriars Bridge…"

"One of my favourites," she said. "I thought you might appreciate that one. She was the model who tried to destroy you after that thing you did in Lambeth with her."

"I know. And the old judge? Skinned and laid out on the park bench?"

She shook her head this time. "That was Gareth," she told me. "He did that one himself. Took him a long time to do it. I wouldn't have known where to start but he was like an expert, cutting the old man and peeling off his skin. I took the pictures of his son while Gareth worked on the old guy in here. It took him a whole day and a night and just before dawn he carted the body off to Hampstead Heath. So then I thought I could do better. And I did the girl with the nail in her head. Roses in her belly. Just like your Saint Rita. You remember the saints? You were obsessed with them. I remember you telling me about the saints. And Saint Rita has such a beautiful, tragic story."

"You empathised with her?"

"I guess so."

"And the little girl in the church?"

She nodded casually and I started shaking even more.

"And… Stephen. What about him? Did you kill Stephen Craine?"

"Who? Oh! Your boyfriend? Your experiment? You always were a bad judge of character weren't you? Did you know what he did after you dumped him?"

I stared at her terrifying face as she rose in the shadows against the wall.

"When you broke up with him he went crazy. He went to a bar, got drunk and raped a girl. She was one of the staff. Maybe he wanted to see what fucking a woman was like, what all the fuss was about. He tried it on with her but she wouldn't have it. So he waited outside the bar and took her in the car park. She was with the manager but he beat the shit out of him, and the guy had to watch while your boyfriend threw the girl to the ground, ripped her jeans off and beat her almost to death. He stuck his cock in her and fucked her while he held his whole hand over her face, pressing her into the ground. I saw it happen. We were both there, me and Gareth."

This wasn't true. Stephen wasn't like that.

She continued.

"I stepped in. Gareth tried holding me back but I walked over to your boyfriend and booted him in the face. He got off her pretty quick then. I told the girl and the manager to get the fuck away, and then when Stephen came at me Gareth caught hold of him, grabbed him by head and put a knife into his neck. After that, we took him to your lock up and finished the job. That was Gareth's idea. He said we needed to send you a message."

My voice was hoarse when I spoke. "So what was the message?"

"I thought you'd want to join us," she said.

I had no idea what the hell I was going to do here. This woman was my sister.

And she was the Camden Killer.

7.38

But she wasn't working alone. Someone calling himself Gareth Evans completed the double act. Has to be someone I know, I was thinking, otherwise he'd have chosen a different name.

It was always going to come down to a confrontation between me and this manipulative killer. He'd been steering me towards this for God knew how long and it was inevitable. But I hadn't counted on Jenny's complicity in the murders. Who was I kidding? It wasn't just simple complicity; she had killed these people herself.

7.39

The sack landed on the metal plates flooring the gallery with a clang.

"You can have this one, Jason," Jenny whispered. "My present to you."

"Give me your torch," I said, holding out my hand.

Jenny passed it over and I shone it into the sack.

A face was looking up at me.

Dirty and dishevelled but still recognisable.

I held out a hand.

"Come on, Harriet," I said, as gently as I could. "It's all right."

She didn't move.

Just stared at me with her big eyes under a matted fringe of hair.

"Come on," I said. "It's over."

Then I heard Jenny's voice.

"What are you doing?"

I rounded on her. "Why would you kill her?" I snapped. "And why would you think for one minute that I'd want to do it?"

"Because you're like me," she answered, sounding confused. "Jason – why are you being like this?"

"I'm nothing like you, Jenny."

"We're the same."

"No! We're not the same. You're not even my sister!"

"Don't say that."

"You know what our parents did," I said. "You know the lie they sold us. We grew up together, that's all."

I turned back to Harriet. "Get up!" I roared. But she didn't. If anything she seemed even more frightened.

"I let you fuck me," said Jenny.

I turned to face her now and she looked broken, her back against the wall, knees slightly bent.

"You can't just… you just… can't just…"

"Kill people? I can do what I like. My universe, JJ. Remember? My universe, my rules. You said that to me years ago when you pulled out of that fucking Bedlam and it's the code we lived by when we were kids."

"We never had a 'code', Jenny."

"Not a spoken one maybe, but that's how we lived. You expect me to give that up? You think I should be weak so that someone else can do to me what he did to Jane? Or maybe I should have stayed in that hospital and let them 'counsel' me, shoot me full of drugs or put me back in a padded fucking cell. Well fuck you, JJ, that isn't going to happen."

"You can't do this, Jenny."

"Don't get moral on me, JJ," she said. "You're not exactly an innocent yourself. You're the one who destroyed everyone you touched. Jane Gordon, Jamie, my dad…"

"No," I said. "I made bad decisions, that's all. I never … I never killed anyone."

There. I'd said it.

All these years living with the guilt of those decisions, and I think that was the moment I realised I couldn't be responsible for those deaths. Maybe they'd never have happened if I'd made better choices, but I wasn't responsible for those horrors.

I turned back to Harriet, reached down for her hand.

She drew away, terrified, and in that moment my stomach kicked. I saw in her the same expression I'd seen on Donna Llewellyn's face in the station house and Bethany at Lambeth, the real Gareth Evans tied to his chair in Balloch, Jane Gordon on the video tapes and me, my own face in the mirror telling myself I wasn't a victim. The frightened animal.

And this was the difference between all of us and Jenny. Jenny had the look of an animal about her, I'd seen it earlier. Difference was that she was a predator.

It was something Theo had tried to tap into inside himself when he'd tied me up in St Leonard's. He'd had to wear a mask to put himself in that headspace, but even then he couldn't do it.

He'd come close, he'd carried the thing through almost to the end but he'd let me go, falling short of delivering the final blow, of crossing that line. Jenny had crossed the line a long time ago, maybe she'd been born the other side of it. There was no way back for her.

But by saving Harriet, maybe I could walk away from my own line, the one I'd treaded dangerously close to in Balloch, the one James had pushed me away from by taking my place as the murderer. The same one Jane Gordon had rescued me from merely by holding my hand in the old station house in front of Donna.

"Harriet!" I snapped, reaching out. "Come on…"

There was a moment, and then she finally grabbed my hand. I pulled her up and I realised she was wearing the same clothes I'd last seen her in, getting on the bus a week or so before Christmas.

Had she been in here since then?

Jenny's ice-cold whisper ripped the moment apart.

"You can't do this!" she hissed.

"It's got to stop, Jenny," I said, rounding on her. I tried to hold

Harriet but my hands were shaking so much I could barely do it. I didn't have to. She pressed herself against me like a dead weight.

"Jenny, whoever this guy is he is not Gareth Evans. Gareth Evans is dead so who is he? Tell me!"

I was in danger of losing it.

"I was so wrong about you," Jenny said.

"I'm not a murderer."

"Unlike me you mean? Well fuck you, JJ, for being so noble."

"I don't get why you're doing this. Is it him? This guy calling himself Gareth Evans? Did he make you this way? What did he tell you? What did he promise you?"

She didn't answer.

"Jenny, we've got to turn him in. Whoever he is! We have to tell the police and they need to put him away or put him down or fucking hang him for all I care. He's dangerous."

"Not your decision."

"For Christ's sakes!" I almost screamed. I felt Harriet clutch me tighter round my back. "What do you think is going to happen now? Huh? You think he won't turn you in? Look, Jenny. He told you he's Gareth Evans but he can't be. He can't be the same guy we went to school with but he must be someone who knows me. Which means he's using you, and when he's finished he'll either kill you or give you to the police. You become the Camden Killer and no matter how much you tell them that someone else was with you, once they look into your history they're not going to believe you. So you go to prison as a lone serial murderer and that sonofabitch walks free. That's you, in life imprisonment, Jenny."

"I won't go to prison," she said.

I tried to bring my voice down, but it was difficult. I was caught in an impossible situation that nothing I'd been through in life could prepare me for.

"Jenny," I said, "you've murdered people. You kept Harriet in this fucking bag down there for days and … and you killed a twelve year old child…"

Harriet was shaking now.

I pulled her head close to my breast, ran my hand through her hair. "Shush," I whispered to her. "You're going home now."

I think I felt her nodding but I wasn't sure. I looked at Jenny. "You've got to tell the police, Jenny," I said, calmer. "You've got to tell them everything you know about this man. Maybe they'll … I don't know…"

"Maybe they'll what?" she shrieked. "Strike a deal? Slap my wrists?" She scoffed. "No. I'm walking out of here and I'll live how I want to live, and do whatever I want to do."

She stepped forward and Harriet shuddered.

Jenny looked at her. "Put him down, bitch."

Instantly Harriet drew away, her back against the railing.

"You should kill her, JJ," Jenny said. "You think she was ever your friend? You don't know anything about anybody do you? You spent a night in her flat. Did you read her diary?"

"Shut up, Jenny," I said.

She was closer to me, but her eyes were locked onto Harriet. "If I can't have him, no one will," she said to Harriet. "Isn't that what you wrote? Why don't you tell him how his cat died?"

"Jenny," I said. "Just stop. It's over. It doesn't matter."

"She tried to kill that French bitch. Laced her tea with rat poison. She wasn't to know that it ended up in the cat food but it was her nonetheless. Just shows you doesn't it? Her, Stephen Craine, Theo your best friend. Even Gareth Evans. You attract destructive personalities and fuel them up. Somehow you give them just what they need to go further. Don't worry. It's not your fault. It's who you are, it's who we are – you, me, James. Even Jane, and who knows what she'd be doing now if she was still alive."

"Jenny, stop," I said. "I'm taking Harriet away from here. I want to get her home. You too. Come with me and then we'll find 'Gareth' and together we'll– "

"You can't hurt him, JJ," she cried, reminding me of what she'd said not so long ago. And now I realised what she meant by it.

"Anyone can be hurt, Jenny. And it's like you said, we're the powerful ones right? We're the ones who change people. Not him."

She paused and it looked like she was listening.

Then I realised that she had the metal bar in her hand, the one I'd picked up earlier and dropped so I could take the wheel and hoist Harriet to safety.

"First things first," she said.

Then she lifted the bar, lunged past me and swung it violently at Harriet's head.

7.40

At that moment the world exploded and several things happened seemingly at once. Only now, thinking back on it, can I put it into some kind of order.

7.41

Firstly I went for Jenny, shouldering her away from Harriet. Caught off balance she missed, and the bar crashed against the railings with a reverberating bell-like clang. Enraged by what I'd done she swung round, fast, and slammed the bar into my kidneys.

I wasn't prepared for that kind of pain. It near felled me. Down on my knees, I grabbed for the railings. Tried to haul myself up whilst gasping for breath; but the railings moved under my weight and something fell off, clattering down the shaft.

The next thing that happened was that the tower was flooded with light from above: a powerful, burning spotlight that shone brilliant white through the dirty Toblerone-shaped skylight. Shadows spun wildly, wheeling around the interior. A thudding sound accompanied the light, hacking and chopping at the air outside: A helicopter with a spotlight bearing down on the tower.

It distracted Jenny; just enough for me to rush her and grapple for the bar. But she wasn't letting it go and I began to realise how strong she really was.

"Come on, Jenny," I growled through gritted teeth, our hands on the bar, faces almost touching from either side. "It's over."

"I can't believe what you've done," she said, and I could see tears in her ruined eyes. "I can't believe you've sided with them. After everything we lived through, after everything I did for you. Your face, my face – the same person split! I thought we were the same, JJ! I thought we were the *same!*"

With a scream of pure, animal rage she smashed the bar into my mouth. Hard.

I let go, my head ringing, and fell back against the railing. The thing gave under me again and I thought I was going to fall. I looked up only to see her coming at me, beads of sweat flying from her face, teeth bared, brows furrowed in rage and the bar held high, already on the downswing.

Terrified I rolled to one side and the bar crashed against the railings once more. It didn't feel like I was quick enough or strong enough for this. Jenny was both fast and strong. She swung a sudden backhander which caught my roll, slamming the bar into one or two of my ribs. I screamed with pain and dropped like a stone to the floor, every bone and every nerve in my body howling, shrieking with pain.

I rolled onto my back and now she stood over me, her dark eyes wet with tears, her body shaking with fury.

I caught sight of Harriet, cowering against the railings, just a few feet away.

"Get up!" Jenny yelled at me, pointing the bar down at my head. "I said get the fuck up!"

"Jenny!" I gasped.

She smashed the bar down on me again and again, swinging hard and fast repeatedly, and all I could do was lift up my arms to protect my face. The bar hit my left lower arm and although it hurt, I got the feeling she was holding back. I think if she'd really meant to hurt me properly, I'd be a bloodied mess on the floor. She was a killer, a real killer.

"Get up!" she screamed, standing astride my hips.

I couldn't.

"Fine," she said, and her legs scissored in front of my face as she stepped over me.

Turning my head, painfully, spitting blood and snot, I saw that she was pulling Harriet up by her hair. Harriet was screaming, out of control.

Using the unstable railing for support I climbed to my feet, adrenaline dulling the pain with its own energy.

This was not the Jenny I knew. I couldn't even think that this animal, this murderer, was my sister. Maybe it was someone who'd taken her place, maybe the real Jenny was still in Swindon dreaming about God and Saints and reading children's picture books in the common room.

"You're a fucking idiot," she sobbed, looking back at me as she shook the screaming Harriet. "It's always about you isn't it? Everything revolving around Jason fucking Jones." She was shoving Harriet up against the railings. "That's why Jamie died," she yelled, "and that's why Jane died. It's why dad died and why I ended up like this. No wonder your best friend tied you up and tried to put you out of…"

A door to the outside opened on the other side of the tower – the one I'd entered by – and the helicopter light shone right in from above, a brilliant shaft of light pinning us down. The thunderous concussion of the helicopter's engine and its rotors echoed around the interior of the tower and now a voice from the open doorway shouted out: "Stop! Police!"

Bootsteps reverberated around the metal gallery. Torchlight flashed.

Yellow light seeped up from below.

Jenny stared at me.

Fuck you, Jason, she mouthed, and with a terrific scream of pure rage and hatred she slammed Harriet's face hard into the railings. She pulled her away and threw her against the back wall of the gallery. Then she came at me.

The police were running from two directions around the gallery.

The helicopter hovered overhead.

Jenny was murderous. She swung the bar and hit me in the stomach. This time it was hard, much harder than before and I felt weak. I couldn't breathe. She wasn't holding back now. With a scream she came at me again, the weapon going straight for my head and there was nothing, nothing I could do to stop her.

Blood streaking her face Harriet got up and rushed Jenny from behind. She slammed into her, carried her forward and to one side of me, straight and hard into the railings. Jenny swung round and headbutted her. Harriet collapsed backwards, holding onto one of the railings instinctively for support.

Now Jenny reached forward, grabbed her head and pulled her towards her. Teeth bared it looked like she was going to bite Harriet's face off.

"Jenny, no!" I screamed.

In trying to move away Harriet panicked and backed against the railing she was still holding onto, but right at that moment the thing broke and both women fell.

Harriet screamed as she pitched over. Jenny was going the same way, the momentum carrying her over the edge. Harriet was still holding onto the piece of railing, just about still attached, but her feet had slipped off the gallery completely and she was dangling.

Terrified I scrambled round on my knees. Looking down I saw the both of them hanging either side of me. Jenny looked like she might be able to swing round and get her feet back up but Harriet was ready to fall any moment. She was hanging from one hand and her legs were cycling below her.

The yellow barge light increased, lighting the terrifying scene from below.

If I could help one of them at least…

I lunged forward, reached out and made a grab for Harriet's free-swinging hand. I caught it and, holding onto her with every ounce of strength I still had, I started pulling her up.

"JJ!" Jenny screamed. She tried to swing her legs back up onto the gallery but the railing she was holding onto slipped quickly away from its support, angling sharply downward.

It didn't even occur to me that I should let go of Harriet in order to rescue my sister.

I clawed Harriet up onto the gallery, using my own weight as leverage for the final pull.

Then the fragile railing holding Jenny broke off entirely. She slipped and fell, tumbling down the shaft as the barge rumbled into view way below.

"Get away from me!" Harriet snapped and pushed me away.

The police rushed us. One or two of them were looking over the broken railings, barking into the radios on their lapels.

Dazed, I crawled towards the edge of the gallery and looked down the shaft.

A whole train of barges was passing by, way below.

"Jenny..." I collapsed to my knees. Felt like my whole body was shutting down. If I could dive down there after her...

The barges slid through, transporting their noise, their light and possibly the life of my sister away with them.

What have I done? I wondered.

DI Hershey pushed her way through the ranks of police.

"Arrest him," she barked. "And get someone down there quickly."

7.42

Hours later I was back in a police station. Not sure which station it was, but it was new; modern and gleaming. Even during the dead of night it was a busy place, with coppers rushing up and down corridors and stairwells exchanging jokes and songs, keeping their spirits up for tomorrow's New Year's Eve. I'd been examined by a police doctor and now I was washed, bandaged and wearing some poor fucker's clothes – a purple jumper, fresh underwear, a pair of faded Levi's – all given to me in a sealed plastic bag stencilled with a Metropolitan Police graphic.

They put me in a cell which could have been worse, and I fell asleep easily.

Burrows came for me some time in the night and walked me through the station. He showed me into an interview room where DI Hershey was already sitting down at a table. A man in a suit was on his way out. He nodded at me and Burrows as we entered.

Within minutes of me sitting down I was telling Hershey and Burrows in my own words what had happened.

It took a while, but I explained that Jenny had confessed to the murder of the twelve-year-old girl found in the church of St Mary Magdelene. I told them she'd confessed to killing Nugent Fry, Bethany-Jane Swann and Rachael Clarke.

I also told them that she'd been 'working' with someone else. They didn't seem surprised by this.

"She was vulnerable," I told Hershey. "And he took her from the hospital. He made her into this killer."

Hershey nodded. "What about the others? Judge Grace?"

That was all she wanted to know. Fucking ice maiden bitch. All she wanted was to tick off the cases. Put a name against each one and stamp it 'closed'.

"That was the other guy," I said, tiredly. It felt as though the fight had left me. "Same with Stephen Craine…"

"Names, Jason. Did she give this man a *name*?"

"He told her his name was Gareth Evans," I said, and left it at that. It was a popular name and they didn't need to know the rest.

But Hershey didn't want to leave it there. She pushed for more.

"Did Jenny describe him? Do you know if Harriet saw him? What does he look like?"

"I don't know."

"Is he young? Old? White? Brown?"

"I said I don't know! I don't know who this other person is!"

"Come on, Jason! The guy abducted your sister from the hospital. Signed her out in your name."

"Then ask at the hospital! See if anyone remembers, or see if they had any CCTV. That's what it's there for right?"

"What about Harriet?" she pressed. "Did *she* see this other man?"

Now I was angry. It was all I could do to keep it down and stay in control. "You'll have to ask her yourself," I snapped.

"We can't," Burrows interjected. "We can't ask her anything yet."

Hershey sighed with what I took to be impatience. She was tapping a broken fingernail on the tabletop. Leafing through some pages out of a buff foolscap file with the other hand.

"But I'm OK right?" I laughed, though not through humour.

"You're a tough guy, Jason," Hershey mumbled, still looking through the papers.

I snorted. Shook my head. Dragged my fingers down my face and breathed in deeply. With the dressing over my nose and stitches in my eye and my cheeks, my entire face ached and throbbed with pain.

"She was my sister," I whispered, emotions bubbling.

Hershey was frowning. Then she started comparing two different pages against each other. "You sure about that?" she said.

I snorted again. Shook my head. Half-sister? Whatever the fuck, I didn't care about Hershey and her fucking attitude. She certainly didn't give a shit about me.

At that moment Hershey's mobile rang on the tabletop. She looked down at it, contemplating whether to answer. "Excuse me," she said, then picked it up, answered it and left the room.

I looked at Burrows.

"What did she mean by that?" I hissed.

Burrows pulled the file towards him and leafed through the pages.

I sat back in the chair and breathed out heavily. "Oh, this is …" I shook my head again. "How did you find me?" I asked Burrows, not for the first time. "Who told you where I was?"

"Nobody."

"Nobody?"

"Nobody told us where you were. I mean we knew you were looking for your sister. We had a bulletin out on you which a couple of the shelters and the bedsit you stayed at picked up on, not that the information reached us quickly."

"But…"

"We recovered your laptop," he said.

I frowned at him. "My laptop?"

"You threw it out of the window when you legged it from Harriet's flat right?"

"I dropped it."

"Really?" His eyes flickered up. "Well, we found it. On the street. Powered down, screen and case broken. But it was a MacBook right?"

I nodded and Burrows grinned.

"Solid aluminium chassis," he said, almost proudly as though he'd invented the damn thing himself. "Solid-state flash drive. So the IT boys powered it back up, had a look, hacked your emails and eventually found the message from someone calling himself 'Shitpolice'. We got in touch with Harish Patel and he told us you were hunting this guy down. Took us a while because we went to the other location first."

"That's him you know. He's the other guy: Shitpolice. Working with

Jenny."

He was nodding.

I said, "I mean it's crazy right? The guy was on Twitter, joining the conversations on the Camden Killer. He even had a blog on the police investigations. I thought he knew so much because he was a police, but actually it was because … all this time… he was the one directing events, he was the bloody killer."

Burrows was still nodding. "Yeah we found all that," he said. "Fits a profile, so I'm told. He's what they call 'an exhibitionist'."

I looked at him as he did the thing with the fingers.

Frowned.

What did he say?

An exhibitionist?

Exhibition?

Burrows was still talking, saying how they'd secured this guy's Twitter account and ripped open his blogs to see if there was any clue as to where the guy lived or wrote them from. But apparently not. "It all goes through servers in India," he said. "And from there, who knows? That's the trouble with the internet, it's makes things easy for the bad guys. Harish is a useful kid, mind."

I stared at him again. Hershey was still out of the room. I could hear her voice just outside the door but I couldn't make out what she was saying.

I leaned over the table. "You arrested me back at that tower," I said.

He nodded.

"So am I under arrest?"

"You're in a police station aren't you?"

I wasn't in the mood for his shit.

He seemed to pick up on this. "Jason –" he began, then stopped.

The door opened and Hershey was back in the room.

"Grab your coats," she barked. "River Police think they've found a body." She looked at me. "You come with us," she said coldly. "We need an ID if it turns out it's your sister. We don't have time to mess around."

She snatched the papers out of Burrows' hands and put them back in her folder. She closed it and tucked it under her arm, then we all left.

River Police. A body.

I stood slowly, shaking and short on breath. I didn't know what was going to happen next, but I guessed there was no way Jenny could have survived that fall.

Time

Just a couple of hours later, they pulled the corpse from the Thames. London was still dark and frozen around me.

The divers dragged the body across the mud and I looked down. Caught my breath as the forensics guys carefully, delicately, pulled weeds and silt away from its mouth and eyes to reveal a fish-bitten face.

She looked just like me. Her face was my face.

Hershey glanced at me for confirmation but I don't think she needed it: It was Jenny.

Time marches on and I'm done here. It's time to leave the warehouse because now I know, I'm *sure* of it. I'm more certain of this than anything in my life.

Standing on the rooftop in the night, the freezing wind picking at the tails of my coat, I know now that it can *only* be him.

All this time…

Time to go.

8

Escapism

A painting's meaning lies not in its origin, but in its destination.

Statement.
Sherrie Levine.
Style. A catalogue of the exhibition Mannerism; A Theory of Culture
Vancouver Art Gallery, March - April 1982

8.1

London is busy. On New Year's Eve everyone comes out to join the party.

Police hover at street corners on horseback, their hi-vis waistcoats rippling with light from hundreds of mobile phone and camera flashes. In the streets of Deptford and then Greenwich, tourists and locals mix and mingle, some more obviously drunk than others. There's even kids out here. Some slicing through the crowd in pushchairs and buggies, some transported high on their dad's shoulders. Teenagers larking about, shaking hands with the cops.

There's a good feeling about the place but I'm not part of it. Not in the same way they are.

As I make my way through them all, I keep my head down. Woolly hat over my ears as far as it'll go. I'm nothing and no one, just a face in the crowd, a single element in the complex swarm massing around London's landmarks. The CCTV cameras on the lampposts and street corners can twitch and blink as much as they like. For all their face-recognition software, they're not going to find me. This is *my* moment now.

It was like Jenny had said; she and I were agents of change. We transformed people. And like Eve Gordon we were elemental, of a higher order than everyone here. Throughout my life I'd never answered to any laws, I'd never done what people wanted me to do. I did what I wanted to do and behaved according to me, myself and I.

And it feels like ... like this crowd is moving in patterns that externalise my thoughts, driving me on towards the inevitable. They don't even know it! They're like cattle, just as Jenny had said, grazing on whatever the government and the media threw at them to keep them docile and dumb. Give them a firework party on New Year's Eve and you'd be guaranteed that nothing would ever change. Resolutions would be crushed, candles of hope snuffed out in favour of that DIY job that had needed doing for years. Same old holiday as last year.

Well fuck them. Fuck them all.

And fuck this 'Camden Killer'. He isn't running my life now.

Jane, James and now Jenny are gone. My dad and Eve Gordon too. Which just leaves me, heading towards the realisation of James' Zero-sum Equation at terminal velocity.

8.2

The approach to the Dreadnought Gallery is a theatre of noise and life. Completely different to when I was here with Arnold walking towards Starbucks in the cold. It's packed with people: visitors to the concourse and the exhibition itself. Street performers are pulling their own little crowds; unicyclists, the inevitable juggler, a musician or two busking by the river.

High up on poles I can see television screens showing images of different clock-faces, ticking away the minutes to midnight.

Nearby, the O2 Arena is shining with green searchlights. It looks more than ever like the Emerald City from the Wizard of Oz. The whole place is transformed into something magical and deadly. Full of anticipation.

And then I see my face on the TV.

It takes me a while to register it, but it's me nonetheless. The clock faces slowly morphing into the haggard face of an artist I barely recognise now. An older me, a younger me.

I'm in a chair, in a church crypt, and Liselle is dancing around me in something that looks like a white-lace wedding dress. Behind her I see a man in black wearing a terrifying mask splashed with blood around the eyes, and now there are plenty more of them surrounding me on the concourse: Harlequins, clowns, Pierrots, a bunch of performers mingling with the masses, wearing masks like the ones I'd seen in Theo's Studio. Miming and producing bunches of flowers from nowhere.

Enough of this. It shakes me up but I need to be strong, so I make my way into the gallery, losing myself inside the throng of people spilling into the lobby. I didn't have my e-ticket but it didn't seem to matter.

Inside the gallery there are more TV screens connected to twisting, metallic sculptures spiralling into deformed shapes. The TVs hang like windows onto other worlds, of dreams and nightmare.

The place is heaving, packed with people looking at the screens. One more body in amongst them isn't going to make much difference.

But this is my work they were using. This is my *Castle Mechanics*. Adapted and transformed because they've incorporated my incarceration in the church into the video. They are actually using footage from that horror as … as *art*!

And no one here knows! They think that this is art.

But there I am. On every TV screen inside the gallery. Strapped into the chair and superimposed onto landscapes and backgrounds that have been pre-filmed by me.

Shaking with anger I slip through and make my way to a door, heading upstairs. Eventually I find what I'm looking for: an office.

The name-plate on the door reads simply: 'Hugh Donovan-Smith. Director'.

8.3

Time marches on.

A while later and I'm sitting in an office of chrome and glass at the Dreadnought. A few minutes after midnight, UK time.

The New Year is just getting underway, multi-coloured explosions are lighting up the sky outside: fireworks animating the details in the office with tiny, dancing rainbows.

The office is like a Captain's cabin in an old frigate, with great, bowed glass windows extending over the Thames like the stern of a ship, just like the gallery space beneath it.

I'm sat here in the big chair, toying with a heavy, stone paperweight designed to look Celtic. I keep looking at the door, willing him to enter.

Here on the Greenwich Meridian, at the zero hour, *The Odyssey Exhibition* began, and in around four hours' time the other half of it will explode through New York in what Brian Cavendish calls his 'Simultaneous Event'.

Time is not an exact science I guess… It's all relative.

Midnight here, midnight in in New York. Four hours of null time in-between, ticking down.

And yes, I'm sitting in the office of the Camden Killer. The *real*

Camden Killer, not my sister. Jenny could have been so many things, and maybe she always was a killer-in-waiting. But *he* was the one who found that fire inside her, *he* was the one who blew on it, fed it fuel and made it grow strong until it burned her up. He was the one who took her from the hospital and made her into his tool.

Just to get at me.

So here I am. Surrounded by his things, waiting for him to open the door and see me here.

Eventually the door opens and he walks in.

It seems to take him a moment to see me, even though he's just switched the lights on.

He frowns.

"Jason?"

I rest the paperweight back on his desk carefully and then I smile, beaming right at him.

"Hello Arnold."

8.4

He walks into the room. Staggering slightly. Face flushed like he's been on the champagne. He's wearing a dinner jacket and dress-shirt, open at the collar with the bow tie dangling like he's James Bond or something.

"Wh… what?" He clears his throat. Stares at me again. "What are you doing here? You look like shit."

"I feel like it," I tell him.

There's a silence between us. One I'm in no rush to fill. What is he thinking? Does he know, does he even suspect why I'm here?

I'm sure he does. After all, he's the one who made this happen and I'm sure he knows by now what happened with Jenny.

"How did you get up here?" he asks.

"I used the stairs." Simple enough. "I'm pleased you decided to use the *Castle Mechanics* piece in the end – or at least some of it. Not so pleased that it seems to belong to Theo now."

He shrugs.

"We'll pay you something I'm sure," he says, and now there is no sign of the friendly, slightly bemused Arnold Evans I've known for so long. The mask is wholly absent and at that point I know for certain that I'm right, that I'm looking at the man who orchestrated my downfall.

He wrinkles his nose.

"You stink," he tells me. "Why don't you go home? We'll talk about this in the morning."

It's all I can do to keep the rage from exploding.

I keep it down. Bite on it hard. I need to stay in control here. If I'm going to live through the night then *I* need to be the one conducting events.

"This isn't about the exhibition," I say to him. "It's just about you and me. Couple of days ago I looked at my face in a mirror and saw a man I could hardly recognise. And yesterday morning I saw it again, in a body dragged from the Thames."

He clears his throat, scratches at his chin with a thumbnail.

"She's dead, Arnold. My sister. Jenny."

Is that a flicker of something in his face? He's looking down at the floor, walking towards the windows looking out over the river.

I swivel the chair round to face him.

"I'm sorry to hear that," he whispers, his back to me.

His voice is shaking.

"I'll get it over it," I tell him. "One day. But what about you? You two got pretty close from what she told me."

He snaps his head round. *Go on*, I'm thinking. *Let it out, you know you want to.*

But he doesn't. He pulls it all back inside himself and all I can see are his eyes, burning with contained rage.

"It's all about your son isn't it?" I say to him. "It's all about Gareth?"

Another silence.

I stand up and now he faces me, on edge. Tense, like he thinks I'm going to punch him or something.

"I can understand," I tell him. "I get that. I can appreciate why you think I'm responsible for your son's death. What I don't get is everything else. The killings, Arnold. Why the killings? And the stuff in the church with Theo. What the *fuck* was that all about?"

He turns his back. Relaxes and faces the window again. I'm looking at his profile, the side of his face lit by fireworks bursts.

"I wanted you to know what it was like," he mumbles. "I wanted you to feel what he felt when he was tied in the chair before you killed him. Tortured. Brutalised. Disoriented, de-humanised and *humiliated*!" Spit flies from his lips. He gathers a breath. "I told you once that the only thing that got me through the pain of his death was the thought of revenge. And the only way to make that happen was to take control. Over my life, and yours."

"Graduation day at the Barbican," I say to him. "You came to me and Theo. Has this been going on since then?"

"It was too good a chance to miss," he says.

I start thinking about all the times we talked, all the things he'd said and done, and I remember the time I walked in the house to see him sitting on the sofa with Theo watching a video of… something…

Jesus! It was the video from Balloch! Theo sat him down and let him watch it?

I feel my blood draining from my face and I think I'm about to faint. Arnold is still talking and it's all I can do to stand up straight and not be sick.

"… Once you start it's hard to stop," he's saying. "Once you move away from the law you can't easily walk back towards it. So you make a choice. You turn either one way or the other. You force yourself back, or you push on ahead."

He turns to face me.

"You'd know that right? You know about choices, control and manipulation. It's what you've done all your life. You're no innocent, JJ."

"Difference is that I managed to walk away," I croak, still feeling sick and giddy. "I never crossed that line no matter what Theo showed you."

He shakes his head. "Theo? Look at what you did to him. Look at what you made him become by getting him involved in the murder of my son. Look at what happened to your sister because you neglected her. Look at all your friends and look at what's left of your family. You're like an explosion going off slowly, drawing everyone you know into your field of destruction. This *Castle Mechanics* piece is what that's all about. Your intention was to pin people into the screens, surround them with disorienting landscapes and environments, situations they have no experience of – for what? Why? Nothing to do with art, Jason. You said it was a metaphor but you never admitted what it was a metaphor *for*. So I'll tell you. It's an expression of your own destructive, manipulative personality. Your own deep horror. And now you're in there. Caught like that girl at Lambeth between nightmares of your own making."

"Sure," I tell him. I can agree with this. It's fine. I know what I am. But I know now what he is, and there's one big difference. "But I'm not a serial murderer, Arnold," I tell him.

He laughs. Kind of.

"You made me this person," he says.

"Bullshit! I don't even know you! I didn't make you this way, the same way I never made Gareth into a cunt who killed … who killed… Fuck this! Do you know what your bastard son did to Jane Gordon? He stripped her of everything. He cut pieces off her and fucked her. He filmed it all because he was a perverted fucking savage and then he killed her. Where did he get that from? Not from me. So come on!" I'm shouting. "Like father like son. Right? He was a murderer and so the fuck are you. I didn't kill him, Arnold. But God knows if my … my *brother* hadn't been there then I would have done. I'd have taken him apart and I'd have made him suffer a thousandfold for what he did to Jane. And if I find him in the afterlife, I'll do it properly. Myself."

I'm holding a hand to my forehead now.

"Don't tell me you don't know what he did to Jane," I say to Arnold, quieter.

"She wasn't the first," he answers, after a moment.

"*What?*"

"It's why I sent him to a shit school in the backyard of Wales," he tells me, his voice strengthening. Then, "He started school in the States. When he was six he pushed other kids off the climbing frame. When he was nine he threw a six-year-old girl into a river. When he was ten he – I sent him to child shrinks and they told me he was psychotic. He was unable to empathise with other people, and I thought 'that's like me. I'm like that'. The only person I could empathise with was him, my own son, a skinny kid who couldn't win a fight but who had this amazing capacity for what others would call cruelty. I tried to understand why he was the way he was. I wondered how you could take a life so casually, so coolly, and end it by your own hand… That little girl in the river… He watched her going under. Watched her father dive in to save her. Watched as others jumped in and pulled out the dead girl and her dead dad together. It's an amazing thing, to do that, to watch it happen… the moment a life ends at a time of your choosing. The power you feel, right there and then… It's addictive. And once you cross that line…"

He faces me and all trace of the man I knew has disappeared. A stone-cold killer is looking right at me, eye to eye.

"Theo wondered about it," he says. "He tried to go there a few times. He got sooo close, and I was hoping in the church you might even push him over the edge… Damn but I tried hard with him. He really wanted to kill you."

"And you gave him every chance to do it," I whisper.

I take half a step backwards and inwardly swear at myself for showing weakness.

"I thought it would be easier, but Theo's stronger than you think."

He's laughing, but then he stops. Suddenly.

"Just you and me now though," he whispers. "Just the two of us."

I don't know what to say. I can't say anything. Seems I've quickly lost control.

He asks me, "So what do you want to happen, Jason? I mean you came up here to face me. You worked it all out and here you are, just like Balloch only there's no one left to do the deed for you this time. If you want to kill me you'll have to do it yourself. Have you thought about what happens next? Did you have a plan? Come on! You want us to slug it out?" He looks me up and down and scoffs. "No. Look at you. I'm not a boxer but you wouldn't stand a chance, my friend."

"Try me," I challenge, but I know he's right.

"So, do you want me to go to the police, hold my hands up and confess to the murders? 'Sorry, coppers, it was me all along'," he laughs. "Sorry. No. There's no need for that. Besides that won't work because as far as the police are concerned your ex-sister is solely responsible for the murders of the Camden Killer."

My own rage is building.

"Maybe I should kill you," I tell him. "Just have done with it once and for all. It's the only way to stop you right?"

"Talking sense at last," he says buoyantly, now in complete control of the situation. "So how are you going to do that?"

"Throw you through the fucking window? You know... I could have killed you before," I tell him. "Years ago in your cottage in Scotland. I found a gun in your wardrobe. I took it when you crashed out on your bed and I pointed it right at your forehead while you slept."

He looks surprised at this. It seems to check his sudden enthusiasm and he looks serious again.

I keep talking. "I should have pulled the trigger. Wish I had. It was meant for me, right?" I continue. "It was your plan to shoot me up there in Scotland, either that year or the one before, I don't know. You were going to take me out on some fake fucking fishing trip and blow my brains out with the gun. But you never did."

He's smiling again. Shaking his head. "Jenny was right, JJ. You think it's all about you don't you? Every time. The gun, you prick, was for *me!*"

His voice cracks with emotion and he's shaking with rage now.

"You get that?" he shouts into my face. "I was going to shoot myself, JJ, not you. And you should have done it because if you had... if you had..."

He's almost crying.

He wipes his eyes. "Fuck this," he says. "I'm done with your games. This, my friend, is what happens next!" Suddenly he swings a punch at me so fucking hard and fast I don't even see it coming. Last thing I see is the room spinning. Last thing I feel is the back of my head cracking on the desk and then, nothing.

Nothing for a while until…

8.5

I'm on a boat. I can feel it rocking under me as people move around.

Someone is slapping my face, trying to get me to wake up.

"Hey," says a familiar voice. "Hey, come on."

Through the blur a shape, a face, resolves itself, takes form and becomes solid.

I don't know what I'm looking at. It takes a long time to make sense of the colours, the strangely-shaped eyes and hard cheekbones. It's a mask. A beautiful, bejewelled, gorgeously painted mask covering her eyes and nose.

"There you are," says the voice. French accent.

It's Liselle. Unmistakable. The bottom half of her face is uncovered, and I'd recognise those lips anywhere.

Arnold looms into view behind her wearing a long, black coat. He's batting his gloved hands together in a show of keeping them warm.

For a minute I panic, and I'm slapping the deck of the boat with my hands. At least I'm trying to, as they're tied up and trapped between my back and the deck. I can't move my feet either; feels like something's been wrapped around my ankles, binding them together.

My mouth has been taped up, so I can't move my lips.

"Chilly night, my darling," Arnold says, breath steaming from his lips. He sounds buoyant.

I struggle, pulling at the bonds.

"It's colder in the water," Liselle answers in her singsong voice.

And this is strange now, because I don't know how she fits into all this. I guess she's just another soul Arnold has been able to manipulate and control. Someone he used from the very beginning.

I stare at him, which is about all I can do. I'm thinking: *So what are you going to do now?*

Seriously, they're not going to throw me into the river are they?

Arnold hunkers down next to me. He looks around for a bit, then right at me. The hem of his coat brushes against my cheek.

"Just so you know, throwing you into the river wasn't part of any grand plan that I had," he says. "To be honest I've dreamed up so many ways to finish you over the years that whatever I do now feels like a bit of an anti-climax. Fact is, Jason, I've just had enough of you. You've no friends, no family. Even your fucking cat's dead!" With a mighty kick he shoves me down the boat.

The back has been let down to drop into the water. My eyes widen in horror and I'm rolling unstoppably.

At the last moment, Arnold catches hold of me. "Whoops!" he says, sadistically.

Liselle moves behind Arnold. She tilts her head to one side and I'm just a foot away from falling into the Thames. Panicking inside.

If I could speak maybe I could try and reason with her, I mean she knows what's going on right? She isn't just going to stand by and watch him kick me into the water.

"I've thought about gutting you," Arnold says, "stringing you up, having you watch while I fucked then killed your sister. I've thought about running you down in a car, a bus, a fucking tube train. Oh... yeah we stood on a platform a few times didn't we? And every time a train came through I thought to myself 'one push, one nudge, one single motion of my hand and it's all over for Jason Jones and his little universe'. Yeah. All of that stuff," he sniffs. Then stands, his foot ready to deliver that final kick.

I'm trying to roll myself back up the boat, all the time looking at Liselle, at the beautiful mask already marking her as a victim-in-waiting.

Come on, Liselle. You can't let him do this. The guy's a nutter.

"What are you looking at, Jason?" Arnold asks.

Liselle! You're not a murderer! Help me!

"Oh I see..." He reaches into the inside pocket of his coat and casually pulls out a pistol with a silencer attachment. Might have been the same one I saw in Scotland, maybe not.

I'm staring at Liselle.

Arnold aims the gun down at me. Almost imperceptibly, he winks – then quickly swings his gun arm round to point his weapon at Liselle. Right at the side of her face.

And then he fires.

Liselle's head sprays out and the body collapses.

"Looks like you two had a disagreement," he says, moving forward.

I want to be sick. I can't believe what he's just ...

Arnold aims the gun down at me and I know now exactly what he wants to do. I can see his finger tightening on the trigger. I'm breathing hard through my nose in panic, terror. Absolute animal fear because it can't end like this.

"I've probably had too much champagne, Jason," he says. "Because it wasn't part of any plan to kill Liselle either. She's been a good earner for me that girl but to be honest, I've no need for that life anymore. No more Arnold Evans, no more Hugh Donovan-Smith – that was my first wife's name by the way." Then he adds, "Not Hugh, Hugh was my dad. Donovan-Smith was the wife's name." He's laughing again.

There's a sudden commotion from the bank and I hear the chimes of Big Ben. Arnold looks at his watch for a second.

"Midnight in New York," he tells me, straightening the gun. "The world restarts. But this time, without you in it. Goodbye, Jason." He pulls the trigger.

Fuck you!

With a surge of energy I roll myself off the boat and hit the darkness.

I think he fired same time as I hit the water but it's difficult to know for sure. All I heard was the concussion as I went under.

Now I'm in the water, going down down down … Fulfilling my part of the Zero-sum Equation.

8.6

Cold! Freezing, freezing liquid in my mouth getting in through the tape. It's in my ears, in my nose. Everything fills up quickly.

Down, down down I go. Oh shit this is so cold. I never thought it would be this cold.

Dark too. So dark it's frightening. Can't see … can't breathe … can't …

Can't even cough. Nose spluttering. Lungs filling up with the thick, dark, freezing pain.

I want

I am.

What? What am I?

Don't panic.

They say your life flashes before you when you drown, but all I see is darkness.

Nothing but darkness.

Buzzing in my head and in a minute I'll be dead.

Should've been a poet. Who needs artists anyway? All they do is lie and murder people. Or is that just their agents?

Drowning.

Sinking.

Colours flashing in my eyes, head hurting, hurting.

Can't - *can't fucking breathe*. The buzzing gets louder in my head and I think I might be thrashing around, sinking faster, rolling end over end in the darkness searching for a way out.

But at least he didn't kill me. It was a decision I took away from him.

Now I'm doing the dying thing.

Breath bubbling up from my nose. Weight crushing me from all sides. Hands tied behind my back so I can't reach out for anything to hold onto.

Maybe I'm already dead.

A corpse who ... who ...

A corpse who doesn't know who he is ...

Or even who he was ...

I'll be dredged up from the river in the early hours, zipped into a body bag like Jenny in the mud.

Like, is this all it comes to? Everything I've done in my life, everything I laughed at, everything I raged against – it all comes down to this moment right here and now.

There's a boom from above that thunders through the water and I'm aware of another body hitting the river. Arnold? It has to be Arnold. His shadow is vast, spread-eagled, growing like a cloud of black ink as it sinks to one side of me.

It doesn't matter right? I'm already dead. I know this because I've given up fighting.

I just can't breathe anymore.

All I can do is sink...

But I.

I am

I...

Not over yet.

There's a weight around my chest. Then something grabs me, pulls me up in its jaws.

Panic! Fuck!

Look at it, a giant fucking whale coming right at me!

It opens its mouth and *chomp*, it has me, carries me away and we're moving quickly upwards.

I feel giddy as we move quickly ... *quickly quickly* ... up through the murk –

Oh! Air Air Air ... *FUCK!*

Gasping ... fighting ... coughing vomiting choking on air hands slapping down on the hard surface of the water don't let me go under again please oh fucking hell I don't want to die I don't want to die don't let me go under again...

"Jason!"

Angels and demons scream above my head. The stars are wheeling and the moon spins through air and water. Cough it out of my nose, spit it from my mouth as the gag is ripped savagely and some fucking beast has me.

No. It's a woman. Soaked through.

She's sitting on my hips and she's hitting my chest, pumping water out of my lungs, making me cough, splutter choke and ... here it comes.

I'm sick as she turns me onto my side and the dirty, stinking river comes spewing out of my mouth.

I'm shaking, shivering, soaking wet and in pain like I never felt in my life... gasping at the air that fills me up almost as painfully as the river.

Trying to make sense of this...

Blue lights strobe, spin, reflect and refract and I'm almost blinded. Droplets of water cling to my lashes and the foul taste of shit from the water makes me want to be sick again and ... oh christ ...

I'm ... alive. Aren't I?

I'm fucking alive!

I don't believe it. Someone saved me, someone pulled me out of the water.

Someone, somewhere ... who ... ?

Who?

The woman is shivering violently, sitting to one side of me. Scraping hair away from her face, out of her eyes and hooking it over her ears. She hacks, spits and coughs at the ground.

Someone throws a towel over her, then one over me.

Flashing blue lights.

Still on a boat.

Police radios squawk.

Someone says, "Ma'am," and the woman looks up, lifts a hand and nods at the copper. Then back at me.

Her face is covered in wet slime and her hair hangs like thick curtains either side of it. She's still shivering. Snot and water bubbling at her nostrils. "Thank God for CCTV and face-recognition," she croaks, shivering and gasping, in what I think might be an attempt at humour.

Then Burrows appears. Hunkers down next to us.

"Two bodies, Allie," he says. "Both are gunshots to the head. One

looks self-inflicted."
 This 'Allie nods and jerks her thumb at me.
 "Couldn't have been him," she says. "He's still tied up."
 I know the voice, and now I know the face.
 It's DI Hershey, the ice maiden bitch herself.

Closure

Fourteen days later…

I've just walked into a room in the hospital. It's a dedicated meeting room the police have converted to look like one of their own. Blinds are down over the windows so it's darker than it ought to be. There's a large conference table planted dead centre with chairs around it. Medical stuff shoved over to the sides.

Hershey is sitting at the table, dressed up in a smart, blue business suit. Her hands are on the table and she's talking, laughing with an older man sitting on her left. There are others around the table also.

The doctors have told them I'm good to talk now, so without any further ado here I am.

I take a vacant chair and sit down at the table, looking across at the face of DI Alison Hershey, the woman who rescued me from the river. Saved my life. It's the first time I've seen her since that day, and now she looks different.

Human.

She smiles when I take the seat, and I relax. Painful formalities ahead no doubt, but I'll get over them.

My brief sits next to me. Young guy. Tall, blond. Dark suit, no tie. Looks like he works out. I've just spent the last hour or so going over some things with him. A sequence of events leading up to Jenny, and Arnold. Throwing myself into the river…

I'm in no way ready to go through all this, but the police don't wait until you feel comfortable. I guess they need to move on.

Burrows isn't here, and it feels wrong without him.

The guy next to Hershey, the one she was sharing a joke with when I walked in, looks much older. He's grey. Dark. Dour. The folds of his face look like they've started to ooze away, falling like wax off a face-shaped candle.

It begins.

I'm being recorded, I'm told, and I need to state my name and my age. I'm told I'm not under arrest but that I'm required to answer questions truthfully and as fully as I can. Withholding information is punishable by fines or imprisonment etcetera etcetera. All of these things are calmly ticked off by the brief in his big notebook.

Just doing his job right? When this is over he's back off down the gym.

"Jason," Alison Hershey starts quietly. Measured. "This is Inspector Watts of the Police Service of Scotland. He wants to ask you some questions concerning an unsolved crime which happened in Balloch in June 2002."

Blood roars in my head.

My hands clench like claws.

I don't hear much else. I know my brief is going crazy at Hershey, shouting across the table at her. The Scottish guy is trying to calm things down and Hershey is smiling, because she made this happen.

The shouting continues around us and now I'm being hauled to my feet. It's my brief and he steers me out of the room.

There's no mistaking her expressions of triumph, but if Hershey thinks she's beaten me then she can think again.

I'm nobody's victim and I did not kill Gareth Evans.

ACKNOWLEDGMENTS

There are so many people I need to thank here because no matter how solitary an activity Writing A Novel is, it really doesn't happen alone, especially on an independent title where the writer is mostly begging favours from friends who have plenty of their own stuff to do.

So I need to thank Chris Butler for taking time out of his busy schedule to edit a good chunk of the text, and the extraordinarily talented Tanja Hehn for letting me use her *Dark Mask* image, both for the cover and for the website. As soon as I saw her work I knew I had to use it and she was gracious enough to let me do so. Please take a look at Tanja's incredible work at www.tanjahehn-art.de

Huge thanks also to Ed and Jade at *Doubleshot.tv* not only for the awesome cover design, but also for first-class beer and brainfood. Here's to our future collaborations!

Special Mention to Laura and Dools at *PurpleFuji* for sharing advice, encouragement, and marketing expertise with no complaints.

To my Mum, for always believing I could do this, and to my two gorgeous daughters for bringing me back to normality after I'd spent hours inside Jason Jones' head.

Thanks to everyone who shared, liked, posted, commented, tweeted, pinned, poked and prodded on FB, Twitter, G+ etc, and to all those early readers who downloaded, rated and reviewed the Kindle edition and fed back comments. You've no idea how much I love you all for that.

But most importantly, big hugs and kisses to Sarah, my fantastic wife who supported me throughout the entire creation of this novel. Without her support and encouragement I'd never have finished this (or found all the typos!).

Finally, I want to thank You, the Reader, for choosing to spend some time with my book. I hope you enjoyed it and will recommend it to all your friends. There'll be more on the way so watch this space.

Paul Laville
February 2015

ABOUT THE AUTHOR

Paul is a family man. It's true. And thankfully nothing in this novel is even remotely similar to his own life.

Except for his love of Art, that is…

www.goodreads.com/plaville

www.awdk.wordpress.com

www.facebook.com/AWDK.novel

@PaulLaville

Made in the USA
Charleston, SC
01 March 2015